A Wretched Man

A NOVEL OF PAUL THE APOSTLE

To my friends @ Glendon
Congregational church.
Enjoy your journey
with Paul!
Obie Holmen
June 2, 2011

RW Holmen

A Wretched Man
A Novel of Paul the Apostle
www.awretchedman.com

BASCOM HILL
PUBLISHING GROUP

Bascom Hill Publishing Group
212 3rd Avenue North, Suite 290
Minneapolis, MN 55401
612.455.2293
www.bascomhillpublishing.com

"Saint Paul the Apostle" by El Greco is used in the cover design with
the permission of Casa y Museo del Greco, Toledo, Spain.

Biblical texts imbedded in the narrative or the dialogue are from the
New Revised Standard Version Bible, copyright 1989, Division of
Christian Education of the National Council of the Churches of Christ
in the United States of America. Used by permission. All rights reserved.

ISBN - 978-1-935098-21-8
ISBN - 1-935098-21-7
LCCN - 2009940687

Cover Design by Alan Pranke
Typeset by Melanie Shellito
Map designs by Aaron Fruit

Printed in the United States of America

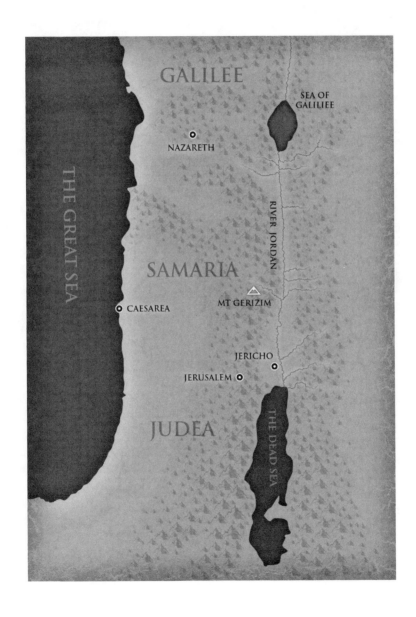

To Lynn,
MY WIFE OF NEARLY FORTY YEARS.

WITHOUT HER PATIENCE AND SACRIFICE,
THIS BOOK WOULD NOT BE POSSIBLE.

Foreword

In 332 BCE, the Greek armies of Alexander the Great defeated the Persians and swept swiftly through Palestine, destroying several cities, but Jerusalem surrendered peaceably. For the next two centuries, the Greeks were the masters of the Hebrew lands and people, importing their culture of philosophers, gymnasiums, universities, and a plethora of Greek gods and goddesses. From the ancient name for Greece, *Hellen*, this transplanted Greek culture was termed Hellenism. Even the Hebrew language scrolls of the ancient Jewish holy writings were translated into Greek.

Eventually, the Romans replaced the Greeks. The Romans were soldiers--keepers of the *Pax Romana*-- who functioned as road builders, administrators and bureaucrats. But they did not replace Greek culture, and the gymnasiums remained along with the Greek language as the *lingua franca* of the entire Mediterranean world, the language of commerce and the culturally elite. The common spoken language of the Jews remained a Hebrew variant known as Aramaic.

Jesus would have called himself *Yeshua* in his spoken Aramaic tongue. To the Greek-speaking, he was *Iesou*. His brother, known as James in English language Bibles, would have understood himself to be *Ya'akov* according to the Aramaic. Similarly, Simon Peter was *Cephas* in Aramaic and *Petros* in Greek. Paul, who penned his papyrus scroll letters in Greek, was *Saul* in Aramaic and *Paulos* in Greek.

This novel is set in the first century Mediterranean world of the Roman Empire. Along the eastern shores of the Great Sea, stretching from the cosmopolitan Greco-Roman cities of Antioch in the north and Alexandria in the south, the *Pax Romana* was anything but peaceful, and Hebrew culture and religion struggled for survival against the seductive influences of Hellenism.

Hebrew reaction to Hellenism and the *Pax Romana* ranged from violence to complicity: assassinations by the secretive daggermen of the zealots: banditry and brigandage in the hills and country-side of the Galilee; messianic claimants, including the one called Yeshua of Nazareth; Pharisee schools where the Torah traditions of the elders were taught as a bulwark against Hellenistic assim-ilation; escape from foreign pollution to isolation in the desert sanctuary of Qumran; and collaboration by the aristocratic priests and Sadducees, only too happy to be propped up in positions of power and wealth by the occupying Roman legions.

Into the swirling currents of bloody oppression and resistance, factionalism, and clashing cultures, appeared an outsider, a man from Tarsos of Cilicia. This is his story.

I am of the flesh, sold into slavery under sin. I do not understand my own actions. For I do not do what I want, but I do the very thing I hate. I see in my members another law at war with the law of my mind, making me captive to the law of sin that dwells in my members.

Wretched man that I am! Who will rescue me from this body of death?

From the 7th Chapter of Paul's letter to the Romans

Prologue

A goatsucker soared on the evening breeze above the Judean countryside. To the west, a smear of purples on the far horizon was all that remained of the day; to the east, a pale aura of lamplight over Jerusalem struggled to hold back the night. The sharp eyes of the creature searched the rocky hill beneath its wings as it circled on the currents and updrafts. Suddenly, the raptor tucked its wings and dove toward a pair of intruders. When it neared the ground, it spread its wings in a booming surge of air before flying away.

Paulos ducked and raised his hands as the nighthawk swooped past his face. Did even the beasts of the air oppose him? When his fist flew open, he loosed a silver coin that sparkled in the moonlight as it slowly tumbled toward the dust. He retreated a step, but his gaze quickly returned to his adversary; he would retrieve his *belonging* coin later.

In the first skirmish between the would-be leaders of the Yeshua movement, Paulos faced off against Ya'akov. Four years had passed since the death of Yeshua of Nazareth, the one they called the Mashiah, and the combatants dueled atop the desolate hill known as *the skull*, the place where the Romans had crucified him.

Paulos was a Jew of the dispersion, not yet aged thirty years, who had experienced a conversion on the road to Damascus. Ya'akov was a Jew of the homeland, Paulos' senior by a handful of years, and the brother of Yeshua.

Hot breaths steamed on the chilly hilltop. Ya'akov continued his verbal assault. "Who do you think you are, coming here with your Greek tongue, claiming to be a Pharisee, claiming to be a follower of my brother? You weren't there!"

Paulos strained to find the right words for a response. Even in the cool air, sweat beads worried down his dusty face, disappearing into a snarled beard.

"You never heard him speak," Ya'akov growled. "You never mingled with the crowds, and you didn't witness the stinking Romans murder him on the cross—

Ya'akov's voice cracked, and his hand braced against a boulder.

At Damascus, Paulos had glimpsed the form of a human in a flash of lightning, but Ya'akov had seen the blood seeping from his brother's hands spiked to a cross. At Damascus, Paulos had heard whispers on the wind, but Ya'akov had heard the death rattle of his brother, suffocated under his own weight. Against Ya'akov's lifetime with his brother, Paulos offered a single moment on the road to Damascus, a year after Yeshua's crucifixion. What had happened to him then? What did it mean? Paulos *believed* he had experienced a heavenly encounter, but his claims only angered Ya'akov.

Ya'akov's voice rose, shrill for a man his size. "You're like an uninvited stranger at a burial," he said, "boasting that you knew the dead man well. How dare you share my grief? How dare you!"

Paulos forced himself to speak. "Yeshua called to me from the clouds," he said, but the words seemed too thin for the truth of Damascus.

"That was but a dream," said Ya'akov. "Who can trust a vision? I tell you, he was *my* brother, and *you* didn't know him!"

Paulos' thumb and forefinger rubbed together as if the *belonging* coin was there. Damascus now seemed a dim memory, and the truth of it eluded his hollow speech. There was nothing more to say.

"You don't belong here," said Ya'akov, and then he stomped off toward Jerusalem, leaving Paulos standing alone on the forlorn hill. Except for the distant barking of a pair of hounds, the night was silent.

Unwelcome in the land of his forbearers, Paulos would leave Jerusalem and Judea to return to the city of his youth and his parent's home. Along the way, he would revisit the creek side trail on the Damascus road where the heavens had opened to him three years earlier. Ya'akov's stinging rebuke had jarred him, and he would seek reassurance on the holy ground of his conversion.

There was truth in Damascus beyond what eyes could see and ears could hear. On that glorious day, God had transformed him, setting his life on a new course, and Damascus was in his heart and soul. Paulos would study the holy books in the synagogue to unriddle his heavenly encounter and to find the words to tell the tale.

Paulos dropped to his knees to search for his belonging coin, the one that he had carried since his youth, the one that tied him to his Hebrew ancestry, the one that reminded him that he belonged to God's chosen family—the Lord's own portion. It didn't take long before he spied the gleaming shekel in the light of the rising moon. He rubbed the dust off and held it to the moon to catch its glint. He kissed the coin and returned it to his goatskin purse that hung from his sash. Even if he didn't belong in Jerusalem, he *belonged* ...

After descending to the bottom of the hill, Paulos tugged on his long nose to remember the path that had brought him to this time and place. He passed through a grove of palm trees and moon stripes of light and dark.

Come, follow along.

PART ONE
TARSOS
23-33 C.E.

When the Most High apportioned the nations, when he divided humankind, he fixed the boundaries of the peoples according to the number of the gods; the Lord's own portion was his people, Jacob his allotted share.

Deuteronomy 32:8-9

Chapter One

A caterpillar rafted down the river aboard a silvery olive leaf. The larvae had not yet become a moth, a butterfly, or whatever it was destined to be. Speeding through the ripples, slowing in a pool, and spinning in an eddy, the hairy pilgrim drifted with the current.

Perched on a rocky outcropping along the River Kydnos, the teen-aged boy named Paulos dangled his feet in the cool alpine waters, coursing toward the sea from the nearby mountains. Snow-capped peaks loomed over the Cilician plain and the city of Tarsos like white-haired eminences in vigil over their domain. Here was the young man's sanctuary: a maze of rocks, pools, and small waterfalls just upriver from Tarsos, his home.

A spindle-legged stork stalked the shallows, hunting frogs or minnows. Some called the boy "Stork," teasing him about his too long legs and pointed beak-nose. He wished they would call him by his name, Paulos, or "Saul" as old Eli the sage called him, using the Hebrew form of his Greek name.

It was the ninth year of the reign of Emperor Tiberius Caesar Augustus; according to the Hebrew calendar, the year was 3783, the number of years since God had created the earth, 23 C.E. The night before, a thin slice of a new moon appeared: *Rosh Kodesh,* the start of a new month, the month of his fifteenth birthday. A shooting star had arced across the heavens before the crescent moon swallowed it—an omen, he was sure.

His dark eyes stared vacantly into the deep, still water of a river pool. According to his habit, he tugged on his pointed nose to form his thoughts; he knew that his life was about to change. Perhaps it would be the end of his apprenticeship as a tentmaker. Perhaps it would the beginning of new studies. As a Hebrew Pharisee? A

Greek scholar? Soon it would be a new bride. He shuddered.

Perhaps God intended something else ...

* * * * * * * *

That same day, many leagues around the corner of the Great Sea, another young man reached the end—and the beginning—of his journey. Twenty-year-old Ya'akov had hiked the roads of Palestine toward Jerusalem to begin life as a student. The midday sun blazed hot, and he paused to rest in the shade of a hilltop olive grove that overlooked the valley of the River Kidron and the city of God atop the opposite slope. The burly man puffed heavily as he wiped his sweaty face with the sleeve of his robe.

He tied his donkey to a gnarled olive tree. God didn't use his builder's square when he created olive trees. Short. Squat. Bent. Twisted. Chaotic. Tall and sturdy cedars from mountain forests were real trees. Straight and true.

The soon-to-be-student tapped his builder's bag. The goatskin sack hung on the donkey's haunches and carried the tools of his trade that Ya'akov would use to support himself while he studied. Examining the well-earned calluses on his hands, he hoped he would not grow soft as a student.

For three days, he had led his donkey along the road from Galilee—three long, hard, hot days. Traveling far distances was not easy for a heavy man like Ya'akov. He was exhausted as he lowered himself onto a grassy patch in the shade of the olive branches. The road ahead trailed west down the hill and then ascended the slope across the river where Jerusalem, his campus, awaited him. He had traveled this way before with his family to attend Passover in Jerusalem.

The Galilean's family always rested in the shade of this olive grove before entering Jerusalem. His eyes welled at the memory of his mother wiping his sweaty face in this very spot, many years earlier. He clenched his eyelids tight to remember her face, glowing with pride as she foretold his life in Jerusalem. *You will be an important man one day, a scholar, and a Pharisee.* Only a mother could be proud *before* the son earns esteem. Pray that he would be worthy.

His eyes popped open as he remembered his father's voice spewing angry words at the Roman Fortress Antonia, a festering sore on the Jerusalem cityscape. *Stinking Romans.* Ya'akov was a young man before he knew these were two words, not one, for his father never spoke of the Romans without the epithet.

"Stinking Romans," Ya'akov mouthed the words; they tasted good. One day soon, God would restore justice; Ya'akov was sure.

His parents had named him Ya'akov, the second son of Yosef of Nazareth and his wife Maryam. At great sacrifice, his family sent him to Jerusalem to study Torah as a Pharisee, a profound honor, and he hoped to reflect esteem back upon them. He promised himself to heed the sages who would teach him Torah: God's own law and way of life for his chosen people.

Ya'akov rolled his shoulders to flex his neck and back while envying his carefree donkey that dozed in the shade. Ya'akov's muscles were taut as if he, and not the jackass, had carried his packs all the way from Galilee.

He bowed his head and whispered, "The Torah of the Lord is perfect, reviving the soul." Torah is straight and true, he thought. "The decrees of the Lord are sure, making wise the simple." The humble man prayed for wisdom. "The precepts of the Lord are right, rejoicing the heart." The self-doubting man needed assurance. "The commandment of the Lord is clear, enlightening the eyes." Show me the way, he prayed. "The ordinances of the Lord are true and righteous altogether." Straight and true. Amen.

The privilege of an education rightly belonged to Yeshua, his older brother, the firstborn son, who was also smarter than Ya'akov, but Yeshua had deferred to Ya'akov. An impatient dreamer, Yeshua was not for classroom study. A critic of the priests. A critic of the Romans. Ya'akov worried about Yeshua's irresponsibility and willingness to flaunt authority.

Yeshua and Ya'akov were similar in appearance. Like their father, the brothers boasted ample bellies on their pear shaped bodies, big men in girth but not height. Yeshua spoke in a deep booming voice that commanded attention, but Ya'akov spoke softly. The tight curls of their hair were the color of sand on the shores of Lake Galilee, and their beards were dark like muddy riverbanks after springtime rain. Following the labors of his journey from Galilee, Ya'akov's sweaty, sun-stained face was puffy.

When the sun reddened in the dusty haze over the city, the weary traveler knew it was time to complete his journey. He must arrange a room in an inn before sunset, the beginning of the Sabbath, the seventh day. His donkey smelled the river water and pranced about as Ya'akov staggered to his feet. Ya'akov checked his packs one more time, especially his bag of builder's tools. His joiner's square, his norm, was safely there.

The iron norm was the one indispensable item in his builder's bag: two flat arms, each three palms in length, joined to form a perfect right angle. Straight and true. The norm ordered and disciplined a builder. He pulled the norm from his bag and rubbed his fingers against the cool, hard edges.

He rejected the thought of allowing his animal free rein to trot down to the river, and the donkey followed his measured gait with its snout pressed against its master's back. Ya'akov allowed his donkey to drink its fill before he tied it under a swaying willow tree. Ya'akov then stripped to his loincloth and bathed. He rinsed one more time then dressed in fresh clothing for the last short climb into the life of a Torah scholar.

He hung the norm around his neck. His father had given him his norm. The norm tied him to his past and guided his way forward. As Torah was to life, the norm was to work. Straight and true. Everyone needed a norm to follow. He rolled his shoulders again to loosen his tight muscles before he hiked up the hill toward the Jerusalem gate. Halfway up the path, he glanced back at the way he had come.

Chapter Two

Paulos had dallied too long at the river; the morning sun polished his apple cheeks, and a bead of sweat dangled from his lone, scraggly whisker. It was time to deliver his jars of fresh water to his parent's home.

The wooden wheels creaked and clattered as Paulos' two-wheel cart trundled down the narrow city street. Each turn of the wheels spun dust into the arid morning air. The water in the tall jars sloshed about on the bumpy roadway. Paulos had filled two for the family livestock—goats, sheep, a few sorry donkeys, and egg-laying chickens—in the River Kydnos, and two more for the household at a public well.

The whole process took the better part of an hour, and Paulos performed this task each morning six days a week. Today was the sixth day, and Paulos would fill the amphorae a second time later that afternoon in preparation for the sundown arrival of the Sabbath, a day of rest when he could do no work.

The aroma of fresh bread baking on the stone hearth welcomed Paulos into the courtyard as he returned to the two-story house of Kleitos, his father, and Olympia, his mother. His mother squatted on a small stool by the hindquarters of a she goat, gently pulling the goat's teats and squirting warm milk into a bucket. A rooster crowed and strutted confidently in front of his hens. Paulos grasped the handles at the top of the heavy, thigh-high amphorae and emptied two into the animal trough. He placed the two household water vases inside the front door before ascending the stairway to the veranda for his breakfast of porridge, sprinkled with raisins.

The brown mud-brick house was a typical residence of Tarsos. On the first floor were kitchen, storeroom, and Paulos' bedroom that he seldom used, preferring the fresh air of the rooftop. An outside courtyard enclosed their animals and contained a stone cooking hearth. The bedroom of Kleitos and Olympia was on the second story, accessed by an outside stairway. The rest of the second story was a spacious veranda covered by a roof thatched with palm fronds. The family dined here around a short-legged oaken table ringed by three-legged stools, pillows for Kleitos to recline on, and the high-backed matriarch's chair for Olympia. Paulos' favorite spot was up six rungs of a wooden ladder to the flat mud-brick rooftop of his parent's bedroom where he slept on his goatskin mat under the stars—unless it was raining, and then he slept under the rooftop of the veranda.

Paulos had finished his porridge when the soft footfalls of his mother's sandals on the steps signaled the arrival of fresh bread. She squeezed her bread warm hands on his shoulders and kissed the top of his head. Acrid wood smoke lingered in her bunned hair along with fresh bread smells.

They sat together at the short-legged table and broke apart the small flat loaves. Only later in life would he realize how much he'd loved munching on his mother's fresh bread dipped in honey.

"Leave your father's shop early to do your *agora* shopping. Your sister and her husband will take their Sabbath meal with us."

"I know," he said without returning her gaze.

The sixth day was always the same. He didn't need reminding. He swallowed the last of the fresh bread with honey, gulped down a cup of goat's milk, still warm from the udder, and then hustled off toward the *agora* and a short day of work in his father's shop. Why would this day be any different?

"Spices! I have exotic spices. Spice up your dishes. Spices here!"

Itinerant peddlers hawked their wares from mats under tents or awnings placed in the central pavement of the agora, their shrill voices rising above the din.

"Glassware! Glass bottles. Glass jars. I have glassware!"

Goats and sheep bleated for a rescuer that did not come. Dogs barked for the joy of it. Roman soldiers on patrol swaggered about in pairs; the feathers in their bronze helmets wagged with pompous authority. "Helmets"—the name his father used for the legionaries but only in the privacy of his shop.

The agora aromas coaxed Paulos. Fresh bread smells reminded him to buy flour from the baker for his mother's baking. He bought a thick chunk of tuna despite the foul odors that always clouded around the fishmonger's booth. How did the fishmonger stand it? A savory aroma from a pudding vendor's pot tempted Paulos' nose, but Paulos knew this vendor to be a Gentile whose skewered meats were prohibited foods for Torah observing Jews. Paulos held his breath as he passed the pudding pot. Torah decreed that he should not eat the prohibited meat, and he would not smell it either.

Paulos neared his father's shop where Paulos had spent the morning. Only successful vendors and tradesmen boasted a permanent wooden building in a prominent location on the agora quadrangle. Such a workshop—proud pine walls and plank flooring! Kleitos, the leather smith, sewed tents, new ones of his own making and old ones in need of repair; Paulos was his father's apprentice. Many caravans passed near their city demanding the services of a skilled tentmaker, and the ever-present Roman soldiers required saddle and tack repair. Father and son enjoyed a prosperous tent and leather smith business.

A group was leaving the shop, led by a foreigner in a red turban, a Nabatean spice merchant. Slaves carried a huge tent their master had rented. Caravans often encamped on the grassy plain on the edge of town while their camels rested and replenished their stores of food and water; renting tents produced extra income for the leather smith. Whenever foreigners came into the shop, Paulos' ears enjoyed the exotic tales of faraway lands. It was an especially good day when Paulos delivered a tent to the staging area where he could mingle with the caravanners while setting up the tents.

Clutching bundles of goatskins, a pair of herdsmen disappeared into the shop. Except for their wrapped headdresses reflecting their outdoor life spent under sun and stars, they dressed in the familiar dull-gray garb of the men of Tarsos: knee-length tunic held tight to the waist by a leather belt or cloth sash with open robe over the tunic and sandals. In Tarsos, the Gentiles and Jews dressed alike, for the Jewish men seldom wore a fringed garment as Torah prescribed. Paulos was different. He followed the command of God to wear the tassels known as *tzitzit*. The sages promised that one who meticulously wore *tzitzit* was worthy of the divine presence.

The Jewish men of Tarsos gathered in the leather smith's shop in the mornings to gossip, to argue Torah, or to tell bawdy stories. They perched on stools near the front or leaned against one of the benches strewn with leather and linen. Hunched over his workbench with an assortment of knives, awls and needles neatly arranged in front of him, Kleitos would listen and nod or grunt while he worked. Paulos would receive his own tools upon completion of his apprenticeship. When would that be? Not soon enough.

Levi, the stout butcher in his blood-spattered apron, was usually there. The seller of meat, the father of seven unmarried daughters, intimidated Paulos with watchful eyes that seemed to be taking his measure. Malachi, the wine merchant and town gossip, would be broadcasting the latest news in his piercing voice while waving his arms like a fledgling attempting flight. He hopped about and cawed like a crow too. *Koraka,* the raven, was Paulos' secret name for the seller of wines.

Paulos moved past his father's shop and paused at the booth of Arasteh the widow, a produce merchant; olive-green eyes peeked from beneath her hood. The friendly old hag always offered the freshest fruit, and Paulos was a regular customer. He gingerly squeezed purple plums in baskets.

"Try one," she said. "Pick a nice ripe one and taste its sweetness."

He bit into a dark skinned plum, sticky-sweet juices dribbling down his chin and his fingers.

"Hey, Stork!"

A few Gentile friends from primary school days approached Paulos. From age six to age twelve, he had learned Greek grammar with the silly boys who consistently unnerved their teacher. An unknown boy in colorful robes accompanied Paulos' former classmates. Paulos straightened his hunched shoulders as they approached.

"This is Arsenios who recently arrived from Greece," said one of the boys. "His father will teach at the university."

The other boys wore simple white tunics covered by open robes, but the Greek dressed in a flowing, ruby-red *himation* wrapped around his torso and grasped by one hand at the waist. The Greek's oiled and fragrant blond hair curled tightly. His dimpled, beardless face glowed with a healthy tan, and a slight smile tugged at one corner of his mouth. But more than anything, his penetrating eyes dominated his features: deep, dark, intelligent and inquisitive.

Paulos shifted his weight from one foot to the other and licked the nectar from his fingers. Why did the Greek stare at him, into him, through him? Pointy nose? Arms too long? Feet too big? Sticky chin? Flushing cheeks? What did he see?

Paulos caught a whiff of scented lotion from the fair hair of Arsenios the Greek. Paulos said, "I am Stork—no, no. My name is Paulos."

"The Stork was the teacher's favorite," said one of the boys, "because he always completed his lessons, and he scored better than the rest of us."

Was Arsenios impressed?

"Will you be starting rhetoric classes at the university?" Arsenios asked.

"No. Yes. Well, maybe. We haven't decided." Why did he sound the fool? "I mean, I haven't decided." He would soon choose between studying Greek rhetoric in Tarsos or Pharisee training in Jerusalem.

"The Stork is going to Jerusalem to study Torah," said one of the boys.

"Maybe not," Paulos said, jerking his head toward the speaker. "I might stay in Tarsos to study at the university." He quickly glanced back at Arsenios.

With his free hand, Arsenios placed a copper coin in the palm of Arasteh the widow and selected a plum from her basket. Pursing his lips, he nibbled at the luscious fruit, sucking the juices before they ran down his chin. Oblivious to the jabbering silly boys, Paulos and Arsenios slurped their last bites of plum as they gawked at each other.

"I hope," said Arsenios, "that you enroll at the university with me." He followed the others but not without looking back to offer a firm wave of his refined hand with long, graceful fingers.

Paulos had to squint as Arsenios departed in the direction of the blinding afternoon sun.

"How many plums would you like?" asked Arasteh.

"What?"

"How many plums?"

Paulos bought several handfuls of plums; he tapped on melons and purchased several ripe sounding specimens; as usual, he purchased figs. He filled his basket with onions, carrots, peas, lentils, and garlic.

He walked past Levi's butcher shop; since he had fish, he did not buy meat. He stopped at Malachi's wine shop where an assistant filled Paulos' two empty bottles from an amphora of local wine. As he exited the wine shop into the glaring sun of mid-afternoon, Paulos glanced around the agora, but he did not see the Greek.

Paulos departed the agora, balancing his produce basket on his right shoulder while grasping the necks of the two wine bottles with the fingers of his left hand. Turning down a quiet street, he felt a chill draft as he passed the alleyway just before his home. A familiar apparition squatted in the dust. The sallow skin of the phantom beggar named Jubilees stretched tight against his hairless skull-head. Paulos couldn't help but stare, and the ghastly face rotated slowly toward Paulos, revealing white eyes without pupils, staring blankly from deep in their recesses, seeing but not seeing.

"Beware the Gentiles," said Jubilees.

Paulos jerked his head forward and quickened his pace. He looked back as he turned the corner, but what he'd seen was there no more. Paulos shivered as he paused at the stoop before entering the house.

Chapter Three

Paulos delivered the fresh fish and produce to his mother. Somehow, he felt vaguely conspicuous, like the time he had swiped an apple from a vendor's stand and his face gave him away. He kept his head bowed low, and he mumbled something about the tuna before he ducked out to fetch water from the river and the well for the second time that day. Fortunately, his mother was preoccupied with curdling goat's milk for cheese and yogurt and didn't pay attention to him.

By the time he returned from the river, he felt better. His older, married sister had arrived and helped Olympia prepare the Sabbath meal. Euthalia lived with her husband in a room in his father's house. She was Paulos' only living sibling, others had died in childbirth.

Mother and daughter were short and slight with thick black hair gathered in a bun. Olympia's hair contained a few gray flecks. Both women wore plain tunics that extended to their ankles, drawn at the waist by a sash.

"I see no beard on your chin," his sister said. She smiled as she looked up from cutting vegetables and glanced at Paulos. "I saw Esther, the butcher's daughter, in the agora. She shows the curves of a woman. Are you man enough for her?"

Paulos ignored her; he didn't want to think about such things.

"I need to send you back to the market. Take your cart with an empty amphora to the oil vendor. Half full only," Olympia said. "Fill the lamps before sunset."

They would use the olive oil for many purposes: cooking and eating, lamp lighting, and personal grooming. Paulos gladly avoided his teasing sister and returned to the agora.

By the time Paulos returned in late afternoon, neither Kleitos nor Euthalia's husband had arrived. The women had bathed and donned finer clothing for the Sabbath. Their hair had been let down, carefully combed, and lightly oiled. Paulos filled the oil lamps then climbed the ladder to his favorite perch atop the house.

The city of Tarsos sat on the plain of the River Kydnos, and Kleitos' hilltop house offered a panoramic view from the rooftop. Paulos leaned against the short wall that enclosed the rooftop while he surveyed his domain, a pleasant ritual of the sixth day as he awaited the Sabbath.

He held his hand at arm's length to shield the sun and to measure the gap from sun to horizon with his long and slender fingers. The gap measured four fingers; sundown was an hour away when the Sabbath would begin. The Taurus Mountain range, less than a day's journey from Tarsos, defined the western horizon. A black blanket of forest warmed the slopes beneath snowy summits. What lay beyond the mountains? Did the setting sun know the hidden place of God?

The River Kydnos trailed out of the mountains and crossed to the right. The mountain stream sluiced down from the rocky gorge known as the Cilician Gates. A cloud of dust marked a caravan heading toward the Gates, the only passageway through the rugged mountains. Their journey beyond the gorge would take them to the plains and cities of central Anatolia, which meant "sunrise" in the language of the Greeks, but to Paulos, it was always sunset in the direction of Anatolia.

To the east lay the fertile plains of Cilicia, beyond the river as it flowed past the city. Fields and flocks dotted the flatlands. Grapes. Olives. Goats. Wheat. Flax. Like the sails of ships at sea, a multicolored patchwork of caravan tents floated on a sea of green, marking the staging area tucked into the grassy wedge between the city and the river.

There was more to the east than his eyes could see. Antioch. Jerusalem. Pharisee school. Paulos and his parents would soon decide the next phase of his education; he leaned toward Pharisee training in Jerusalem, but remaining in Tarsos to study at the university was also appealing; Arsenios the Greek would be studying rhetoric.

The main portion of the city was to the south. Rising plumes of hearth smoke flattened into a dusky haze. Dockworkers hustled on the waterfront of the inland harbor of Tarsos, and boats at anchor floated idly in the calm lagoon. Beyond the harbor, the river ribboned its way southward to the Great Sea some ten miles distant, well beyond his vista.

What was the fate of the caterpillar on the olive leaf, bobbing down the river? Did the pilgrim reach the Great Sea? Where did the wind and waves take him?

Euthalia's husband shouted a greeting from the street. "Hey, Paulos!" Paulos waved back.

The daytime din of the city seeped away, followed by evening calm. Following his survey, Paulos was satisfied that everything was as it should be.

A new goatskin pouch hung from the sash around his waist. The fresh goat leather was buff colored and stiff as he opened the purse strings to pull out his solitary coin. He rubbed the shekel on his robe to brighten the luster of the dull silver. Framing the coin between thumb and forefinger, he held it to the sun for close examination. A palm tree with a cluster of dates on the one side symbolized Palestine. A big "χ" was on the other side. Why would a Hebrew coin from Jerusalem contain a Greek inscription, the letter *chi* in the Greek alphabet? What did it mean?

The coin wasn't worth much, but it was a special trinket to Paulos, a gift from Eli his sage and mentor. "I give you this shekel as a token of Jerusalem and the homeland," Eli had said. "Remember your roots, remember your heritage, and remember that you belong to God."

Along with many Jewish boys in Tarsos, Paulos had learned at the knee of the sage for many years. From the first day and every day thereafter, the elder had reminded the students of their legacy:

"Together with all the Jews born of Abraham, who, with Moses, escaped from captivity across the Red Sea, and who covenanted with God on Mt. Sinai, you belong to the Lord's own portion, his chosen people that he has blessed."

Paulos squeezed the shekel, his *belonging coin,* in his palm before tucking it safely into his pouch.

Just before sunset, Kleitos appeared on the still street with his long, purposeful strides. Paulos often heard that he resembled his father—tall, thin, and beak-nosed. He supposed it was true, and that pleased him. The late day sun highlighted the red tinge in his father's auburn hair, another feature Paulos shared with his father. Would Paulos' whiskers grow thick like his father's strong beard? Did they call him "Stork" when he was a boy?

As Paulos turned toward the ladder down to the veranda, the porticos and domes of the university caught his eye. The buildings had always been there, but now they seemed bigger, bolder, and more dominating of the city setting. University study in Tarsos held a growing allure for him, but it came with a vague sense of unease. As the sun dipped behind the mountains, he was of a different mind than when it had climbed the morning sky, even if he didn't understand.

Steaming food adorned a short-legged table under the veranda roof. The Sabbath feast included boiled tuna, a tangy smelling vegetable stew seasoned with coriander leaves that simmered in a blackened cooking pot, bread, goat cheese, olives and green onions. Competing aromas hung in the humid air of dusk. Plums, figs, melon, and curdled goat's milk waited on a small side table to follow the main courses. Kleitos and the son-in-law reclined on pillows, Paulos and Euthalia sat on stumpy-legged stools, and Olympia took her place on the single high-backed chair that was hers alone, towering over the table.

The meal began with a prayer. "Blessed are you, O Lord of

Israel," intoned Kleitos. "And it was evening and it was morning,
the sixth day. And the heavens and the earth and all their hosts were
completed. And God finished by the seventh day His work, which
He had done, and He rested on the seventh day from all His work,
which He had done. And God blessed the seventh day and sanctified
it, for on it He rested from all His work."

The others responded, "Amen."

"I saw Eli the sage today," Kleitos said as he filled each plate with
a slice of tuna and steaming stew. "He is as excited as we are for
your plans to study with the Pharisees in Jerusalem."

Paulos did not make eye contact with his father as he passed the
filled plates to the others.

"I also spoke to the harbormaster to arrange ship passage to
Palestine." Kleitos looked at his wife. "It'll be safer than travel by
caravan."

Olympia's eyes glistened as she accepted her plate from Paulos.
Her fingers lingered for a moment on his hand. He looked into her
face and realized she would be an ally in the discussion to come, but
not tonight. He wasn't ready.

Paulos picked at his food, and his plate was still full when his
father finished his second helping. Kleitos leaned comfortably into
his pillows and burped.

"Just my compliment to the cooks," he said.

After the meal, Paulos lay on his sleeping mat, searching the
heavens. The moon peered from behind the sailing clouds. As a
young boy, he believed he saw the face of God on the moon, but he
no longer sensed the presence of the hidden God so easily. On this
night, the crescent slice seemed empty.

He fell asleep. In his dreams, he saw the silly boys—and Arsenios.
*The Greek bit into a plum before offering it to Paulos. Paulos
reached for the fruit as pleasure rippled through his body.*

In the middle of the night, a chill wind disturbed his sleep. Moon and stars had disappeared behind a bank of dark clouds. He reached for his wool blanket and discovered that his loincloth was wet and sticky; he had soiled himself with his seed, and he was unclean. Eyes wide, he searched the darkness for the icy presence that he felt. His jittery breaths steamed in the cold night air. Despite the Sabbath prohibition against activity, he snuck down to the main floor and washed himself from a vase by the door.

In the troubled sleep that followed, the leering face of Jubilees the blind beggar taunted him from the alleys of his dreams.

Chapter Four
26 C.E.

"Let's stop now. I'm tired of riding this stupid donkey. My rump hurts." Joses, the youngest son of Yosef and Maryam, complained.

Under a blistering midsummer sun, Ya'akov retraced his steps to Jerusalem with an entourage that included his mother, three younger brothers, and two younger sisters. After three years in Jerusalem as a student of the Pharisees, Ya'akov had returned to Nazareth to bury his father.

While Ya'akov resolved his father's affairs in Galilee, Ya'akov's wife and child remained in Jerusalem, awaiting his return. Three years earlier, Ya'akov had traveled to Jerusalem as a young man alone, but he soon married Shera and sired a daughter named Seema. He had studied with the Pharisees and gained influential friends who helped him to flourish as a builder. Now, following the death of his father, Ya'akov had become the head of the family, a heavy burden for a young man barely twenty-three years of age. The oldest brother, Yeshua, remained in Galilee as Ya'akov escorted the family to Jerusalem.

Ya'akov wiped the sweat from his brow as he scowled at Joses, his whiny young brother. Raising a callused hand against the bright sun still high in the sky, Ya'akov measured the hour. An ominous cloud of smoke smudged the heavens over Gerizim, the mountain that loomed over the passing donkey caravan. Sacrificial fires smoldered atop the heights, the sanctuary of the Samaritans. Ya'akov regretted his decision to return by way of the valley that snaked along under the evil eye of unholy Gerazim. Ya'akov considered the Samaritans to be half-breed Jews and blasphemers who worshiped on Mt. Gerizim instead of revering God's holy Temple in Jerusalem. But for the imploring look in Maryam's eyes, Ya'akov would have traveled further toward Judea and away from Samaria while they still had good light. He set up camp behind a grove of trees to shield his family from the gaze of abominable Gerizim.

Ya'akov and his brothers were heavy-set like their father, but Maryam was a slender woman, and her daughters favored her. Wisps of silver hair added to Maryam's appearance of dignity despite her widow's grief. Tiny wrinkles creased the corners of her eyes, giving her face a worn, soft look.

Jude was nearest Ya'akov in age and temperament, and he took charge of the six donkeys that carried the family's possessions. The donkeys drank their fill in a nearby stream, and Jude staked them in a grassy patch and allowed them to graze. Maryam and the two girls, Asenath the older and Mahalia the younger, began to prepare a simple meal of porridge and dates. Simon, a young teen, tended the child Joses; together, they gathered sticks for a fire.

After ensuring that the family had settled into their chores, Ya'akov, alone with his thoughts, walked to the stream to fill water-skins with fresh water. How would Shera react to an extended family? He had married well, and Shera, his strong and hardy wife, belonged to a solid Jerusalem family. City dwellers. What would she think of his Galilean family from the tiny village of Nazareth? *Will your family return with you?* Even though he had denied it, she knew. Would she accept these country folk into her home?

As Ya'akov knelt on the creek bank to fill his water-skins, Seema smiled at him from the water's sheen, his beautiful child with sandy curls like her uncle Yeshua. Seema, his treasure, whom he missed dearly. Was he being fair to her, splitting his allegiance, multiplying his responsibilities, and filling her young life, and not merely her tiny home, with strangers? *Abba (papa).* Her first word. Two moons had waxed and waned since he had departed Jerusalem. Had she forgotten him? Had she forgotten his name? *Abba.* Ya'akov blew his runny nose and washed his face in the creek. *Abba.*

Ya'akov trudged back to the camp with the bulging water skins slung over his shoulders. The sky darkened as black clouds blotted out the sun. He sniffed the air, smelling a storm.

"Why is Yeshua such a dreamer?" Ya'akov was shocked to hear himself mumble these words aloud, and he glanced about to be sure he had not been heard. He reached to touch the builder's square, his norm, that usually hung around his neck, but it was not there. He hurried to drop the water-skins so he could rummage through the packs to find the norm. When he found it, he hung it around his neck. He would be a full time builder now, no time for further studies as a Pharisee. As a builder relied on a norm, a man must rely on Torah as a guide to life. Straight and true. Responsible men followed God's pattern.

He knelt amongst the donkey packs and prayed, "Abba father, keep us safe. I accept my responsibility. It's my duty, and the right thing. I'll do what I must do."

Thunder rumbled low and distant. Supper was over, and the younger children were fast asleep. The older ones, Jude and Asenath, whispered together, leaning against an olive tree while Maryam and Ya'akov sat around the embers of the fire.

"Jude can join me in my work. Jerusalem has plenty of jobs for a good builder. Simon can help too."

Maryam nodded and smiled.

Ya'akov continued to think aloud, "It'll be cramped in our humble house. I must add rooms and a veranda on the roof."

"And will you add a room for Yeshua when he comes to visit?" asked Maryam.

Ya'akov kept his eyes fixed on the glowing coals. He would not judge his brother Yeshua, but he indirectly questioned his impractical lifestyle by criticizing his friends. "That wild man who wears animal skins is a bad influence on Yeshua."

The man they called the Baptizer was dangerous he was sure.

Loose talk. Revolutionary talk. *The kingdom comes.* Romans should not hear such words. Even as Ya'akov's disgust for the Romans had swelled, his three years in Jerusalem had taught him to respect the keen edge of their swords. Just before Ya'akov left Jerusalem, the new Roman Governor, Pontius Pilate, had raised Imperial flags in the holy city, a desecrating sacrilege. *Stinking Romans.* The voice of Yosef, Ya'akov's deceased father, spoke the truth.

As usual, Maryam defended her eldest son. "Yeshua is different. He hears God's voice, and we must not question that. We must trust that God is leading Yeshua." Maryam placed her hand on Ya'akov's knee and laughed, "You and Yeshua look so much alike, yet you are so different. I love you both for who you are. You're my practical one, and it's a great comfort to know that you're here for your sisters and brothers."

And then the smile on her face faded. Even in the dim firelight, her rosy cheeks paled and sunk in against her cheekbones. "Your studies. There will be no time for your studies," she said as she raised her eyes to meet his.

He allowed himself only a brief glance, and then he looked back at the hot coals. He was satisfied. Her brief acknowledgment of his sacrifice was sufficient. It was best if he took responsibility for the well-being of the family, and he knew it. He would do his duty even at the cost of curtailing his studies with the Pharisees. Straight and true.

Ya'akov kicked apart the dying embers, and he and Maryam lay on mats next to the sleeping children. For hours, he heard Maryam's soft breathing as he waited for sleep that did not come. His neck and back were stiff, and he frequently sat up and rolled his shoulders, trying to loosen tight muscles. For a while, he stalked around the olive grove, framed on one side by the brooding shadow of Gerizim and on the other by flashes of lightning over the far off hills of Judea. Half breeds to the north and Gentiles polluting God's holy city. When he returned to his mat, he hardly slept, dreaming of Roman flags flapping in the lightning flashes; Yeshua was tearing them down.

Chapter Five

When Paulos had chosen Tarsos and Greek rhetoric over Jerusalem and Pharisaism three years earlier, Eli the sage stewed for a day, but then he offered to teach Paulos the wisdom of the elders under his direct tutelage. In the mornings, Paulos studied Greek rhetoric, learning skills of oration and argumentation; Arsenios the Greek became his classmate and friend. In the afternoons, Paulos learned Torah interpretation as a Pharisee from Eli, his mentor. Eli's solution salved Kleitos' initial anger over his son's choice. With his father's blessing, Paulos became a full-time student and rarely worked in the tentmaker's shop.

Now, the three years of his dual studies were nearly complete. Soon, he would finish his Greek university training, and he would return to his father's shop as his partner. Torah training as a Pharisee would continue. A Pharisee never stopped learning.

The late spring month of *Iyyar* was upon the land: green, lush, and expectant with budding flowers and ripening heads of grain. Arsenios stood knee deep in the River Kydnos. He shook his head, and his blond curls sprayed sparkling rainbow droplets of water. He cupped his hands and splashed water at Paulos. He laughed and pranced onto the shore. As he pulled his tunic over his head, Paulos discreetly glanced at the uncut flesh of his foreskin.

Arsenios was tall and smart like Paulos but that was the end of it. He was blond with tight curls—Paulos had straight brown hair; Arsenios' dimpled face was bare—Paulos' face was scraggly with budding whiskers; Arsenios was muscular and well proportioned—Paulos was puny and his legs, arms, and nose were too long; Arsenios was light-skinned but tanned—Paulos was dark-skinned but pale; Arsenios was a Gentile—Paulos, a Jew.

A random gray cloud in an otherwise blue sky drifted across the sun, casting a shadow over the river.

Paulos' friendship with Arsenios was his one little sin, a mixing of the unlike that the spirit of Torah prohibited. Worrisome, but Eli taught that Torah was to be a light to the nations; that the Jews, the descendants of Abraham, were to be a blessing to all the families in the earth; and that Gentiles could join the family of God through the time-honored practice of proselytization. Was it not Paulos' duty to spread God's own story to the Gentiles? In this way, Paulos often persuaded himself that his friendship with Arsenios was just a *little* sin and maybe no sin at all.

The gray cloud floated away, and the shadow passed. The hot sun barely warmed the chilly water. Yellow-bellied larks serenaded the eighteen-year-old men from the bushes, their melodies lilting over the gurgling rhythm of the brook. The men breathed heavily, filling their chests with the fresh vapors of springtime.

"God is good and generous and chooses to be in relationship with mere humans, is that correct?" asked Arsenios as he sat down on the rock next to Paulos.

Arsenios had become a God-worshiper, a *theosebes,* a Gentile attracted to the One God of Israel instead of the variety of impersonal Greek and Roman deities who treated humans as playthings. The alluring promise "I will be your God" drew Arsenios and many Gentiles to the threshold of the synagogue door, anxious yet hesitant to enter.

"Of course," Paulos said. "God calls, God invites, and God reaches for us."

"So, the initiative for this relationship comes from God?"

"Yes," said Paulos.

"And God wants this relationship to include all humans?"

Paulos hesitated to consider his answer. The question was complicated, as he knew well from his many discussions over years of study with Eli the sage. Boundaries defined God's family. Joining the family entailed a commitment to accept, honor and obey the boundary requirements.

"God wants his chosen people to be a blessing to all persons by bringing others into relationship with God," Paulos said. He then added the all-important caveat, the threshold that Gentiles must cross. "But this relationship must be on the basis of obeying Torah and following the commands of God."

"So, I must become a Jew before I am acceptable to God? Is God the God of the Jews only? Is he not the God of the Gentiles also?" Arsenios raised his familiar criticism of Torah boundaries.

"Torah is the badge that defines the family of God," Paulos replied softly, without conviction.

Arsenios rose from his perch and wandered to the edge of the river. He heaved a large stone high into the air, and it landed in the pool with a loud *whomp.* He watched in silence as the circles of the splash rippled outward. When he returned to sit next to Paulos on the boulder, he repeated the question that he had raised many times before, one which Paulos had struggled to answer.

"Why must I become circumcised in order to be acceptable to God? Circumcision is the mark of the Jews."

They came to a familiar impasse—the bloody ritual of cutting the foreskin. They sat together on a rock at the Kydnos pool, Arsenios, an uncircumcised Gentile, and Paulos, a circumcised Jew. Paulos pointed down the only path he knew—the path of Torah, the path of obedience, the path of living God's commands. Would Arsenios find God down that road?

It seemed as if the larks stopped singing as Arsenios plopped pebbles into the stream, and Paulos heard only the hollow plunking of the stones. He stroked his beak-nose as if to coax answers from deep within.

Did God not create the Gentiles in his own image? Do Gentiles belong to God's family? Should the Lord's own portion include the uncircumcised? But … Torah is clear; Torah is from God; Torah must be obeyed. God decreed that a man must cut off the flesh of his foreskin; Paulos could see no way around it.

Paulos feared that Torah boundaries would one day drive his friend from the synagogue doorstep—and from him. Sometimes he wondered why Arsenios remained his friend. Was there more than religious curiosity? Perhaps it was an intellectual attraction; after all, they were the two brightest students in the rhetoric class.

Paulos stole a glance at the Greek. He felt puny next to his muscled classmate. Only God knows what makes a friend a friend, Paulos thought with eyes closed. Only God knows a man's heart. Only God knows …

Arsenios repeated his question, breaking the silence. "Why must I become a Jew in order to be acceptable to God?"

The taunt hung thick in the air like a foul odor, and Paulos struggled for breath. He wished he could respond with a favorable answer.

"Let's catch fish." For the ever-exuberant Arsenios, the somber moment quickly passed. He scurried into the brush, looking for a crude fishing net they had stashed there together with a rusty iron pot. The net was fashioned of linen from Kleitos' shop and shaped by branches.

Paulos waded into the water and grabbed one end of the net. "Ow!" He stepped on a sharp clamshell in the riverbed, and he nearly lost his balance, causing Arsenios to chuckle.

They moved into current and plunged the net to the bottom of the river. Success! Two small round silver fish with orange bellies flopped in the net. The fishermen deposited the floppers into the old pot. They repeated the process as they moved to different spots on the river and soon the pot was full. When Paulos reached the shore, he realized the clamshell had sliced his heel, and he pressed the wound with his palm until the bleeding stopped.

Paulos gathered sticks and started a fire using a bow drill. The leaf smoke stung his eyes as he bent over to blow a flame to life. He boiled the fish to a delicate softness that allowed the men to pick the blanched meat from the bones. After they finished, Arsenios splashed in the shallows, stepped on a clam, and threw it onto the shore—then another and another. He dropped them next to the cook-fire.

"Let's eat clams."

Paulos' head jerked up. It was questionable enough that he ate fish with Arsenios the Gentile. His friendship with Arsenios was his one little sin. But to eat boiled clams! That was too much!

God is One. Unity, Wholeness, Order, Purity, Perfection, and Completeness: characteristics of the holiness of God. Torah established borders and categories that reflected the holiness of God. A clam was an imperfect anomaly. It did not have fins, it did not have gills, and it did not swim as a fish should swim. It was incongruent with its category; it did not reflect the wholeness or holiness of God; it was an unclean abomination.

"We cannot eat clams. Clams are unclean," Paulos said.

"I'll wash them in the river, and the water in the pot will boil away any dirt," replied Arsenios.

"Ritually unclean, I mean. We can't eat shellfish. It's a command of God," Paulos said to convince himself as much as Arsenios.

Arsenios stared blankly at Paulos. He shook his head and methodically threw each clam back into the river before departing without speaking. With a rush of beating wings, the flock of larks took flight, and then all was silent.

Paulos walked alone back to the city. Why not eat shellfish, he wondered? What was God thinking? Paulos tried to chase the questions from his mind. If he doubted Torah, was he not questioning God? He looked at the sliced heel of his foot, which had begun to bleed again. Leaning against a vacant house, he pressed his linen sleeve against the wound. Blood seeped into the threads, and a dark stain spread through the fibers of the white cloth.

"Beware the uncircumcised male who is not circumcised in the flesh of his foreskin on the eighth day!" The cold voice of Jubilees the phantom beggar hissed from beneath a tattered awning of the empty building.

Paulos couldn't help himself; he turned to face the probing of the unblinking white eyes that saw but didn't see.

Chapter Six

Levi the round butcher, father of seven daughters, lingered in the tentmaker's shop after Malachi, the gossiping raven, and his listeners had departed. Levi and Kleitos engaged in whispered but animated conversation with frequent glances toward Paulos. He could not hear their words, but he knew what they were saying. Levi waddled to the back of the shop to speak directly to his cornered prey. His wide body blocked the light from the windows, and he reeked of blood still fresh on his apron.

"I invite you to a meal with my family. I wish to discuss personal business with you," Levi said. With a thick hand scarred with nicks and cuts and one missing finger, he waved toward Kleitos, "Your father has agreed to come as well."

Paulos did not need to look at his father to know that he nodded. Levi had trapped Paulos who could not refuse the honor of sharing a meal with Levi's family. With a false smile, Paulos accepted the invitation. What else could he do? After all, he was well into marrying age.

When the evening arrived, Paulos intended to make a marriage contract. Not that he was eager to do so, but it was expected. As he left home with his father, Olympia handed him a fresh baked cake dripping in honey, a gift for Levi and his family. The evening sun squatted on the western mountains, watching them as they meandered toward the butcher's home. They arrived early.

"No need to knock yet," Paulos said to his father.

They passed by, but before long, the impatient sun could wait no longer and disappeared behind the mountains with a frightening suddenness. Dark alleys loomed before the bridegroom-to-be.

Barking dogs, bleating goats, and squawking chickens retreated into the dusky stillness. The soft glow of lamplight seeped through shuttered windows onto the dust-settled streets. It was time.

Paulos tapped lightly on the front door to Levi's house. When the door swung open, lamplight spilled over him, clinks of dishware and cookware filled his ears, and aromas of the feast to come swirled about his nose. It was all too much. He almost turned and ran, but he entered, stumbling on the stoop.

"Welcome. Welcome."

Levi appeared odd in this setting; he belonged in the busy agora, wearing a bloody apron, surrounded by butchered mutton hanging on meat hooks. At home, he wore a clean white tunic with a red sash around his abundant middle and an ankle length brown robe hanging open in the front; he appeared even more massive in domestic garb.

"Sit. Sit here at my right hand," Levi gestured at Kleitos who squatted down and leaned against pillows on the reclining couch. "Son, you may sit here," Levi said to Paulos and gestured to the spot at his left. The three-sided couch was U-shaped with a low table in the center. A single chair with a stiff back sat empty on the fourth side of the table.

Sitting at the couch was a new experience for Paulos. A simple stool for boys, a place on the reclining couch for men. The elegant Roman practice of reclining while dining had spread empire wide, even among many Jews. Paulos must learn to lean on his left arm while using his right hand to eat.

Levi jabbered about trivialities with Kleitos, and Paulos nodded appropriately or responded with one-word answers to questions posed to him. After the women finished their preparations for the feast, Levi's wife took her place on the chair, and the girls stood in a semi-circle behind her for the opening prayer. Esther, the eldest daughter, stood directly across from Paulos but kept her eyes low.

"Blessed are you, O Savior of Israel," began Levi as the meal commenced. "Blessed are you, O Lord, who gave Abraham his loving wife Sarah; blessed are you, O Lord, who made Abraham a blessing to the nations through his son Isaac. May you continue to give loving wives to the young men and offspring to their union."

"Amen," said Paulos with the others as he avoided eye contact with Levi.

Steaming dishes filled the room with rich aromas of spiced veal, nutty coriander in a vegetable stew, and green onions. Levi the butcher offered both mutton and veal from a fatted calf. Paulos had never dined at a meal that offered two meats, and he had never sampled veal, but the choice meats tasted bland to him that evening.

Each of the seven daughters flitted back and forth bringing this, attending to that, and always stealing a giggling glance at Paulos. Levi's plump wife clucked instructions to the daughters from her roost.

Esther the eldest should be the first sister to marry, according to custom. Paulos had known Esther for many years but had never seriously looked at her before that evening. Her nut-brown hair draped forward over her shoulders onto her breasts. A shiny green robe flowed elegantly from her neck to her sandaled feet, open at the front to allow her tight fitting tunic to reveal the shape of a woman. Balsam scented perfume delighted Paulos' nose as she leaned over him to refill his cup with dark red wine. Her silk robe brushed his cheek. Paulos could not probe her bashful eyes because she avoided his gaze. Her pinched cheeks glowed pink above a wisp of a smile.

Levi droned on about the finer points of butchering. "It is the proper removal of the blood from the animal that is of vital importance," explained Levi, who bore the traditional name of the tribe of priests in old Israel. There were no priests in Tarsos, but Levi the butcher played a religious role nevertheless by ensuring that the meat eaten by the Jews of Tarsos was pure, according to Torah. "Blood is life. Life is from God. Blood is holy and cannot be eaten."

Levi wiped his lips with a loud smack, signaling the end of the meal. He drank the last of his wine then refilled his cup from a jar of barley beer for the discussion to follow.

"More wine? Or do you prefer beer when talking amongst men?"

"Beer for me," said Kleitos.

Paulos shrugged, and Levi filled Paulos' cup to the brim with frothy beer.

Levi's wife and daughters left the room. Paulos looked again at Esther as she hesitated at the door; for the first time, she looked back at him, blinking her long eyelashes. Esther and Paulos had never spoken a word to each other. Yet, in that moment, her emerald green eyes promised him.

In the twinkling of her eye, Paulos knew she was an ideal match for him, but in a rare glimpse of self-understanding, Paulos realized that he would never marry. She was perfect for him, but his heart did not stir.

For years, Levi had stalked Paulos. Even as he avoided Levi, Paulos had expected to become favorably inclined toward marriage when the moment arrived, assuming that the mantle of matrimony would fit comfortably upon his shoulders. Now, in the alluring glance of the beautiful Esther, his perfect match, he realized that marriage was not for him. What had been merely a twinkling premonition now burst forth in a dazzling flash of insight.

Not that he understood the why of it. All he knew was that he would never marry. If the loving glance of Esther did not stir his passion, he knew that his heart was hardened against marriage to any woman. The stark certainty of the revelation surprised him. That he calmly allowed that insight to direct his actions surprised him even more.

"Isn't she beautiful? And strong! She'll bear you many sons. What do you think, shall we make an engagement?" Levi's fleshy face glowed red and sweaty as he spoke through the strained smile of a nervous father-in-law to be.

"I'm still young. I'm not sure I'd be a good husband to your daughter." Paulos floated over the room, listening to words he had not planned to speak.

"I was your age when I became engaged to my dear wife. An engagement does not mean an immediate marriage."

"True enough," said Kleitos. "Your dear mother and I were engaged for several years before we married."

"I might leave Tarsos. It wouldn't be fair to take your daughter from you." The idea of leaving Tarsos just occurred to Paulos. He risked a glance at his father, and he was not surprised at the dark scowl cemented on the paternal face.

"Of course, you could expect a substantial dowry," said Levi.

Kleitos added, "We have the details worked out. It's a fair arrangement."

Paulos replied in a soft voice without looking at either of his elders, "You're known as a generous man and successful in your trade. I have no doubt that your dowry would be more than sufficient."

Levi gulped down the last of his barley beer. Beads of sweat glistened on his forehead, and his loose jowls tightened as he leaned toward Paulos and lowered his voice.

"Of course, Esther is our oldest and should be married first, but perhaps you have more interest in a different daughter?"

A muffled groan escaped from behind the door.

"Esther is a fine woman, and I don't mean to suggest any dissatisfaction with her." Paulos glanced in the direction of the moan. "But ..."

In the blink of Esther's eye, his life had changed. Paulos arrived intending to conclude the engagement that Levi, his parents, and his culture expected. In the glance of Esther, Paulos realized the path of marriage, children, and grandchildren was not for him.

"I don't mean to say no, but I'm not yet able to say yes."

Levi slumped against the couch, his portliness melting over the edges. Kleitos glared, and his lips moved silently, but Paulos heard his anger anyway.

Paulos stood and thanked Levi profusely for the fine meal. Levi stared blankly without standing. Levi's wife and the six younger daughters, but not Esther, appeared and thanked Paulos and Kleitos for coming to their home.

For the first few paces through the dark streets of Tarsos, neither father nor son said anything. Paulos had followed his heart and flaunted convention. Perhaps it was merely the barley beer, but he was giddy despite the brutal scolding he knew was coming.

It was not long before Kleitos erupted. *"Be fruitful and multiply. That is the command of God!"* Kleitos said. *"I will make your offspring as numerous as the stars of heaven and as the sand that is on the seashore.* That is our destiny as sons of Abraham."

Paulos knew these words of Torah well, and his father's arguments had no effect. But when Kleitos dropped his voice and spit out his last words like rancid meat, Paulos' heart sagged.

"You bring dishonor to me and your mother."

Chapter Seven
33 C.E.

"Yeshua is coming!"

Ya'akov stopped sawing the pine board and jerked his face toward his youngest brother, Joses. Ya'akov, Jude, and Simon sweated together raising a house, and Joses had scampered to their worksite with the news he had heard in the agora.

"Yeshua is coming! Yeshua is coming to Jerusalem!"

"So, the rumors are true. I heard that many Galileans are with him," Ya'akov said to his brothers. He felt the same swell of pride that he heard in the voice of Joses and that he saw in the smiles of his brothers, but the leering face of the Roman governor, Pontius Pilate, shadowed his thoughts and soured his excitement.

It had been ten years since Ya'akov arrived in Jerusalem to become a student of the Pharisees and seven years since the death of his father, Yosef, when Ya'akov had become head of the family. Now, he was thirty years old.

Ya'akov's success as a Jerusalem tradesman these past ten years had lessened his resentment that he had become the responsible head of the family, rather than Yeshua the oldest son. With influential contacts gained through his training as a Pharisee scholar, Ya'akov and Jude prospered as tradesmen in bustling Jerusalem, assisted by younger brothers Simon and Joses. Theirs was not the only home in Jerusalem that had once swelled with too many inhabitants, but extra rooms and a rooftop veranda soon appeared. Shera, Ya'akov's wife, had treated his family as her own. Seema had become the spoiled favorite of all, but especially Maryam, her doting grandmother.

It had all worked out well; Ya'akov's dependability had allowed his idealistic older brother to follow his own calling, which had proven to be less irresponsible than Ya'akov once thought. Yeshua had visited the family in Jerusalem a few times, and his words rang true in Ya'akov's ears. His brother was a deep thinker with a pure heart.

Still, in those early years, Ya'akov saw Yeshua as nothing more than an insightful Torah teacher. Later, when Ya'akov first heard the rumors of a growing movement in Galilee, he had not paid close attention. According to the whispers in the street, there was a man in Galilee who attracted a massive following in the countryside, whose voice echoed the prophets of old with a call for justice and mercy, who criticized the hollow rituals of the priesthood, and who taught according to the pure spirit of Torah. Most importantly, he promised the imminent arrival of God's own kingdom, and his followers believed. Hope was alive in Galilee.

But when Ya'akov heard the name of the man, Yeshua from Nazareth, he had dropped a hammer on his toe, splitting it open with blood spurting into the dust, yet he felt no pain. *Yeshua of Nazareth.* The name on the lips of many.

That was the previous summer, nine months earlier, and the news of his brother's huge following prompted Ya'akov and his brothers to return to Galilee to visit Yeshua, the firstborn, and to witness his ministry firsthand. They sat with the simple folk of Galilee and listened to his mesmerizing words:

"Blessed are the poor; blessed are the meek; blessed are those who hunger and thirst; blessed are those who are persecuted, for theirs is the coming kingdom of God."

Yeshua's booming voice bounced off the sides of the valleys, engulfing the swelling crowds—mostly poor peasants who had no reason to hope—but Yeshua gave them hope; Ya'akov could see it in their eyes. Yeshua walked among his people, touching them as he passed. "Yours is the coming kingdom of God." Yeshua's voice roused the faceless masses like a noontide breeze across waving fields of grain, stirring the yellowing stalks to life.

"That's my brother," said Joses to anyone who would listen, and Ya'akov would smile and nod. He also was proud of Yeshua and glad that his own responsible behavior had allowed Yeshua to grow into the important man he had become—famous, too, with a growing reputation that reached Jerusalem. Ya'akov didn't mind the newfound respect he received from his circle of Pharisees.

And Ya'akov dared hope that Yeshua's promise of the imminent coming of the kingdom of God was true. God must see the oppression and injustice under the Romans and their aristocratic puppets. If Yeshua's movement could hasten the day that the Gentiles were rooted from God's holy land, well, praise God, thought Ya'akov.

Now, Ya'akov again had doubts about his brother's good sense. It was one thing to speak as a prophet in far off Galilee, but leading a throng of Galilean peasants to Jerusalem was foolhardy.

"Yeshua is coming to Jerusalem."

With Joses' announcement, the brothers babbled with excitement, but Ya'akov issued a stern directive.

"Gather our tools and return home," he said.

Yeshua faced danger in Jerusalem. The king of a nearby region had recently beheaded Yeshua's mentor called the Baptizer. Rumors crept through the back streets of Jerusalem that Yeshua was the long awaited Mashiah sent by God to restore the throne of King David and to throw off the yoke of foreign oppression. A foolish notion, Ya'akov was sure, but how would Pontius Pilate react to popular clamor for a new king of the Jews, a rightful king, a true king, God's own anointed? How would Pilate respond to the swelling crowds?

Ya'akov hurried into the city to speak to his Pharisee friends in the Sanhedrin, the Jewish leadership council of seventy. He arrived at the meeting place of the Sanhedrin, a private villa, just as the council was adjourning. Recognizing the green turban worn by Yosef of Arimathea, Ya'akov merged into the flow of pedestrians to reach his friend. The green turban, ringed by a gold band at the base, made the short man appear taller. Nicodemus, another Pharisee member of the Sanhedrin, was with Yosef.

"We must speak," whispered Ya'akov as he joined his Pharisee friends.

Nicodemus was heavy, broad, and soft, and the fleshy jowls of his face jiggled as the trio hustled to Ya'akov's house to speak in private. This was no matter for discussion on the streets of Jerusalem, and the sanctuary of Ya'akov's home was near.

Packs of legionaries roamed the streets like wolves stalking prey; Governor Pontius Pilate had sent extra soldiers from Caesarea to maintain order during the upcoming Passover. Ya'akov and the two Pharisees encountered four of them teasing a young dog, jabbing at the pup with their lances. The poor animal's yips were more fearful than threatening. *Stinking Romans.* It seemed the words of Ya'akov's father had lost their bite. Much as Ya'akov despised the Romans, he feared them more. He turned away from the Romans and led his friends along a different route to his home.

"We, too, have heard the rumors," said Yosef after draining the cup of water that Ya'akov poured from a pitcher. The three men sat on stools around a solid oak table on Ya'akov's veranda.

"There may be hundreds of Galileans, maybe more, traveling with him," added Nicodemus. "The Romans will certainly fear an uprising. They'll see the peasants as insurrectionists, an army of revolutionaries marching on Jerusalem."

Yosef was the optimist. "There are whispers in the agora that Yeshua is the Mashiah coming to overthrow the Romans. Pray that it is true! Praise God if it is true!" He pounded his fist on the table as he spoke.

The Pharisees were no friends of the Romans. The Pharisees were no friends of the aristocratic Sadducees and the puppet High Priest who served at the pleasure of the Romans. Yeshua's criticism of the Romans and the religious establishment found a sympathetic ear among the Pharisees, who believed in the redemptive promises of God to restore Israel through a legitimate king and heir to King David. Through his prophets, God had promised a new King David, his anointed, the Mashiah, and the Pharisees were hopeful.

"Praise God if it is true!" Yosef said again.

Yeshua promised the coming kingdom of God, but he made no claim that he would be the Mashiah, and Ya'akov considered such foolish rumblings to be an absurdity. The preposterous claims of the peasants deluded some of his Pharisee friends such as Yosef, caught up in their own hopes, unable to think clearly on the matter. Ya'akov's brother Yeshua, from a poor family in a country village, would be no king. His brother, who taught love of neighbor, would be no warrior to lead God's avenging army.

For a moment, they sat in silence. Nicodemus slowly began to shake his head, his breathing quickened, and his jowls swayed. A deep sigh interrupted the portly man's rapid breaths. "Yeshua and his followers will be crushed. The Romans are a mighty army."

"What if this is from God?" Yosef asked. "What if God miraculously intervenes on behalf of Yeshua and his followers? What if Yeshua is right and the kingdom of God is at hand? Can the Romans stand up to God?"

Ya'akov both envied and scoffed at Yosef's willingness to hold onto hope in spite of circumstances. In Ya'akov's sitting position, the leather cord around his neck was too short to allow his norm to dangle freely, and the iron measure rested awkwardly on the shelf created by his belly; the sharp metal edge poked his chest over his heart.

Yosef rolled his knuckles on the tabletop with a sound like a galloping horse.

Rrump.

Rrump.

Ya'akov wanted to hope. He remembered the crowds listening to the words of Yeshua the previous summer, and he yearned for the fresh country breeze on his face, for the buoyant optimism that lifted the Galileans, for the trust that swelled confidence in the faceless masses. *Yours is the coming kingdom of God.* He wanted to hope, but he could only fear. He closed his eyes and attempted to pray, but he saw Pontius Pilate and centurions and swords and lances and … his eyes jerked open. Nicodemus was right—the mighty Roman legions would crush Yeshua and his followers.

Rrump.

Rrump.

Finally Nicodemus spoke. "If it's God's will that the time is at hand, then it matters not what we say or do. Praise God if that's his will, but if this isn't the time or place for God's Mashiah, then Yeshua is in great danger. Ya'akov, you must warn your brother."

A muffled whimper came from the back of the room where the family had been listening from the shadows. Ya'akov went to them. Tears streamed down the beardless face of Joses, the youngest, and Simon's lips quivered. Jude stood with his jaw clenched tight. Maryam smiled serenely, but her eyes were moist. His wife, Shera, clutched their eight-year-old daughter, Seema, close under her robe.

"Go to him," Maryam said. "Tell him of the danger in Jerusalem. Tell him—Maryam broke down and sobbed on Ya'akov's shoulder.

Once again, it had come to him, the responsible one who must account for his brother's irresponsibility. His back ached. His muscles felt tight like the bowstrings of a legion of archers, drawn and ready to loose a thousand arrows. He rolled his shoulders and spoke. "Jude and Simon will come with me. Joses will stay and protect the women."

Rain began to fall as the brothers departed the city, hiking north to intercept Yeshua and the Galileans. As the night darkened, they trekked through pelting raindrops that stung their faces. In the wet blackness, they stumbled up the path to the hilltop outside the city where they huddled briefly under storm tossed olive branches. Ya'akov glanced at Jerusalem as a lightning flash backlit the stone ramparts of Antonia, the Roman fortress that blighted the city of God.

They didn't linger. Turning their faces to the wind and rain, they slogged through the small town of Bethany, past the city of Jericho, and up the Jordan River valley; many miles passed beneath their feet before the first slivers of gray dawn appeared over their right shoulders.

By daybreak, the storm had ended, and they encountered other foot travelers who reported that Yeshua was near. The brothers quickened their pace. Campfire plumes guided them to his encampment: tents and trees dotted the west slope of the Jordan River valley; storm-soaked pilgrims huddled close to crackling campfires; and wet robes hung drying on sticks, resembling crucifixes.

Suddenly, a shout, "Ya'akov, come here!"

Ya'akov, the brother of Yeshua, turned to face his namesake, Ya'akov, the brother of Yochanan. Yochanan and Ya'akov, the fishermen sons of Zebedee, were close friends and confidants of Yeshua. The Sons of Thunder he called them. From the first time they had met months earlier, Ya'akov—brother of Yeshua—and Ya'akov—brother of Yochanan—shared a kinship based on their common name.

"Have you come to join us?" Ya'akov the brother of Yochanan asked. "Yeshua will be pleased. He climbed to the mountaintop with Cephas and Yochanan to pray. Sit by the fire and eat something. You look a sight."

The wet, shivering brothers welcomed the invitation to sit on logs and stones while soaking up warmth from the campfire. Fresh-cut green branches hissed in the fire with sap bubbling out the ends. A woodsman's axe leaned against a stack of logs.

There was movement in the tree line, and Yeshua emerged from the shadows. On one side of Yeshua was his best friend named Simon, but some called him Cephas, and the Greeks called him Petros: long-limbed, slender as a reed, and half a head taller than Yeshua. On the other side was Yochanan: sinewy and muscular with square shoulders and an angular frame, half a head shorter than Yeshua.

Yeshua was in the middle. He has lost weight, thought Ya'akov as he patted his own potbelly; Yeshua must not eat well in the vagrant life he has chosen.

The brothers stood as Yeshua approached. When he recognized them, he lunged the last few paces, and the four brothers embraced as one before they sat down and ate figs and hard bread around the campfire. Yeshua peppered his brothers with questions about the family.

"How is Mother? How are the girls? Where is Joses? How is Shera? How is Seema?"

"They are well," said Jude.

"You all look a bit worn."

"We walked through the night in the rainstorm," Jude answered Yeshua's questions as Ya'akov waited for the right moment to speak.

"What a large group of followers," said Simon as his eyes surveyed the camp.

Yeshua quickly scanned the crowds with a surprised look as if he had not noticed the horde that accompanied him. Yeshua returned his gaze to the fire as he poked a stick in the coals. Without looking up, he spoke to Ya'akov. "Why are you here?"

"Danger awaits you in Jerusalem." Ya'akov blurted the reason for their midnight dash.

Yeshua shrugged his shoulders without looking at Ya'akov. He continued to poke in the fire without speaking. He arose, grabbed a log from the pile, and threw it onto the coals.

As he sat down, he looked Ya'akov in the eye and spoke. "Why are you worried? Do you not trust God? Do you not see that I am following the path laid out by God?"

Smoke swirled in the rising breeze and stung Ya'akov's eyes. Of course, he trusted God. Did Yeshua alone hear God speaking? Ya'akov wiped his eyes and brushed aside Yeshua's rebuke.

"I know Jerusalem," Ya'akov said. "I know the dangers that await you there. The Romans will feel threatened. Pontius Pilate, the Governor, is a cruel man. The bastard High Priest who empties the piss pots of the Romans is evil."

Jude added, "Your ragtag followers cannot resist the Romans. The Romans will crush these poor people. I see a few axes, and I am sure there are knives, but this is a rabble and not an army."

Yeshua slowly looked around at the many tents and many people. He placed both hands on his forehead, threw his head back, and ran his hands back over his sandy, curly hair. Finally, he spoke. "I do not want to risk harm to these faithful Galileans. They will do nothing to provoke Roman violence."

"And what of you dear brother? Will you provoke the Romans? Can you hold your tongue? Can you control this rabble? Even if you act peaceably, you're still in danger," Ya'akov said. "I urge you, I plead with you, please turn back."

Yeshua was silent. He inhaled deeply and ran his hands through his hair. He shut his eyes as if lost in thought—or prayer.

Simon poked at the fire with a stick, and a hissing log rolled toward his feet.

"Be careful. Stop playing around before you burn yourself," Ya'akov scolded.

Yeshua stood on his feet and stepped toward the morning sun that ascended the eastern sky. After a moment, Ya'akov joined him, and the two brothers walked alone to a small rise overlooking the River Jordan.

Ya'akov gazed upriver to the north. For a moment, they were boys again during the carefree days of their youth, splashing in the Jordan where it poured out of the Sea of Galilee to begin its southward journey. They were chilled to the bone until Maryam opened her outer robe and pulled their quivering bodies close against her tunic, like a hen gathering her chicks under wing.

The down slope of the ridge fell away toward the river that crossed in front of them. Mist lifted from the sheen of the clear waters like billowing incense. Mourning doves offered their haunting plainsong from the terebinth shrubs on the riverbank.

The river trailed off to their right. They could not see the end of it. Far beyond their vista, past Jerusalem, the river emptied itself into the Dead Sea.

"I must go to Jerusalem," Yeshua said.

Framed by sandy curls lifting in the breeze, Yeshua's weathered face glowed warm and brown in the morning sun. Ya'akov saw their father in the eyes and the smile—the same reassuring glance he had seen when Yosef had gripped his hand tight before sending him to Jerusalem to study as a Pharisee. Ya'akov's resistance and resentment melted away. He only wished he had his brother's faith.

"God be with you," Ya'akov said softly.

"And with you."

Chapter Eight

"Make a low bellowing sound like a dying bull, releasing all your breath and straining your sides." The nasal drone of the leader echoed in the narrow cave. The ceremony in the secret cave of the cult of Mithras, hidden in the Taurus Mountains near Tarsos, celebrated the sacrificial death of the star god, Taurus, the bull.

Shadows danced in the flickering candlelight as chanting male voices filled the chamber. The initiated sat on benches lining the cave, facing inward toward a narrow aisle with inlaid mosaic images of spirits ascending to the stars. The mosaics progressed up the aisle to an altar. Behind the altar, Mithras stabbed Taurus the bull in a sprawling mural. Stalks of grain sprouted from the tufted tip of the bull's tail—new life from the sacrificial death of the bull-god.

The leader walked down the aisle offering a sip from a bowl of wine that he said was the blood of the bull. He stopped before reaching Arsenios, a mere novice attending his first and only Mithras ceremony. The existence of the cult with a cave in the mountains was a poorly held secret in Tarsos, but only participants knew what actually took place. Arsenios had bragged to Paulos that he would feign interest to secure an invitation. His purpose accomplished, he ran to share the delicious experience with Paulos.

Arsenios' report rattled in Paulos' head as his long legs carried him quickly to the synagogue to report to Eli the sage. Now twenty-five years old, Paulos still thought of Eli as his mentor.

The stooped elder hobbled into the spacious room that served as Sabbath meeting place. The chamber had also been the scene of group Torah classes for Paulos as a youngster and later his individual instruction as a Pharisee. Eli's willow cane stabbed the cadence for his ambling entrance. The sage's long, white beard was unkempt. Eli taught Torah, the five books of Moses: the teaching, the law, the basic understanding of God's revelation and will for his people. Ancient scrolls preserved written Torah. The mind of Eli the Pharisee preserved oral Torah—interpretation and adaptation of the written word.

Paulos held his mentor's elbow and eased him into a squat on the tile floor. Paulos sat next to a stumpy-legged table with a flickering oil lamp and smoldering incense. A shaft of sunlight streamed through the window, catching a billowing haze that danced before disappearing into the cavernous high ceiling above.

As a young man, Eli had received Pharisee training in Jerusalem, learning the art of Torah interpretation. "You will follow my steps to Jerusalem one day, Saul my son," he often said to Paulos, using the Hebrew form of his protégé's name. When Paulos had decided against Pharisee training in Jerusalem, he knew that Eli was disappointed, but Eli's offer of personal instruction in the wisdom of the Pharisees had been more than an acceptable substitute. At least, Paulos thought so.

In the ten years since he began Pharisee training with Eli, Paulos' immersion in Torah and the other holy books served both his intellect and his soul. He scrupulously followed the commands of Torah with great vigor. His confident Torah religiosity had buried youthful self-doubt deep beyond the reach of his conscience, where it rarely intruded upon his self-satisfaction. The only shadow was his friendship with Arsenios the Gentile, but he had convinced himself that he served God's purposes by proselytizing the Greek to Israelite religion.

"Teacher, a Greek friend claims knowledge of the secret Mithras cult," Paulos reported to Eli. "Tell me about the mystery religions."

Eli frowned at Paulos. "I have heard of this one or that one," Eli said. "From Egypt comes Isis and Osiris, from Galatia comes

Cybele and Attis, and right here in Tarsos we have Mithras. Stay away from such nonsense."

Paulos expected such an answer, but it did not satisfy his curiosity. It was not the mythology of the pagan cult but the mystical experience that intrigued him. "What of Jewish mystics who see visions?"

Eli tugged at his beard without looking at his curious protégé. The flesh of his cheeks stretched taut as he pursed his lips. "Fetch the scroll of the prophet Ezekiel."

In the room that served as the library for the synagogue, Paulos found the Ezekiel scroll on the shelf for *The Prophets*. The library cabinets also supported shelves for *Torah* and *The Writings*. Together, these scrolls comprised the holy books of Israelite religion, compiled by ancient priests half a millennium earlier, copied and recopied by unknown scribes countless times since then, and now translated from Hebrew into Greek. Paulos returned to Eli and unrolled the scroll of Ezekiel, one of the major prophets of old.

"Begin at the beginning." Eli sat in his familiar cross-legged posture with the backs of his hands resting on his knees with open palms facing upward.

Paulos skimmed the words: "The heavens were opened, and I saw visions of God ... As I looked, a stormy wind came ... a great cloud with brightness around it and fire flashing forth." Paulos raced through the words of the text that described bizarre images of half-human beasts, spinning wheels, spirits, and clashing thunder.

Eli's voice called him back. "That is enough."

Paulos was breathless, and his heart was pounding. Undoubtedly, he had read these words earlier in his training, but now the words thrilled him. "Tell me more," said Paulos, probing the nearly sightless, cobwebbed eyes of his mentor.

"The Prophet Ezekiel describes the God who is indescribable. How do we see the God that is beyond sight? How do we know the God who is beyond knowing? The absolute holiness of God is greater than a mere human can bear and more than we can comprehend.

These are words beyond words with meaning beyond meaning."

"I understand," said Paulos.

Eli scowled. "Do not be overconfident, my young friend. Self-doubt is the blossom of wisdom. When Moses faced God in the burning bush, he asked, *What is your name?* We must all pursue the same question," Eli said, and then his voice dropped to a whisper, "but we err if we believe we have the answer."

The oil lamp flared and briefly chased the shadows, but then the flame died, leaving the room dark except for the shaft of light that fell across the scroll in Paulos' hands.

"As soon as we name the one whose name is unknown, we create the one who created us," Eli said. "Ezekiel the prophet painted colorful pictures that point to the truth, but they are untrue."

Paulos squinted into the nearly blind eyes of the old man. Had the fuzziness that coated his eyes reached his mind? Paulos began to doubt his mentor who spoke in silly riddles. He tugged on his nose and his gaze returned to the written words. His finger traced the scribed marks with care not to touch the holy scroll. He read aloud, "This was the appearance of the likeness of the glory of the Lord."

The wizened old man rhythmically tapped his willow cane on the tile floor. First, he offered a promise. "One day *you* will see the glory of the Lord."

Tap. Tap. Tap.

And then, he issued a challenge, "What words will you speak when you tell the tale? What picture will you paint?"

Tap. Tap. Tap.

And finally, he uttered a warning, "But retain your humility and self-doubt. Do not pretend to answer Moses' question or paint truer pictures than Ezekiel. Do not commit idolatry."

Eli extended an unsteady hand toward Paulos, and Paulos cradled it between his own. Paulos welcomed the promise and accepted the challenge even if he didn't hear the warning of the old man whose age was telling.

Paulos was ready for whatever God had in store for him. Despite his mentor's admonition, he brimmed with self-confidence. He had learned his Torah lessons well, and he lived what he had learned, fulfilling every word, every letter. As to righteousness under Torah, he was blameless. Nothing could separate him from the chosen of God, the Lord's own portion. Nothing.

Chapter Nine

The cool damp of the Tarsos winter lingered beyond its welcome that year, the nineteenth year of the reign of Emperor Tiberius, and the twenty-fifth year of Paulos life, 33 C.E. When the winds of spring finally warmed the Cilician plain, Paulos and Arsenios celebrated with their first swim of the season.

Paulos leaped into the chilled waters that had been a mountain snowfall just a few waterfalls and torrents ago. "Aaaah," he exhaled audibly as his head bobbed above the surface. Holding his breath, he submerged before exploding into the fresh air, shaking his head, and spraying droplets from each dark hair. "Aaaah," he breathed again, softer this time, as he climbed onto his familiar rocky perch. He tossed his head back and ran splayed fingers through his thick brown hair with a reddish hue that glistened in the noonday sun. Water dripped from his beard onto his chest, coursing tiny rivulets that dried and disappeared.

Arsenios continued to frolic in the cool stream. The sun reflected at the spot where he splashed, and the spray glistened with rainbow colors. His blond curls drooped in a tangle.

He ascended to the rocky perch and sat next to Paulos with a hearty laugh. A droplet of water dribbled from a dimple down his chin. The chill river water had stolen the breath from their lungs, and they breathed heavily, watching the sun sparkle on the water.

Paulos felt Arsenios' gaze wash over him, and he lifted his face to his friend's stare. Paulos drank of the eyes deep as the city well. What was there, at the bottom, in the Greek's heart? He was about to have his answer.

Arsenios leaned forward and kissed Paulos on his lips.

Paulos flinched. Arsenios tilted his head as a smile broadened across his face. He leaned forward and kissed him again; Paulos did not resist at first, but then his eyes burst open, and he looked down at his swelling loins as if awakened from a dream. A bad dream. A nightmare. He was naked and exposed.

Paulos stumbled to his robe to cover his shame; the words of Torah clanged in his ear like an accusing alarm bell, "You shall not lie with a male as with a woman; it is an abomination." Torah was clear. He was unclean. His shame was uncovered.

"Come back my friend," called the naked man on the rock who invited Paulos back with a wave of his hand.

Paulos risked a glance and nearly yielded to the temptation, and that was what shook him to the core: it was not merely the kiss but that he wanted another. The frightened Jew turned his back on his Greek friend.

Paulos wandered aimlessly back to the city, and he found himself in a dead-end alley facing Jubilees, the blind beggar. The searing glare of the phantom held him transfixed, unable to resist the probing of the eyes that did not see but that saw too much.

"The uncircumcised belong not to the children of the covenant but to the children of destruction, destined to be destroyed and slain from the earth," the toothless mouth barely moved as it uttered the icy words.

Paulos saw it clearly now, Arsenios and the Gentiles were beyond redemption. Eli's teaching was too lenient, too tolerant, too forgiving, but the damning words of Jubilees rang true. There could be no muddled compromise of the stark requirements of Torah. Even a late circumcision could not satisfy the strict requirement that a male child must be circumcised on the eighth day. The Gentiles were the children of destruction not the children of the covenant, destined for annihilation. The Lord's Own Portion did not include the Gentiles.

"God's people should cover their shame, and should not uncover themselves as the Gentiles uncover themselves," said Jubilees.

The toneless voice of Jubilees cut deep, slicing away the veneer of Torah fastidiousness that had protected Paulos from seeing his true self: guilty, unclean, corrupt, impure, defiled, and contaminated. Paulos' one little sin had rendered him an abomination unto the Lord, incongruent with humanity, inconsistent with his own kind. He had exposed himself, and he was exposed. He had uncovered himself, and his shame was uncovered. Through the blind eyes of the seer, Paulos saw himself, his true self, for the first time.

"There will be great wrath against the children of Israel who turn aside from God's word so that they may be removed and rooted out of the land. And there will no more be pardon or forgiveness unto them for all the sin of this eternal error." A slight twitch of Jubilee's pale, thin lips hinted at a smile as he uttered condemnation of the self-reliant, self-righteous, self-confident Torah scholar.

With the last words of his accuser, Paulos collapsed to the ground. He was beyond hope, beyond redemption, outside the family of God. No pardon for him. No forgiveness for him. Accursed. God would root him out. Paulos had always feared this judgment, mostly unconsciously and usually buried by his religiosity, but now he lay in the dust, naked and exposed, before the God-Who-Judges.

Paulos stared through bleary eyes at the linen swatch in his hands. He had barely slept the night before.

"Redo this stitch. Do it right this time," his father said.

"Go to Hades!"

An awl slipped from Kleitos' surprised fingers and stabbed the floorboard, quivering like a dagger.

Paulos was immediately ashamed at the disrespectful words that had spilled from his mouth, and he stormed out the tent maker's shop and ran to the river. He lunged into thigh deep water and scrubbed with sand until his skin bled.

"Hello, my friend." Arsenios watched from the riverbank.

"Damn you! Damn me!" screamed Paulos as he picked up a

pebble and hurled it at Arsenios, missing by a wide margin.

Arsenios had a quizzical look on his face. "Stop playing around," he said.

A second pebble whizzed by the Gentile's head, and his mouth dropped. "What're you doing? Be careful."

The third throw found its mark; the pebble thrown by Paulos glanced off Arsenios' leg. Arsenios dropped to his knees, his eyes welled with tears, and the color drained from his face.

Paulos' heart flipped at the confused, betrayed look on his friend's face. Paulos knew that the pain felt by Arsenios was deeper than the bruise on his leg. A fresh wave of remorse washed over Paulos, his unsteady legs buckled, and he collapsed in the stream.

Both men struggled to their feet at the same time. When Paulos stumbled out of the water toward Arsenios, the Greek turned and ran. Paulos fell on his face in the sand and sobbed.

Branches whipped his skin as Paulos wandered aimlessly. He sat on sharp rocks and then wandered again. Clouds slid off the snowy crags, seeped down the valleys, and spread across the plain as a suffocating blanket. Darkness fell on Paulos, and he spent the night alone in the thicket near the river.

Raindrops roused him from semi-sleep. Night blackness turned to gray dawn; leaves quaked in a rising breeze. Shivering, he turned his back to the pelting rain. His empty stomach growled, but he doubted that hot porridge would heal the ache. He spied the dried up skin of a snake, rotting in the rocks. If only he could shed his sinful flesh as easily as the asp. He was condemned to live in his body filled with decay.

He followed his feet to the city; he removed his sandals before stepping over the doorstep into his parent's home and instinctively reached toward the "Sh'ma" affixed to the doorpost—before he pulled his hand back; he was unworthy. Olympia turned silently to face him; Paulos looked away, unwilling to face her questioning eyes. He brushed past her, fearing that she saw deep beyond the surface layers of filth into his contaminated soul.

He carried a vase of water into his first floor bedroom that he seldom used, and he washed himself and his clothes. He would have scrubbed bare to the bone if he could have removed his sinful flesh. He rubbed a damp cloth over every inch of skin before dressing in fresh clothes and rushing out the door.

"Paulos?"

He didn't hear the concern in his mother's voice, mistaking it for the condemnation he deserved. He was convinced that he had always dishonored his parents. The wretched man wandered the streets of Tarsos, lost and alone, accursed and condemned.

Chapter Ten

Ya'akov sat straight up in bed. Since Yeshua's death several weeks earlier, the slightest noise awakened him. What had he heard? What had disturbed his sleep? He cocked his head and listened for the sound that had roused him.

From his closed bedroom on the second floor of his house, Ya'akov heard muted thumping on his front door. Shera looked at him with tears running down her cheeks, clutching their daughter Seema close. Since Yeshua's crucifixion, their grief mixed with fear. Was it the stinking Romans come to arrest him?

The bedroom door creaked open, and Maryam and the others stepped into the room with eyes wide and faces gray as cold ashes from the hearth.

Ya'akov's mind raced as he considered what to do. Why hadn't they fled to far off Galilee with the others? He regretted his decision to remain in Jerusalem after his brother's execution. His gray-haired mother was shaking; he had never before seen her afraid. She seemed to have shriveled in the weeks since the crucifixion. She had lost one son, and the knocking on the door signaled danger to the rest of her family. The fear in her face pained him. It was his fault; he had failed as head of the family. He should have led them to safety. The pounding on the door continued.

Ya'akov rose from the bed, exited the bedroom, and walked to the edge of the veranda where he spied from the shadows to the street below. If necessary, he would surrender as his family slipped out the back door.

Dark figures lurked in the shadows, but they were not soldiers. A mob? The jeers of the unwashed scum at his brother's crucifixion still echoed. Ya'akov leaned over the edge to gain a better view just as the moon appeared from behind a sliding cloud. An arm jerked from the shadows to point at him, and Ya'akov recoiled back.

"There he is!"

A harsh whisper called to him from the street below.

"Ya'akov! Open your door!"

Who called his name? Was it a friend? Ya'akov bolted down the stairway to the front door and opened it a crack; he staggered back at the sight of the tall thin man with a mischievous smile.

"Cephas?" Ya'akov's voice squeaked.

Ya'akov recognized Yeshua's best friend, the one with several names—Cephas, Simon, and Petros. Here too were brothers Yochanan and Ya'akov—the one who shared his name, Maryam of Magdala, and other Galileans who had fled to Galilee after Yeshua's death. Standing in the back was his own cousin Symeon from Nazareth.

"Come, come. Come inside all of you." Ya'akov looked up and down the street and saw no one watching. Why had the Galileans returned to Jerusalem? Had they lost their senses? The fools endangered his family.

Ya'akov led them up the steps to the veranda, the only place in the house large enough for such a crowd. His frightened household stared wide-eyed at the Galileans. Over the rising din of excited murmurs, Ya'akov climbed atop a table and gestured for quiet; "shhhhh," he whispered, placing a finger over his lips. "Be quiet or you will raise the dead!"

Cephas stepped from the shadows into the bright moonlight and spoke boldly, "Yes, the dead shall be raised! Yeshua is alive!"

Part Two
Damascus
34-37 C.E.

There the angel of the LORD appeared to him in a flame of fire out of a bush; he looked, and the bush was blazing, yet it was not consumed... But Moses said to God, "If I come to the Israelites and say to them, 'The God of your ancestors has sent me to you,' and they ask me, 'What is his name?' what shall I say to them?"

Exodus 3:3, 13

Chapter Eleven

A Sabbath passed by and then another. Paulos and Kleitos worked side by side in their shop, but they rarely spoke except for matters of business. Paulos avoided conversation and questioning eyes. The strained silence had begun the day Paulos swore at his father. Paulos stopped taking meals with his parents, exiling himself to the rooftop when not at the shop; he visited neither synagogue nor river sanctuary.

He had become the alien. He didn't belong. The accusing finger of God wagged at Paulos from the mountains, the river, the synagogue, the agora, even his parent's home, and the brooding young Pharisee chose to flee. He would be rooted out of his land as Jubilees had warned. After a fortnight of seclusion, he climbed down the ladder from the rooftop with an announcement.

"I plan to leave Tarsos."

A tin cup clattered on the floor. Olympia's eyes welled and each tear carried a question: *What's the matter? How can I help? How have we failed you? Why must you leave? Where? When?* But she couldn't speak.

Kleitos cleared his throat, and he spoke for his wife. "Where will you go?"

Paulos expected anger; he was prepared for anger; he deserved anger; and he couldn't handle their sadness. He had tears but no words. Finally, he stammered. "I don't know why or where, I just know I must leave this place for a time."

Kleitos breathed deeply and looked into his wife's eyes. His own eyes welled, and he quickly looked away. He rose to his feet to retrieve the cup, and he set it on the table. Olympia wiped the tears from her son's face.

Kleitos again cleared his throat to speak. "Damascus. You will find Gaius there. Gaius is a Jew and a tentmaker originally from Tarsos. Go to Damascus and find Gaius." Kleitos had apprenticed with Gaius many years earlier.

Olympia listened with moist eyes but said nothing.

Paulos slipped away one morning while his mother shopped in the agora and his father toiled at the shop. He said no goodbyes. He filled a bag with food for three days: bread, figs, dry salt fish, and a small jar of olive oil. He tucked the few coins he called his own into his purse after first removing his special coin, his gift from Eli. He looked at the shekel from Jerusalem briefly and then flipped it onto the table, intending to leave it behind, but it rolled onto the floor. He immediately retrieved it and stuffed it in the bottom of his tool pack.

He traveled by land caravan rather than by sea. Unstable weather shut down the shipping lanes of the Great Sea from late autumn to early spring. "The sea is closed," said the harbormaster. His favorite donkey carried his possessions, including his tools and bulging water skins. His mood brightened as he began his escape.

Paulos joined a caravan of the *cursus publicus,* the Roman postal and messenger service. The caravan mix included a few Jews, a few Gentiles, and a dozen Roman soldiers. Two of the Romans led the way mounted on sturdy horses, two more drove a heavy wagon pulled by draft oxen, and the rest of the soldiers marched in a loose formation. Paulos and the others trailed behind for the four day, one hundred mile journey to the great city of Antioch around the corner of the Great Sea.

Under the heat of the midday sun, Paulos chugged the last of his water. When the caravan forded a river, he lagged behind and refilled his skins before pissing into the stream. He plopped a couple of figs in his mouth as he jerked his donkey's tether, and they quickly caught up with the caravan.

"How far will the Romans travel today?" He asked the Jew who walked next to him.

"Weary already?"

Paulos felt strong and fresh, his long legs and big feet were good for something.

"Just curious."

"Don't be stupid and run off alone again."

Paulos looked at him but did not speak.

"Bandits. Bandits wait for stragglers. Stay with the caravan."

Paulos imagined bandits behind every rock and tree.

"We'll travel thirty miles today. There's a *mansione* ahead where we'll stop for the night."

A *mansione* was a Roman rest house, a way station set up at intervals along the caravan trails to provide a roof over the heads of Roman officials together with food for man and beast. Unofficial members of caravans such as Paulos slept under the stars or in a private inn that often operated next to the official *mansione*.

With the passing hours, his strides grew longer, and Paulos never looked back, his moping melancholy receding mile by mile. By late afternoon when they arrived at the *mansione*, the inviting peaks of the Amonos Mountains loomed on the eastern horizon, signaling the caravan's arrival at the corner of the Great Sea. The Amonos Mountains were not nearly as tall or formidable as the familiar Taurus Mountains to the west of Tarsos, and the pine peaks seemed warmer and softer than the snowy crags of the Taurus that he left behind.

Together with the other Jews, Paulos laid his sleeping mat under trees near a stream. The tethered donkeys grazed nearby. The rest stop offered lean-to stalls for the soldier's horses and a pen for their oxen. Two Romans, the ones on horseback, slept in the hut while the others pitched two man tents. Other travelers also pitched small tents. Only a few slept under the stars like Paulos.

Two crackling campfires lit up the wooded glen—one Jewish and one Gentile. Meanwhile, the Romans ate hot food and drank barley beer in the *mansione*. Their laughter spilled from the *mansione* well into the night. Paulos feasted on dry salt fish and chunks of bread dipped in olive oil; he finished with figs washed down with large gulps of water. He fell asleep to a cheerful chorus of croaking frogs.

The next day, the caravan curled around the northeastern corner of the Great Sea. Spiny ridges joined mountaintops to sea, and the trail to Antioch hugged the coast. By nightfall, the caravan reached a riverside mansione at the scene of Alexander's great victory over the Persians that opened Palestine and Egypt to the Greeks. On the third day, they made slower progress, leaving the humid coast and climbing into the cool pine forests, exiting Cilicia and entering Syria. They spent their third night at an encampment high in the mountains next to a fresh spring. Sweet smelling pine needles made a fine mat, and Paulos slept well in the cool mountain air. The caravan arrived in Antioch on the Orontes late the following day.

"Can you direct me to the synagogue?" Paulos asked his mostly silent walking partner.

"Which one? There are many."

"Many synagogues?"

"There is one right there," he pointed before disappearing, leaving Paulos alone with his donkey.

The city stretched in all directions, and he could not see the end of it. Tall stone buildings. Market stalls all around. Paved streets. Musicians. What a magnificent city, he thought. He briefly considered changing plans and remaining in Antioch instead of continuing on to Damascus, but the comforting letter of introduction he carried to Gaius, the Jewish tentmaker and friend of his father, prevented a change in plans.

Paulos spent a few coins and replenished his food supply. He slept on his mat at a synagogue with his donkey tied in the alley behind the building. The next morning, he eagerly walked to the edge of the city and waited at the edge of the caravan trail to the south. Before long, a caravan passed, led by three rich men riding camels, followed by many pedestrians leading donkeys. He slipped to the rear with the slaves of the rich men. For a fortnight, he walked with the Jerusalem bound caravan of Jewish aristocrats and their entourage. Their route would pass through Damascus where he planned to leave them.

Paulos walked next to Abdel, a Hebrew slave: a tiny man with springy bowlegs who seemed even shorter because he hunched over; a bald man with a tanned spot on the top of his head, edged by bristly, sand-colored hair; and a poor man who wore only a sweat-stained, grimy brown tunic without cap, sandals, or robe.

"Azariah is his name," said Abdel, identifying his master, the aristocrat who wore a tall scarlet hat with golden bands and a matching robe of silk. He is a Sadducee, a cousin of the High Priest in Jerusalem." Azariah sat astride a camel at the front of the caravan with men walking on each side brandishing knives and swords.

"Why does a Hebrew serve as slave to another Hebrew?" Paulos asked Abdel.

"What else can I do? I have no land and no cattle or goats, but I do have a wife and hungry children. I sold myself to the rich man for seven years servitude. At the end of seven years, I still had nothing so I sold myself for another seven years. One day I will sell myself for another seven years, and my children ..." His voice trailed off. He shrugged his shoulders and mumbled, "At least we have food to eat."

"Who are the men with swords?" Paulos asked.

"Bodyguards. This caravan will be safe from bandits, and Azariah will be safe in Jerusalem."

"Why does he need protection in Jerusalem?"

Abdel glared at Paulos and said nothing.

After a week of walking, Paulos' coin purse lost its jangle. Food purchases from villagers and farmers along the way depleted his meager supply of coins, but an important client accepted his standing offer to provide leather smith services to caravan travelers.

"Azariah wishes to speak to you. Follow me to his tent."

Paulos followed the man with the sword scabbard hanging from his belt.

The manservant of Azariah spoke to Paulos outside the tent of the rich man. "It is said that you are a leather smith. You will be paid a denarius if you repair the saddle of my master."

Paulos sewed the frayed saddle cinch and received his silver coin in payment. Others came to him with repair requests and his coin purse bulged by the time they reached Damascus, but the familiarity of sewing and stitching rekindled the recent tension of Kleitos' shop, and Paulos' enthusiasm began to slip away.

As the caravan neared Damascus, the countryside turned dry and rocky, matching the return of Paulos' melancholy. Barren desert supplanted fields and vineyards, and his water skins hung limp on the back of his thirsty donkey. The tedium of the arduous trek had dissipated his fragile, high-spirited wanderlust. Drudgery replaced eagerness as one heavy footstep followed another.

Finally, after a fortnight on the road, Paulos entered Damascus, the frayed border of the Roman Empire. Roman soldiers of this edgy frontier outpost lacked the swagger of the helmets of Tarsos. Damascus teetered atop a fault line grinding West against East, the Roman Empire against the Arabic Kingdom of the Nabateans. The scent of anarchy hung in the air; pickpockets, thieves, and prostitutes were open for business.

Damascus had sprouted in a highland oasis on the edge of the desert. This region was the ancestral homeland of the nomadic and pastoral Arameans who passed their Aramaic language down to Jews of Palestine and Nabateans of Arabia; Aramaic remained the common language spoken in Palestine whenever Greek was not. *A wandering Aramean was my ancestor.* Paulos remembered the Torah stories of Jacob the Aramean, son of Isaac, grandson of Abraham, father of the twelve patriarchs of the tribes of Israel.

Paulos explored the maze of crooked and narrow streets of this tired city, older than memory. Some said Damascus was a lush garden city, but his eyes saw dilapidated market stalls tucked under faded awnings, mangy dogs panting in the sun, and a naked toddler caked in dirt and striped with rivulets of sweat. Paulos first roamed the Nabatean neighborhoods before he finally made his way to the Jewish sector and a large synagogue.

"I seek Gaius the tentmaker."

"He's long dead."

Paulos had journeyed a far distance seeking a dead man. He wished he had stayed in Antioch, or continued to Jerusalem.

"I'm a leather smith seeking employment."

"Ezer. Go to Ezer's stall at the wall of the city." The men at the synagogue pointed the way.

Ezer's shop fronted a busy street on the edge of the Jewish sector and butted against the high wall of stones and mortar that ringed the city. The two-story building doubled as shop and home for the leather smith and his wife.

Ezer the leather smith was nearly as wide as he was tall. An undersized sleeveless goatskin vest, split wide in the front by his protruding belly, covered his sweat-stained tunic. He spoke with a deep gravelly voice.

"Tell the son of a whore that he can have his tent when he pays for it and not a moment before. If ya return without coins, I'll kick my foot up yer bunghole."

The servant slunk out of the shop without his master's tent.

"What in Hades do ya want?" Ezer bellowed as he looked at the gangly, road-weary traveler from Tarsos who slouched in the corner.

Ezer paid Paulos a denarius a week, daily breakfast and supper, and a room to place his mat with a roof over his head. Paulos shared this room with Uri, an apprentice, a few years his junior.

Ezer's gray-flecked beard suggested he was older than Paulos, but his wife, Azubah, was nearer Paulos' age. She was tall and busty with broad hips and a heavy boned frame. Ezer and Azubah had no children but not for lack of effort. Uri and Paulos listened to shrieks and sighs of lovemaking from the adjacent room on a nightly basis. Paulos never noticed the way her eyes explored his gangly frame from head to foot, or the teasing way she pursed her lips when he passed, or the low cut sleeping gown she wore on the mornings he ate his porridge alone without Ezer or Uri.

Ezer's shop remained open on the Sabbath, a good excuse for Paulos to stay away from the synagogue. He once met the synagogue leader, a Jerusalem trained Pharisee named Mordecai, but Paulos didn't even mention his own Pharisee training.

Paulos' meager pay was well earned. He often worked into the night after Azubah's tasteless suppers. On the rare occasions when they didn't work after their evening meal, Uri disappeared into the night, smelling of wine and women when he returned.

"Come with me. We'll find you a Jewish whore." He taunted Paulos with the same invitation every time he went out.

Life was merely a succession of days, but Paulos accepted his exile as his due. He often thought of his parents, but the fear that he had failed them darkened the memories. Eli too. He had escaped Tarsos, but not himself, nor the wagging finger of God, nor the leering grin of Jubilees the beggar. And always nipping at the fringes of his slumber—like a yipping, yellow cur—the dimpled visage of Arsenios haunted him, alluring and repugnant at the same time. Paulos came to dread closing his eyes.

Chapter Twelve

"Yeshua is alive."

At first, the exuberant claims of the Galileans left Ya'akov to wonder. Were they drunk with new wine? Yet, the Galileans believed.

"Yeshua appeared to Cephas." They spoke the words as a simple matter of fact.

What happened to them? What transformed them? They ran to Galilee like whipped hounds only to return, boldly proclaiming that Yeshua lived. Ya'akov barely dared hope.

Before his death, whispered rumors on the streets claimed that Ya'akov's brother was the long expected Mashiah of God, a new King David, God's own anointed, who would restore Israel. With the return of the Galileans only weeks after his death, the rumors ignited like a lightning bolt sparking a dry forest. Fanned by the windy claims of Cephas and the Galileans, messianic hopes blazed hot in those heady days. Cephas and the Galileans openly proclaimed Yeshua as Mashiah, soon to return to restore God's justice. The Galilean's enthusiasm was like a wildfire that hopped from one burning tree to the next. The messianic conflagration consumed large numbers of Jews including many of Ya'akov's Pharisee friends—and his own family.

"Some say you should ascend to the throne. Since Yeshua was the king of the Jews, his eldest brother should succeed him," Jude said to Ya'akov.

"I'm unfit to be king."

"Less fit than Herod's sons and grandsons?"

"I won't have any of my brothers speaking such words."

Ya'akov stared down each of his brothers and cousin Symeon as they sat around the table in his veranda. "Let's get to work," he said.

Questions swirled in Ya'akov's head. What did it mean to be a follower of Yeshua? What did it mean that Yeshua <u>was</u> the Mashiah? That he <u>is</u> the Mashiah? He knew that the Nazarenes must be faithful to the words of his brother to bless the poor and humble. He also knew that they would have trouble with the aristocrats and the Romans; the proclamation of a returning, conquering king would only raise the heat on tensions that already simmered.

A few months passed before the cauldron boiled over.

"Cephas and others have been arrested! The High Priest sent Temple police to arrest them!" Joses reported the news to his brothers at their worksite where they were building a thatched lean-to that would serve as a stable. "Our friends are frightened and confused. With Cephas arrested, who will lead?" Joses echoed the questions he heard from other Nazarenes: the name attached first to the Galilean followers of the man from Nazareth and then to the entire Yeshua movement burning in Jerusalem.

Ya'akov plopped down heavily on a workbench and wiped the sweat from his face with his sleeve. He knew Cephas and the loudmouths were in for trouble; he had warned them.

"Some say it is up to you as the head of the family, the successor to our crucified brother," Joses said.

Ya'akov said nothing as he picked up a small board, cocked his eye at one end, and sighted down its length, checking for straightness. "This is a good cut," he said to Jude whose skill as a carpenter was nearing his own. He rubbed his finger along the hewn edge as he nodded his approval. Why did it always come to him? He was a carpenter, and a good one; was that not enough?

"What're you going to do?" Joses said.

Ya'akov looked at the sun to measure the hour. Long shadows stretched across their worksite, and it felt good in the shade. Shera would soon have the evening meal prepared. He pictured Seema cutting vegetables as she gleefully jabbered to all within earshot.

His neck and back stiffened as cool minutes passed, and he twisted his torso to loosen up. He took hold of the norm that dangled from his neck, and lined it up with the edge of the board. "Good cut," he said again.

He looked into the eyes of his brothers that implored him to action even as they held their tongues. He could see Yeshua in each one. With Jude, it was the curly, sandy hair; with Simon, it was the nose with a hint of upturn at the tip; with Joses, it was the eyes: soft, brown, trusting.

Yeshua is alive, they say, and he will return soon. This would be a good time. But if this is not the time, what will the Sanhedrin do to Cephas? Will the good men in the Sanhedrin oppose the bastard High Priest? A simple carpenter could not do much, but a word to his Pharisee friends might help. He could do that, at least.

"It is time to quit for the day," he said. "Run home and stay close to each other and the rest of the family. I'll be home late."

His brothers fumbled with their tools.

"Go, I said!"

With both palms flat on the workbench, Ya'akov pushed himself to a standing position; it seemed a tremendous effort as he raised his own massive bulk and more. He rolled his shoulders again when he stood on his feet, trying to loosen his tight muscles.

"It's my responsibility; I'll do what I can," he said, and he departed without further explanation.

Ya'akov pounded on the door of Nicodemus, his rotund Pharisee friend and Sanhedrin member. Yosef of Arimathea and other Pharisees were there already. These men and others of the Sanhedrin, the judicial council of the Jews, would place Cephas on trial, and Ya'akov lobbied the jurors on behalf of the Nazarene prisoners.

"Yes, yes, we have heard the news," said Nicodemus. Yosef, Nicodemus, and other Pharisees had openly joined the cause of the Nazarenes. The Pharisees nodded as they listened to Ya'akov's entreaties on behalf of Cephas.

"Don't worry. The Pharisees control the Sanhedrin," said Nicodemus. "The Sanhedrin acts according to majority rule, and the Pharisees outnumber the Sadducees."

The trial occurred two days later. Jews on the street jeered the Temple police who paraded their Nazarene prisoners through Jerusalem to the Court of the Sanhedrin. Ya'akov watched discreetly, followed from a distance, and observed the proceedings.

"Fellow Israelites, consider carefully what you propose to do to these men." Gamaliel himself, the Pharisee leader of the Sanhedrin, defended the cause of the Nazarenes. "I tell you, keep away from these men and let them alone; if their movement is of human origin, it will fail; but if it is of God, you will not be able to overthrow them—in that case you may even be found fighting against God!"

The Sanhedrin dismissed the charges and freed the prisoners. Gamaliel, the leading Pharisee of Jerusalem, proved to be a valuable ally of the Nazarenes. After that day, he became Ya'akov's friend as well. If only Gamaliel and the Sanhedrin had heard of the shameful action of the High Priest, the night the temple police arrested Yeshua. If only ...

Ya'akov had successfully intervened on behalf of Cephas. He had worked in the background, but he was the one with Pharisee influence, and his role soon became widely known. As he walked to work one morning soon after this incident, he overheard a voice on the street, "There goes Ya'akov ..." He listened for but did not hear the usual refrain, "the brother of Yeshua." Instead, he heard, "the leader of the Nazarenes." His pace quickened as he straightened his slouch.

Chapter Thirteen

In the months that followed, the ranks of Yeshua's followers swelled with many Jews of Jerusalem—and others as well. Diaspora Jews on pilgrimage to Jerusalem, Greek-speaking foreigners with Greek names and Greek customs, joined the Yeshua movement. "Hellenists," Ya'akov called them, and the tone of his voice spoke of his contempt.

If it had been up to him, he would not have accepted the Hellenists' request for an audience, but he reluctantly agreed to hear what they had to say only because Cephas was sure it was a good idea. As he waited for Cephas to deliver the Hellenists, Ya'akov ranted to his brothers and cousin Symeon.

"Why do Jews not live in Palestine—God's holy land? Why do they choose to live in far off places, speaking the language of the Gentiles, and following Gentile ways?" Ya'akov said. "Are they really Jews? Did anyone check their circumcision?"

For Ya'akov and many Jews, the glory of Israel was her past—the idealized days of King David, a holy king leading a holy kingdom, a time of power and prosperity for God's holy people—but Torah disobedience led to decline, decay, and dispersion in the present. God's Mashiah, the new King David, would restore the glorious days of an earlier millennium; his people would return to Zion, God's holy land; and they would return to the holy path of Torah.

The Hellenists did not fit the picture unless they *permanently* returned to Palestine and not merely for a *temporary* visit to offer sacrifice before returning to their foreign lands and foreign ways, leaving Torah behind when they departed Jerusalem. Jews in foreign lands who forgot the ways of the elders were barely Jews.

Ya'akov was civil when Cephas arrived with the Hellenists even though he immediately noticed neither of the foreigners wore fringed *tzitzit.* Jude offered cups of wine all around, and after introductions, Barnabas from the island of Kypros spoke first.

"I am a man of means having been richly blessed by God. I have arranged to sell land owned by my family, and I am pleased to offer a sack of gold in support of the poor of Jerusalem."

Ya'akov studied the tall man from Kypros. He seemed genuine and sincere enough, with a solid voice and clear manner of speaking, and Yeshua would be pleased with a generous offer to help the poor. But what do these Hellenists want in return?

A man named Stephen stated the condition. "Our only request is that the distribution to the poor includes those of a Hellenist background whose numbers are great and whose needs are many."

"Of course, of course," blurted Cephas. "It shall be done."

Ya'akov had misgivings. Was this not an implicit acceptance of the Hellenists and their Hellenistic ways? Besides, he didn't trust this Stephen with the whiny voice and clean-shaved face. Cephas shouldn't have spoken so quickly.

Ya'akov's intuition proved prophetic when Stephen outraged the Jews of Jerusalem a few days later. Ya'akov was shocked when he heard what Stephen said at a synagogue.

"The law of Moses has been set aside by Yeshua of Nazareth. Torah no longer has any claim upon us or meaning for us!"

Ya'akov suspected that Stephen ate unclean foods and neglected the Sabbath long before he became a follower of Yeshua. To blame Yeshua for such an outrage—well, it was a damned outrage!

Stephen also spoke against the Temple, the greatest symbol of Israelite religion. "The Most High God does not dwell in houses made with human hands."

****

Cephas had messed up, and he knew it. His round shoulders hunched more than usual on his reed-thin frame, his ever-present smile turned into a pouting downturn of the corners of his mouth, and a low monotone replaced the high pitched twitter in his voice. Slowly, he ascended the stairs to Ya'akov's veranda, followed by the sons of Zebedee, Yochanan and his brother Ya'akov, trim fishermen from Galilee, friends of Yeshua during his lifetime. Ya'akov had summoned all the Nazarene leaders, including his brothers and cousin Symeon, to his rooftop veranda for a meeting to consider the news of the arrest of Stephen the Hellenist.

There had been no discussion—much less a formal decision—but leadership of the Nazarenes had shifted from Cephas to Ya'akov. It just happened, and Cephas was the happier for it. As Yeshua's best friend and confidant, the others naturally looked to Cephas after Yeshua's death, but in the months that followed, Ya'akov had proven his mettle, and he was Yeshua's own brother, after all. Who got Cephas out of prison? Who arranged for jobs for the Galileans? Who had the important contacts in Jerusalem? And now Cephas had embarrassed the Nazarenes over this matter with Stephen and the Hellenists. Best to let Ya'akov wriggle the Nazarenes out of this difficulty; Cephas would support him.

Stephen's loose talk had resulted in charges of blasphemy, potentially a capital offense. Cephas expected that Ya'akov would again lobby his Pharisee friends in the Sanhedrin on behalf of this foreign follower of Yeshua just as he had done for Cephas himself; Cephas regretted the embarrassment he had caused by promoting Stephen, but Ya'akov would smooth things over.

Ya'akov faced the others sitting on stools in a semicircle. "Is it not true that he denied Torah, God's holy word for his people, the way of life for God's own family, the very essence of what it means to be a Jew?"

Cephas shifted restlessly on his stool, head bowed, neck burning under the hot glares of the others.

"Did he not attack the Temple?" Ya'akov asked a rhetorical question. "For a thousand years, God's people have revered the Temple as God's own house. Just because the priests are bastards doesn't mean that God has abandoned the Temple."

Ya'akov paused, poured water into a clay cup, and drank it down before he finished. "Let the Sanhedrin do with this blasphemer as they will," he said, and he slammed the clay cup on the table so hard it smashed into pieces.

Cephas jerked his head up to see the large man. He knew that Ya'akov routinely wore an iron norm around his neck, but it was as if Cephas now saw it for the first time—cold iron with a hard edge, straight and unbending.

Cephas cleared his throat as if to speak, but under Ya'akov's glare, he held his tongue.

Ya'akov made no appeal to the Pharisees, and the Nazarenes stayed away from Stephen's trial. The Sanhedrin convicted Stephen, and a handpicked mob of Jews stoned him to death the same day.

Cephas and Ya'akov sat alone on Ya'akov's veranda after the sunset on the day of Stephen's death. "Pardon my honesty," Ya'akov said, "but he brought it on himself. Let this be a lesson for the rest of the Hellenists. God's kingdom on earth will respect the traditions of the elders and will be a kingdom whose people honor the covenant with their God." Ya'akov rubbed his norm as he spoke.

Cephas poured himself another cup of wine. Troubled by the affair, troubled that Ya'akov seemed pleased with the outcome, but mostly troubled by his own guilty contribution, Cephas drank heavily that night.

The Hellenists disappeared from Jerusalem. A few, including Barnabas, retreated to the great city of Antioch, some fled to Caesarea by the sea, and others escaped to Damascus.

Chapter Fourteen

Paulos squatted with legs crossed on the synagogue floor, prepared to listen to a boring Sabbath sermon delivered by Mordecai. The hard-edged Pharisee who had trained in Jerusalem thought highly of himself, but he seemed a dullard to Paulos. Paulos rarely attended Sabbath at the synagogue, but Ezer said he needed a day off from the monotony of the shop.

Before Mordecai began, a stranger uttered the shocking claim of a crucified Mashiah, setting the synagogue abuzz. "Yeshua is the Mashiah! Yeshua was crucified but has been raised from the dead!"

Mordecai attempted to quiet the stranger, but the Jews were curious.

"Speak man!" yelled one listener.

"Tell us more!" yelled another.

The barefaced speaker wore no *tefilla* or *tzitzit*. As he spoke, he maintained a posture of arms outstretched to his sides. The young man, no older than Paulos, told a strange tale of a Galilean peasant who led a rabble to Jerusalem where the Romans arrested and crucified him. When he appeared alive, Jerusalem burned with excitement.

"The kingdom of God is at hand!" the speaker concluded with a shout.

For a moment, the congregants of the synagogue sat in silence, not sure what to make of the shocking claims. Then, the crowd began to stir, and low mumblings grew into a steady hum of animated conversations. The Jews crowded around the stranger, and Paulos strained to hear his words. Finally, as the murmuring crowd disbursed, Paulos caught the sleeve of the speaker.

"Man, tell me more," Paulos said. Paulos listened with great interest but also with skepticism. He knew the messianic promises of the Prophets well enough, and a crucifixion did not fit the picture. As the stranger talked, Paulos' unease swelled at vague hints at the edges of the story.

Then the stranger said it. The words nearly knocked Paulos over. "Yeshua welcomed sinners and ate with them."

"Sinners? What sinners?" asked Paulos.

"Tax collectors, adulterers, those who do not keep Torah—

"Why man, you're unclean!" Paulos' voice threatened. "Are you a Jew? You defile this holy synagogue. Begone! Get yourself away from here while you're able!" Gangly and awkward, Paulos nevertheless stepped aggressively toward the defiler who retreated.

Paulos stood alone in the late afternoon sun that slanted through the windows of the synagogue, surprised by own belligerence, and warmed by self-satisfaction. He had protected God's holy place from pollution.

The next Sabbath, he bounded to the synagogue early with eager strides, hoping the defiler would return. He did, and Paulos was ready to attack.

Paulos shouted as the infiltrator stood to speak. "You wear no fringes on your garment or prayer box on your arm."

As the man attempted to respond, Paulos shouted again. "Do you keep Torah or not?"

Every time the man attempted to speak, Paulos shouted him down; others added taunts of their own until the young defiler departed to jeers from the Jews. Even Mordecai nodded approval of Paulos' passionate defense of Israelite religion.

Paulos, the defender of orthodoxy, had acquired a proud identity and a status; self-righteousness became the dressing for his wounds, masking his inner torment. For the moment, partisan Zealotry replaced his melancholy. On behalf of God's own Torah, Paulos became a rigid persecutor of the Yeshua people, salving his own self-doubt.

Ezer was away on business, and Uri was out whoring. Paulos was drifting off to sleep when the door creaked open and lamplight seeped into his bedroom. A form loomed in the doorway. Paulos leaned on an elbow and raised his head. Azubah stood outlined in the light; her robe slipped from her shoulders, and she stood naked, her breasts heaving with eager sighs.

As if she sucked all the air from the room, Paulos struggled to breathe. *Arsenios' tanned and dimpled face smiled from the shoulders of Azubah's nakedness. Paulos remembered the kiss, the saltiness of it, the tenderness of it, and the yearning for another, but then he stood naked in the Kydnos pool, scraping away his skin with coarse sand, as stinking pus seeped from his wounds.* Azubah stepped toward him, and he bolted past her into the night where he vomited in the alley.

The next morning, he did not appear for his morning porridge, but he could not hide in his room indefinitely; Azubah taunted him by puckering her lips and smacking a smooching sound as he passed.

When Paulos joined Uri at the workbench, Uri whispered, "You missed a good time last night. I sucked the tits of a dark-haired whore."

Paulos stumbled to the street and retched; his empty stomach turned into knots.

Ezer teased him as he returned to the shop. "A touch of the morning sickness? If yer done puking, deliver this awning to the baker near the synagogue," Ezer said.

Paulos' humiliation deepened, and his guilty heart returned, full of self-hate.

Paulos finished his discussion with the baker who was pleased with the awning Paulos had delivered. Across the street, a small group entered the synagogue led by a woman in a crimson robe. Her tangled scarlet hair was uncovered; it seemed aflame. A Jewess would not enter the synagogue with a bare head; she was an unclean

Gentile who defiled God's holy house.

Paulos saw red. Against a blurry gray background, he saw only red. In his agitated mind, the scene played as a dream. He saw a red demon hovering over the synagogue steps in a crimson gown, hair ablaze. Trailing a wisp of smoke, she slipped into the synagogue in the company of her consorts to pollute God's holy house with a profane orgy.

Paulos ripped a small branch from an olive tree. Wielding the switch like a sword, he charged into the synagogue to purge the contamination. "Unclean! Unclean," he screeched. The switch whistled in his hand as he struck the Gentile woman. He struck her again as she collapsed into a writhing heap onto the stone floor. "Unclean whore!" he shouted as he struck her repeatedly. He saw an unholy demon fall from the air, a hissing, smoldering mound of charred flesh.

The Gentile woman held up her hands to shield herself from the bloody switch that sliced through the air. She became Arsenios, blood spurting from his wounds. Paulos' cleansing sword sliced to the bone, ripping away the Greek's tunic, leaving him naked and uncovered. Gentiles uncovered their shame. Arsenios uncovered his uncircumcision. Gentiles were the children of destruction. Paulos would destroy and slay him.

The Gentile woman dropped her arms, but Paulos continued to flail with the olive branch, now flogging his own body, contorted at his feet. Black, oily contamination seeped out with each cut. He welcomed the wounds. He deserved them. Unclean! Unclean! Polluted beyond reprieve. No pardon or forgiveness for him.

It was over quickly as her friends pulled Paulos away from the woman. They helped her to her feet, and she staggered away from the synagogue. The wretched man sagged onto his back, chest heaving, whimpering.

Chapter Fifteen

"Ya need exercise ya skinny bastard," bellowed Ezer a few weeks later. "Tomorrow, deliver this tent to its owner in a village a few miles upriver."

Paulos barely had the energy to lift his head in response to Ezer's orders. Since the synagogue incident, he had stopped eating with the others, and he barely slept. If Azubah had not left hard, dry bread on his mat, he might have withered away altogether.

With first light the next morning, Paulos traveled west from Damascus up the Barada River valley toward the nearby mountain village. He led a donkey burdened with the tent.

Heavy black clouds shrouded the peak of Mount Hermon. With each hour, the clouds stole further down the slopes. By the time Paulos reached the village, the clouds had filled the valley, blocking out the sun.

The merchant paid with Roman denarii that Paulos placed in the purse in his belt, and he anxiously began his return journey to Damascus. The wind howled, shrieked, and roiled the angry clouds as they pursued him down the valley. He pulled the cowl of his robe over his head, forming a hood as the tempest pushed him forward.

The donkey trotted to keep pace with the long strides of Paulos, but the beast suddenly jerked the loosely held lead rope from Paulos' hand. "Stupid ass!" He grabbed the rope and yanked hard as a hissing viper slithered into the rocks. The donkey limped badly on its left rear leg. Snakebite.

Paulos slowed to a near standstill as the donkey gamely limped along. Paulos would not reach Damascus by nightfall at this pace. If he abandoned the donkey, Ezer would be angry.

Pelting raindrops joined forces with the wind to drive him forward.

The rain puddled the ground to mud and obliterated the path. For an hour or more, the elements pushed him along, and he did not resist. Suddenly, the wind and rain stopped, replaced by an eerie stillness. The dark of night blanketed him. He pulled back his hood, and his ears begged for a clue. He moved toward a splashing stream to follow the river toward Damascus.

Dark shapes loomed around him, and his fear saw what his eyes didn't. Was something behind that rock? Behind that tree? Did something move?

"Who is there?"

His queasy voice was barely audible, and there was no answer except the bubbling river—and the jangle of coins in his purse. The coins! He carried a treasure! Bandits! The clinking coins invited thievery. With his empty hand, he squeezed the coin purse silent.

He smelled wood smoke. With slow, deliberate steps, he followed the scent while straining his ears; soon he heard muffled voices, and he hesitated behind a boulder and listened, but he could not make out their words. He pulled his hood over his forehead for a glance into the clearing framed by tall palm trees. Four or five shadowy figures hovered around a blazing campfire.

Just then, his donkey brayed a betrayal!

The voices stopped, and the shapes peered in his direction. He froze. A burning log popped and spit sparks, breaking the silence.

"Who is there?"

Should he answer? Should he run?

"Who is there?" The question came again, louder, hanging in the still night air.

"A traveler with a lame donkey," Paulos muttered with a dry tongue. He started forward again though he worried that they might hear the jangling coins.

As Paulos moved into the firelight, a short man wearing a white headdress of wrapped linen spoke. "Sit, stranger." He gestured at a log next to the fire.

Clutching his coin purse tightly, Paulos squatted on the log next to several other men seated around the fire.

"I'm Ananias. Are you hungry? Charis, bring bread and wine for our guest." Ananias spoke to a woman in the shadows. Donkeys shuffled in the trees as a dark shape rummaged in their packs. Ananias threw a log on the fire, kicking up a cloud of sparks.

Bearded men wearing dull gray robes sat around the fire, mumbling in low voices. Their hoods hung low over their faces, shadowing their eyes.

At that moment, a young woman stepped into the halo of the fire with a loaf of bread in one hand and a wineskin in the other. She wore a crimson robe. Her hair was uncovered and flickered orange in the firelight.

"This is our Gentile friend named Charis," said Ananias.

Paulos choked. He recognized the woman he had pummeled at the synagogue! He bowed his head and pulled his hood lower on his face. The storm had swept him into danger. Would the Gentiles have their revenge? "My times are in your hand; deliver me from my enemies," he prayed silently, but he feared that he faced God's own vengeance, that these pagans would be the instrument of God's judgment. He tried to appear calm. He dropped the tether, allowing the donkey to wander over to the others, freeing his hands to cover his face.

Charis sat next to him. From under the hood of his robe, his eyes watched her closely. She broke off a piece of bread and gave it to him. He should not eat food despoiled by the hand of a Gentile, but this was a matter of life and death. With one hand, he rubbed his nose to cover his face as his other hand accepted the bread chunk. He gnawed without tasting.

Charis poured wine into a crude tin cup and handed the cup to him. He brought the cup to his lips and tilted his head back slightly to sip. The wind gusted and blew the hood from his head!

Paulos stared helplessly into her eyes, green and wet like a desert oasis. She raised no cry of alarm. He wanted to pull his hood back over his face, but he could not move.

"Have you heard of Iesou the Christos?" asked Ananias, speaking in Greek and using the Greek words "Iesou" for "Yeshua" and "Christos" for "Mashiah".

His words floated above Paulos. Paulos said nothing but continued to stare at the woman and her inscrutable smile. Why didn't she recognize him? Or did she? Why didn't she claim retribution? Why didn't she accuse him before his enemies? He was confused yet drawn into her soft, smiling, calming eyes.

At first, he saw only her eyes, then her face, then her upper torso. Uncontrollably, his eyes diverted to her wounded arms. He stared. She ran the long fingers of one hand over her opposite arm, softly caressing the scabs. She crossed both arms and pulled them tight against her bosom with a deep sigh and a slight smile.

Ananias droned on about the man from Galilee, but Paulos listened without hearing. Ananias finished by boldly proclaiming, "Iesou has been resurrected by God and has appeared to many persons."

Charis stared straight into Paulos' eyes, nodding to add weight to Ananias' statements. He did not hear the words, but somehow he felt them.

"Time to sleep," announced Ananias as he moved to the donkeys. He pulled out a blanket for himself and one for Paulos and tossed it to him. The blanket struck Paulos in the face, causing laughter all around. "It appears our friend is already asleep!"

Charis took Paulos by the hand and led him to a grassy spot where everyone would sleep. She spread out his blanket. "You may sleep here," she said, "and I will be over there."

His lips moved but his words caught in his throat.

Charis touched her fingers to his lips, and she whispered, "I know, but do you think that matters to me or to God?"

Paulos lay on the blanket. The sky had cleared and a full moon filled the eastern sky that seemed aglow. Minutes passed. Or was it hours? Or days? Or a lifetime? Or, was time standing still?

Suddenly, the palm trees bowed under the force of a fierce wind; lightning crackled through the clearing; thunder shook the ground where Paulos lay. In the fiery flashes, he saw a shape, a visage, an appearance of the likeness of a man, and he heard a voice on the wind. He cowered on the ground, but then the voice beckoned to him.

"Mortal, stand, and I will speak with you; I will send you to the Gentiles; let those who will hear, hear; and let those who refuse to hear, refuse."

Paulos rose to his knees and bowed before the voice that boomed in the thunder.

"Take wheat and barley, beans and lentils, millet and spelt, put them in one vessel, and make bread for yourself."

In the flashing images, he saw himself holding a bloody sword over the limp body of Charis—no, it was Arsenios—no, it was Paulos himself with oily, black contamination seeping from his wounds. The formless shape in the clouds grabbed the weapon and tried to wrest it from him. Paulos held tight and pulled back, but then he could resist no more. He was defeated. He let go and fell, drifting slowly through the starry skies—a clean and healthy babe floating in the heavens.

Paulos jerked up on the blanket, shaking and choking for air. Sweat soaked his tunic and dribbled down his face. He surveyed the peaceful encampment: coals glowed in the fire, donkeys' heads bowed as they slept while afoot, snores rose from Ananias and the others, and the yellow moon smiled down on him.

Charis rolled over, and her eyes met his. Without saying a word, they walked back to the embers of the once blazing fire. They sat in the pale aura of the coals and talked.

"I am your persecutor, forgive me!" With his first spoken words to Charis, his body began to quiver and tears streamed down his face.

Charis removed a scarf from her neck and wiped the tears from his cheeks.

"You're not the only Gentile I have harmed," he sobbed. "I also hurt my closest friend."

Charis, his confessor, was a sponge absorbing his words; her gentle demeanor inspired him to speak boldly. The floodgates opened and words spilled from his mouth; he confessed what he hadn't dared think.

"I kissed him," he said; his body convulsed again, and his chest heaved with sobs. Tears washed away the dust on his face, leaving it shining and pink. After awhile, he was empty but full.

Ananias was the first to arise, and he joined Paulos and Charis at the burnt out fire.

"Please baptize our friend?" asked Charis.

"Of course, of course. Hey, you snoring fools! Arise; there's God's work to do."

The others sat on the banks of the Barada River as Ananias and Paulos waded up to their waists. Paulos leaned back and fell softly into and beneath the water.

Chapter Sixteen

"My mother was a prostitute. She was an Aramean woman, and my father was a Roman soldier that I never knew." Charis spoke without emotion or embarrassment. It was two days after his experience on the road to Damascus, and Paulos and Charis wandered the streets of Damascus, walking and talking.

She looked to be about twenty years old, half a dozen years younger than Paulos. Her reddish orange hair was uncombed yet it was just right. Green eyes danced above high and prominent cheekbones in a ruddy, freckled face without wrinkle. Paulos thanked God that his switch had not cut her face, and he hoped the scabs on her arms would leave no scars.

She told her story. When she was around ten years old, she had been caught stealing fresh bread from a courtyard hearth by the woman of the house. Her captor marched her around the city slums until Charis identified her mother. For twenty denarii, the woman purchased Charis from the prostitute who would have accepted far less. Charis never saw her mother again. Charis green eyes glistened.

"That was the first, best day of my life. The woman bought me to save me even though she was a Jewess, and I was an unwashed Gentile. She raised me as her own daughter."

The Jewess had a daughter named Demetria who had married Ananias, the man who had baptized Paulos in the Barada River. Ananias had been in Jerusalem where the fervor of the Yeshua movement had touched him, but there had been trouble. A friend named Stephen had been stoned to death, and Ananias had escaped back to Damascus.

"The second, best day of my life was when Ananias returned from

Jerusalem. He was so excited! He talked so fast we could not keep up. He was filled with the spirit of God, and joy radiated from his face." Charis wiped a tear from her freckled cheek and brushed back her wayward, strawberry hair. "'Iesou has broken down the barriers between Jew and Gentile', Ananias exclaimed to us. For the first time, Demetria and I truly were sisters!"

They arrived at the edge of the city and walked through the countryside along the banks of the Barada River. Although a child of the slums, she seemed more natural here, fresh as the noontide breeze, radiant as a midsummer rose, cheerful as the mice that scurried in the bushes. She hummed a simple tune, but she sounded like a heavenly chorus to Paulos, her joyous alleluias answered by the praise songs of reed warblers.

In the warm glow of a golden sun, they stood knee-deep in the Barada River, splashing cool water in their faces. Ripe apricots hung heavy in trees along the riverbank, and they plucked and ate their fill. Sweet yellow juice clotted in his beard, and he stuck his face in the water and shook his head as he let loose an underwater shout. Charis laughed. Honeybees buzzed about drinking nectar of yellow lotus flowers that smiled wide in the midday sun. Charis and Paulos sat in the shade of a palm grove, and he methodically plunked pebbles into the river.

"You look different," she said. "In the synagogue, your eyes were full of hatred; in the wilderness, I saw sadness and fear. Today I see only peace." As she finished speaking, she turned and looked deeply into his eyes.

She was right. A serene joy filled him, a mysterious wafting of his soul upward and beyond. He was humbled yet exalted, circumscribed but also extended beyond himself. To be sure, his head was still spinning following the Damascus road experience, and he did not fully understand what had happened to him.

What did he know right then? He was changed. Outwardly, he had been angry, judgmental, and moody: inwardly, wracked with self-doubt, anxiety, and depression. Now he was upbeat and joyous; quiet assurance replaced his inner torment, a confident sense of well-being. He was transformed—no more and no less than that.

Finally, he spoke. "A wise sage taught me. He promised me that I would encounter God face to face, and he teased me that I would struggle with explanations. 'What words will you speak when you tell the tale? What picture will you paint?'" Paulos chuckled softly as he shook his head, remembering old Eli. "It seems the elder has cursed me with the truth, but I'm not yet ready to paint the picture. I'm less sure of what my eyes saw and my ears heard than that my heart beats anew."

The hues of his Damascus road experience blended with Charis' coloration of the Iesou stories, reported by Ananias from Jerusalem. Paulos believed he had encountered God, who redeemed him and restored him to God's beloved family despite his Torah unworthiness. What of these claims from Jerusalem of a crucified but resurrected Christos? Had he seen the risen Christos in the shapeless form in the clouds?

The agent of his transformation had been a Gentile: according to Torah, an unclean outsider. What is more, she was a woman, a lesser person on the Torah purity scale. According to Torah, he was an unworthy abomination. The voice in the wind told him to mix different grains to make bread. According to Torah, there was no mixing. Up was down and down was up.

Was Torah wrong? Misunderstood? Outdated?

Questions rattled in his mind but fewer answers. He was different; he was changed; he was new—*apart from Torah*. He attributed his transformation to Iesou the Christos, and he would become a follower of the crucified man. He also believed that his theophany was more than personal; it was cosmic, and he must report his encounter to others, especially to Gentiles. There was good news in his experience, good news for the Gentiles, good news that he must share.

Paulos remembered the nagging question of Arsenios, "Must I first become a Jew in order to belong to the beloved family of God?"

"NO! NO! NO! Can you hear me, Arsenios? NO! NO! NO!" Paulos stood knee deep in the river Barada and shouted, and then he laughed at himself; he laughed so hard he sat down in the flowing stream.

A man and a woman stood nearby watering their donkey, eyeing Paulos with suspicion. "A little early in the day to be drunk," the woman mumbled, shaking her head.

Paulos jumped to his feet and pranced to the shore kicking and splashing water at Charis, but he stopped suddenly in ankle deep water and shivered. As the sunlight splashed across her beaming face, Paulos briefly saw the dimpled smile of Arsenios.

Chapter Seventeen

As they returned to the city, aromas of fresh baked bread and wood smoke triggered a memory of home and hearth. Paulos almost returned to Tarsos in the days following his experience on the Damascus road, but there were too many questions to resolve before he was ready to return to Tarsos, Eli, his parents, and—Arsenios.

The allure of exotic Petra, the Nabatean capital city, beckoned to the exuberant new follower of the Christos. Paulos decided to carry the good news to the Nabateans, the spice merchants of the caravans, who shared a border, a language, and Semitic bloodlines with the Jews of Palestine. The three-hundred-mile caravan route from Damascus to Petra traced the frontier between Palestine and Arabia—east of the Sea of Galilee, east of the Jordan River, east of the Dead Sea, east of the Negev wilderness area of southern Palestine, and finally to Petra. Paulos arranged to join the next caravan headed south.

Ananias attempted to dissuade him. "The Nabateans are a suspicious people, my innocent friend. Your enthusiasm won't overcome centuries of mistrust and hostility."

Realizing they could not deter him, his new Damascene friends offered a small sack of Roman coins for his journey. While packing his leather smith tools, he spied his *belonging* coin lying in the bottom of the goatskin satchel. Even though it had languished for months in the bottom of the bag, forgotten since he had departed from Tarsos, it sparkled when he pulled it out. He turned it over in his hand, rubbed it to feel the Greek letter "χ" inscribed on one side and the date palm tree on the other, and then framed it between thumb and forefinger for close examination. He returned it to his coin purse where it belonged and gave the purse a gentle tap. Eli had been right; he belonged to God but—*apart from Torah.*

He also packed a bag with his few tunics and robes and other belongings. He held up his fringed garment, his *tzitzit* that signified that the wearer was Torah observant, and looked it over before deciding to leave it behind.

The radical change in Paulos' demeanor had puzzled gruff Ezer, but Azubah his wife said it was better than the morose ghost that skulked around the shadows of their home, and she persuaded Ezer to loan a donkey for the journey, the same donkey that had now recovered from snakebite. With goodbyes all around, Paulos enthusiastically set off to spread the good news to Petra.

For nearly three weeks, he traveled with the caravan. "Iesou is the promised Christos sent by God to redeem and restore the world. All peoples will share in God's kingdom including the Jews and Gentiles." He tested his missionary message on a camel tender.

The young Arab snarled at him, "Get away from me Jew. I have no interest in your Hebrew gods."

He tried the message on a merchant with similar results. To his surprise, his message offended his fellow travelers. A few listened politely at first, but by the end of the trip, everyone avoided him, and he trudged along in silent tedium, wondering why they didn't hear the good news he offered them.

His spirits lifted as the gully mouth into Petra swallowed the caravan, signaling their arrival in the great city of the Nabateans. Sheer cliff walls loomed on either side of the gorge as they passed, one by one, into the hidden city of the mountains of the Negev desert.

Ancient engineers had created a mountain oasis through an elaborate system of dams, ducts, and reservoirs that controlled the flash floods of the wet season. Conduits channeled rainwater and natural springs into cisterns and ponds, allowing a plentiful year-round supply of life giving moisture.

The Nabateans had tamed nature and created civilization in the mountainous wilderness of the Negev. The Nabateans were skilled engineers; they were also artists who had carved tombs, dwellings, banquet halls, altars and Temples out of the soft sandstone. Pastel buildings splashed against the backdrop of rose-colored cliffs. As alluring as Petra had been to his imagination, the reality was ten-fold more exotic.

He wandered the city alone, leading his donkey, but he found no synagogue and few Jews. Finally, Achishar, a Jewish widower, a glassblower who blew glass bottles from a shop in his courtyard, reluctantly agreed to rent him a room. The crumpled old man warned Paulos against drunkenness and carousing, and Paulos assured him that would not be a problem. Achishar insisted on one denarius per week, two weeks payment in advance. Achishar also agreed to stable Paulos' pack donkey. Water and hay was another denarius per week, two weeks payment in advance.

After three weeks of sleeping under the stars, the comforts of a house with a roof did not result in a restful night. Paulos barely slept that first night at Achishar's home, too eager to tell his tale in the morn. Cocks crowed as he confidently arrived at the market early; vendors chattered as they set out their wares.

"Kind sir, may I tell you of the coming kingdom of God?" Paulos said.

The spice merchant in a crimson robe and a crimson headdress knelt, spreading his frankincense, cassia, cinnamon and myrrh on his blanket. Paulos cleared his throat, but the merchant did not acknowledge his presence.

Paulos repeated himself, "Kind sir, may I tell you of the coming kingdom of God?"

"Are you here to buy or to sell?" the merchant grunted without raising his eyes from his blanket.

"The God who is One sends me to spread the word of his coming kingdom."

"Which one?"

"The God who is One."

Finally, the merchant raised his head and looked at Paulos. He spat in the dust. "Move on. Unless you are here to buy my spices, I have no time for you."

Paulos moved to the shaded awning of a vegetable vendor. "How much for a cabbage?" he asked.

"Two copper for a cabbage head," the woman replied.

"Perhaps I will stop back later when I return home. May I tell you of the coming kingdom of God?"

The hag blew her nose on the sleeve of her robe. She turned away from him, muttering to herself and shaking her head.

At the end of the day, Paulos slowly trudged to the house of Achishar as the dusty sun hovered over the Negev desert. Not a single merchant had listened to him. Nabateans were suspicious of Jews, their frequent border enemies, suspicious of Greeks, who had once colonized their city, and suspicious of Romans, a powerful empire that was dangerously close. As a Greek speaking Jew and Roman citizen, Paulos was an unwelcome stranger in a strange land, just as Ananias had warned him, an admonition Paulos had ignored.

Paulos returned the next morning with a new strategy. "Friends, the kingdom of God is at hand!" he stood in a central spot of the marketplace and shouted with cupped hands in front of his mouth. At first, there was no response, but after awhile, he received an occasional jeer. About the time his throat gave out, two burly men appeared and escorted him to the edge of the marketplace, one on each side, grabbing his arms.

"King Aretas orders you to leave our city immediately," said the man with one eye. A scar crossed the furrowed flaps of skin that sunk into the socket of the absent eye.

Paulos sulked through back streets and returned to the house of Achishar.

"You were a fool to come here in the first place," Achishar said. "This isn't a friendly place for Jews, and you foolishly flaunt your

Jewishness for all to see. Must you parade like a peacock? You've come to the attention of the King himself!" Achishar looked out his window and down his street. "You must leave immediately before harm comes to you. Your behavior threatens all Jews. I was a fool for allowing you to stay in my house." The shriveled old Jew stomped around, waving his arms as he spoke, accidentally knocking a glass bottle to the floor where it shattered into a thousand pieces. "Now, see what you made me do. I want you out!"

"God called me here! Why do these stiff-necked Nabateans resist the good news I bring? Do they not have ears to hear?"

"God sent you here? Hmmph. You're a cocky bastard."

Paulos resisted the impulse to rake his arm across the table, sending glass bottles crashing to the floor. Of course, God sent him here. Hadn't he?

Paulos agreed to return to Damascus with the next northbound caravan scheduled to depart in two days. If the stubborn Nabateans chose to remain outside God's family, so be it.

He would give them one last chance, their last chance for redemption, his last chance for validation. On the one day that remained to him before departing, he would warn them. The next morning, he returned to the agora, climbed atop a stone and mortar wall, cupped his hands, and shouted, "By your hard hearts, you are storing up wrath for yourselves on the day God's judgment will be revealed." He repeated the warning a second time and then a third before a tomato splattered against his chest, hurled by a nearby produce vendor. His initial spike of anger quickly became embarrassment at the spectacle he had become and the chorus of jeers that burned his ears. He retreated.

Alternately blaming the stiff-necked Nabateans and questioning himself, Paulos shuffled toward the home of Achishar when he sensed stalkers. He cocked his head slightly and listened without looking back. He heard footsteps behind him. He quickened his pace but so did his pursuers. He detoured down a side street, loped to the next corner, and turned again. He stopped and peered around a corner of a building.

There they were, four of them, coming his way, with swords, led by the thug with one eye. Paulos wheeled about, looking for an avenue of escape. He spied a ladder to a rooftop, and he scrambled up, nearly falling when his foot broke a rung, but he slithered over the rooftop wall just before his pursuers passed. He prayed they could not hear his heavy breathing or heart thumping or notice the broken step lying on the street. With rhythmic clomps, they marched past.

Paulos waited until the last faint glimmers of dusk before climbing down the steps and finding his way in the darkened streets. He paused outside Achishar's house, peering through the crack in the door into the dim lamplight. Achishar sat alone eating a cold supper. Paulos entered.

"You're a bigger fool 'n I thought, you stubborn bastard." Achishar was calm but resolute. "Pull your robe over your head to cover your eyes. Take your bags and your donkey and head to the edge of town where the caravan will gather on the morrow. Don't say nuthin' to nobody." Achishar had stuffed all Paulos' belongings into his bag, and his donkey was haltered and ready. "I'll keep your payments for my troubles. Don't say nuthin' to nooo-body—ya hear?"

Three weeks later, Paulos poked along the dark Damascus street, leading to the house of Ananias. Cheery beams of light seeped through windows and cracks. He knocked. Demetria swung open her front door, spilling warm lamplight over the failed missionary. A hearty stew and warm friends immediately buoyed his spirits. His first missionary journey had been a failure, but he would soon experience his first missionary success, purely by accident.

Chapter Eighteen

Demetria sent him to the market with Charis for fresh produce. They stopped at the booth of Omar, a Nabatean vegetable merchant and his wife, Deborah, a Jewess. Both were short and squat. Omar's nose bent sharply as if broken long ago. He sat on a tall stool on the side of their stall with crumbs littering the shelf of his belly. His triangular face broadened into jowls that jiggled as he chewed a stalk of celery. Deborah's smile revealed missing teeth. She wore layers of clothing—robes, scarves, and tunics—as if she carried her whole wardrobe with her.

Charis held up a pale yellow melon. "This is what your face looked like on the road to Damascus." She laughed.

Paulos plucked a green grape and threw it at her.

Deborah watched them with a smirk. "Are you young newlyweds?" she asked.

Paulos looked at Charis, and they laughed.

"No, we are just new friends," replied Charis. "What makes you think we are newlyweds?"

"Silliness," Deborah said.

Paulos looked at Charis, shrugged his shoulders, and then proceeded to tell Deborah about his experience on the Damascus road. Deborah lowered her eyes and fumbled with her vegetables. She looked up with pursed lips and a wrinkled nose as if searching for words to speak.

Before Deborah said anything, Charis spoke. "Will you honor us by breaking bread with us? The followers of Iesou will gather when the first day of the week begins at sunset."

Deborah's mouth dropped, and her lips moved without speaking. Then she said that this was the first invitation they had ever received to share a meal in another's home. As a mixed couple, they never felt welcome in either the Nabatean or the Jewish community. She looked at Omar who rolled his eyes and shrugged his shoulders as if to say, "You decide."

Deborah again fumbled with her vegetables. Finally, she looked up and stammered, "Yes, yes. We will come." Paulos' first converts were attracted not persuaded.

For the next three years, Paulos lived in Damascus, returning to work for Ezer the leather smith. The Damascus *ekklesia*, the gathering community of the followers of Iesou, flourished even though Paulos' own missionary successes were meager. Children were born and baptized into the *ekklesia,* including Markos, the son of Charis and her new husband, a Hellenistic Jew, the "defiler" Paulos had chased from the synagogue. Paulos considered himself an uncle to young Markos. Ezer, Paulos' employer and landlord, and his wife, Azubah, joined the *ekklesia*—but not Uri who still preferred women and wine to religion.

With lost innocence came greater cunning, and Paulos evangelized to Jews and interested Gentiles, *theosebeis*, in the synagogue. He had learned a lesson in Petra about evangelizing to strangers to Israelite religion—best to seek those with a footing in the Hebrew traditions, appealing to their pre-existing expectations, relying upon his own grounding in Torah, learned at the knee of Eli the sage.

Through his Prophets, God had promised to bring the nations together through a new King David, his anointed, the Christos. Paulos spoke the words of the Prophet Isaiah to the synagogue gathering:

"On that day the root of Jesse shall stand as a signal to the peoples; the nations shall inquire of him, and his dwelling shall be glorious … The wolf shall live with the lamb, the leopard shall lie down with the kid, the calf and the lion and the fatling together."

Of course, many Jews at the synagogue knew Paulos as the

persecutor, and his new role both attracted and offended. For some, his earlier stance lent credibility to his startling conversion. Others saw him as a traitor.

His chief antagonist at the Damascus synagogue was Mordecai the Pharisee. Thin, wiry and completely bald, he hopped about and crouched on spry legs as he mocked Paulos' words.

"The messianic king is to be of the family of King David, not a peasant from Galilee, and everyone knows that nothing good can come from Galilee!" Some Jews snickered at Mordecai's rebuttal.

"Tell us how a Mashiah who dies a humiliating death is a triumph of God?" He continued without allowing an answer, "When I look around, I do not see lions lying down with lambs."

More snickers. Mordecai's tone then changed from derision to warning. "The claim that Torah observance is unnecessary is far more serious. Paulos encourages you to break God's command. He threatens your own standing before God. Under Torah, this is the gross offense of apostasy, leading others astray. Paulos is a law-breaking apostate!"

The opposition of a fellow Pharisee might have stung Paulos more deeply except that it came from Mordecai, a tiresome dullard unable to comprehend the obvious fulfillment of Jewish messianic expectations in Iesou. The Nabateans were not the only stubborn deniers of the Christos, thought Paulos. There were stiff-necked Jews also, and it was unfortunate that a mediocrity such as Mordecai thwarted his missionary efforts in the synagogue.

Three years in Damascus passed quickly, and Paulos might have made Damascus his permanent home, but events across the Great Sea rippled toward Palestine. When the news reached Damascus that old Emperor Tiberius was dead, Paulos didn't pay much attention. Tiberius had been emperor since Paulos was a youngster in Tarsos, and he didn't know anything different. He had no reason to believe that life in the far regions of the empire under Caligula would change. He certainly didn't expect that a political change in far off Rome would endanger his own life.

When Paulos first arrived in Damascus, the city had been under control of the Romans, but the desert oasis was a frontier town adjacent to the Nabatean kingdom of Arabia, and the border was fluid. The absence of Roman soldiers in the marketplace and streets of Damascus signaled a change in the balance of power following the death of Tiberius.

"The Roman officer is late picking up the saddle I repaired for him," Ezer said to Uri. "Take it to his quarters and be sure to collect a denarius for payment. Don't give him the saddle without payment."

Uri returned a short time later still carrying the saddle.

Ezer bellowed at Uri, "Where in Hades is the payment?"

"The soldiers are gone. The quarters are empty."

Ezer quickly left the shop to speak to other vendors in the marketplace. He soon returned and reported, "Rumors are that the Romans snuck away in the night and that Nabatean solders of King Aretas of Petra will soon arrive."

Paulos swallowed hard as he realized his own stake in the political change; he had made enemies during his brief stay in Petra. He rubbed his nose as he remembered Achishar the glass blower who had ushered him out Petra and out of danger. *Don't say nuthin' to nooo-body—ya hear?*

Paulos intended to keep a low profile, but as he walked through the market one afternoon, he felt the glare of three Nabateans watching him. He cast an uneasy glance in their direction, and his breath caught in his throat. A burly Nabatean with one eye stepped from the shadows toward him. Paulos ducked behind a vendor's booth then slipped into the crowd. He snuck home, glancing back occasionally; he did not see anyone following him.

A few days passed. As Paulos hunched over his workbench, pushing hard to penetrate stiff leather with a needle, Ananias burst into the shop.

"Nabateans asked about you at the synagogue," he said. "Mordecai told them where you live, and they could be here soon. Hurry, you must leave!"

His words stunned Paulos, and his heart raced. Leave? Where would he go? Before he could speak, loud voices in the front of the shop signaled it was too late; they were here.

Azubah dashed down the stairs from the living quarters, yanked Paulos by the sleeve, and pulled him back up the stairs; Ananias followed. The rear windows looked down to the ground outside the city wall—too far to jump, but Azubah had a plan. She tied a rope to a large basket.

"Climb into the basket, and we'll lower you to the ground. Take these coins and run!"

Paulos protested. "Where shall I go?"

Ananias answered. "You're a Roman citizen and you must escape to a Roman city. After you're safe, head to Jerusalem. Cephas and the others will take you in. Go!"

Still unconvinced, Paulos climbed into the tipsy basket, and Ananias and Azubah lowered him to the ground with a thud. Paulos scrambled out, and they pulled the basket back into the house while Paulos hesitated and watched.

"Run!" shouted Azubah.

His eyes welled up as he gathered his bearings. He started to trot slowly but picked up speed; he followed the wall until he turned onto the Jerusalem road. He jogged until he overtook three men and a donkey heading in the same direction. They looked at him with curiosity as he slowed, gasping to catch his breath.

"I'm escaping," he stammered, "an angry husband."

The three laughed and one slapped Paulos on the back.

"Then join us as we travel to the next village."

PART THREE
JERUSALEM
37 C.E.

In Judah God is known, his name is great in Israel.
His abode has been established in Salem,
his dwelling place in Zion.

Psalm 76:1-2

Chapter Nineteen

Paulos departed Damascus reluctantly but journeyed toward Jerusalem eagerly. His long postponed pilgrimage was at hand. For the first time, he would behold Jerusalem: the mother city, the dwelling place of the Lord, Mount Zion, the scene of the crucifixion of the Christos, and the hub for his followers. A pilgrim's heart beat a hurried cadence to his long strides as he journeyed southward along the well-traveled road from Damascus to Jerusalem.

Signs of early summer surrounded him: ripening fields of grain; fruit trees laden with green figs, apples, and apricots; and suckling lambs bleating after the ewes. Each evening, he watched the waning crescent moon grow smaller as the Hebrew calendar month of *Lyyar* passed; with the new moon, the month of *Sivan* and summer would begin.

Following his hasty escape from Damascus, Paulos would seek Cephas, the companion of Iesou the Christos and leader of his Jerusalem followers. He reminded himself to speak Aramaic and to call him Yeshua the Mashiah now that he was in Palestine.

"Is Nazareth nearby?" he asked a stranger in Galilee. "Did you know Yeshua of Nazareth?"

The stranger looked him up and down without answering before stalking away, jarring Paulos' enthusiasm. Paulos slowed his pace as he remembered the martyrdom of Stephen—stoned by his fellow Jews. Paulos suddenly worried that he was walking into a complicated, unfriendly political situation.

Doubt frayed his optimism further as he began to question his reception by Cephas and the Nazarenes. Who was he, to seek an audience with the friends and family of the Mashiah? Why? What was his purpose? He stroked his nose as he shortened his steps.

On top of everything else, with his coin purse nearly empty, he could not turn back. A hot breeze whistled up the valley of the River Jordan, blowing dust in the face of the uncertain seeker.

When he entered Jerusalem, he aimlessly followed the foot traffic. With his last coins, he rented a room in an inn, filled with pilgrims in Jerusalem to offer sacrifice at the Temple. He stripped naked, bathed, and washed the clothes he had worn since he left Damascus, hanging his tunic, robe, and loincloth from a rafter to dry. As evening settled on the city and the din from the street receded, Paulos brooded on a mat in his room without windows. Why should Cephas—leader of the disciples, best friend and confidant of Yeshua, the one who saw the resurrected Mashiah—receive him? What credentials did he offer besides a few converts and a vision? He felt a fool for coming to Jerusalem as a beggar—no clothes, no tools, and an empty coin purse—depending upon the mercy of a stranger.

The morning brought false courage, and Paulos set out early in his freshly cleaned clothes to find Cephas. He headed to the agora and mingled with the crowd. His ears caught snatches of discussions of the Nazarenes, and when he overheard a pair of boys speaking to a wine vendor about Yeshua, he took his chance. Paulos waited until the boys were alone before approaching them.

"Are you friends of Cephas from Galilee?"

"Yes, I know Cephas," the chunky boy with curly, sand-colored hair responded. "Would you like to meet him?"

Finding Cephas was as easy as that. The boys escorted Paulos away from the hubbub of the agora down a quiet side street, a short distance to Cephas' house. Paulos' heart raced faster than his steps. Cephas himself answered Paulos' nervous knock on the door.

Slender as a mountain aspen, Cephas appeared shorter than Paulos because his spindly legs bowed out at the knees, and he hunched over. For no good reason, Paulos expected him to be much bigger. His curly red hair with flecks of gray encircled a tanned bald spot, and his beard was mottled red and brown. Paulos was a year short of his thirtieth birthday, and Cephas was nearly a decade older but with a boyish face and a mischievous smile. Cephas cocked his head slightly as Paulos introduced himself; Cephas' warm grin melted Paulos' icy apprehension.

"Why yes, I remember Ananias. Is he well? Are the others well? Is your Damascus group safe and well? It's growing you say? Wonderful, wonderful. Praise God!"

The boys started to leave. "I must bring this wine to my mother," said the thickset boy.

Cephas placed his hand on the shoulders of the boys and spoke to Paulos. "Have you been properly introduced to Joses? Joses is the youngest brother of Yeshua, and this is his cousin, Symeon, who has joined their household here in Jerusalem."

It had not occurred to Paulos that Yeshua had a brother so young, so chubby, and so flesh and blood normal. The boys nodded a greeting and then hurried away.

"Invite the man in," said a woman behind Cephas. "Where are your manners?"

Cephas chuckled, stepped to the side, bowed low, and with a sweeping motion with his hand, gestured for Paulos to enter. The tall, buxom woman stepped forward to introduce herself.

"Since my husband seems to have forgotten his woman, allow me to speak for myself. I am Raziah, the man's wife for more years than he can remember. We hail from Capernaum of Galilee. His name is Simon, but his friends call him Cephas, which means 'the rock'; hmmph!"

Cephas winked at Paulos. Paulos recognized the name "Cephas" to be Aramaic; in Greek, it would be "Petros."

"Please sit down both of you at the table. You must sup with us."

Raziah offered simple fare: a steaming vegetable stew, fresh bread, green onions and yogurt. Her barley brew was especially dark and sweet—the best Paulos had tasted, much better than his mother's recipe, which seemed pale and flat by comparison.

Paulos and Cephas enjoyed a lively discussion, often interrupted by Raziah, as they broke bread together. Cephas was easy to talk to and not at all intimidating. Paulos told of his early life in Tarsos, his Pharisee education, his persecution of Charis, his Damascus road experience, and the last few years of missionary activity in Damascus. He skipped over his failure in Petra. Paulos thought he detected approval, or at least hoped.

"What do you intend to do next?" asked Cephas.

"Not sure." Other than fleeing Damascus and seeking a safe haven with the Nazarenes of Jerusalem, he had no plans, and a fresh wave of insecurity washed over him.

"I'll introduce you to Ya'akov, the brother of Yeshua. He can use a good man like you. He's a Pharisee, too," Cephas said. "In the meantime, you must stay with us. I'll walk with you to the inn to collect your things." Cephas pushed himself away from the table with a resolute nod.

Paulos welcomed the invitation. His coin purse was empty. "I have no belongings due to my hasty departure from Damascus," he said.

Paulos and Cephas drank Raziah's sweet barley beer and talked late into the evening. Raziah retired early, her relaxed snores from the back room a counterpoint to the beery chorus of the male voices.

When Paulos finally climbed a ladder to the rooftop, he found extra tunics and robes on a sleeping mat placed there by Raziah. He circled around the rooftop to see what he could see of Jerusalem; even in the dark, it seemed grand. *Ya'akov could use a good man like you.* Ya'akov: the brother of Yeshua, the leader of the Nazarenes, a Pharisee.

Hours earlier when he had timidly knocked on Cephas' door, he expected to be dwarfed by a giant, but now as he yawned and stretched his lanky frame and long arms, he felt much taller.

The punishing mid-morning sun awakened Paulos. He squinted into the piercing rays, barley beer throbbing in his head. He dressed in fresh clothes. Cephas was already out, and Raziah offered Paulos flat bread and dried figs washed down with water. He chomped down the bread and fruit and waited for Cephas to return while visiting with Raziah. He had known this Galilean husband and wife for less than a day, but they already seemed old friends, their hospitality as comfortable as his borrowed robes.

"Simon and I lived in Capernaum on the shores of Lake Galilee where Simon and Andrew, his brother, were fishermen. We live alone here in our humble house as God has not blessed us with children."

Raziah's plain, box-face matched the square-shouldered, thick frame of a woman of the country accustomed to hard work. Nearly as tall as her beanpole husband, she certainly outweighed him, but without being fat—just solid. A slight upward curl at the corners of her lips hinted at an impending smile that never quite appeared. Her modest clothing fit the wife of a poor fisherman: a loose fitting gray tunic extending to her ankles, a darker gray outer robe, and a faded maroon sash gathering the garments around her waist. She had coiled her long brown hair into a bun.

"They may call him Cephas, but he'll always be Simon to me." A slight grin suggested amusement at the elevated status accorded her husband by the followers of Yeshua.

Paulos sat in the cluttered main room of the modest, one-story home; a second room served as bedroom for Cephas and Raziah. There was no courtyard but merely a tiny back porch with a thatch roof and cooking hearth. A crude ladder next to the porch provided access to the flat rooftop where he had slept. Except for a small table, a few stools, and a tattered awning in one corner, the rooftop was bare.

Finally, Paulos decided that Cephas must be busy so he would not waste time sitting around. The affability of Cephas and Raziah had dispelled his anxiety, allowing his pilgrim curiosity to return. Paulos would visit the Temple.

Chapter Twenty

The gleaming white marble wall towered above humble mud-brown single and double story residences. Paulos shielded his eyes with his hands, unable to look directly at the radiance of the sun on the ramparts. The Temple sprawled before him so that the gates appeared as mole-holes along the base of the wall. He darted into one of the tunnels and followed a staircase up three stories toward the Court of the Gentiles, an outer court that encircled the Temple proper.

He initially passed by a ritual bath but changed his mind and returned to wash himself in the purifying waters. The baths offered a last opportunity for Jews to cleanse themselves of any impurity before entering the holy realms—only the Torah observant and ritually clean could access the Courts of God. On the road to Damascus, he had been washed in the waters of baptism, a lasting cleansing, but he would honor the Temple rituals out of respect.

He continued up the tunnel where he emerged onto a platform of giant white stones that supported an area the size of a small village. It seemed a village, too, with cackling chickens, bleating goats, and pilgrims whirring about. Minor priests wearing white linen robes and tall hats directed traffic and offered guidance. Sacred melodies from the inner courts floated over the profane buzz of the outer Court of the Gentiles.

The Court of the Gentiles was a place of commerce: pudding vendors offering braised meats, merchants selling sacrificial animals and religious souvenirs, and moneychangers converting unclean foreign coins into Jewish currency suitable as payment for the sacrificial animals. At the far end of the platform, carpenters and masons toiled in the ongoing task of reconstruction and expansion that had begun nearly fifty years earlier under King Herod the Great.

Like the profane world surrounding God's holy land, the Court of the Gentiles ringed the sacred Temple proper. As Paulos moved through the chaotic outer Court of the Gentiles toward the orderly inner courts, he saw signs posted at regular intervals on the boundary wall. He stepped forward to read, but he did not understand the Latin sign so he moved along to the next sign printed in Greek: "Gentiles, refrain from entering the Temple enclosure, on pain of death."

Boundaries of stone and boundaries of circumcision. There were always walls to keep the Gentiles away from God, but Yeshua changed all that. Paulos had come out of curiosity, but the boundary and purity rules of the Temple kindled a growing resentment toward its exclusionary practices.

Paulos slowly walked a complete circle around the Temple proper. Massive plates of gold flashed in the rays of noonday sunshine. Sharp, golden spikes on the top of the Temple prevented birds from perching, and golden vines draped the main entrance.

Paulos stepped through the main gate, exited the profane Court of the Gentiles, and entered the first inner court of the sacred Temple area, the Court of Women. Ritually clean Jews, male and female, frequented the large court where musicians and dancers performed throughout the day. Golden-veiled dancers in purple silks glided to breathy melodies of flutists and plucked tones of harpists; jangling tambourines measured the cadence. A Temple worker carried firewood from a storage room into the inner courts for the sacrificial fires. Aromas of wood smoke and incense floated in the air.

Paulos did not linger in this court long, and he soon moved into the next court through the Nicanor Gate. The next court, a step closer to God, was the Court of Israel—only ritually clean Jewish males entered this court. Women were not as holy as men. Paulos slowly shook his head as he thought of Charis.

Paulos ventured no further than the Court of Israel, but he spied into the next level. The next court, where the wood bearer dropped his armful of wood, was the Court of the Priests, the location of the altar of burnt sacrifices and a "sea of bronze" for ritual washings. A feather of gray smoke from the sacrificial fires plumed upward toward heaven. A staircase behind the altar ascended to a porch flanked by two ornate bronze pillars. His eyes could not probe the room behind the porch, but he visualized it from the stories told by Eli: a small altar for offering incense, ten golden lamp stands—five on a side, and a golden table for the "bread of the presence."

There was still one room beyond that, the "Holy of Holies," the dwelling place of God according to Israelite religion. Once a year, on the Day of Atonement, the High Priest entered this chamber alone, face to face with God, with a rope around his waist for pulling him from God's presence in case he fainted or died.

Paulos admired the majesty of the place, but did he sense the nearness of God? He listened to the songs of the musicians, smelled the incense, and watched the priests performing their sacrificial rites, but did he sense the nearness of God? His people, his culture, his religion had revered the Temple for a millennium, but did he sense the nearness of God?

Paulos shut his eyes and breathed deep, cleansing breaths. After a moment, his eyes popped open. Nothing.

For Paulos, the Temple had become an artifact, merely an interesting relic of the past. The sacrificial functions of the priests had become hollow. The purity system that defined boundaries and degrees of holiness had become meaningless. The old had passed away and everything had become new, *apart from Torah.*

Paulos departed the Temple satisfied of the truth of Damascus, unaware that many followers of Yeshua still honored the ways of old. He would soon meet Ya'akov, Yeshua's own brother.

Chapter Twenty-one

When Paulos returned from the Temple in the late afternoon, Cephas was still out. Raziah frequently searched through her kitchen window. "Where is that man?" she muttered to herself as Paulos sat at the table. "Where is that man?" she mumbled again a few minutes later.

Just then, Cephas appeared at the doorstep with a leg of lamb and wine bottles. "It has been a stressful day," Cephas reported. "Were you in the agora? Did you hear the news?"

Paulos shook his head.

Cephas continued, "Peasants assaulted a Sadducee in the agora. They began by taunting the rich man's entourage as he passed by, and one of them threw a rock which struck the man. Fortunately, Azariah the Sadducee was not injured."

"Azariah the cousin of the High Priest?" asked Paulos, remembering the rich man from the caravan from Antioch a few years earlier. He also recalled the comment of Abdel, the slave, who said Azariah needed the protection of bodyguards in Jerusalem.

"His henchmen drew swords and threatened the crowd, Roman soldiers rushed in, vendor's booths were knocked a kilter, goats ran loose, chickens got underfoot, and—well, it's a miracle no one got hurt."

Cephas filled two cups with fresh wine without bothering to mix with water, as was the normal custom. "They'll blame us you know. Every time a Sadducee gets a sliver in a finger, he runs off and tattles to his Roman masters, and the Nazarenes somehow get blamed." He settled heavily into his chair, his chipper smile replaced by a scowl.

Cephas continued. "The rich and powerful stick together. They like things the way they are. When the Roman Emperor sends a new

Governor who then appoints a new High Priest from the Sadducee aristocrats, is it surprising that the High Priest and his Sadducee friends are friendly toward the Romans?"

Raziah nodded.

"Even King Herod the Great suckled at the breasts of the Imperial courtesans in Rome." Cephas said. "His sons and grandsons gamble away their day at horse races in Rome, biding their time until the Emperor dispatches them here or there to rule over this or that province. Are the Herodians Jews or not?"

Raziah shook her head.

"On the other hand, the poor do not like things the way they are. Zealots, like the one who threw the stone today, are willing to pick up the sword against the Romans and their puppets."

Cephas gulped a swallow of wine and exhaled a deep sigh. "Who knows what to do?"

"The Essenes run to the desert, cursing the rest of us because we're not pure enough. They think they're the only chaste remnant of God's beloved family, and they believe the Gentiles have contaminated the rest of us. These are the fringes. Right in the middle, the big mass in the middle, the rest of us muddle about."

Raziah interrupted. "Tell Paulos about the Pharisees. The Pharisees are popular with the people."

Before Cephas could continue, Paulos spoke up.

"I myself am a Pharisee so I understand the written and oral Torah, and I understand how the covenant God made with Moses on Sinai defines God's relationship with the people. But don't you think that Yeshua has changed all that?"

Cephas stared at the Pharisee from a far off land. Paulos knew that Cephas was sizing him up, and he felt small again. Cephas did not speak but merely clucked his tongue a few times before draining his cup of wine.

"Stop talking," Raziah said. "Wait while I get this lamb roasting." She stepped to the porch to place the leg of lamb on the hearth.

Cephas winked at Paulos. For the first time that evening, Cephas' familiar smile returned. He leaned back and ran his hands over his head, scratching the bald spot. Cephas refilled his own cup, but Paulos had barely touched his wine.

Raziah returned and immediately began speaking, "The Pharisees are not just popular; they have power too," she said with a firm nod. "The Council, the Sanhedrin, has seventy-one members and most of them are Pharisees including Gamaliel the leader. If it wasn't for the Sanhedrin, the High Priest and the Sadducees would have their way with everything, but the Pharisees keep them in check." Raziah smacked her lips twice to emphasize her point.

"Tell Paulos about the Nazarenes," said Raziah, "about us."

"The Nazarenes who await the return of Yeshua as the Mashiah are closest to the Pharisees. Just like the Pharisees, we despise the Romans and wait for the day God kicks them out of his Holy Land, but neither the Pharisees nor the Nazarenes are rebellious like the Zealots and brigands from the countryside."

Paulos shifted uneasily on his stool at the long dialogue between Cephas and Raziah regarding Jewish factions in Jerusalem. Politics? Why did Cephas drone on about politics? Paulos' picture of Damascus was not about politics. Spirit and soul—not Romans and rebellion.

Cephas continued. "The Nazarenes retain ties with the Pharisees; Ya'akov remains a Pharisee and has influential Pharisee friends, but Stephen set us back a few years ago with his wild attacks on Torah and the Temple." Paulos wasn't aware of Cephas' role in promoting the Hellenists to Ya'akov, and Cephas didn't mention it—nor did he mention the silence of the Nazarenes at Stephen's trial.

Cephas shut one eye and measured the man with Hellenist ties from the Damascus *ekklesia* with the other. Paulos worried that his face had betrayed his skepticism. This was not the time or place to defend Stephen or the Torah free message the Damascus *ekklesia* promoted amongst the Gentiles, and Paulos said nothing.

Apparently satisfied, Cephas continued. "Our greatest problems are with the Sadducees. Ya'akov says, 'A learned bastard takes precedence over an ignorant High Priest'. The Sadducees and the priests worry about their own standing with Rome. We find ourselves as followers of Yeshua floating in a bubbling cauldron that is ready to boil over at any moment."

Cephas continued to discuss local political factions and their differing views for a long time. Paulos nodded and listened but held his tongue even as the question kept rolling over in his mind. What did Jerusalem politics have to do with God's new creation? He was glad when Raziah suddenly jumped up.

"The lamb!" she said. "The lamb must be cooked!" She ran to the hearth and returned with a smile and a steaming roast.

"It's done just right. Stop talking and clear the table. It's time to eat."

Raziah cleaned up after the meal. Cephas invited Paulos to the rooftop into the cool night air. Paulos carried his cup, and Cephas carried a fresh bottle of wine as they ascended the ladder into the starry night. They sat on three-legged stools and leaned against the short wall that enclosed the rooftop.

For a while, Cephas talked about fishing on Lake Galilee while Paulos tugged on his beak-nose without really listening. Paulos gut was queasy. Perhaps the roasted lamb roiled his belly. Or was it the growing realization that he and Cephas saw things differently?

Paulos would ask important questions. Cephas had walked, talked, and lived with Yeshua; Cephas was with Yeshua in the last days; and Cephas was there when the resurrected Yeshua appeared. How did Cephas understand the significance of these events?

"Who do you say Yeshua was?" Paulos asked. "Let me ask that differently, who do you say Yeshua *is*?"

Cephas drained his cup and refilled it. With a big sigh, he scratched his bald spot as he considered his answer.

"Well, of course, Yeshua is the long expected Mashiah, but we didn't know that right away," began Cephas. "Yeshua had a sense of urgency to his ministry. 'The kingdom of God is near,' he said often. The charisma of the man with his message of the imminent arrival of God's kingdom attracted a large following."

Cephas had a faraway look on his face with a wistful smile.

"At first, we believed Yeshua to be God's prophet. However, the crowds wanted more. The crowds wanted Yeshua to lead a rebellion against the Romans. The crowds wanted to make him the new king of the Jews."

Cephas stood, placed his hands on the waist-high wall, leaned forward, and stared down the empty street as if he could see the events playing out in front of him. His smile had faded, and he pursed his lips tight.

"Rabble rousing crowds led to his arrest and crucifixion. There was violence and arrests. Yeshua and those of us who were with him attempted to avoid trouble, but we could not."

Cephas moved to a corner of the rooftop and pointed. "As we gathered together that last evening in the upper room—it's just over there," he said, lifting his cup toward the dark night, "we knew that a crisis was unfolding and a confrontation with the Romans was imminent. Some of the followers armed themselves; if it was to be a confrontation with the Romans, so be it. God would intervene."

Cephas looked up at the stars for a moment before he blew his nose on his sleeve.

"But our hopes and expectations were dashed. Following a brief skirmish, the Temple police sent by the High Priest arrested Yeshua. The High Priest surrendered him to the Romans, and within a day, he was dead." Cephas finished in a half-whisper. "I retreated quietly home to Galilee along with the others."

Cephas returned to his stool and leaned back, tilting the stool on two legs as he inclined against the wall. The back of his head rested on the roof wall with starlight splashing across his face, but his eyes remained closed.

Was he done with his story? Wasn't there more to it? Paulos hesitated to interrupt Cephas' thoughts, so he merely filled his cup with more wine even though it was nearly full. Finally, he dared to break the long silence.

"Why did Yeshua die?"

Cephas opened his eyes and stared at him with a blank look, suddenly in the present. He leaned forward, and the front leg of the stool returned to the rooftop with a jolt. He scratched his head as he pondered the question. Finally, he answered with a shrug of his shoulders.

"It just happened. Chaos, I guess. The crowds got out of control, and the Romans overreacted. It just happened, but God righted this tragic injustice. When we gathered again in Galilee, Yeshua appeared to us. With his resurrection, Yeshua became the Mashiah. Yeshua was, and *is,* the new King David, but even greater than his ancestor. Soon he will return, and we will throw out the Romans and establish God's kingdom on earth."

The streets were mostly dark, but Paulos could see a dim aura of light in the direction of the Roman garrison. Cephas puzzled him. Although Paulos had great respect for the leader of the disciples, his explanations seemed inadequate—too political, too local, too personal. Paulos' own encounter with God on the Damascus road signaled the dawn of a new age: spiritual not political; cosmic not local; universal not individual. This is what he believed. Was it not true?

"Was it not God who appeared to you?" Paulos asked, "God revealed in a resurrected Yeshua?"

Cephas stood and stretched his arms and yawned. "I'm not sure if it's the wine or the conversation, but my head spins. I must be off to bed." Cephas disappeared down the ladder.

Paulos was not ready for sleep. For a while, he watched the stars and the slice of moon that had thickened since his arrival in Jerusalem. Did his mother watch the same sky tonight? Or his father? Why had he turned south toward Jerusalem after escaping Damascus instead of north toward his parent's home? And his own.

Paulos didn't notice the mouse that gnawed at the frayed edge of his robe that lay on his sleeping mat. It scurried away in the dark as Paulos tossed the robe aside and took his place on his mat. Silky clouds floated by as he lay on his back. He tried to remember the sky on the Damascus road. What had he seen in the clouds and heard on the wind that night three years ago? The memories were murky, especially after listening to Cephas for two days. The hospitality extended by Cephas had calmed Paulos' initial insecurity about the reception he would receive from the ones who had walked with Yeshua, but Cephas' stories had rekindled Paulos' anxiety. Doubt gnawed at the fraying edges of Paulos' self-confidence.

And he had not yet met Ya'akov.

Chapter Twenty-two

Ya'akov was tired and grumpy after a long Sabbath at the synagogue. He would have preferred a simple meal followed by an early sleep, but the Nazarene leader had obligations. With the setting of the Sabbath-day sun, the Nazarenes gathered for a common meal in the upper room where Yeshua had shared his last supper with his disciples four years earlier. As the leader, Ya'akov was always present, and no one could blame him for the lagging attendance at these gatherings.

The Mashiah had not returned as expected, and many seasons had passed. Was it only four years? After an early burst of enthusiasm that God's kingdom was near, not much had changed under the Roman colonialists. True, the emperor had recalled Pontius Pilate to Rome just last year, and there were rumors that the Governor had paid a price for his tyranny. Now, old Emperor Tiberius was dead, replaced by Caligula, but the stinking Romans were still here, unclean Gentiles who polluted God's Holy Land.

No one could blame Ya'akov. He did his best to prepare the way for the Mashiah's return. He set an example of strict Torah observance. His knees ached from the hours spent kneeling in prayer. He was just a simple carpenter who had not asked for this responsibility. No one could blame him.

With heavy steps, he mounted the exterior stairway to the second-story upper room. He rested at the top to catch his breath before entering the incense-laden chamber. A dull glow of candles and oil lamps filled the windowless room.

When he took inventory of the early arrivals, he noted Cephas, wine-cup in hand, already aglow with winy affability, in animated discussion with others. The cackling giggle of the man floated over the din of many conversations. A lanky stranger was with him. Cephas always attracted the newcomers. Ya'akov envied the gregarious confidante of his brother whose aura of warmth drew moths to his flame.

Each new arrival added a loaf of bread, or a basket of figs, or some other food item to a large table for their weekly common meal. Ya'akov grabbed a handful of olives and a cup of wine as he made his rounds. He spotted Cephas elbowing his way toward him with the tall stranger in tow.

From the moment Cephas introduced Paulos to him, Ya'akov didn't trust the man although he didn't fully understand the reason. There was something about the man's impudent, elongated nose—prying and eager to poke into matters that were not his concern. Ya'akov didn't care much for the man's boasts about his missionary work, but his ties to Damascus raised the greatest suspicion in Ya'akov's mind. Damascus had connections to Stephen the blaspheming Hellenist who paid for his crimes with his life. Stephen had doused the fiery enthusiasm of those early days like a goat herder pissing on his campfire. If anyone was to blame for the sluggish growth of the Nazarenes, it was Stephen and the Hellenists. No one could blame Ya'akov for refusing to aid the blasphemer who got what he deserved.

"Damascus. Is that where Ananias now lives?" Ya'akov asked as if making polite conversation, but he really probed the stranger's Hellenist sympathies.

"Yes, Ananias is the leader of the *ekklesia* of the followers of Yeshua. However, I'm not from Damascus but from Tarsos of Cilicia. I'm a Pharisee," Paulos said.

"A Pharisee?" Ya'akov's eyes widened and flared black at the insolence of the foreigner. "Who trained you?" Only the Pharisee schools of Jerusalem offered proper training.

Before Paulos answered, a tiny woman joined their conversation. "Ya'akov, who is your guest?" She asked.

"Hello Maryam. So nice to see you. This is Paulos, a visitor from Damascus. This is Maryam of Magdala." Ya'akov lied. He was not happy to see this haughty rich woman from Magdala on the shores of Lake Galilee. As usual, Ya'akov thought she overdressed—emerald green silk robe with a matching scarf wrapped around her neck with one end dangling down her back and the other end draped across her shoulder.

The lines in Paulos' face lifted when she conversed with him in fluent Greek. When he spoke to her, he flailed his arms like a madman; when he listened, he stroked his beak nose as if planning a sinister plot. Ya'akov's own Greek was very poor, and he barely understood their conversation. This is Jerusalem, damn it! Speak like Jews, not Gentiles!

At that moment, Cephas interrupted and ushered Paulos forward to meet others in the room. Maryam extended her hand and touched Paulos' arm as they separated and said something Ya'akov didn't understand. Ya'akov stood awkwardly with the uppity woman and her damned smile that somehow irritated him. He was relieved when she drifted away to join another conversation as the meal began.

Ya'akov plopped down on a stool, but the others squatted on the floor for the meal. He ate his bread silently and alone in the midst of cheerful jabbering. He barely noticed when the service began and singers offered a familiar temple song with the lyrics changed to praise Yeshua, but one line caught his attention: *That we would be saved from our enemies and from the hand of all who hate us.* The optimistic words jarred loose painful images of the Roman garrison that oozed its filth over the Temple next door, of centurions driving chariots through the streets of Jerusalem with Roman flags streaming in defiance of God, and of Roman legionaries pissing in the gutters of the city's poor neighborhoods. Bloody Romans. Ya'akov looked around at the joyous faces of the Nazarenes, but he felt only sadness at hopes unfulfilled. Who was to blame?

After the service, the Nazarenes slipped away by twos and threes. Cephas and the so-called Pharisee from Tarsos caught Ya'akov at the door. "This young man wishes to speak with you about working with us in Jerusalem," said Cephas.

Ya'akov's eyes darted from Cephas to Paulos and back again. A Greek speaking, self-important, pretend-Pharisee? How would that improve the lot of the Nazarenes with the local Jewry?

"I'll drop by tomorrow," Ya'akov said before stomping down the stairs. He would give the beak-nosed man one chance to prove himself worthy, but no one could blame him for refusing to allow a Gentile-loving foreigner to join the Nazarenes.

Ya'akov shuffled through the darkened streets. When he arrived home, Shera, his wife, greeted him with a kiss.

"What's the matter?" She asked.

"I blame myself," he said.

"For what?"

"Everything."

Chapter Twenty-three

By the time Paulos finished his breakfast of melon and Raziah's flat bread, the morning sun had already overheated the city, and the dust hung thick in the breezeless streets. Paulos nervously awaited the arrival of Ya'akov, glancing out the door at every clump or clatter from the street. When the burly figure of Yeshua's brother finally appeared at the open door, Paulos hopped up, eager to learn, eager to impress, eager to find his place.

Breathing heavily and wiping his sweaty forehead with his brown-stained sleeve, Ya'akov moved quickly on his feet; the builder's norm that hung from his neck swayed rhythmically with his steps. Fringed *tzitzit* dangled from his immense belly under a flowing robe, and curly brown hair peeked from beneath a tight fitting black cap. Paulos didn't see his eyes because Ya'akov never looked squarely into his face; when Paulos caught him stealing glances, Ya'akov quickly diverted his gaze, which only increased Paulos' nervousness, unsure what the heavy man was thinking.

"See the Temple rising over the other buildings. We'll go to the Temple later." Ya'akov pointed to the Temple ramparts, visible from many Jerusalem vantage points.

"I've seen the Temple already," Paulos said. He didn't mean to sound brusque, but it came out that way.

They walked toward the agora, followed by a battle-scarred, patchy-haired brown mutt with a stubby tail.

"Who is the sage who taught you? It surprises me to learn that there are *hakhamim* outside Palestine." Ya'akov asked.

"Eli, the sage, was my dear friend and a man learned in the traditions of the elders."

"Was this man from Jerusalem?"

"Must all learned men call Jerusalem home?" Again, Paulos regretted his own impertinence.

"Did you study Torah in Hebrew or Greek?"

"The holy scrolls in the synagogue library were Greek not Hebrew," Paulos confessed. For the first time, his Torah training seemed inferior. Paulos caught a subtle nod of Ya'akov's head. Did that signify approval? Or, had Ya'akov merely confirmed his disapproval?

Each time Ya'akov stopped to point out a landmark, the hound lifted its leg and peed.

In the agora, Ya'akov purchased a basketful of fresh bread and several jars of honey for distribution in the city slums. "Two or three times a week we distribute food to the poor."

For several hours, Paulos reluctantly followed Ya'akov into places he would never enter alone: alleys of stench and filth; tumbledown shacks overflowing with scrawny, naked, bawling kids; and corners cramped with lame beggars. In spite of bodyguards, a stone thrower in the agora had attacked Azariah the Sadducee, yet Ya'akov charged into this den of God's forgotten with nary a worry.

"Blessed are you, my child, yours is the coming kingdom of God," Ya'akov said to each one as he offered a bit of bread and honey.

Their hard faces softened with familiarity. They knew this man, and there was trust in their eyes. Ya'akov mellowed too, with a relaxed smile that had not been present the night before in the upper room.

The sun slowly crawled across the sky and passed far beyond its midpoint by the time they departed the slums and approached the Temple. The dog claimed a shady spot and lay on its belly, pale tongue hanging low and drooling, awaiting their return. The men entered through a mole-hole gate in the Temple wall and ascended a stairway to the Court of the Gentiles. Paulos followed Ya'akov to a spacious room in the north wall that had the appearance of a legislative chamber, with seats in a semicircle, facing a speaker's platform in the center.

Ya'akov explained the significance of the chamber. God commanded Moses to gather seventy of the elders of Israel. With Moses as seventy-first member and leader, he convened the first ruling council of the Hebrews, called the Sanhedrin. This chamber, known as the Hall of Hewn Stones, was the traditional meeting place for the Sanhedrin.

Ya'akov looked quickly from side to side before speaking. "Stinking Romans. They control the High Priest and the Sadducees, but they don't control the Sanhedrin. There are good men in the Sanhedrin," he said, "good Pharisees, and they keep the High Priest in line. In protest of Roman rule, the Sanhedrin has removed itself from this Hall and meets elsewhere in a private villa."

"Is this where the Sanhedrin tried Yeshua?" Paulos asked.

"Damn it man! Don't you see? The trial of Yeshua wasn't before the Sanhedrin at all. It was a rigged trial," he said, "held before the High Priest in the middle of the night. The bastard delivered Yeshua to the Roman Governor, Pontius Pilate, before the Sanhedrin leadership got wind of the arrest. Had Yeshua been tried by the Sanhedrin," Ya'akov said, voice rising, "the result would certainly have been different."

He pounded the speaker's podium with his clenched fist. "Damn that bastard," he said, "and the stinking Romans." He stalked out of the hall, kicking an empty seat as he passed.

A rat scurried from under the seat, trailing its long tail across Paulos' feet. Paulos jumped back, tangled his legs, and tumbled in a heap on the hard stone floor, ripping the seam of his robe from its hem upwards a span of more than a few hands. He scrambled to his feet and inspected the damage. He pulled off loose threads and threw them in the corner. He smoothed the torn seam as best he could.

As Paulos hurried out of the chamber, the rat squatted on its haunches, chewing on Paulos' discarded threads. The day was not going well.

Paulos caught up to Ya'akov where he waited in the shade with the slobbering dog. Paulos averted his eyes when Ya'akov stared at him. Paulos smoothed his robe again and followed Ya'akov as he set out toward the upper city where many fine villas were located. Ya'akov did not speak until he stopped in front of a stone villa with a red tile roof, hesitating to catch his breath. Lean and long-striding, Paulos breathed normally.

"Is Gamaliel here?" Ya'akov said to the servant who answered the knock on the thick oak door. "He is expecting us."

Gamaliel? The leading Pharisee of Jerusalem? Paulos cast a surprised glance at Ya'akov. Gamaliel was the *Nasi*, the seventy-first member and leader of the Sanhedrin, the one who stood in the sandals of Moses.

A servant escorted the men into a large inner courtyard, lush with green flowering plants and shaded by a trio of palm trees. Paulos straightened his stooped shoulders and worried about the rip in his robe. Gamaliel squatted on a mat in the shade; the tiny man, white teeth flashing through his chest-length gray beard, jumped to his feet to greet his guests. His expectant eyes sparkled as he extended his hand in greeting, soft but firm. His confident voice commanded the courtyard.

"And how is my friend Ya'akov, the disciple of Shammai?" asked Gamaliel, the grandson of the great Pharisee sage named Hillel. Ya'akov had received his Pharisee training in the school of Shammai, a sage and contemporary of Hillel. The House of Shammai and the House of Hillel continued to educate students in the ways of the Pharisees but always with a hint of competition and nuanced differences in point of view.

"Allow me to introduce a visitor from Tarsos via Damascus. Paulos *says* he received Pharisee training in Tarsos under a sage named Eli."

"Tarsos of Cilicia?" said Gamaliel, lifting his eyebrows. "My grandfather Hillel was also from the Diaspora. He returned from

Babylon to Palestine, first to Galilee and only later to Jerusalem."

Paulos beamed at the first good news of the day.

"Please allow me to share a favorite story of my grandfather, Hillel. A Gentile came to Shammai and said to him, 'You may accept me as a proselyte on the condition that you teach me the whole Torah while I stand on one foot.' As the story goes, Shammai refused to play such a game with the Gentile and drove him away with a builder's square."

Ya'akov removed his fingers from the norm that tilted on the shelf of his belly.

"The Gentile then came to my grandfather, Hillel, and made the same promise. My grandfather accepted the challenge stating, 'What is hateful to you do not do to your fellow: that is the whole Torah; all the rest is explanation; go and learn.'"

Gamaliel teased Ya'akov further, "Did not your brother Yeshua say that the whole Torah hangs on the command *to love your neighbor as yourself?* Yeshua and my grandfather said much the same thing. Yes, I believe Yeshua favored the more tolerant Hillel."

Gamaliel finished with a laugh. Paulos wiped his own smile away with his long fingers when he saw Ya'akov's scowl. Gamaliel's servant returned with a bottle of wine, three clay cups, and a tray of sliced pears together with cracked almonds.

"That was nasty business in the agora with Azariah the Sadducee. We can be sure his Roman friends will take notice." Gamaliel shook his head as he spoke.

"Undoubtedly, the bastard deserved it and more," Ya'akov said, "but the Nazarenes will be blamed for the fanatical actions of the Zealots."

Gamaliel looked straight into Ya'akov's eyes.

"If you are serious in your claim that your brother Yeshua was the Mashiah, you should expect trouble with the Romans and their Sadducee friends." Gamaliel made a scolding sound with his tongue between his teeth before continuing. "If you proclaim a kingdom, do not expect the Romans to sit back and offer encouragement. I hope you understand the serious business your brother has begun. Even though I remain skeptical of your messianic claims—after all, your brother was crucified and has not returned as the Nazarenes promised—I will support you when I can, but I can only do so much."

After visiting with Ya'akov's important friend for more than an hour, Ya'akov and Paulos departed for one more stop, the hound again lagging behind. The blood red sun hung in the dusty haze, hesitating on the horizon as the men exited the city and ascended a rocky hill, barren of vegetation. When they reached the hillcrest, Ya'akov gestured with a sweep of his hand as he spoke.

"This is where they crucified him. This is Golgotha, the place of the skull."

Ya'akov sat mute on a large rock, and Paulos sat on another. The desolate hilltop was dead still until a swirling gust of wind choked them with dust before quickly dying down. The sun disappeared, tracing purple edges on silver clouds that piled on the far horizon.

Paulos had begun the day with high expectations for his time with the brother of Yeshua. After a rough beginning, the visit with Gamaliel had salved his bruised confidence. Now, the sun had set, and Paulos waited in silence for Ya'akov to share personal stories of his brother. When Ya'akov stirred from his rocky seat as if he was about to depart, Paulos blurted the question that he needed to ask.

"Tell me about your brother. What does it mean to you to be the brother of the Mashiah?"

The weathered face of the carpenter seemed to soften.

"I miss him a great deal. I wish he had listened to me and avoided Jerusalem. I wonder sometimes if I did enough to persuade him to stay away."

In the twilight, Paulos did not see the tears in the corners of Ya'akov's eyes.

"Yeshua believed strongly that he was following God's will. I take comfort in that. I know that Yeshua is alive, and I'm anxious for his return."

"Why did Yeshua die?" Paulos again broke the silence with a hard question, the same question he had asked Cephas, the same question that nagged his own wonderings. *Chaos* was the answer given by Cephas, but that hadn't satisfied Paulos. Paulos leaned toward Ya'akov to hear the answer of the brother of the Mashiah.

The lines in Ya'akov's face grew hard again. Finally, he spoke. "Evil. Evil forces caused Yeshua's death. The Romans. The Sadducees. The High Priest." The answer spilled from Ya'akov's mouth.

His voice rose as he continued. "But God overcame the evil. God raised Yeshua from death to life. Yeshua will establish his kingdom on earth, freeing Israel from its oppressors. God will reign through his anointed."

Ya'akov rose from the rock as his words raced. "Our plight in Palestine cries out for relief. The Romans and their lackey high priest won't be here forever. Soon and very soon, Yeshua will return and Israel will be restored and the kingdom of God will arrive."

Paulos' head tilted slightly to one side with his chin resting on his chest. With wrinkled forehead, Paulos pulled hard on his nose as he mulled Ya'akov's answer. Cephas had said *chaos;* Ya'akov said *evil.* Paulos was unconvinced; there was more to it than that.

Ya'akov continued. "Although we look forward to the overthrow of the Romans, we're not an insurrectionist group like the Zealots. Until Yeshua returns to lead God's kingdom, he calls the Nazarenes to prepare the way by building up a following for the kingdom. We must work for justice and offer mercy. There is much work to do, much work to do." Ya'akov's voice trailed off as he sat down again with sagging shoulders and a bowed head.

"You ask what it means to be the brother of the Mashiah." Ya'akov whispered. "It's a heavy burden. I pray unceasingly that I may be worthy of my brother."

The first stars appeared as Paulos wandered to the edge of the hilltop. To the north were Damascus, Antioch, and Tarsos of Cilicia. To the west, the Great Sea and Rome. He mumbled something with his back to Ya'akov, but another dust devil swirled about him, catching his words and throwing them back on him.

He wiped dust from his eyes then turned to Ya'akov and asked his question again, "What about the Gentiles? On the road to Damascus, Yeshua called me to go to the Gentiles."

Paulos stood on one edge of the hilltop, looking at Ya'akov on the opposite side. They were far apart, and Paulos did not see Ya'akov's hot glare. Paulos stepped toward Ya'akov, waiting to hear his answer. Ya'akov started to speak but hesitated. Paulos walked closer. Ya'akov mumbled, but Paulos did not hear what he said and moved closer still. Ya'akov's breathing quickened, hot breaths steaming in the cool evening air, and then he erupted.

"Gentiles?" Ya'akov said, in a mocking, derisive tone. "You're a foreign-born, foreign-taught, and foreign-thinking, so called Jew!"

Ya'akov stepped toward Paulos, his massive bulk blocking the last purple hues of the sunset. Paulos shrank back.

"Do you not see the oppression of your own people under the hobnailed heels of the damned Gentiles from Rome? You worry about the oppressors and forget the victims! Stinking Romans! Damn the stinking Romans!"

A goatsucker soared on the evening breeze above the Judean countryside. To the west, a smear of purples on the far horizon was all that remained of the day; to the east, a pale aura of lamplight over Jerusalem struggled to hold back the night. The sharp eyes of the creature searched the darkness as it circled on the currents and updrafts. Suddenly, the raptor tucked its wings and dove toward the intruders on the hill below. When it neared the ground, it spread its wings in a booming surge of air before flying away.

Paulos ducked and raised his hands as the nighthawk swooped past his face. Did even the beasts of the air oppose him? When his fist flew open, he loosed a silver coin that sparkled in the moonlight as it slowly tumbled toward the dust. He retreated a step, but his gaze quickly returned to his adversary; he would retrieve his *belonging* coin later.

Ya'akov paid no heed to the bird and continued his verbal assault. "Who do you think you are, coming here with your Greek tongue, claiming to be a Pharisee, claiming to be a follower of my brother? You weren't there!"

Paulos strained to find the right words for a response. Even in the cool air, sweat beads worried down his dusty face, disappearing into a snarled beard.

"You never heard him speak," Ya'akov growled. "You never mingled with the crowds, and you didn't witness the stinking Romans murder him on the cross—

Ya'akov's voice cracked, and his hand braced against a boulder.

Against Ya'akov's lifetime with his brother, Paulos offered a mere moment on the road to Damascus. At Damascus, Paulos had glimpsed the form of a human in a flash of lightning, but Ya'akov had seen the blood seeping from nails in his brother's hands. At Damascus, Paulos had heard whispers on the wind, but Ya'akov had heard the death rattle of his brother, suffocated under his own weight.

Paulos' confidence had begun to unravel on Cephas' rooftop when he realized that he and Cephas saw Yeshua differently. Now, Ya'akov's tirade had ripped his certainty completely apart. What had happened to Paulos at Damascus? What did it mean? Damascus seemed so far away and long ago.

Ya'akov's voice rose, shrill for a man his size. "You're like an uninvited stranger at a burial," he said, "boasting that you knew the dead man well. How dare you share my grief? How dare you!"

Paulos forced himself to speak. "Yeshua called to me," he said, "from the clouds." The words seemed both too thick and too thin for the truth of Damascus.

"That was but a dream," said Ya'akov, "who can trust a vision? I tell you, he was *my* brother, and *you* didn't know him!"

Paulos' thumb and forefinger rubbed together as if the *belonging* coin was there. Damascus now seemed a dim memory and the truth of it elusive. There was nothing more to say. When he pulled his robe tight against the chill air, he realized the main seam up the back had ripped apart from hem to hood.

"You don't belong here," said Ya'akov. He opened his mouth as if to say more, but spun on his heels and stalked off, leaving Paulos alone in the dark on Golgotha. A decade would pass before the men would meet again. The dog followed Ya'akov. When the mutt heard another hound howl in the distance, he barked back.

Unwelcome in the land of his forbearers, Paulos would leave Jerusalem and Judea and return to the city of his youth and his parent's home. Along the way, he would revisit the creek side trail on the Damascus road where the heavens had opened to him three years earlier. Ya'akov's stinging rebuke had jarred him, and he would seek reassurance at the scene of his conversion.

Was there not truth in Damascus beyond what eyes could see and ears could hear? On that glorious day, God had transformed him, setting his life on a new course, and the truth of Damascus was in his heart and soul. Was it not so? Paulos would study the holy books in the synagogue to unriddle the truth of his heavenly encounter and to find the words to tell the tale... to convince himself if not Ya'akov.

Paulos dropped to his knees to search for his *belonging* coin, the one that he had carried since his youth, the one that tied him to his Hebrew ancestry, the one that reminded him that he belonged to God's chosen family—the Lord's own portion. It didn't take long before he spied the gleaming shekel in the light of the rising moon. He rubbed the dust off and held it to the moon to catch its glint. He kissed the coin and returned it to his pouch. Even if he didn't belong in Jerusalem, he belonged ...

After descending to the bottom of the hill, Paulos tugged on his long nose to remember the path that had brought him to this time and place. He passed through a grove of palm trees and moon stripes of light and dark.

Chapter Twenty-four

Leaden clouds smothered the city and hid the morning sun. The marble walls of the Temple appeared gray and dull. The din that rose from the streets had a tinny, metallic ring.

"I must take my leave," Paulos said without looking at Cephas.

The men lingered on Cephas' rooftop after breakfasting on Raziah's fresh bread.

"I've decided to return to Tarsos."

"Why?" Cephas blurted as his head jerked toward Paulos.

"I think God calls me to go to the Gentiles," Paulos said, unconsciously speaking the words in Greek and not Aramaic.

"What?" Cephas asked. "What happened yesterday?"

Paulos said nothing.

Cephas leaned back and spoke knowingly in a half-whisper, "Ya'akov can be an ass, sometimes, a stubborn ass."

"Don't blame Ya'akov," said Paulos even as Ya'akov's harsh words echoed in his ears. "Coming to Jerusalem has confirmed my calling to the Gentiles," he said as much to himself as to Cephas. "I'll leave on the morrow."

"But I've more to share about Yeshua," Cephas said, "and his teachings."

"I appreciate what you have taught me, but God spoke all that I need on the road to Damascus," Paulos said.

Cephas narrowed his eyes. After a moment, his familiar grin returned. "You will miss the PAR-ty," he teased.

"A party for me?" Paulos asked, looking at Cephas for the first time.

Cephas laughed. "If you say so."

Paulos was anxious to leave. He needed the reassurance that

he hoped to find on the Damascus road, and he wanted to search the holy books to prove the truth of Damascus, for himself if not for Ya'akov. The synagogue library of Tarsos beckoned, but he extended his stay in order to placate Cephas. It would be rude to abandon the hospitality of Cephas and Raziah so abruptly. Besides, when Cephas told him the party was a Nazarene adaptation of a traditional Hebrew festival, he was curious.

The Feast of Weeks, *Shavuot,* celebrated the early summer grain harvest. Paulos knew the Hebrew festival by its Greek name, *Pentekoste.* Cephas explained that the Nazarenes had their own reason to celebrate. When the Galileans returned to Jerusalem after a resurrected Yeshua appeared to them, the Hebrew Feast of Weeks was underway. The high spirits of the festival coincided with the enthusiasm of the Galileans, and in the four years since then, the Galileans celebrated the anniversary of their own beginnings along with the Feast of Weeks parties.

"We also observe the traditional Temple sacrifices that accompany the feast day," Cephas said. "Ya'akov insists that we offer two loaves of wheat bread at the Temple before we begin our PAR-ty. 'Remember the gift of Torah', he reminds us every year."

Three days later, Paulos, Cephas and Raziah watched from the rooftop as a parade of farmers danced through the streets of Jerusalem to the Temple, where the country folk presented their offering of the "first fruits" of their grain harvest. Ox carts hauled the grain, accompanied by boisterous singing, horn blowing, and toasts of freshly brewed barley malt. If the first fruits went to the Temple, the next portion of the barley harvest became fermented malt. The oxen, with gilded horns and floral garlands hanging from their shoulders and haunches, appeared bored by it all.

When Cephas and the Nazarenes went to the Temple to offer their wheat loaves, Paulos stayed with Raziah. He had borrowed needle and thread and mended the seam on his robe. The familiarity of the sewing tools gladdened his nimble fingers.

Later, when the Nazarenes gathered for continued revelry in the streets, celebrating the heady days following their return to Jerusalem, Paulos observed from the calm sanctuary of Cephas' rooftop; he did not want to bump into Ya'akov after their encounter on Golgotha.

When it was time for the pilgrim to return to his own land, Cephas offered encouragement. "When you pass through Antioch, you should look for Barnabas," Cephas said, "he'll be a good man to know—even if Ya'akov doesn't like Barnabas' Hellenism."

Two weeks and a day after his arrival, Paulos departed the holy city. He had arrived seeking purpose and a place, but the brother of the Mashiah had rejected him, and he had failed to gain standing among the Nazarenes of Jerusalem. What is more, Ya'akov doubted his Damascus road experience. Yet, Paulos had gained a friend in Cephas, whose hospitality included a weighty measure of respect, and Gamaliel, the greatest sage in the land, was of a like mind as the Pharisee from Tarsos.

His first stop on his homeward journey was the hallowed ground near Damascus where the heavens had opened to him three years earlier. He wasn't sure what he sought there, a reoccurrence, perhaps, but certainly reassurance of his belief that he had met God there.

Late in the day, Paulos stepped into the empty glade that now seemed small. A breeze sighed in the palm trees, and they bowed like penitents. Long shadows splayed over river pools. He licked his dry lips and breathed the scents of creek water and spring flowers. He wandered and wondered and waited.

There was no flash of lightning and no crash of thunder, yet he sensed that God was there, ambling in the cool of the evening. That night, Paulos felt rejuvenated as he slept under the stars of Damascus, his mended robe pulled snug against his bearded chin.

The next morning, he sent word to Ananias that he waited outside the city on the banks of the Barada. He dared not enter Damascus, but he wanted to say a proper goodbye following his hasty escape from the Nabateans several weeks earlier. His friends from the Damascus *ekklesia* brought food and drink. Charis was there with her two-year-old son, Markos, a handful who splashed in the river shallows. The smile on Charis' freckled face cheered him, and her moist, green eyes brought him nearer to that night on the road three years earlier. Paulos and the Damascenes had a joyful reunion but a tearful parting; it was uncertain when, or if, they would again be together.

Ananias asked Paulos to deliver a message to his old friend, Barnabas, in Antioch. "Tell that black-headed Kypriot that our Damascus *ekklesia* boasts nigh unto a hundred members. See if he can match that!"

After more than a dozen sunrises and sunsets, Paulos settled into the rhythm of the Antioch-bound caravan. If the spice traders had continued beyond Antioch toward Tarsos, he would have naturally followed along, but then he would not have met Barnabas.

After arriving in Antioch late in the day, Paulos knocked on the door of an elegant villa of Antioch. "A visitor from Jerusalem to see you, sir. He says he is a friend of Iesou the Christos," the servant announced to Barnabas.

Clad in a crimson robe of silk, Barnabas greeted the road-weary traveler: dusty, smelly, crumpled, and quite the contrast to the finely scraped and buffed Kypriot and leader of the Antioch *ekklesia*. Barnabas ordered a tray of fishes and figs for his guest. Paulos briefly summarized his journey that had brought him to this place and offered greetings from Cephas in Jerusalem and Ananias in Damascus.

"A hundred? Only a hundred?" Barnabas closed his eyes as if scouring a list of his own flock that he kept inside his eyelids. "Yes, I'm sure we have more than a hundred," he said as his eyes popped open. "Mostly Gentiles, I might add."

Paulos awoke well before Barnabas the next morning, and accepted a servant's offer to draw a warm bath. The servant snatched Paulos' smelly robes and whisked them away for cleaning. When he finished his bath, Paulos had no choice but to dress in the elegant silk robes that had replaced his own.

Paulos then observed Barnabas' curious morning ritual. The servant would request a song, and Barnabas would sing it. His baritone voice filled the marble room where he enjoyed his daily shave, dispensed by a servant. Barnabas followed the Roman practice of sporting a clean-shaved face. The servant smeared Barnabas' face in myrrh-scented olive oil, and then he scraped the oil away with a sharp utensil, removing his master's black stubble along with the lubricant. Barnabas completed the session by admiring himself in front of a silver mirror while he ritually combed his oiled, shoulder-length, charcoal-black hair.

Over breakfast of sliced peaches and yogurt, Paulos recounted his visit to Jerusalem, daring to mention the anti-Hellenist, anti-Gentile attitude of Ya'akov.

"I've never understood," Barnabas said, "why Ya'akov and the Nazarenes didn't support my good friend Stephen." He rubbed the back of his hand over his smooth cheeks.

"Have you come to join me in Antioch? You would fit in well with our *ekklesia*."

You don't belong here. The words of Ya'akov and his scowling face flashed through Paulos' thoughts but faded quickly, replaced by the glowing countenance of his clean-faced host who reclined on thick pillows in front of him. *You would fit in well,* Barnabas said. Paulos believed that he would.

Paulos spent a second night at the home of Barnabas. Cephas had been right; Barnabas was a good man even if Paulos didn't accept his invitation to remain in Antioch. Paulos would return to Tarsos as planned, but he would remember Barnabas of Antioch. When Paulos departed for the four-day journey to his Tarsos home, he was sure that he had found a fellow traveler on the road to a Gentile mission.

Paulos awoke before dawn on the last day of his journey home. The crisp air smelled of wood smoke from caravan campfires.

In the dimness of the starlight, the low ridge of the Taurus Mountains on the western horizon was a vague shadow. To the east, from where the caravan had traveled the day before, pale slivers of early sunlight filtered through the Amonos Mountain passes with peaks haloed by the yet invisible sun. Paulos rummaged through his pack and found dates and raisins; he ate his few morsels slowly as he watched the sun climb over the mountains.

The caravan was stirring. A camel tender led his foul-smelling beasts back from a nearby stream where they had drunk their fill. Paulos waded to his knees in the cool creek, bending over and cupping his hands to splash water onto his face, rinsing away sleepiness.

The bubbling stream sang to him, stirring happy memories of Tarsos. He imagined his river refuge in the rocky rapids of the River Kydnos. He saw Arsenios splashing in the sun-drenched water, but then, like a dark cloud passing over the sun, the image of the kiss shadowed his memories. God had transformed him on the road to Damascus. God had healed him. Why did he still yearn for the smile of Arsenios—even his touch? Was he ready to meet him?

Paulos cursed aloud and shook his head. A bit of the old guilt gnawed at him. He turned his eyes toward the heavens, and he prayed. "Heal me, O God. Remove this thorn from my flesh."

Just then, a loud shout called him back. The caravan snaked forward, and he hustled to catch up. As the caravan plodded westward, he watched the Taurus Mountains slowly, ever so slowly, fill the western sky. The caravan passed through flaxen fields of the Cilician plain; the familiar sights, sounds, and smells swelled his anticipation with each step. Before he saw the city, smoke plumes from many hearths flattened into a low cloud, marking his journey's end.

As the caravan neared the city, Paulos' eager long strides carried him ahead of the rest, and the sandals of a solitary man slapped across the concrete bridge above the rushing Kydnos—a double arched span built by the skilled artisans of the Roman army. His heart pounded as he raced through the agora: a rainbow of tents, robes, and skin colors; a hum of chattering shoppers and hawking vendors; and an aromatic blend of fresh bread, foul-smelling fish, and spicy pudding pots. This was the place he first met Arsenios. He breathlessly arrived at the familiar stoop of the tent maker's shop—his eyes, nose, and ears telling him that he was home.

He burst into the shop; Kleitos his father sat at his workbench with his back to the door. Malachi, the town gossip, stopped in mid sentence, his flailing arms suspended as he stared at Paulos; for once, he was speechless.

Abihu, Paulos' former helper, spoke first. "Paulos? Is that really you?"

The long anticipated scene played out like a dream. Paulos' saw his father's lips speak his name, but he didn't hear the voice. He saw himself fall into his father's arms for a long embrace. When Kleitos' gnarled fingers grasped Paulos' shoulders tightly and held him at arm's length, it was all real again, and he heard his father's voice.

"Your mother. We must go to your mother."

They hurried out the shop and through the agora—the father's arm hanging over the son's shoulder, the father's voice proudly proclaiming the son's return.

"Paulos is home. My son is here!"

Paulos had long imagined this day, and now it was all real and joyous. Familiar faces smiled in doorways. He was home again, in the place that he belonged. Ahead was the house, his childhood home; Olympia stepped onto the front stoop as if she sensed his arrival. Paulos tasted fresh loaves dipped in honey, and remembered her bread-warm hands on his cheeks as he picked her up and swirled her around.

"Look at you!" she exclaimed as they stepped inside. "What're you eating, you're too thin. Father, run to the butcher and buy mutton; we must feed this boy."

Homecomings, especially after a lengthy absence and especially the first time, are sweet. It was as before, but it was different; he was still the son, but he was also a man. His father *asked* him if he would like to return to work in the shop, he did not *tell* him. He sensed that his parents accepted him back without questions or reservations. Although he would tell them of Damascus, he would not explain the reasons he had left home three years earlier, and they never asked.

Paulos had disrespected his father on the day that he swore at him years earlier, and he owed an apology. As father and son sat together on the veranda while Olympia prepared the meal, Paulos spoke.

"Father, that day. That day that I failed to honor you—

Kleitos cut him off with a dismissive wave of his hand and a simple statement that warmed Paulos' heart and ended the matter. "You are my son and that pleases me."

When Paulos raised questions about his Tarsos friends, he received two bits of unexpected news.

The first was that Eli the sage was dead. Somehow, Paulos had expected that old Eli would always be at the synagogue ready to debate the finer points of the holy books. Paulos regretted that he had never expressed his appreciation for the sage's tutelage much less his fondness for the old man.

The second bit was even more surprising; Arsenios the Greek had departed the city to accept a teaching position in Rome. There were words that Paulos needed to speak to the Greek, and now he might never get that chance.

Paulos slept again on his parent's rooftop. He surveyed his world the morning after his return home. Everything was comfortably in its place and the colors seemed brighter, the sounds of the city seemed sharper, and the agora smells seemed more savory, but the sight of the empty university buildings pinched his heart.

PART FOUR
TARSOS REVISITED
37-39 C.E.

For the life of the flesh is in the blood; and I have given it to you
for making atonement for your lives on the altar;
for, as life, it is the blood that makes atonement.

Leviticus 17:11

Chapter Twenty-five

Eli the sage, mentor to Paulos and Pharisee leader of the Tarsos synagogue, had died during Paulos' absence. Soon after his return to Tarsos, Paulos poked his head into the room at the synagogue that had been the elder's quarters; he knew it would be empty, but he had to look anyway. A mat lay bundled in the corner with a willow cane lying on top. The room smelled of burnt oil, incense, and old man.

Paulos walked down the hall and opened the creaky door to the synagogue library. He ran his fingers over the cabinet edges, touching the shelf for Torah scrolls, then the shelf for the Prophets, and then the shelf for the Writings. He picked up a scroll and blew the dust off. Was no one reading these holy books?

He replaced the scroll, gently closed the creaking library door, and traipsed through the central chamber, once the dining room of the rich man who had bequeathed his villa to be a synagogue. The Jews of Tarsos preserved their Jewishness by gathering together for prayer, instruction, and worship in their synagogue. The Psalmist lamented, "How could we sing the Lord's song in a foreign land?" The synagogue was the answer. The room was quiet, and his sandals *clap, clapped* on the hard stone floor as he exited the building.

He stepped out to the portico where five young men sat on the steps arguing Torah; he overheard snatches of their conversation. He missed the mental exercise of Torah debate, the delight of a new insight, and the serenity of contemplation. He would always be a student.

Paulos recognized boys who had become young men. They sounded more serious than he remembered them. Others were strangers to him. Paulos smiled at the debaters as he skipped down the steps.

"Must we first become Jews before we are acceptable to God?"

Paulos whirled about, half-expecting to see Arsenios speaking these words. He bounded up the steps and asked, "Who said that? Who asked that question?"

The frightened boys were silent, but their glances at the speaker gave him away. The yellow haired boy was slight of build and frail with eager eyes, like those of a young pup, dominating his soft face.

He haltingly raised his hand as Paulos looked at him, "I asked the question, sir."

"Do you have a name, boy?"

"It is Titos, sir."

"You are to be commended. That is a hard question, but I have an answer."

Paulos gestured for the boys, three Jews and two Gentiles, to follow him into the synagogue. They squatted together on the stone floor, and Paulos introduced himself.

"We know who you are. Where have you been?"

With the opening offered by the question, Paulos eagerly told his story of Damascus to listeners with open ears, not stiff-necked skeptics like Ya'akov. Paulos stopped himself part way into the story and lit incense that billowed in the shaft of sunlight that pierced the room. Later, he retrieved Eli's willow cane and tapped a cadence to his story on the stone floor. The telling of his story reinforced the certainty of it, even if the truth was not in the details.

"What did the face of God look like?" a student asked.

Paulos struggled with a response.

"What was the sound of his voice?"

Again, the answer was beyond explanation. He could not describe the indescribable. No, the truth was not in sight and sound but in cause and effect, before and after. His eyes had not seen nor did his ears hear what God revealed in his heart. "What happened on the road to Damascus?" Whether the questioner was Ya'akov, or Cephas, or the starry-eyed boys of the Tarsos synagogue, or even

Paulos himself, the truth of Damascus was not a burst of light or whispers in the wind but the transformation of his soul.

In the room where Eli the sage had fathomed the depths of Ezekiel's visions, promising his protégé that he would one day experience his own divine encounter while teasing him about the difficulty of describing the indescribable—*what picture will you paint?*—Paulos began to sketch the broad strokes of his masterpiece.

"In a flash of lightning and a clap of thunder," Paulos said, "God revealed himself to me in the form of a human, Iesou the Christos, crucified but raised from the dead, the first fruits of God's new creation and the promise of God's new covenant."

"According to Torah, I was an unclean sinner." Paulos didn't identify his sins—that part of the story would never be told.

"My sin burdened me with guilt, more than I could bear." Paulos hesitated and cleared his throat.

"In a remote mountain vale, I encountered a Gentile woman, unclean according to Torah." Green eyes in a freckled face beamed at him. "The spirit of God touched her heart and she forgave my rage against her." At Damascus, not only had God been in the thunder and lightning but also in Charis, the one who forgave him.

"On the road to Damascus, God healed me. God transformed me. Not because I was worthy, according to Torah, but in spite of my unworthiness, *apart from Torah. Apart from Torah* ..."

His voice trailed off as the memory of the Damascus road faded, and he again saw the wide-eyed students seated in front of him, hanging on his every word. Paulos stood and stretched as he exhaled a deep breath; he turned and looked squarely at Titos. "You are blessed by God, and you are part of God's beloved family."

Paulos fumbled with the goatskin purse that hung from the sash around his waist. He reached in and removed the single shekel that was there, his *belonging* coin that Eli had given him many years earlier. He held it to the shaft of light for examination. On one side was a palm tree with a cluster of dates, emblematic of Palestine, the home of the Jews and of Iesou. On the other side was an "χ", the Greek letter *chi,* the first letter of the word, "Christos." χριστου. The silver coin caught the sun and sparkled as he handed it to Titos.

"Keep this piece of silver as a reminder that you belong to God. You are part of the Lord's own portion. You are acceptable to God just as you are, without circumcision... *apart from Torah.* You belong not because of who you are or what you have done but because God is who God is."

The five young men, including two Gentiles, became students of Paulos the sage, Paulos the Pharisee, Paulos the heir to the legacy of Eli, Paulos the one who had encountered God on the road to Damascus—last of all, as one untimely born, Paulos the one called by a resurrected Christos even if he never knew Iesou of Nazareth during his earthly life. When Paulos departed the synagogue that day, he stabbed the dusty lanes of Tarsos with Eli's willow cane. Eli would approve of the new sage.

Chapter Twenty-six

It had been the kind of summer that the farmers of Cilicia expected every year, but which seldom happened: the days were not too hot or too cool, the rains came as the budding heads of grain began to thirst, and the ewes all dropped a *pair* of healthy lambs. Now, the season had turned and the aspens in the foothills yellowed, the granaries swelled with the fruits of the fields, and the ewes no longer gave suck to the lambs that had learned to graze on green grass. The cool nights of autumn had come to Tarsos after a bountiful harvest.

The new synagogue sage enjoyed teaching the Jewish boys and the Gentile boys from the holy scrolls in the synagogue library. From the original five boys Paulos had met on the synagogue steps, the group had grown to twelve—six Jews and six Gentiles—in their late teens. The respect he sensed from the mixed group bolstered his self-assurance. He especially appreciated the inquisitiveness of Titos, the tiny boy with the loyal eyes.

"Why did Iesou die?" Titos the Gentile student asked the question, eyes sparkling with curiosity. His question floated on the billowing incense. It would seem that the students were like the lambs, ripe for solid food.

Why did Iesou die? Paulos had asked the same question of Cephas who had merely shrugged his shoulders. It happened, Cephas said, when crowds became unruly, when order broke down, when events spiraled out of control. *Chaos.* It was chaotic circumstances run amok that had caused the death of Iesou, in the mind of Cephas.

Why did Iesou die? Paulos had also put the question to Ya'akov. Ya'akov angrily blamed the evil Roman Empire, the evil High Priest, and the evil Sadducees. *Evil.* The forces of evil had conspired to cause the death, according to Ya'akov.

Both Ya'akov and Cephas had hastened to add that God righted the wrong by restoring Iesou to life. God ultimately triumphed over chaos and evil. In the end, God proved to be in control—but if God was in control, why did Iesou die in the first place? The question had vexed Paulos, and now Titos, his student, had raised the same question.

"What do you think? Why did Iesou die?" Paulos asked the class. The question spurred a robust discussion among the students. Paulos shared the answers of Cephas and Ya'akov, chaos and evil.

The debate ended when the least inquisitive student, bored of the discussion, said matter-of-factly, "I'm sure God had a reason."

God had a reason. God had a reason. The thought fermented in Paulos' mind; unable to sleep, he paced on the rooftop under the stars, pondering God's inscrutable ways. God had a reason. God had a purpose. The death had meaning. The death was the meaning. The meaning of the death was ...

With the first glimmers in the east, announcing the arrival of the day, Paulos hustled to the river and swam in the chilly autumnal water. He returned home invigorated and ate bread loaves dipped in honey, washed down with warm goat's milk.

He headed to the synagogue, leading a goat that he borrowed from his mother's courtyard herd. He passed Levi the butcher, he of the blood stained apron, on a dusty street of the agora. Levi looked at him, then the goat, then back to Paulos.

"The goat and I are going to the synagogue," Paulos said.

Levi shrugged his shoulders and shook his head.

The bleating goat, tied to the portico of the synagogue, drew snickers from passersby. The arriving students looked at the goat with curiosity.

"What Jewish festival began this week?" Paulos directed his question to the Jewish students. Several quickly blurted out the answer, "*Yom HaKippurim* ... the Day of Atonements."

"Let me tell you about all that happens at the Jerusalem Temple on the Day of Atonement," Paulos said.

****

As Paulos described the Day of Atonements to his Tarsos students, Ya'akov was attending the Temple proceedings, along with his younger brothers and cousin Symeon.

Much as Ya'akov despised the High Priest, he respected the ritual. He made sure his family carefully followed the traditions of the elders, and *Yom HaKippurim* was the holiest day of the year.

"Hand me the incense, be quick!" Theophilus ben Ananus gave orders to the Temple assistants. Theophilus, like his father and brothers before him, was the High Priest, the *Kohen Gadol*, of the Jerusalem Temple. Every one of them a bastard. Why, even his name was Greek and not Hebrew.

Theophilus wore pure white linen garments including his tunic, sash, and turban. Earlier in the day, he had worn golden robes with gold braid. In one hand, Theophilus carried incense and in the other, a shovel filled with glowing coals. His hands trembled, and sweat streaked his chalky face. He was about to enter into the presence of God, and he had a rope tied around his waist in case he should pass out so his assistants could drag him from the room. Only the High Priest could enter into the presence of God in the Holy of Holies, and only once a year, on this most Holy Day of Atonements. Once inside, he would place the hot coals in the mercy seat, sprinkle the coals with the incense, and wait until smoke filled the room. Torah prescribed the ritual:

He shall take a censer full of coals of fire from the altar before the Lord, and two handfuls of crushed sweet incense, and he shall bring it inside the curtain and put the incense on the fire before the Lord, that the cloud of the incense may cover the mercy seat that is upon the covenant, or he will die.

Theophilus remained in the Holy of Holies a long time, and the crowd began to murmur, "Has he fainted? Has he died? Should they pull him out with the rope?", but Theophilus finally appeared. Some said the face of the High Priest glowed upon exiting the presence of God, but he looked pale from fright to Ya'akov.

"Hand me the bowl," Theophilus said. "Yes, yes, the bowl filled with bull's blood."

Jude reached out and tapped Ya'akov's knee, and all the brothers exchanged smiling, knowing glances. The incompetence of the bumbling assistants proved the unworthiness of the whole lot of priests and Sadducees. Theophilus returned to the presence of God a second time to sprinkle blood with his finger as Torah commanded:

> He shall take some of the blood of the bull, and sprinkle it with his finger on the front of the mercy seat, and before the mercy seat he shall sprinkle the blood with his finger seven times.

Theophilus exited the Holy of Holies with an audible sigh. He would return a third time later in the day to remove the shovel and burnt ashes.

The rituals of this Day of Atonement had started hours earlier and would continue for hours yet. It was hot standing in the sun, and Ya'akov wiped his brow with his damp sleeve. His stomach growled since the brothers had fasted since sundown the day before. Earlier, priests had slit the throat of a bull; Theophilus sprinkled the blood of the bull in the Holy of Holies. The priests had also slain a goat, and the High Priest sprinkled goat blood around the exterior of the Holy of Holies.

After the sprinkling of the goat's blood, Theophilus went to a second goat, still alive. He laid his hands on the goat as he spoke confession of sins on behalf of the people. Along with the rest of the crowd, Ya'akov and his brothers remained in the Temple while priests led the scapegoat outside the city where they killed it by pushing it over a cliff, carrying the sins of the people along with it. Cleared of their sin, the people were reconciled to God. Atonement.

When word came back that the priests had pushed the goat over the cliff, Theophilus changed his garments, removing the pure white linen in exchange for his golden robes. More Torah readings and sacrifices concluded the ceremonies late in the day, and Ya'akov and the others returned home just before sunset. The aromas of roasted goat and coriander greeted them as they entered the house. A pleasing odor to the Lord.

****

Paulos concluded the discussion with the students. "The goat tied outside our synagogue is a reminder of the sacrifices and the scapegoat of the Temple ritual. Iesou is like the scapegoat, and his death was sacrificial. Iesou died to atone for our sins. In Iesou's death, we have been reconciled to God once and for all time."

Paulos had returned to the Tarsos synagogue to search the holy books for the truth of Damascus. He believed he found it in the ancient stories of sacrifice and atonement. Like a good Pharisee, Paulos retold an old story with a fresh meaning for a new time. He recast symbols of Israelite religion to interpret the meaning of the Christos. Cephas was wrong: Iesou's death was not *chaos*. Ya'akov was wrong: Iesou's death was not *evil*. God had a purpose. The death had meaning. Iesou's death on the cross was sacrificial, and his blood atoned for humankind's sinfulness.

One by one, the students nodded—they got his meaning! Paulos handed several copper coins to Titos and sent him to the agora to buy honey cakes while other students carefully returned the holy books to the synagogue library. This called for a celebration! Laughter filled the meeting room of the synagogue. Paulos strutted amongst the high-spirited boys, joking with this one then that one, enjoying a second helping of gooey cake, laughing as he licked the sweetness from his sticky fingers.

Months before, Ya'akov had questioned Paulos' Damascus road experience, prompting Paulos to wonder as well. With his synagogue study and teaching success, Paulos' self-confidence swelled. The voice in the thunder continued to speak to him, and he grew more certain that the opening of the heavens had revealed a glimpse of a human image grander than merely a new earthly king. Iesou was more than kicking the Romans out of Palestine, and Jewish messianic expectations were just a starting point for understanding him. Paulos concluded that Ya'akov was too close to Iesou, too personally involved, to see the cosmic significance of what God had wrought. It was true enough that Paulos had not walked with Iesou, but God had revealed all on the road to Damascus. To have known the earthly Iesou was no advantage—Ya'akov's deficient understanding was proof of that—Paulos was sure.

What Ya'akov failed to understand, Paulos reasoned, was that the new covenant in Christos had replaced the old covenant of Moses— opening the kingdom to all peoples: apart from circumcision, apart from the boundaries of Israel, *apart from Torah*. The Lord's Own Portion included Jews and Gentiles, circumcised and uncircumcised, saint and sinner.

Ya'akov's criticism had put Paulos on the defensive, but time and study made Paulos even more certain that God had called him to deliver a message of good news to the Gentiles. With the call came the challenge of articulating the good news, of interpreting the good news, of communicating the good news.

For Paulos, the key was not the life of Iesou but the death on the cross. Iesou's death was the atoning sacrifice that restored a broken humanity to a right relationship with God. Christos crucified became his central theme. On the day he spent with Ya'akov in Jerusalem, Paulos had seen the frustration of injustice, anger, and finally grief. These human feelings of Ya'akov were all misplaced—the death of Iesou was in truth the triumph of God!

The interpretation of it was the triumph of Paulos.

Chapter Twenty-seven

The seasons passed quickly, and Paulos entered the second year of his return to Tarsos and the second year of the reign of Emperor Caligula, 39 C.E. The newborn spring arrived without any grand announcement. The lower slopes of the mountains greened as the blanket of snow receded to the peaks and crags. The flatlands blackened as if thousands of crows alit at once, but it was only the plowmen preparing the soil for seed. When the seedlings bashfully greeted the sun, they blushed a shade of pale green, and leaden skies blued as the mists of winter dried up. After a season of rest, the caravans and the ships returned, bringing strangers and old friends to Tarsos. The sea of multi-colored tents on the edge of town swelled each day, and the dockworkers returned to the waterfront.

On a day well into the season, hot and humid and a harbinger of summer, Paulos mindlessly stitched two swatches of linen together while engaging in small talk with Abihu his helper.

"Do you remember Arsenios the Greek?" Abihu asked.

Paulos stuck a needle into his palm, but he tried to appear calm.

"Why?" Paulos' response came out as a squeak, and he cleared his throat. He kept his eyes low even though he didn't see the linen, thread, or needle in his hands.

"Arsenios has returned to Tarsos," Abihu said. "I saw him climb off a barge onto the docks in the harbor."

Abihu's words whirled around Paulos' head, and then the whole room spun and teetered. He dipped a rag in a water vase. "I poked myself," Paulos said, to make an excuse. He stepped outside and leaned weakly against the wood-framed wall with the wet cloth pressed against his forehead.

Paulos did not rest easy that sultry night, caught in a foggy, fretful, hybrid that was neither sleep nor wake. Cloud shadows assailed him, and then Arsenios returned from Rome to visit his dream:

The fair-haired Greek stood beneath a small waterfall with the waters of the River Kydnos cascading over his naked body. A rainbow glowed in the misty spray. Paulos squatted on his favorite rocky perch, methodically throwing rocks at Arsenios who didn't seem to notice; a large rock struck Arsenios on the head, and he slumped out of sight beneath the water.

Suddenly awake, Paulos sat straight up on his mat; he shook his head to clear the nightmare. He walked to the edge of the rooftop to reset his bearings: to the west, snow capped peaks glistened in the moonlight, to the north, fog hung over cool water, tracing the course of the River Kydnos.

He returned to his mat but worried through the night about Arsenios' response to his message. He had invited Arsenios to a meeting at their river refuge in three days.

****

Rebellion stalked the streets of Jerusalem. As Ya'akov walked from his home to meet his friend Gamaliel and other leaders of Jerusalem, he watched Jews openly jeering Roman soldiers and pelting them with rotten tomatoes. The outnumbered troops retreated to the Fortress Antonia, which seemed a victory to the rabble of Jews and encouraged them further, but Ya'akov knew better. Roman reinforcements were on their way from Antioch. A massive army of two legions, thousands of armed infantrymen, marched on Jerusalem, led by the Governor of Syria.

Emperor Caligula was such a disappointment to Ya'akov; when Tiberius had died a couple of years earlier, Ya'akov hoped Caligula, his successor, would soften the harsh oppression of the Judeans. Now this. Caligula had ordered that a statue of himself be placed in the Temple—not just the Temple but in the Holy of Holies. The prospect of such a desecration sparked anti-Roman demonstrations and open talk of rebellion. Ya'akov knew that Jews would die. as martyrs before accepting this unholy command of the Emperor, but he also knew that the mighty Roman legions would slaughter any Jewish rebels.

In response to the crisis, Gamaliel organized a group of emissaries to intercept the Roman Legions. The delegation would attempt to persuade the Syrian Governor against placing the statue in the Holy of Holies.

What would Ya'akov do as leader of the Nazarenes? How would he lead his flock? Would they join their Jewish brethren in taking up arms against the Romans if it came to that? This was not the time, or was it? Would Yeshua return if a rebellion unfolded? These questions nagged at Ya'akov as he met with Gamaliel.

"Ya'akov. Ya'akov, are you listening?" Gamaliel said.

"Yes. What did you say?"

"Will you join our entourage to meet with the Governor?"

The group consisted of Sanhedrin leaders, both Pharisees and Sadducees, in an unusual alliance of competing local factions. Even the bastard High Priest had reportedly summoned the courage to stand up to his masters.

"Do you really think it wise that I join your contingent?" Ya'akov asked. "The Romans believe the Nazarenes are rebellious troublemakers as it is," he said, "and I might damage the credibility of your group."

So, the Jewish leaders, mounted on horseback for speed, departed for Galilee to intercept the Roman legions led by the Syrian Governor. Ya'akov remained behind and prayed for success for their mission, fearing for the fate of the Nazarenes and all of Jerusalem if the mission should fail.

"Yeshua, where are you?" He pleaded, "Is the time at hand?"

Chapter Twenty-eight

Tiny raindrops, not much more than a mist, tickled Paulos' face, awakening him from a dreamless sleep. He had not slept until the wee hours of the morning when he finally lapsed into a deep slumber. Today was the day for the meeting with Arsenios at the river. Would he come? Was he angry? What would Paulos say to him? The mist roused Paulos from his deep sleep, and he descended the ladder to the dry veranda.

A poppy colored sun lifted over the lush plain to the east, an emerald ocean of flowering grain stalks—flax, barley, wheat, and spelt—flowing like sea swells in the early morning breeze. To the west, the weather and landscape were starkly different. Black, gray, and silver clouds rolled and swirled and tumbled, growling an angry low rumble of far off thunder, spitting sheets of rain on a dreary landscape of rocks and dark shapes of cowering trees.

Paulos' rump ached from sitting on the boulder overlooking the pool, watching memories splash by as bubbles on the stream. Five years had passed since he last saw Arsenios when he had thrown stones at him right here in this spot. Paulos had arrived over an hour earlier, but Arsenios was late. Paulos paced, he waded in the stream, he plunked pebbles, he built a fire, and he fretted on the rock. He was about to leave when Arsenios finally appeared.

"Hello, stranger," Arsenios said. "Welcome home."

As usual, Paulos could not fathom the deep eyes of the Greek.

Arsenios spoke first. "That's a nice thick beard. You look like a sage. But, I see that you're still puny and weak," he said with a nervous laugh. His own face had a hint of dark stubble. The curls on his head were less oiled and fixed and more tangled and natural.

Arsenios sat on one side of the rock, and Paulos sat on the other side. Arsenios appeared a bit sturdier, but the extra heft was all muscle. Arsenios told Paulos that he was a university teacher, in Tarsos for a visit, but he would soon return to Rome, his new home. Paulos said he had been in Damascus except for a short time in Petra and Jerusalem. Paulos wanted to tell him about his experience on the Damascus road, but he waited for the right moment that didn't seem to come in their forced conversation. Paulos measured Arsenios' every word, every sigh, every grin and grimace. What was in his heart?

Paulos walked from the rock to the brush to find sticks to add to the dying fire. "Look what I found," he said as he held up the old pot that they used to boil fish. He also picked up the rotting linen net that fell apart as he lifted it.

"Gather clams," Paulos said as he handed the rusty old pot to Arsenios, watching for a reaction.

With a bemused look, Arsenios accepted the familiar artifact, searched in the sand shoal, and plunked clams into the pot as Paulos built up the fire. Arsenios retold a familiar anecdote from rhetoric class; Paulos laughed, and shared another. The stories eased the awkwardness between them. By the time Arsenios filled the pot with clams, the easy affability of their youth had returned.

Arsenios handed the clam-filled pot to Paulos for boiling, and his fingers brushed Paulos' hand. A gentle breeze from the verdant plain of the east carried the lush scent of ripening heads of grain and stirred the quaking bushes.

As they ate the boiled clams, Paulos had the opening to tell Arsenios of his Damascus road experience, concluding with the story of shouting to Arsenios while sitting in the Barada River. "You don't need to be circumcised, I hollered to you," Paulos said with a laugh, hoping for the same from Arsenios.

He wanted Arsenios to feel the same joy that he had known at Damascus, and to share the same excitement at the good news that

Gentiles could belong to God's own family, *apart from Torah*. But Arsenios kept his eyes fixed on the fire without any sign of either joy or excitement at the good news.

"I forgive you for your former zealotry," Arsenios said, "and for your rage when you struck me with a stone." He withdrew from the fire and waded in the edge of the river, facing west toward the roiling dark clouds, occasionally brightened with flashes of distant lightning, too far away for thunder.

"I forgive, but I cannot forget, and I'm not interested in a God that separates us."

Arsenios' words dampened Paulos' hopes for this long-anticipated moment. Paulos had expected that he and Arsenios would be best friends again like before ... best friends to laugh together, to debate together, and to wade across the rivers of life together. Best friends, like before... before the kiss. Rain fell on colorless clumps of trees in the foothills of unseen mountains, obscured by rain, mist, and clouds.

The university teacher skipped flat stones across the water and spoke with his back to Paulos. "It is you that brings me to Tarsos," he said as he turned to face Paulos. "Return with me to Rome."

Paulos' heart leaped.

Arsenios returned to the fireside and tossed dry sticks onto the coals. The kindling quickly flared. The flicker of flame that reflected in Arsenios' eyes appeared as a leaping gazelle. The fragrance of blossoming figs floated in the air; in the bushes, a turtledove cooed, *Arise, my love, my fair one, and come away*. Paulos slowly unfilled his chest, exhaling through pursed lips. He knew then that his hopes had been naïve; they could never be just friends.

The images in Arsenios' deep eyes darkened. Torah scrolls rolled off their shelf, incense roiled in shafts of sunbeams, fire exploded on a mountaintop. Paulos swallowed hard and coughed and set his face toward the angry clouds of the west.

Smoke swirled in the breeze, stinging his eyes. Paulos walked away from the fire, unable to see. "Give me a day or two to think."

Paulos bounced from one wall to another on the rooftop. Yes or no? His heart said go, but his head said stay.

Was Torah now meaningless for him after Damascus? He no longer observed Sabbath or the festivals, he ate what he wished, and he counseled Gentiles that circumcision was not necessary. What of the rest of Torah? Was he free to disregard the rest of Torah also? What of the future King David and young Jonathan in the stories of old? Did God not smile on them?

What of his mission to spread the good news to the Gentiles? That was the least of his worries. There could be no better city than Rome, the largest city in the Empire, the hub for travelers from around the Great Sea, a center of culture and commerce, and a place of learning and erudition. A blooming *ekklesia* in Rome could pollinate the entire Empire.

Two days later, Paulos' squeezed the reed pen in his hand, chewed on the tip, dipped it in water, and then drew it slowly across the dry ink. His shaking hand splotched a blot of black ink onto his papyrus sheet, but he continued and carved out the one, short word. He blew it dry then rolled the sheet and handed it to a courier for delivery to Arsenios.

"What's this?" asked Arsenios.

"Paulos the tentmaker sends you a message."

Arsenios unrolled the papyrus and mouthed the single word: *YES.*

Chapter Twenty-nine

The morning of their departure dawned bright, clear, and chilly. Paulos arose early and scurried through the quiet agora carrying his possessions, including his tools, in two goatskin bags. He arrived at the harbor's edge and hustled onto the docks, his sandals clunking on the bulky wooden planks. Harbor odors of fish, seaweed, and refuse mingled with all the other pleasant and unpleasant smells of the Tarsos riverfront. He chased a sleeping sea gull, leaned against a post jutting up from the bed of the dock, and waited for Arsenios.

"Hail, fair Cleopatra," teased Arsenios as he joined Paulos. The fragrance of his oiled curls preceded him. "Marc Antony requests permission to board your Royal barge." This stretch of the River Kydnos had witnessed the spectacle of Cleopatra cruising upriver for a rendezvous with Marc Antony several generations earlier.

Arsenios wore a *himation* banded with gold weave, folds held tight at the waist with long fingers on a strong hand. Early morning sunbeams radiated off his blond locks with the illusion of a halo. Tanned, smooth skin on a clean-shaven face framed an incessant grin.

Arsenios' servant trundled a cart, heaped with four trunks and several leather bags. Paulos, Arsenios, and the servant lugged the trunks onto a barge under the stern gaze of the barge captain who gestured with his hands and grunted to indicate where the cargo should be stowed.

A grimy goatskin cloak hung loosely over the short and slight captain who repeatedly coughed and spit overboard. A round, flat hat with a prominent bill tilted forward over his river-rat eyes. More than one scar marked his weather beaten face.

The harbor fleet of Tarsos consisted of two species of craft: tugboats and barges. Both types employed oarsmen to provide locomotion up and down the ten-mile stretch of river between the city and the sea. Small sails added power when the wind was right. Teams of oxen marched a riverside pathway pulling larger craft upriver.

Paulos had been a riverboat passenger many times, and it was always an exhilarating experience, but never more so than this day. His first sea voyage would be another matter, and apprehension tinged his enthusiasm. An image of a caterpillar floating on the currents of the Kydnos flashed across his mind.

The crew of eight foul-mouthed oarsmen loaded a cargo of victuals for delivery to the company of three Roman warships, beached on the seashore ten miles downriver. Sleek and narrow warships did not have the capacity for carrying significant supplies nor for bedding their crew of over one hundred sailors, mostly oarsmen plus a few archers; each night they encamped ashore, purchasing their daily provisions from local vendors. Several times a week, a Tarsos barge delivered provisions for the Roman navy, and the two Rome-bound passengers booked passage aboard such a barge that would transport them to the sea and a rendezvous with a westbound merchant galley.

Paulos and Arsenios secured seats in the aft of the stubby vessel, next to the captain who manned the large stern oar that dragged behind the boat and served as the rudder. The oarsmen set a leisurely pace, with the assistance of the downriver current and a pleasant breeze in the barge's small sail, while the captain entertained Arsenios and Paulos with tales of the famous pirates of Coracesium, a Cilician port city just down the coast.

"Twas Julius Caesar," the captain began his story, "near a hunert year ago, a young nobleman captured by the pirates and held fer ransom." The captain's words hissed out his clenched jaw through the gaps in his broken teeth. "'Twenty talents of gold fer yer neck', said the pirate. 'Not nearly enough,' boasted the brash Caesar. 'I'm worth much more than twenty talents. Ask fifty, and you'll receive fifty.'"

Arsenios winked at Paulos as they listened to the tale. His yellow hair glistened in the sun; a loose curl dangled down his forehead. Paulos' anxiety was growing as the barge bobbed on the current that carried him ever closer to the unknown sea.

"The pirate drew his short sword," the captain said, voice swelling for dramatic effect, "and held it tight against his hostage's neck. 'Mock me not young fool or I'll slit yer throat as easy as pissin' on an anthill.'" The barge captain's mouth split open into a broad grin.

"Twas the smell o' gold held back the pirate's sword. Fifty talents was asked, and fifty talents was paid—just as Caesar boasted."

Arsenios gracefully moved from port to starboard placing his hand on Paulos' knee as he squatted next to him.

"Tis nothin' sweeter'n revenge," the captain said, nodding for emphasis. "Caesar returned with warships and hung his kidnappers on crosses in the noonday sun, watchin' from the shade whilst eating peeled grapes." The barge captain coughed and cleared his lungs and spit into the eddying waters behind the boat. The story was over.

Against the slowly passing background of grain fields, Arsenios leaned against the gunwale, tilting his head back over the rail with eyes closed as he soaked up the sun. A smile tugged the corners of his mouth upward. He was handsome, spirited, and self-assured. Happy—he is happy, Paulos thought.

Am I happy? Paulos asked himself. *Yes. Yes, but ...* the wind suddenly switched and blew cold from the mountains, scrambling the crew to pull down the small sail that had leisurely pulled the barge toward the sea. Paulos shivered.

"You look ill," Arsenios said. "Your face looks the color of the dung of the sea gulls." Arsenios' words melded concern and teasing.

Paulos wiped his sweaty, chalky face with the sleeve of his robe and forced himself to smile.

"The gangly one's not fer the high seas," the captain announced to the oarsmen with a gloating snicker. He scowled at Paulos and said,

"Just ya wait till the ship bucks under yer feet, tossed like a bug on a leaf in the howlin' gales whistled from the mouth of Poseidon, waves bigger'n a house 'n going sideways, slammin' agin ya, nails apopping like fuzz off a dandyline."

Paulos wished it was merely seasickness, but he knew better. Perhaps something in the pirate story triggered his unease. Capture. Ransom. Punishment. With each passing mile down the river, a war within him raged stronger. A torrent of doubt flooded his thoughts.

God claimed him, *apart from Torah*. Did this mean he could disregard all the commandments? He ate unclean foods. But could he steal? He didn't keep Sabbath. But could he kill another? To lay with a man as a woman: was that akin to eating unclean foods and disregarding the Sabbath, or was it more like stealing or killing? His gut answered, and he stumbled to the rail of the barge and vomited over the side, serenaded by the hoots of the crew.

"I can't go with you," Paulos said to Arsenios, and then he turned to the barge captain, "take me back to Tarsos." Paulos deserted the Greek without further explanation.

Twice, Paulos had rejected Arsenios. What did Arsenios think? Paulos hoped he thought sea travel and seasickness scared him, a silly fool frightened by the captain's tales. Perhaps he realized that Paulos again had allowed his religion to come between them. Paulos cringed at the thought that Arsenios believed he did not care for him, that Paulos rejected him based on the feelings in his heart and not in spite of those feelings.

Another image would torment Paulos' dreams—the ashen face of Arsenios, with tears on his cheeks as the barge pulled away from the ship. Would they ever speak again? Would Paulos ever find the right words? If God forbade his feelings for the Greek, why did he create his unclean heart?

PART FIVE
ANTIOCH
39-49 C.E.

Hear, O Israel: The Lord is our God, the Lord alone.

Deuteronomy 6:4

Chapter Thirty

Paulos stopped stitching and listened closely to Malachi, the wine merchant and gossipmonger of Tarsos. The usual crowd filled the tentmaker's shop: a few herdsmen, a few merchants, and a few who never seemed to have much to do except hang around and gossip. Today, the Hebrew men were not in a joking mood as Malachi the Raven narrated a frightening tale from Alexandria, the grand metropolis of Egypt across the Great Sea, the second city of the Empire behind only Rome itself.

"A young child screamed," Malachi reported, "'the house is afire! Mama! Mama!'"

Paulos' leather-cutting knife slipped from his lap and clunked on the floor. Malachi stopped speaking and waited for Paulos to pick it up and set it on his workbench.

Then, he continued, "The young mother nursed her scorched son as best she could, but they had been forced from their charred house and lived on the streets of the rapidly filling Jewish ghetto."

The men in the shop shifted from one foot to the other or leaned heavily against workbenches. When Malachi paused before finishing his story, the shop was silent except for the heavy breathing of the Hebrew listeners.

"The boy's screams ended when he died in his mother's arms, one of many Jews murdered by the Egyptians."

On this day, Malachi the Raven did not hop about, arms flailing, voice cackling; instead, his hands hung limply at his side as he finished the sober tale in a muted voice. He explained that Egyptian mobs murdered Jews with stones, clubs, and with fire. The Roman Governor of Alexandria stood by and watched the bloodshed. Perhaps he even encouraged it. He certainly did not attempt to stop the pogrom until it had run its course. Mobs torched homes and synagogues and herded the Jews into a ghetto.

Jews had always been respected citizens of Tarsos and many other cities of the empire, but it appeared as though times were changing. Organized persecution in Alexandria—under the approving eyes of the Governor—who could imagine such a thing?

Malachi then reported that the Jews of Jerusalem also dealt with a Roman outrage. The Roman Emperor, Caligula, had ordered the placement of a statue of himself in the Holy of Holies of the Jerusalem Temple. Jewish leaders had persuaded the Governor of Syria to stall the march of the Roman legions, at least for now, but thousands of legionaries remained in Galilee with lances pointed at Jerusalem. A Roman assault on the holy city of Jerusalem was unthinkable, and Paulos muttered a brief prayer that someone in Rome would intercede with the Emperor to stop these outrages.

The last words from Malachi's mouth were mere whispers. There were no jokes that day. The men in the leather smith's shop departed one by one into the late afternoon shadows. Kleitos and his son were the last to leave, nearly bumping into a pair of patrolling helmets. The vain peacocks now seemed an ominous presence; for the first time in his life, the power of the Roman Empire created apprehension in the young Jew, and even though he and his family were Roman citizens, he worried. Pray God that someone in Rome would intervene with the Emperor.

"Damn it! We'll be blamed for sure." Barnabas feared for his *ekklesia* in Antioch. The empire-wide hostility that flared between Romans and Jews afflicted Antioch also. A mob of Jews had stoned three Roman soldiers; two were badly injured, and one had died. Wild rumors and accusations clouded the reality.

"The Christians did it! The Christians did it!" The enemies of the Antioch *ekklesia* mockingly identified the followers of Iesou the Christos as "Christians."

The *ekklesia* in Antioch was under siege, caught between the Romans and the Jews. Members of the *ekklesia* felt threatened and some had left the *ekklesia*. Evangelization was difficult. Barnabas felt overextended, putting out one fire after another. He needed help—an assistant, maybe even a co-leader. He remembered the bright and eager Jew from Tarsos.

It was then that Barnabas traveled the short journey to Cilicia to ask Paulos to help lead the Antioch *ekklesia*.

Olympia sobbed. Paulos was leaving her home a second time, the final time, and her motherly instincts knew that. Her wailing said she feared she would never see him again.

"Mother, dear Mother," Paulos said. I'm only going to Antioch a few days journey away. I'll return to visit often." He brushed away her gray hair and caressed her cheek.

Paulos had lived in Tarsos for nearly two years when Barnabas arrived from Antioch with an urgent request. "Please return with me," he had pleaded. "The *ekklesia* needs leadership and encouragement, and you can provide both."

Of course, Paulos would go to Antioch. His return to his parent's home in Tarsos had been a pleasant interlude, but Antioch on the Orontes! Paulos was confident that the small cell that developed from his Tarsos synagogue teaching, the first *ekklesia* he could call his own, would prosper under the tutelage of tiny Titos, the brilliant one. Surely, God was calling Paulos to the grand city of Antioch where he would be a leader of men and not merely a teacher of boys.

Twice he had peered over the precipice with Arsenios before shrinking back, and twice he would leave Tarsos soon after rejecting him. Earlier, he sought to escape the wagging finger of God and the leering face of Jubilees, his accuser. Burdened by crushing guilt, he had been afflicted with a crippling melancholia. What was different this time?

Paulos knew he was guilty as before, but he no longer felt condemned. On the road to Damascus, God had pardoned him. His sinful attraction to Arsenios remained as his "thorn in the flesh" that he neither understood, nor chose, and could not remove; but which no longer defined him before God. God had broken through his corruption and claimed him, transformed him, justified him not because of his purity but despite his impurity. And God's action was final, complete, determinative, and eternal. Nothing could separate him from the love of God. The angst of the day on the riverboat was short-lived, and he departed Tarsos, not to escape the wrath of God but to embrace God's mercy. Paulos had good news to share in Antioch!

Kleitos placed his aged, stiff fingers on Paulos' shoulders. "God be with you, my son." His lips quivered, and his eyes glistened. He hugged his son long and hard.

Then Paulos was gone with Barnabas.

"Get out of the way, fool!"

Paulos jumped as the horse drawn chariot clattered by on the hard marble street of Antioch. He stood in the middle of the thoroughfare, marveling at the *stoa*, a covered sidewalk lined with a colonnade in the front and storefronts in the back. Artists, musicians, and dancers entertained the passersby. Into this modern and cosmopolitan metropolis, the third largest city of the Empire behind only Alexandria and Rome itself, Paulos arrived to serve as a leader of the local *ekklesia;* he would remain happily ensconced in Antioch for more than a decade.

"Eeeeyowww!"

The short, round man with a matching round head shrieked. Droplets of sweat beaded on his forehead and dribbled down his face through several days of uneven reddish stubble. He wrinkled his face, shut his eyes, and winced at the pain of running a large sewing needle into the fleshy tip of his thumb. The needle protruded from his thumb with small drops of red blood trickling from the wound around the edges of the needle. He opened his eyes, looked at the bloody needle, and woozily slumped to the floor.

"Eeeeyowww! Take it out! Somebody take out the needle!"

Paulos had just stepped under the awning of the small shop. No one else was there. He stepped forward and easily pulled the needle from the round man's thumb; a droplet of blood congealed at the pinprick, and the bleeding stopped. The short, round man lay on the floor with his eyes closed, panting heavily, his tunic soaked in sweat.

"Am I hurt bad? Have I lost much blood? Ooooh the pain!"

Paulos smiled and shook his head. The pinprick was of no consequence, and the man was grossly overreacting.

"Please man, help me to my quarters. I must lie down. Ointment. I must have ointment."

He pointed toward a shelf where Paulos found a healing balm, a mixture of aloe and myrrh, and he rubbed a dab on the man's pinprick. Paulos grasped the man's hands and pulled him to his feet; he was heavy and didn't try to assist himself, content to let Paulos lift him. Paulos draped the man's arm over his shoulder and half-dragged, half-carried him to a mat in the rear of the shop. The little round man lay on the mat, sucking deep breaths for a few minutes before he opened one eye slit and squinted at Paulos.

"Who are you man? I don't know what might have happened to me if you hadn't been here to help. You saved my life."

Paulos shrugged. "I'm Paulos a tentmaker; I seek employment."

"Well, who knows when I will be on my feet and able to work again. Of course, of course. You're a godsend. Praise Mercury, the god of the marketplace!"

That was how Paulos secured employment and lodging with Julius, a Roman leather smith and widower of more than a few years. Just as Julius had overestimated his injury, he also overestimated his need for convalescence, and he sat back and watched Paulos handle the workload that he had also overestimated.

There was barely enough work for one smith, much less two. When Julius finally returned to work, each of them performed less than half the workload of an able leather smith. Paulos slept on his mat in the widower's kitchen and received a few denarii for a week's work. Part time employment freed him for *ekklesia* work, and Julius preferred a lighter workload, too. The arrangement suited each man well.

Chapter Thirty-one

Barnabas was an imposing preacher: slick, black hair draped over broad shoulders, a sharp-featured face, and bushy dark eyebrows over animated eyes. He modulated his rich baritone voice as the mood demanded.

At the end of the Sabbath worship service, his tone changed to a soft lullaby of farewell. Forty or fifty persons sat on the stone floor of the synagogue; Paulos squatted in the rear with eyes shut in quiet contemplation, mouthing the words sung by Barnabas and tasting their sweetness.

> Master, now you are dismissing your servant in peace, according to your word; for my eyes have seen your salvation, which you have prepared in the presence of all peoples, a light for revelation to the Gentiles and for glory to your people Israel.

The Sabbath service at the synagogue was a delicious blend of old and new: Hebrew traditions flavored with Iesou stories and songs. When the *ekklesia* service ended, Paulos stood up and stretched his too long legs, gently swaying back and forth to get the blood moving.

"Come, come here and meet my friends." Barnabas beckoned to him. "This is Lucius and his wife Agathe. They are Gentiles from Cyrene."

Cyrene was prominently located where Africa jutted into the Great Sea pointing toward Rome. Lucius and Agathe were dark-skinned North Africans, nut-brown not black. Agathe's round belly revealed a soon-to-be new member of the *ekklesia*. Paulos had seldom seen dark-skinned persons, and he greeted the North Africans with eager curiosity. It was good to be in Antioch and part of an *ekklesia* that rightly proclaimed the good news of the Christos to all, despite the rigid self-righteousness of Ya'akov and the Nazarenes of Jerusalem.

After Paulos met many of the *ekklesia* regulars, Barnabas and Paulos departed the synagogue together in the early evening; the sun had set, and a full moon peeked over the eastern horizon in a cloudless sky. Even though Barnabas was as tall as Paulos, he walked with muscle-bound short steps, and Paulos shortened his strides to slow his pace for Barnabas.

"That was a fine sermon you delivered." Paulos said. His compliment was sincere. Barnabas was an able and effective speaker with a commanding voice and presence. "And your voice. You sing like an angel." The compliment was again sincere.

"But I'm not sure I agree with that point about 'King of the Jews.'"

Barnabas shrugged, and Paulos was encouraged that he didn't seem to be one to argue. Paulos dared to press his point further.

"'King of the Jews' doesn't mean much to your Gentile listeners. Wouldn't 'Lord' or 'Son of God' be a more suitable description of Iesou—and better understood by the Gentiles?" Paulos watched closely for a reaction to his criticism. He didn't mean to overstep, but it was important that Barnabas speak effectively to the Gentiles. "Come, let me show you," Paulos said.

Barnabas and Paulos turned around and returned to the synagogue that boasted a full library of sacred scrolls. Paulos read from the ancient coronation liturgy in the Psalms scroll, recited when a new king ascended to the throne:

"You are my son; today I have begotten you. "

The king was God's earthly agent, the son of God; the Christos was the new king; the Christos was son of God; Iesou was Christos; Iesou was son of God.

"Don't you see? Iesou is the Son of God sacrificed once and for all time for the atonement of God's beloved people."

Barnabas looked at Paulos with one eye half-closed. He pursed his lips but said nothing. Paulos read another passage from the Psalms scroll:

"The Lord says to my lord, sit at my right hand until I make your enemies your footstool. "

Sitting at the right hand was the place of honor. Sitting at the right hand of God was an honor signaling importance beyond that of any mere king. It was an honor for one and one only. "Don't you see? Iesou is sitting in the eternal heavens waiting with God for the right time to return in glory. Iesou is Lord."

Again, Barnabas listened skeptically without responding.

"Iesou is so much more than the Mashiah, a mere political king of the Jews. Iesou is the Christos, the Son of God, and the Lord." Paulos looked at Barnabas with pleading eyes, willing the tall preacher to understand his teaching. He continued:

"If the atoning sacrifice of the crucifixion is the once and for all time triumph of God, the dawning of the new age of the new covenant for God's new creation, then the sacrificial lamb must be more than a mere human martyr—kings and prophets have been martyred before."

Paulos expected Barnabas to see what was so clear, but Barnabas scowled without speaking.

"Don't you see, the lamb must be like no other, and the names 'Son of God' and 'Lord' as they are written in scripture, better describe the once and for all time importance of the Christos. The Son of God. The Lord. Don't you see?"

"Show me those verses again," Barnabas said.

Paulos pointed to the verses in the scroll of the Psalms. Barnabas' lips moved silently as he read the verses to himself. He read each one several times pausing with deep sighs between readings. Barnabas was a charismatic leader, an effective speaker, and an inspirational singer, but he was not an innovative thinker.

Barnabas and Paulos were complementary opposites. Barnabas was muscular, well groomed, and proud of his good looks, but self-effacing regarding his intellect. While Paulos cared little about his raw-boned, scruffy, and homely appearance, he flaunted his imaginative mind.

"I'll think about it," Barnabas finally said.

They departed the synagogue for the second time that evening. The full moon brightened the streets of Antioch. Paulos was satisfied that Barnabas would eventually see things his way.

"Slow down man, do we need to walk so fast?" Barnabas reached out and grabbed the sleeve of Paulos' robe.

Barnabas pouted. He seldom disagreed with Paulos' visionary teachings, but this time Paulos was going too far, he thought. "I received it from the Lord," Paulos claimed as he argued with Barnabas.

Paulos' first two years in Antioch had passed quickly. The thirty-three year old Jew quickly became strategist for the Antioch *ekklesia* that numbered many Jews but even more Gentiles. Barnabas presided over worship at synagogue Sabbath services, but Paulos was his intellectual superior, and Barnabas usually acceded to the innovations of the younger man ... until now.

Barnabas protested. "When I was in Jerusalem shortly after Iesou's death, no one related a tale such as yours." Barnabas was frustrated that Paulos planned to ritualize a recollection of the Lord's last supper—except that Paulos wasn't there.

"But I received it from the Lord," Paulos said again. "It's of no consequence to me what the Nazarenes said to you. I received it from the Lord. The only thing I learned in Jerusalem was that those who walked with Iesou have no advantage; I trust my face-to-face with God to inform my understanding."

Barnabas clenched his jaw with his lower lip pouting out. "If you must, you must. Just don't expect me to lead the service."

He knew that Paulos was a capable worship leader who would ably lead this innovative service. Barnabas' refusal to lead the

service didn't mean much, and the imaginative theoretician of
the Antioch *ekklesia* would go ahead with or without him. Even
when he disagreed with him, Barnabas marveled at the artist who
painted colorful pictures of the Christos, based on his own visionary
experience.

The day after the Sabbath, the Antioch *ekklesia* gathered late in
the afternoon for the special service planned by Paulos but opposed
by Barnabas. Each person brought fruit or fish or bread or wine for
a banquet. After the festive meal, the men moved a table to the front
of the room and placed a bottle of wine with a cup and a loaf of
bread on the table. Agathe lit candles around the room, and Lucius
burned incense that billowed in the dancing candlelight.

Paulos opened with a prayer: "Blessed are you O God for
sacrificing your son on the cross. May his act of atonement redeem,
restore, and transform all the nations."

The husband and wife team of Lucius and Agathe sang a traditional
Jewish Psalms-hymn associated with the sacrificial liturgy of the
Temple. Their curly-haired cherub, Loukas his name, clutched his
mother's robe as she sang.

> Then I will go to the altar of God, to God my exceeding joy;
> and I will praise you with the harp, O God, my God.

Paulos spun a tale of Iesou's final night with his friends in the
upper room. "Iesou took a loaf of bread, he gave thanks, he broke
it, and gave it to all saying, 'This is my body that is for you. Do this
in remembrance of me.'"

Paulos broke off a piece of bread from the loaf on the table and
gave it to the nearest person, and then another piece to the next
person and so on until everyone in the room had eaten a piece of
bread. Grumpy Barnabas sat in the back, but he chewed on a chunk
of bread when Paulos offered it to him.

"After supper, Iesou took the cup of wine and gave it to them, and they all drank from it. Iesou said, 'This cup is the covenant in my blood. Do this, as often as you drink it in remembrance of me. For as often as you eat this bread and drink the cup, you proclaim the Lord's death until he comes.'"

Paulos passed around the cup of wine that he refilled several times until all in the room had drunk from it. Barnabas swallowed a big gulp from the cup when it came to him. Sacrifice. Covenant. Paulos' keen knack for proclaiming the Christos in the language of Israelite religion was again on display, thought Barnabas. Barnabas felt aglow, strangely warmed by the bread and the wine.

Lucius and Agathe sang another Psalms-hymn from the Temple liturgy of sacrifice:

Blessed is the one who comes in the name of the Lord. We bless you from the house of the Lord. O give thanks to the Lord, for he is good. For his steadfast love endures forever.

After they finished, the room fell silent except for a few sniffles. The bread and the wine had filled Barnabas, and a calm elation welled within him. He didn't mind that a tear trickled down his cheek. He looked at his neighbor who also had weepy eyes. Instinctively, they reached for each other and embraced, and then they each hugged another and another.

In the dancing flames of the candles, the scent of the incense, the tang of the wine, the chewy lumpiness of the bread, the melodies of the praise songs, and the teary smiles of his fellows, Barnabas sensed that the Lord was near. Barnabas looked across the room at Paulos who smiled at him. Barnabas knew that Paulos was right; Paulos *had* received it from the Lord.

Chapter Thirty-two

Paulos shivered as a winter draft whistled through the cracks in the walls of the tentmaker's shop. Paulos set his sewing on his workbench, flexed his stiff fingers, and gently rubbed his hands together to keep warm blood pulsing against the biting cold. For a fortnight, rare freezing winds had chilled Antioch. Paulos chinked his clay cup through the thin glaze of ice atop the water vase near the door just as Julius burst into the shop with the news.

"Caligula is dead!" Julius screeched. "Assassinated by his guards!"

Paulos didn't expect such a violent answer to his prayers for intervention. For over a year, the Roman legions had threatened to march on Jerusalem to implement Caligula's order to erect an unholy statue in the Temple; only the good sense of the Syrian Governor held them back. The Governor had been sympathetic to the entreaties of Gamaliel's emissaries and temporarily halted his troops, disobeying Emperor Caligula at his own peril, but now prayers had been answered in far-off Rome. Caligula was dead.

Paulos stepped outside with Julius as they watched the hubbub in the streets. They shared the mood of the citizens of the city: relief that the eccentric and erratic emperor was dead but uncertain of Claudius, his replacement. Would the sickly Claudius have the power to control the fractious Romans? Even more importantly for Paulos and the Jews of the empire, would Claudius continue the oppressive Jewish policies of his crazed predecessor?

"Who knows what foul wind will blow from Rome," Julius said, as his shoulders hunkered down, and he pulled his woolen shawl close under his chin. Snow flurries danced on frosty currents like wintertime butterflies. Julius raised one hand over his eyes as he measured the featureless sky that seemed like a pale sheet of papyrus waiting for ink.

Several months later, the spring westerlies filled the maroon and white striped sail of a sleek warship from Rome, racing across the Great Sea. As if the dispatches on board demanded haste, dozens of oarsmen added their muscles to the strength of the wind. After the naval vessel arrived in the port of Seleucia, a troop of marines marched twenty miles inland to Antioch to deliver the Edict of Claudius, the new Emperor.

Paulos and others from the *ekklesia* watched as the Roman soldier pounded tacks to hang the Edict for public review. As soon as the soldier finished, Paulos stepped forward.

He read silently, *Tiberius Claudius Caesar Augustus Germanicus, pontifex maximus, holding the tribunician power, proclaims ...*

Then, he read aloud, "Therefore it is right that also the Jews, who are in all the world under us, shall maintain their ancestral customs without hindrance."

Barnabas whooped in delight. "No more hobnailed heels at our necks! 'Without hindrance,' it says!"

Men grabbed each other by the arm, and there was plenty of backslapping, but Paulos continued reading silently, *to them I now also command to use this my kindness rather reasonably and not to despise the religious rites of the other nations, but to observe their own laws.*

Paulos detected an ominous caveat; toleration of Israelite religion was at the cost of reciprocal tolerance for others. Proselytizing to Gentiles had become a crime, and Paulos knew he would become a criminal. He glanced toward the heavens and wondered at God's ironic humor.

The naval vessel had also carried mail from Rome. To Paulos' surprise, one of the rolled scrolls was for him. Paulos had received letters before, but never from Rome, and his fingers fumbled with the waxed seal. The look on Julius' face said that he was suspicious of any letter delivered by the Romans. When Paulos saw that the letter was from Arsenios, he dropped it onto the dusty floor of Julius' shop, and Julius' nod said he knew that his misgivings were justified. Under the critical gaze of Julius, Paulos rerolled the scroll quickly without reading and exited the shop without speaking.

Paulos wandered outside the city, in the hills alongside the fast-flowing Orontes. His ears didn't hear the rushing river, his face didn't feel the noontide sun, his nose didn't smell the spring blossoms, his tongue didn't taste the salt when he licked his lips, and his eyes saw only the scritches and scratches of ink on papyrus. His feet carried him forward according to their will, not his.

Dear friend, Paulos. I hope my letter finds you in good health and spirits ...

The first lines contained mere trivialities, and Paulos' gaze fell to the second smear of wax that sealed the inner contents of the letter. He desired to rip the seal and hasten to the heart of the message, but paralysis gripped him. He read and reread the salutations as if that which was inside would seep out diluted and harmless. With a flick of his finger, the seal would be broken, but he didn't have the will to pick the scab, and he nearly cast the unread scroll into the swirling currents.

But he did not, and the waxed seal unloosed itself. The scroll unrolled and the words spilled out.

The ink marks spoke of Arsenios' confusion at the sight of the Kydnos River barge pulling away from the ship as Paulos returned to Tarsos. Had he misjudged Paulos? *Did our hearts not beat as one?*

Paulos nodded unconsciously.

Arsenios spoke of his empty existence in Rome where his teaching filled his mind but not his heart. At that moment, Paulos felt hollow, too, and a tear dripped onto the scroll. Paulos didn't notice the previously smudged ink spot from a tear from the eye of the writer.

Then, the ink strokes grew thicker, bolder, and darker, speaking anger at the god who would condemn the truth of their hearts. *Why must your god build walls of separation? Am I a seed of barley and you of wheat? Am I a woolen thread and you of linen? Am I a fish and you a clam? Even if all this be true, and my foreskin is uncut and yours cut, do not our hearts beat as one?*

Silence swelled and seemed to echo from the cliff walls that encircled Paulos. He could not go forward, neither left nor right, and his path had ended in a box canyon. He could only turn back. He rerolled the scroll and shuffled back the way he had come.

Paulos started to pen a reply letter several times. Finally, late in the fall, he managed to send a short missive on one of the last ships to depart Seleucia before the sea closed for the season. He spoke of the weather, and his new friends, but not of affairs of the heart.

He knew that he was afflicted with a certain inclination, and it would not occur to him to question the ingrained assumption that it was unclean. To lie with a man as a woman was prohibited by God, and that would remain an unquestioned touchstone for Paulos' self-understanding, the beginning of his thought and not its end. Even the sniggering jokes heard in the tentmaker's shop reinforced the preconception that came before rational thought. No, this was an axiom that Paulos accepted without deliberation, a truism not subject to challenge.

Thus, his letter to Arsenios was as bland as the pale papyrus. Did their hearts beat as one? It was Paulos, not God, who judged the truth of it.

Chapter Thirty-three

Abdel, the Hebrew slave, innocently triggered the incident that nearly cost Ya'akov his life—and that of Cephas also. In the summer following the midwinter assassination of Caligula, Ya'akov barely escaped his own encounter with the murderous sword of a Roman henchman.

Abdel was a landless peasant who had sold himself to Azariah the Sadducee, the aristocratic cousin of the high priest, for a seven-year term and renewed several times. While living in Jerusalem as part of Azariah's household, Abdel had heard Cephas preach the message of the ministry of Yeshua: *Blessed are the poor; blessed are the meek; blessed are those who hunger and thirst; blessed are those who are persecuted—yours is the coming kingdom of God.* Like many poor folk encouraged by this message, Abdel the slave and his family joined the Nazarenes.

When Azariah the Sadducee aristocrat made a gift of slaves to a new king, Abdel left Jerusalem for the royal palace located in Caesarea on the seacoast. Herod Agrippa, the newly crowned King of Judea, was barely thirty-years old when he arrived from Rome after his appointment as king. It was the year of Caligula's assassination and Claudius' ascension to the Imperial throne, 41 C.E. Agrippa was the first since his grandfather, King Herod the Great, to bear the title, *King of Judea*. Rome, not Palestine, had been his home from the age of three years when his grandfather sent him for an upbringing among the elite of Rome. The Romans had appointed his grandfather to be King of the Jews generations earlier. The Herodians were not descendants of King David, and to the Jews of Palestine, the Herodians were more Roman than Hebrew. Even as Agrippa sailed to assume his throne in Palestine, his brother

Aristobulus remained in the palatial family villa in Rome.

The trouble started when King Agrippa overhead Abdel speaking in the immense flower garden of the palace. Agrippa wore royal purple robes and much gold—rings, necklaces, bracelets, and armbands—as he strolled about the columns of the castle on the shores of the Great Sea. He was bareheaded only because the sea breeze would blow away the laurel wreath that Emperor Claudius had bestowed upon him. His greased locks clung tightly to his head, impervious to the wind. Agrippa listened from the portico while Abdel and other slaves toiled in the herbarium, unaware of the king's presence nearby.

Abdel told the other slaves about Yeshua and the Nazarenes, and Agrippa heard snatches of the conversation: *King of the Jews, Yeshua, Galilee, coming soon.*

In the conspiratorial world of the Roman Empire, Agrippa ordered the arrest of Abdel and the other slaves. "It is your life if you do not identify your leader," the king said. "Who is the master of this conspiracy?" Agrippa handled the interrogation himself.

"Sire, there is no conspiracy," Abdel said. "We are your loyal subjects."

Brutus, the captain of the guards—short and strong with muscles bulging on his bare arms and head shaved bald—advised Agrippa of the Nazarene stories of Yeshua. Brutus also informed the king that Cephas and Ya'akov were the leaders of the Nazarenes. As Brutus finished speaking, the wife of the king entered the room, carrying their young child in her arms.

Agrippa ranted to his wife. "I am haunted by a ghost. The Romans crucified the man nearly a decade ago, yet there is a widespread belief among the Jews that he lives," he said. "How can I defend my throne against a ghost?" Agrippa stomped to the balustrade overlooking the Great Sea, his voice rising as if Rome would hear his wailing. "The ghost will return to claim his throne. What is worse, this ghost will have the support of the God of the Jews! What nonsense! But they believe it. They believe it." Agrippa's voice trailed off.

"Cut off the head of the snake," his wife said without looking up from her child, tickling his belly.

Agrippa said nothing as he stared blankly out to sea. Finally, he spun on his heels and issued orders to Brutus, "Hold these slaves as prisoners so they cannot warn the Nazarenes. On the morrow, take a troop of soldiers to Jerusalem and arrest and execute Ya'akov and Cephas. Cut off the head of the snake. Cut off the heads of the Nazarenes."

"Open the door or we'll break it down!" said Brutus, pounding on the door with the butt of his sword. Brutus was following orders, seeking Ya'akov, the leader of the Nazarenes.

Yochanan, the Galilean fisherman and disciple of Yeshua, opened the door.

"Identify yourself," Brutus demanded. "Are you Ya'akov of the Nazarenes?"

"No," said Yochanan.

Ya'akov, *the brother of Yochanan,* came from the back of the room and stood alongside his brother. The Romans had found the wrong man, the wrong Ya'akov.

"I am Ya'akov. Can I help you?"

"Grab him. Tie his hands behind his back." The soldiers did as Brutus directed.

Brutus used the butt of his sword to strike Ya'akov in the stomach, doubling him over in pain. Brutus kicked his legs from under him, and Ya'akov thudded to his knees.

"Hold him, hold him there!" ordered Brutus.

Yochanan lunged forward, but the soldiers held him back. Brutus took the bone grip of his short sword in both hands, raised it high above his head and swung violently in a chopping motion. The sword whistled its descent. It was a clean cut and painless. Ya'akov's head rolled in the dust. Yochanan collapsed in the arms of the soldiers who dropped him to the ground and kicked him as he shrieked and writhed on the street next to the headless body of his dead brother that spurted blood into the dust.

As he wiped his bloody sword on the dead man's robe, Brutus gave a further order. "Find and arrest that man Cephas. Throw 'im in jail. I'll deal with 'im in the morn."

The Romans executed the wrong man. They intended to execute Ya'akov the brother of Yeshua and leader of the Nazarenes, but they mistakenly executed Ya'akov the brother of Yochanan—*a* Nazarene leader but not *the* Nazarene leader. Yochanan and Ya'akov, Galilean fishermen, the sons of Zebedee, had followed Yeshua in his life. Ya'akov now followed Yeshua in his death.

Yochanan ran to his leader's home shaken and barely coherent. Ya'akov slumped heavily onto a chair, stunned at the news, as a stormy sea of emotions crashed over him, wave upon wave: his heart ached with Yochanan and grieved for Ya'akov; guilt stabbed him because an innocent man had died in his place; he feared a knock at the door, recognizing that he was still in danger; he worried the pangs of a helpless husband and father, wondering about the fate of his family. Seema, his treasured daughter had married and birthed a daughter of her own, Anina, Ya'akov's granddaughter. All this and more washed over him in an instant, but he also understood that a leader could not afford the paralysis of sentimentality; a leader, even one as inadequate as he was, must lead.

Ya'akov sent his brothers to spread the word among the Nazarenes and many soon gathered in his veranda. They received confirmation that the soldiers had arrested Cephas and dragged him to a jail cell.

"We must run. We must hide." The whispers reflected the panic in the room.

Ya'akov stood atop his table and raised his hands, gesturing for quiet. Despite the personal tempest raging inside, he spoke calmly and with assurance, "Yes, we must proceed with great caution, but we must not abandon our cause. If it is danger and even death we face, then so be it. Can we do any less than Yeshua has done?"

The frenetic swirl of events slowed to a near standstill in his mind; he could see clearly now. For the first time, Ya'akov understood his brother's sacrifice. If God required his life also, he was prepared to offer it.

"And what is to become of Cephas?" came a voice from the rear.

Ya'akov spoke with a serene confidence he had never known. "Go to your homes. Stay with your wives and children. Bolt your doors and pray. Pray that this persecution shall pass. Pray that we may be faithful servants and followers of Yeshua the Mashiah ... and pray for the safe release of Cephas."

Ya'akov prayed, but he also acted.

Late that night, Cephas' cell door squeaked open. A shadow hovered over his motionless body, curled up on the floor.

"Shhhhh. Get up," a voice whispered.

Cephas followed the specter out the cell door and out the prison. There were no guards. Cephas' wife, Raziah, and Ya'akov stepped into the moonlight. The shadowy rescuer was Gamaliel's servant; Ya'akov had spoken to Gamaliel; Gamaliel's influence had pulled the guards; and the servant disappeared into the night. Cephas and Raziah embraced before Ya'akov quickly sent them on their way to the safety of the Galilean countryside. Ya'akov returned home to his own family.

"Cephas has escaped! An angel came to rescue him!" The excited young Nazarene offered his report to Ya'akov the next morning.

Ya'akov smiled, and he saw Yeshua smile too.

The execution quenched the king's thirst for blood. Ya'akov was *an* important member of the Nazarenes even if not *the* leader. Gamaliel, the Pharisee leader of the Sanhedrin, persuaded the king that the Nazarenes were not insurrectionists. The persecution was over as quickly as it began.

The king released Abdel and the other slaves. "I am a fair and generous man," the king said. "I have decided to spare your lives, but I will not allow you to serve in my household. I will send you to Rome where you will serve in my family's villa, in the household of Aristobulus, my brother." The king was pleased at his own magnanimity.

"You and your Nazarene tales will be of no consequence in Rome."

Chapter Thirty-four

"Come with me to Kypros. Meet my family. We'll preach in my old synagogue," Barnabas said.

Paulos and Barnabas walked alone after the regular weekly gathering of the Antioch *ekklesia*. The two leaders hesitated on a rise in the granite-tiled street with colonnades on either side. The city dropped away toward the late afternoon sun; down the street, a throng of Roman spectators departed the racetrack called the circus. Paulos never understood the sport of the chariot competitions held there, but the Romans' blood ran hot at the spectacle, so much the better when the chariots crashed in a jumble of horseflesh and ripped metal.

Paulos tugged on his beak-nose that poked over his salt and pepper beard. "I will go to Kypros with you," he said, "but not for a mere family visit." He raised the willow walking stick that had once belonged to old Eli and gestured toward the haze on the western horizon. The Great Sea beckoned from beyond the purple smears of the setting sun.

"We'll become missionaries."

Paulos had declined Barnabas' previous invitations, but now he was ready to accept in light of the news from Jerusalem. After reigning as King of Judea for merely three years, Agrippa had succumbed to a mysterious illness, and the Nazarenes were chirping that God had punished Agrippa for his persecution. His death was a sign that the Mashiah's return was near, and the gossip from Jerusalem signaled a renewed energy amongst the Nazarenes, but Paulos scoffed at their political opportunism. The Christos would not replace Agrippa; the Christos would be no earthly king; and the Nazarenes were fools.

But, if Agrippa's death was a sign that the kingdom of God was near, then it was time to spread the good news beyond Antioch and Syria. If the Nazarenes' renewed enthusiasm would result in an increased following amongst the Jews of Palestine, then Paulos would seek an expansion of the Gentile *ekklesias* also. Paulos' blood was up, too, just like the Romans who spent the day at the chariot races.

"God calls me to bring the good news to the Gentiles," Paulos said. "God ordains this trip to Kypros; we must go. Lucius and Agathe will be capable leaders in our absence."

Paulos placed both hands on the knob of his cane and leaned forward. He didn't need the cane of old Eli, but it had become his appendage, his own swagger stick. As the last remnants of the Roman spectators filtered out of the circus, Paulos unconsciously set his gaze to his left, toward the south, toward Jerusalem.

Ya'akov's rebuke years earlier still stung. Of course, God spoke to him at Damascus; of course, God called him to the Gentiles; of course, God revealed the new age of the new covenant to him; of course, his scriptural study bolstered his views; of course, his sermons and his services proclaimed the Christos; of course, the successful Antioch *ekklesia* validated his experience; of course, a successful missionary journey to Kypros would further prove the truth of *his gospel*. Who could doubt?

"There is the Temple honoring Zeus," said Barnabas as the recent arrivals from Antioch explored Salamis, the port on the east end of Kypros, "and there is the gymnasium." A large statue of Caesar Augustus stood at the entrance. "There are more public baths," Barnabas said as he pointed. They had seen baths earlier. Finally, they came to an outdoor theatre that seated 15,000 persons!

"There are numerous synagogues in the city and a large population of Jews," Barnabas said, "and Salamis is derived from the Hebrew word *shalom*."

"Let's find a synagogue to ask about lodging," Paulos said. "Perhaps we can inquire about employment." He was not here to be a tourist.

For a day and a night, they had sailed from Seleucia, the port city at the mouth of the Orontes River near Antioch, and Paulos was anxious to settle into Salamis. They found their way to a synagogue easily enough, and the men there directed the travelers to a shriveled old widow who rented quarters in her mud-brick home.

"You can sleep on my veranda," the old woman croaked. "Do you have your own sleeping mats? Good, good. It'll be comfortable in the fresh air." The veranda was large and airy with a solid roof. "For one denarius per week each, you can stay here and also eat bread, cheese, and fruit in the morning. For another denarius per week, I'll cook your supper."

"Breakfast only, thanks," Paulos said.

Paulos guessed that the woman's scowl said she would miss the suppertime companionship more than the lost revenue.

In the days that followed, Paulos secured harbor employment mending sails, but Barnabas departed for the three-day trek across the island to the capital city, the seaport of Paphos, located at the opposite end of the island on the western shores, for a short family visit before returning to Paphos. Once settled, Paulos turned his attention to missionizing in a synagogue.

Sabbath worship included readings from the holy scrolls: Torah, the Prophets, or the Writings, followed by commentary. The first Sabbath after his arrival, Paulos attended a service at a synagogue. He listened intently but said nothing—he reconnoitered. He identified leaders, speakers, and those who asked questions, especially noting the presence of any Gentiles at the door of the synagogue, the *theosebeis*, willing listeners but not full participants; he sensed the "feel" of the synagogue; he shook hands, exchanged small talk, and became acquainted.

The weekly readings followed a repeating calendar from one year to the next. Paulos knew the lectionary well, and he arrived at the Sabbath service the second week prepared to speak. He listened to the readings and the commentary. When he felt the moment was right, Paulos rose from his crouch, stretched his lanky frame, cleared his throat, and addressed the congregants. Pure energy coursed through his veins.

"My name is Paulos, a Jew born of the tribe of Benjamin, and educated as a Pharisee. I have lived, learned, and taught in Tarsos, Antioch, and Damascus, and I have consulted with the great sages of Jerusalem. Please permit me to comment upon the reading we have heard today: *In the beginning when God created the heavens and the earth ...* "

Creation. The lectionary reading was from the first scroll of Torah, the first book of Moses, *In the beginning*—the familiar story of God's creation. Paulos then told the tale anew proclaiming Iesou as fulfillment of the story. "So if anyone is in Christos, there is a new creation: everything old has passed away; see, everything has become new!" Paulos could not read the faces of the dispassionate Jews, but he was encouraged when a few asked questions.

Paulos returned the next week and repeated the process, commenting on the readings and interjecting Iesou the Christos into the story; a few more listeners asked questions.

When Barnabas returned from his family's home in Paphos, he joined Paulos in the forays to the synagogue. After a few weeks listening to Paulos speak, Barnabas said to him, "You find Iesou hidden behind every tree and under every rock of the stories of old. If we read the Torah story of creation, you speak of new creation; if we read the story of the sin of Adam, you speak of new life in the new Adam; if it is a Hebrew festival, you recast the celebration around the Christos." He shook his head and clucked between his teeth. "Mind you, I don't mean to sound critical; it's just that I can't keep up with your fertile mind."

Paulos raised his eyebrows as he listened to Barnabas. It had not occurred to Paulos that he was imaginative in his interpretation; he believed he was merely stating the obvious. "That is the way of the Pharisees, trained to tell the old stories anew according to changing times and new circumstances," he said with a dismissive shrug. His teachings were self-evident. Who could doubt?

Soon, Paulos sent Barnabas to speak at a separate synagogue but not before coaching him in the anticipated Scripture readings and rehearsing his commentary with him. Barnabas provided the style while Paulos provided the substance. After six years working together in Antioch, they had polished sermons that fit the recurring Scripture readings. Their synagogue commentary was seldom spontaneous.

While the focus of the week was the Sabbath, Paulos' day to day life centered on his harbor side employment where his skills as a tentmaker served him in good stead as a mender of sails. Covered by a ragged awning, Paulos labored in a cramped stall overlooking the harbor, provided to him by a shipping company whose sails he mended. From his vantage, he watched the comings and goings of the bustling seaport. He enjoyed the view of the sea and ships, but the odor of the nearby fish-cleaning tables offended him when the wind was wrong. As the days and weeks passed, he made the acquaintance of numerous persons who belonged to the harbor proletariat.

Paulos often ate roasted lamb sold by Draco, the kebab vendor, washed down with barley beer, freshly brewed according to Draco's own recipe. Skewered chunks of vinegar soaked lamb, onions, and vegetables simmered on his charcoal brazier, dripping fat into the coals that spit enticing smells into the breeze. The tall man in the headdress and too short robe—once red but now darkened by sweat, smoke and grime into a deep maroon—hopped around his open stall with a gap-toothed grin and obscene comment for all who came near.

Fabius the fisherman and his brother passed Paulos' stall every day carrying basketfuls of sand smelt, silver fish not much longer than the span of a man's hand, that were sold to fishmongers of the agora. Tangy, pickled smelt were staples of many tables in Salamis.

One day, Fabius stopped to speak with Paulos. "Hail, teacher," he said.

Paulos looked into the weathered face of the fisherman, shaded by a billed cap pulled low over his eyes.

"My name's Fabius; may I speaks with ya?"

"Of course, sit with me. Water?" Paulos asked as he reached for a water skin hanging from a nail in the back of his stall. Paulos poured a cup of water and handed it to the fisherman whose hands were rough from countless pricks of fins and hooks, the chafing of ropes, lines, and nets, and the briny baths of harbor and sea.

"I heared ya in the synagogue where I listens from the edge. I'm not a Jew by birth, ya see, but the ways of the Jews attracts me to Israelite religion, and I attends the synagogue—for my family, ya see."

Paulos often heard such comments from *theosebeis;* compared to the impersonal and amoral Greek and Roman deities, the Hebrew God of the synagogue offered ethical standards within a community relationship, the beloved family of God.

"I wants my kids to know right from wrong, and I wants them to count for something, to belong to something, to have their place in the world. Does ya see what I means?"

Paulos nodded and for the first time noticed that Fabius wore the distinctive tassels of observant Jews. The fringes around his waist identified him as more than a mere *theosebeis*; *tzitzit* was a sign that Fabius was a circumcised proselyte.

"I asked to join the synagogue, and I received instruction in the Torah. When the elders decided that I was ready, they cuts off the tip of my cock in a bloody ceremony." He shifted on his feet as he spoke. "After I healed up, the final step was a water immersion ceremony when the elders declared I was '*like* an Israelite in all respects.'"

With one hand, Fabius removed his billed cap and wiped his

forehead with the sleeve of his robe. The set of his jaw and the hard lines in his sun-ripened face spoke of anger churning inside the man. He pulled his cap down hard over his greasy black hair and leaned in toward Paulos.

"I'm Fabius the proselyte not Fabius the Jew. I'm *like* a Jew, but I'm not a Jew—at least thats the feeling I gets from many Jews; now ya promises that boundaries is torn down. Can I trust ya?"

Paulos heard Arsenios' complaint in the voice of Fabius, *must I become a Jew?* Then he saw himself splashing in the Barada River, laughing, tumbling, and hollering *no, no, no!* Paulos was not surprised that the sweet sound of his good news would resonate in the ears of men such as Fabius.

The time had come for a post-Sabbath meal and service; the missionaries arranged for a festive meal and a celebration of the Lord's Supper in the synagogue the day after Sabbath. Fabius and his family attended, as did a few curious Jews attracted by the missionaries' Sabbath commentaries on the readings. The missionaries invited others such as Draco the kebab vendor and their widow-woman landlord. Most of them returned the second week bringing a few of their own invitees. An *ekklesia* in a synagogue of Salamis was born, consisting of marginalized Jews and *theosebeis* plus a few Gentiles such as Draco.

Paulos was certain that their good fortune confirmed his divine mission, but he would not settle in to nurture the *ekklesia* to life: watering, cultivating, and fertilizing. He had planted the seeds and now he must move on to the next field; that was his calling, and the time was short. He anticipated further success as they departed Salamis for Paphos and new ground.

Chapter Thirty-five

From his vantage point on the porch of a cliff side inn, Paulos fell asleep watching a pod of dolphins frolic in the foamy sea. Rocky sea stacks dotted the shallow waters off the sandy beach, appearing as humans emerging from the sea in the twilight of dusk. For three days, the travelers had walked the south coast of Kypros, and their last night on the road brought them to the western tip of the island, near the capital city of Paphos.

"Are you pilgrims here for the festival?" The innkeeper had asked as Paulos handed him ten coppers.

"What festival?" Paulos replied.

Before the innkeeper could speak, Barnabas interjected, "No, no, we're not pilgrims," he said with a quick glance at Paulos.

Paulos was too tired to notice.

By mid-afternoon of the next day, they reached Paphos and the hillside villa of Barnabas' brother Chariton, the home of Barnabas' youth. Chariton met them at the front entrance. Younger than Barnabas and with shorter and lighter hair, Chariton had the same broad shoulders and the same deep voice. He greeted his brother with a hug.

"Come in. Come in. You're welcome here," he said to Paulos, gesturing with his hand toward the open door.

Overlooking the city below and the sea beyond, the spacious villa boasted a colonnaded portico, multiple rooms, marble floors, and an inner courtyard with a garden around a fountain. Paulos was not accustomed to such luxurious accommodations.

The next morning, Paulos arose before the brothers who had drunk much wine late into the night; he conducted his own tour of the city. The villa was one among many cut-stone mansions with tiled roofs that dotted the hillside, including an ornate Governor's palace. Paphos was the Roman seat of government in Kypros with a noticeable presence of Roman soldiers.

Paulos arrived at the agora, elbow-to-elbow with persons in differing styles of dress and a polyglot of Latin and Greek dialects; Paulos remembered the innkeeper's comment about pilgrims and a festival. He curiously followed the flow that soon converged into a stream of pedestrians climbing a hillside path outside the city.

"Friend, where are you going?" Paulos asked a stranger walking next to him.

"Man, were you only born yesterday? Where did you come from? Why are you here if not for the festival? We go to the sacred grove and altar of Aphrodite, *Venus* if you're a Roman, to celebrate her festival. Come friend and join the fun!" The man pointed to three maidens in diaphanous robes, greeting the pilgrims with a song of Homer, the long-dead-Greek poet:

> Laughter-loving Venus went to Kypros and to Paphos, where is her grove and her altar fragrant with burnt offerings. Here the Graces bathed her, and anointed her with oil of ambrosia such as the immortal gods make use of, and they clothed her in raiment of the most enchanting beauty.

A few moments later as Paulos neared the summit of the hill, he gasped as a giggling nude woman ran past, chased by a nude man. They were all around! Laughing, cooing, fondling, fornicating— men with women, women with women, and men with men!

Ashen-faced Paulos retreated down the hill, bumping against the flow of traffic; his long legs tangled, and he rolled, only to rise and run again; he breathlessly arrived at the villa with skinned knees and elbows. He shouted at Barnabas, "Greek and Roman debauchery! Their degradation is its own punishment and the fate of those who worship themselves and not God. God gives them up to their degrading passions!"

Barnabas attempted to place a calming hand on Paulos' shoulder, but Paulos knocked it away and barked at his friend. Paulos finally stopped shouting and spent the rest of the day pacing on the portico, gulping wine, and mumbling "degrading passions". He skipped supper and kept drinking wine. As the sun sank into the deep, he passed out on the porch, sprawled on pillows. Barnabas laid a blanket over him. From the star splashed sea, Arsenios visited Paulos' dreams again.

Paulos rowed a skiff, pursuing the ship that sailed away. Arsenios stood at the ship's rail, beckoning to him. Paulos stood up, disrobed, and dove naked into the sea and swam toward the ship. The waves choked him, but he struggled on and came near the ship. Arsenios stood naked and uncircumcised on the ship's deck and stretched a hand toward Paulos. Paulos reached for Arsenios but sank beneath the waves. He bobbed up, and reached again for the outstretched fingers. A cold, bony grip grabbed Paulos and would not let go. Paulos stared into the white eyes of Jubilees, the blind beggar. "God's people should cover their shame, and should not uncover themselves as the Gentiles uncover themselves." The voice thundered over the water, carried by crackling lightning.

Paulos awoke, gasping for breath like a drowning man tossed onto a rocky beach. Confused, he staggered about the starlit portico. He slipped on a puddle of spilled wine and fell to the floor, sobbing. "Please, O please, remove this thorn from my flesh," he prayed.

Barnabas strolled from his bedroom, yawning and stretching as he stepped onto the portico. Paulos was already awake, sitting on the balustraded railing, staring at the sea. He didn't notice Barnabas' arrival.

"Figs? Dates?"

Paulos was oblivious to Barnabas' questions, and he didn't see Barnabas saunter into the kitchen either.

"Would you like some dates?" Barnabas said as he returned.

Paulos turned with a start and stared blankly at Barnabas.

"Would you like some dates?" Barnabas asked again, lifting the handful of dates for Paulos to see.

"Oh. No. I'm fine," Paulos said, turning again to stare at the sea. After a moment, he said, "I've decided to leave this place. We must sail away."

"What's that?" Barnabas asked. "What's that you say?"

Paulos turned toward him. "Perhaps we should sail north to Anatolia. Let us spread the good news in Anatolia."

"Man, are you crazy?"

Chapter Thirty-six

The ship sliced through the frothy seas as the wind freshened, producing a rushing, whooshing sound. A slanting rain pelted Barnabas and Paulos who huddled on deck. Paulos learned that sea travel was not always pleasant.

The ship shuddered as it pounded hard on a rising wave with water splashing over both sides and over the bow, adding to the soak of the missionaries. Paulos' belly churned, and he fixed his eyes on the dim line where sea met sky, fighting to keep his supper down. When Paulos' will power gave way to his gut and he spewed hot chunks of fish and bread across the deck, a smug smile briefly chased the scowl cemented on Barnabas' face. He had objected to Paulos' plan to depart Kypros but had loyally acceded to Paulos, as always. His grin said that he felt justice was done.

As gray slivers of dawn appeared after a night that seemed endless, the winds lessened, and the seas calmed. Life returned to Paulos' face, and Barnabas brushed the salt and the wind out of his hair.

The two missionaries had booked passage on a cargo ship departing from Paphos, headed to Perga on the south coast of the Anatolian mainland. The stubby vessel had a square-rigged mainsail and small artemon off the bowsprit. A second, shorter mizzenmast was located aft of the main with a square-rigged sail that was considerably smaller than the mainsail. The beamy ship had a large hold filled with copper ingots from the mines of Kypros.

The sea voyage from Paphos to Perga on the southern coast of Anatolia took three days. During the stormy night, the ship sailed straight northward across the strait of Cilicia for over fifty miles to make contact with the Anatolian mainland. By daybreak, the ship had come within a few miles of the shore, and it pivoted to the west and continued along the coastline toward Perga.

The western slopes of the Taurus Mountains loomed in the distance, sometimes visible and sometimes lost in the clouds. As a youngster in Tarsos, Paulos knew the opposite slope of the mountains well; for him, the range of mountains hid the mysterious land beyond—a place where the sun and the moon set, a place where he imagined the hidden God to dwell, a place of fanciful dreams and aspirations. He now sailed to that place. As the storm clouds lifted, so did the lingering effects of his haunting nightmare of a few days earlier.

By late morning, the ship arrived at the port of Coracesium where Paulos and Barnabas idled for the day while bargemen offloaded the ship's copper cargo. Coracesium was the home of the notorious pirates of a century earlier that had kidnapped the young Julius Caesar. Paulos imagined the bargemen to be pirates with a secret lair in the jagged rocks of the shoreline cliffs that also served as a Temple for the Mithras cult; it was widely believed that the pirates had been devotees of the cult and helped to spread it around the Empire.

It was late in the day before the last ingot was unloaded, and the ship remained in port overnight before sailing westward with dawn's first light. The ship spent the next night at anchor in a small cove along the coast before arriving in Perga late the following afternoon; Paulos was back on the Anatolian mainland but nearly two hundred miles west of Tarsos.

****

In Paulos' absence, Julius the Antioch tentmaker was ill tempered. Without an assistant, he labored harder than he cared to, and he didn't like living alone; he missed Paulos.

"Hello, smith." A yellow-haired young man stepped into the shop.

"I've plenty of business already. Go away." Julius did not look up from his sewing.

"I'm not here with business," the young man said. "I'm looking for Paulos. Does he live here?"

"Yes—I mean no." Julius said. "He did live here, but he's gone, and no one knows when he'll return." Julius threw his sewing onto his bench and looked at his visitor. "Or if he'll return. The last I heard, he sailed to Anatolia."

The tiny, bird-boned young man seemed unsure what to do next. "Please give him a message when you see him—

Julius interrupted, "I'm not going to see him. I don't know if I'll ever see him. Who are you anyway?"

"I'm Titos, a friend from Tarsos. I was a student of Paulos at the Tarsos synagogue."

Julius stood up from his stool. "A friend you say? Well, why didn't you say so in the first place?" He moved around his workbench to get a better look at pale-faced Titos from Tarsos.

"Sit down. Sit down. May I get you water to drink? I've time for a break. Tell me about yourself." Julius' mood suddenly improved. The round man plopped on his favorite chair with his legs up, listening to Titos' story, happy as a bird that had swallowed a bug.

"Do you know anything about the leather smith's trade? No? Well, would you like to learn?"

Titos moved in with Julius, awaiting his mentor's return.

****

Paulos and Barnabas spent eight months walking the roads of the southern Anatolian mainland, reaching as far north as the Roman province of Phrygia; they successfully established *ekklesias* in Perga, Iconium, Lystra, and Derbe. Their methodology was well established. In each city, they initially contacted the local synagogue to secure lodging and employment. After settling into the life of the city and synagogue, they offered commentary on Sabbath readings as a way into Iesou stories; sometimes the Jews were interested but mostly ambivalent, and ultimately *ekklesia* participation included a few Jews but many Gentiles and especially *theosebeis*.

Lystra was different, a small Roman colony whose leading citizens were Roman army veterans. The city had no Jewish population and no synagogue. Neither Paulos nor Barnabas spoke Latin, and their Greek preaching in the marketplace was misinterpreted; some thought they were speaking about the traditional Greek and Roman gods Zeus and Hermes. When the crowds realized the truth, they hissed and booed, and the missionaries retreated to the countryside.

Barnabas cooked over a campfire, and Paulos watered their donkeys at a nearby stream while standing knee deep in the river. Paulos heard a splash in the water, and he turned to the circles of ripples spreading outward. Water splattered over him with a second splash; on the shore, three teen boys tossed rocks in his direction.

"Get out of town, Jew," shouted one.

"Hey, you there, what are you doing?" Paulos began to move toward the boys on the shore.

A rock thumped Paulos on the forehead, and he crumpled to his knees. The hazy faces of the boys on shore all looked like Arsenios. In his confusion, Paulos mumbled, "I'm sorry. Forgive me." When Paulos staggered to his feet, the boys disappeared into the bushes.

Paulos sat on the riverbank, willing his fogginess to pass. He heard a voice on the road, and he imagined that Barnabas had come to find him, but when he heard a second voice, he feared that his attackers would return to finish him. He didn't have the wits to flee, but it was merely a retired Roman soldier and his son that happened upon him.

"Who are you, man? What happened to you? By Jupiter, that's a nasty bump on your head." The soldier wiped blood from Paulos' face.

"Help the man to his feet, and we'll bring him home to your mother," the soldier said.

They collected Barnabas, and the missionaries slept on their mats on the rooftop as guests of the Roman soldier. Except for a headache the next morning, Paulos was fine.

"Are you Jews?" Eunice, the soldier's wife, asked the question as she carried fresh bread to the men sitting at her breakfast table.

After the earlier events, neither man was anxious to confess their Jewishness to their squat hostess.

"I heard about your trouble at the marketplace, and they say that you are Jews. Are you Jews?" She repeated her words but in a way that accused rather than questioned.

Paulos stole a glance at Barnabas who didn't look up but chewed hard on his bread. Paulos tugged his nose and then dropped his hand over his lips, drawing his slender fingers slowly down his beard as if straining it for the right words.

"Yes," he mumbled finally.

"So am I," said the woman, "but I don't keep Torah." Her tone was defiant, and she stood with hands on her broad hips. "I prepare unclean foods. I don't keep Sabbath. I'm married to a Gentile, and our son isn't circumcised. You may consider me unclean, but I don't care what you think," she snorted.

She waited for a response that didn't come. "Hah!" She shrugged her wide shoulders before stoking the fire in her hearth, brushing her long brown hair over her back as she leaned near the flames. She wrinkled her nose and twisted her head away from the smoke as she poked the fire with a stick.

"Do you think that matters to God or to me?" Paulos finally spoke, matching her matter-of-fact tone. If she meant to provoke him, he would turn the tables on her.

Her narrowing, darting eyes said she didn't expect Paulos' nonchalance that matched her own indifference. "You're Jewish holy men who preached in the marketplace, but you don't care if I'm unclean?"

She nibbled at his bait and Paulos set the hook. He explained that Iesou had ushered in the new age of the new covenant. Torah observance was not required to belong to God's family. The kingdom of God was for all persons, even uncircumcised and unclean Romans. Paulos felt the same self-confident surge of energy that accompanied his preaching, and his lips gladly recited his good news.

Timotheos, the twenty-five-year-old son of Eunice, listened from the stoop. He had the military bearing of his father, straight and tall, lean and muscular.

"My parents have raised me as a Roman and not a Jew," he said to Paulos, "but I remember bedtime stories of the Hebrews of old. Tell me more." He would ask Paulos a question in Greek and then receive clarification from his mother in Latin.

An *ekklesia* was born in the household of Eunice, the Jewess who did not keep Torah, and Timotheos, her half-breed son of a Roman soldier, who had not been circumcised.

The merchant galley sliced smartly through the waves, a steady wind astern. Fair winds and following seas—that was the joy of sailing with the prevailing westerlies on the Great Sea. The successful missionaries had retraced their path to Perga and booked sea passage back to Antioch a year after they had departed their home in the city on the Orontes.

Paulos and Barnabas sat amidships along the port gunwale. Since the wind was also over the port side, they were on the high side of the slightly heeling ship with the starboard side lower and closer to the water. The northwest wind cooled their faces with salt spray, and flying fish darted between the sea swells.

With his tentmaker's eyes, Paulos studied the billowed mainsail, a patchwork of odd colored pieces of linen. Massive yardarms near the top of the mast supported the rectangular mainsail, wider than it was tall. A thick rope forestay stabilized the mast, extending from the masthead to the bow. Running rigging attached to the foot of the sail controlled the angle of the mainsail to the wind; Paulos marveled at the sailors who knew just which line to pull and when.

The ship hugged the coastline, and the landform remained a comforting presence on the northern horizon. Paulos and Barnabas carried their own food, as did the other passengers. The two missionaries heartily ate their evening meal of bread dipped in garum. A few passengers pitched tents on deck for sleeping quarters as night descended upon the ship at sea, but Paulos and Barnabas slept under sky and stars. Paulos lay on his back, surveying the constellations and listening to the rhythms of the creaking ship. Like a mother coaxing a baby to sleep, the ship rocked gently as sea swells lifted her up, and she whispered a soothing *shhhhh* of rushing water as the swells set her down.

For three days, the ship raced forward on the friendly sea, triumphantly lifted atop swelling waves before rushing down their back slopes only to rise high again. During the daytime, Paulos stood in the bow of the ship, eagerly anticipating their return to Antioch.

All hail the conquering hero.

The sun had crossed its midpoint and begun its slow descent when the Amonos Mountains that overlooked the port of Seleucia first appeared in the east. Paulos and Barnabas took their position at the front of the ship as if their eagerness would hasten the ship's arrival. By mid-afternoon, the rooftops of the port city came into view, and the ship's crew finally furled sail and manned their oars as the sun set at their backs. Able tugboat oarsmen and deckhands expertly warped the ship into its berth in the harbor using long, thick ropes made of hemp. The harbormaster supervised from his dockside shanty.

"Send for Julius the tentmaker," hollered Barnabas to the harbormaster, "tell him Paulos and Barnabas have returned. Tell him to bring donkeys." Barnabas' baritone voice echoed across the still waters of the Orontes River mouth.

Due of the lateness of the day, the missionaries rented a room at a local inn. After a good night's sleep, they would complete their journey with a twenty-mile trek up the banks of the Orontes to Antioch. With good luck, Julius would receive their message and arrive with pack animals to carry their possessions.

"Hello, teacher."

The snoring man merely rolled over.

"Hello, teacher. Wake up."

Caught between sleep and wake, Paulos was confused at the pale visage that greeted him. He thought he dreamt of young Titos, his protégé from Tarsos.

"Good morning. Welcome back."

Paulos eyes shot open. It was Titos! And there stood Julius, laughing from the open door. Paulos jumped to his feet, hugged Titos, then Julius, and then Titos again. Tears coursed down his wrinkles only to be swallowed up in a slack-jawed grin that touched his ears. It was good to be home in the company of dear friends!

Chapter Thirty-seven

Five years had passed since Ya'akov's great moment following the murder of his namesake, Ya'akov, the brother of Yochanan. Summoning resources deep within his soul, he had bravely captained the Nazarenes through stormy seas, rescuing Cephas from likely death, ensuring the survival of the Nazarenes in Jerusalem.

In crisis, he had acted with confidence. Now, five years later, he struggled with a crisis *of* confidence. The death of King Agrippa had not produced the groundswell of support for the Nazarenes that he had expected. Where was Yeshua? Why had his brother not returned?

A dozen years earlier when Cephas and the Galileans proclaimed that Yeshua appeared to them alive, a wildfire of expectation had engulfed Jerusalem: Yeshua was God's anointed, the Mashiah; through his Mashiah, God would restore his people Israel; the Mashiah would vanquish Israel's oppressors; the Mashiah would rule Israel with justice and mercy; Israel would be a light to the nations. The kingdom of God was at hand. Soon and very soon.

Why had it not happened? More than a dozen years had passed, and the Mashiah had not returned. The Romans were still in Palestine; justice and mercy were not. The messianic claims of the Nazarenes had grown hollow, and new converts were few; earlier converts fell away. Was it Ya'akov's fault? Was he not up to the task of leading the Nazarenes? Was he failing his brother's cause? Ya'akov's knees were callused from the many hours he spent in prayer. He made sacrifice daily at the Temple. What more could he do?

He summoned his brothers to discuss news from Antioch. Jude and Joses answered his call, as did cousin Symeon. Simon, the middle brother, rarely attended these meetings; he had his own family of six children plus a demanding wife.

"Paulos and Barnabas have returned to Antioch after a journey to Kypros and southern Anatolia," Ya'akov said. "They claim great successes in establishing *ekklesias* in far off places. Do you suppose their claims are true?" Ya'akov posed the question even as he feared the answer. Over the years, he had closely watched the successful mission in Antioch headed by Paulos and Barnabas, perplexed by Antioch's growth even as the Jerusalem Nazarenes declined.

Youngest brother, Joses, munched on flat bread and goat cheese. He took a big swallow of wine to wash down the last of the bread. "Why should they lie? If they say they were successful, I suppose it is true," Joses said.

Cousin Symeon, about the same age as Joses, agreed. Jude said nothing and merely sulked.

Ya'akov pressed on. "The reports say that their greatest successes were with Gentiles and not with Jews. What do you make of that?" The question hung in the air. This bit of information did not fit. To the Jew first, then the Gentile.

Joses poured himself a second cup of wine and studied the empty faces of his older brothers. As the youngest, he was the last to speak, deferring to the rank that came with age. Since they sat mute, he broke the silence. "It's a good thing that Gentiles follow the Mashiah. Who are we to question the ways of God?"

Ya'akov's youngest brother was more like Yeshua than any of them—able to question the order of things. Ya'akov regretted his own inflexibility; he was a sturdy man who bent stiffly, afraid of breaking, but Yeshua and Joses were like the willow in the wind. Perhaps Joses was right, the Nazarenes should welcome Gentiles. Ya'akov rubbed his hand over his mouth, straining his beard and pinching the folds of loose skin on his neck as if wiping away his frown and squeezing out his resistance. So be it but—it would be according to Torah, according to the straight and true, according to the wisdom of the elders. His hand continued down his chest until he clutched his norm.

"Are they being circumcised? Are they honoring the Sabbath? Are they avoiding unclean foods?"

Jude shrugged, and Joses bit his lip.

"I'll send someone to Antioch to investigate this mission to the Gentiles," Ya'akov said.

Jude spoke for the first time. "I know the man for the job."

The young Nazarene named Phinehas delighted in repeating the legendary story of his namesake to anyone who would listen. "The Jew took the Gentile whore into his tent," he said. "Phinehas, the son of the priest, ran his spear through them as the man lay atop her. The whore got the lance twice that night!" Phinehas laughed with his listeners and gulped down his cup of beer.

One of his listeners corrected his story. "The woman was merely a foreigner and not a prostitute."

"I thought all Gentile women were whores," Phinehas laughed.

The short man with reddish-orange hair—brushed up to create the illusion of height—honored himself by hosting his own farewell party; pimply-faced Phinehas would depart the next day for Antioch on a mission for Ya'akov.

Ya'akov set his instructions. "Are Gentile converts circumcised or not? Is Antioch honoring the traditions of the elders? Quietly check on these things and report back to me," he said.

Ya'akov was uncertain of the choice of Phinehas whom he knew to be a firebrand. But, he needed a man with the balls for the task, and Ya'akov sent two companions along with Phinehas to temper his zeal. They would sail north along the seacoast and arrive in Antioch within a week of their Jerusalem departure.

Chapter Thirty-eight

Paulos and Barnabas, resident heroes, enjoyed an idyllic summer in Antioch. Springtime rains persisted beyond their season, cooling the city in verdant comfort. Lifelong residents like Julius couldn't remember better weather. Titos' surprising presence delighted his mentor and forced Paulos out of Julius' cramped shop into Barnabas' palatial villa, pampered by servants. He slept late in the mornings in his private bedroom on a real bed covered in colorful damask cloth, lounged in the shade of the lush garden until lunch, and attended to business in the afternoon. It was a social summer too: song-filled evenings, wine and rich food, and laughter—their Antiochene friends feted the accomplished missionaries, eager to be regaled with the tales of the pilgrims. Things were as they should be.

But then three spies from Jerusalem intruded into Paulos' summer of content.

"He was like a demon," said Lucius the North African, a longtime pillar of the Antioch *ekklesia*. "His spiked red hair seemed ablaze when he accosted me on the steps of the synagogue."

Paulos paced as he listened. Who was this evildoer?

"'You there, what's your business in the synagogue?' That's what he said," Lucius reported. "'I'm a Nazarene from Jerusalem here to insist that Torah is observed and the synagogue remains pure before God. This holy place is for circumcised Jews only. You don't look like a Jew to me.'" The nut-brown face of Lucius was pinched in a way that said his insides were tight, too.

Paulos raked his arm across his workbench, spewing needles, awls, and scraps of goatskin leather across the floor of Julius' shop. A Nazarene? From Jerusalem? Did Ya'akov send him?

Paulos paced about, kicked at his tools on the floor, and raged with arms flailing. "Ya'akov sent this agitator to cause problems because he's envious of our successful mission to the Gentiles," Paulos screeched.

Barnabas was calmer. "I'm sure it's not a serious issue. To clear the air, you should send a letter to Ya'akov."

Paulos would not, but a letter to Cephas seemed a good idea. The letter contained a glowing report of the recent trip to Kypros and of the growing *ekklesia* in Antioch. The letter hinted at a trip to Jerusalem for a face-to-face report if the Nazarenes deemed it necessary.

At first, he hoped that Cephas would not invite him. An invitation would signal a problem. He worried that the Nazarenes of Jerusalem might question his Torah free, Gentile mission. Had he run in vain? A chill cloud of concern hung over him. *Apart from Torah*—that was the essence of his teaching and the essence of his Gentile mission. If Jerusalem challenged this essence, why, they ... they challenged his own standing before God. God had transformed him on the road to Damascus, *apart from Torah*.

Paulos shivered under a palm tree as a sudden rain shower deluged Barnabas' courtyard. He stood his ground rather than dashing for the dry villa, and the rain cloud quickly passed by. The summer sun quickly warmed him.

So, too, did his self-doubt dissipate; while awaiting a response from Cephas, Paulos began to hope for an invitation that he increasingly viewed as an opportunity for respect, not that he would boast; a recognition of his calling, not that he needed validation; and a warrant for further missionary activity, not that it was necessary since God sent him directly. This time, he would travel to Jerusalem not as a naked beggar but as an equal, an apostle of God, no less than Ya'akov or Cephas or any of those who had walked with Iesou.

Barely a month passed before Paulos received a reply from Cephas, penned by another since the fisherman was illiterate. "When will you arrive? We will be delighted to host your delegation. I look forward to renewing our friendship."

Paulos accepted the man's word. Cephas was a sincere man and a good friend who had offered his support previously, even in the face of Ya'akov's rejection. Would he support Paulos again in the confrontation to come?

Chapter Thirty-nine

Paulos headed the delegation from Antioch that descended upon Jerusalem and included Barnabas and Titos, the uncircumcised Gentile, as well as other envoys with Greek names. Paulos returned to the holy city for the first time in nearly a decade, seeking recognition for his *ekklesias* and validation of their Torah free status.

A cool breeze whirled around the travelers as they approached a Jerusalem gate. Golgotha loomed nearby where Ya'akov had left Paulos standing alone years earlier. Paulos had been eager for the upcoming meeting, but now that he was here, he had misgivings about subjecting his ministry—and himself—to Ya'akov and the Nazarenes. Why did he seek Ya'akov's approval since God called him directly on the road to Damascus? He trudged into the city less certain than when he had departed Antioch.

Sturdy Raziah greeted the knock on the door, with Cephas at her elbow. A broad grin creased Cephas' face, and he hugged Paulos and Barnabas. His bald spot was larger, but his red hair and beard remained vital with only a few flecks of gray. Had he shrunk, Paulos wondered? Perhaps his sloped shoulders hunched more. His mischievous smile remained as toxic as ever—his high-pitched, twittering cackle infecting all within earshot. Two of the men from Antioch went off to the agora to buy food and wine.

"Kypros! Anatolia as far as Phrygia! What an adventure," Cephas said. "I've never ventured beyond Palestine, and I'm certainly not a world traveler such as the two of you. New converts and new *ekklesias*!" Cephas opened a bottle of wine and then another and personally walked around the room, filling the cups of each visitor as Paulos in turn introduced them to Cephas.

"And this is Titos, a Gentile from my own city of Tarsos. He is a sharp one!" Paulos watched Cephas closely, but there was neither word nor sign to indicate disapproval of the tiny Greek.

Cephas summoned friends, and his rooftop soon swarmed with guests, a convivial party without any hint of tension. Ya'akov was not invited.

With the arrival of the delegation from Antioch, word went out to the followers of Yeshua, in all of Judea, to gather in Jerusalem for an important assembly. Because a large gathering was expected, the venue would be a private villa with a spacious inner courtyard. As the day approached, Paulos and the Antiochenes huddled on a hillside just outside Jerusalem, plotting strategy.

"What will you say about circumcision?" asked Titos. "What will you say about the Torah free Gentile mission?"

"Circumcision is the real issue, and we must get agreement on that; otherwise, why did we come?" Paulos said, wishing they hadn't come.

"Allow me to speak to the assembly," said Titos.

For a moment, no one spoke, but then heads began to nod. It was neither his appearance, frail and slight as he was, nor the words that he would speak that made him the perfect choice. Because he was an uncircumcised Gentile and a follower of the Christos, *he was the message.*

At that same time, Ya'akov led a meeting at his home with the local leaders of the Nazarenes including Cephas, Yochanan, and Ya'akov's family.

"They're not here just to give a report. They want something from us." Ya'akov said.

"I'm sure it has to do with Titos, the uncircumcised Gentile," brother Jude said.

"They pollute our fellowship by bringing this unclean Greek. What will the Pharisees think?" Ya'akov shook his head as he spoke.

Cephas defended the Antiochenes. "I know these people. They're of God, and their mission is from God. Certainly we can all agree that their successes in Antioch and Kypros and Anatolia are from God."

Ya'akov bristled. "If their mission is from God, why not honor God by observing Torah— including circumcision!" He wished he had never consented to this meeting. Bloody Hellenists. Must the Nazarenes cozy up to them and their Gentile ways without insisting that they honor God's Torah? That they honor God?

He changed the argument. "We have difficulty enough with the Romans. Yochanan, your own brother died a martyr under a Roman sword. Emperor Claudius has decreed that there is to be no proselytizing among the Romans, but that is precisely what Paulos and Barnabas do. We will incur the wrath of Rome."

Yochanan's eyes flashed black, and the set of his face stiffened. "We mustn't be afraid of persecution. We shouldn't limit the work of God to Jews only for fear of the Romans," Yochanan growled. He had become edgier since the Romans murdered his brother.

Ya'akov walked silently to the waist-high wall of his veranda, his back to the others as he stared down the street. A blast of hot air stung his face. He peered to the east through squinting eyes where a summertime windstorm—a *ruah qadim*—blew in from far-off deserts, threatening the city with searing winds and foreign dust. He fretted over his present work project, a veranda roof that he and his brothers were building. It was not complete, and the whipping winds would topple un-braced beams and scatter loose thatch. It would be better to finish the project than attend the conference.

Yochanan spoke again. "Let them say what they came to say. When they have spoken to our assembly, I'm sure God will lead us."

Cephas nodded, and Ya'akov merely grunted. That was it; the discussion was over; Cephas and Yochanan departed, leaving Ya'akov and his kin alone.

"Are we to forget everything God has revealed to us?" Ya'akov asked, not expecting an answer. "How are we to be a light to the nations if we fail to obey God's commands, if we fail to honor the covenant, if we fail to be holy as God is holy?" Ya'akov spoke as he stared blankly down the street.

"You must stand fast, my brother," said Jude who had become Ya'akov's most trusted lieutenant. "Paulos is a sly one. He'll make the issue black or white, right or wrong; either we support a Gentile mission or we don't."

Ya'akov listened but did not respond, and Jude continued to rant.

"I'm suspicious of Paulos and his doctrines and his rituals," Jude said. "What tales does Paulos tell the Greeks who know only the cults of Mithras, Cybele, and Isis? What do the Gentiles hear? In Paulos' words and to Gentile ears, has Yeshua our brother become a Gentile god? Paulos blasphemes the God who is One."

Jude was right. Or was he? Who could know? Why was the answer not clear to him? Ya'akov feared that he was failing as the leader. Why must he lead? Why not Cephas? Or Yochanan? Or Jude, his brother? Maybe he would just go and finish the roof. Let someone else take charge.

Ya'akov fumbled with the norm that hung around his neck. He placed the flat edge along the top of the wall, taking its measure. Somehow, that calmed him. Youngest brother Joses appeared at his side and placed a calloused hand on Ya'akov's slumped shoulder. Neither brother spoke, but his brother's touch reassured the Nazarene leader.

Ya'akov set his face directly into the stinging east wind. It was his responsibility, and he would do his duty even if he couldn't hold back the swirling currents.

Chapter Forty

The buzzing, early arriving crowd of Nazarenes hushed as the delegation of foreigners from Antioch arrived. The swirling desert winds of the *ruah qadim* raged over the top of the villa, depositing dust over the courtyard. The hot gusts flushed Paulos' face—or was it the glare of the gawkers? He tugged on his soaked tunic to ventilate his overheated torso.

The Antiochenes stood alone in the corner of the courtyard surrounded by strangers. When Ya'akov ascended to a tabletop to speak, Paulos canted his head and cupped his hand to allow his best ear to hear his nemesis speak.

Ya'akov convened the assembly. "We're here today for an historical meeting. For the first time, we gather as a combined *ekklesia,* bringing together brothers and sisters from near and far. We welcome our brothers from Antioch."

The crowd politely applauded, and Paulos managed a forced smile.

Ya'akov held up his hands for silence, and he continued, "Our friends from Antioch are here today to report on God's work in far off places."

Ya'akov gestured to the Antiochenes—an invitation for a speaker to come to the table-dais in the center of the courtyard. When Ya'akov saw Paulos emerge from the shadows, his face looked like he had bit into a sour apple.

Paulos climbed atop the table, outstretched both hands toward the crowd, and slowly turned in a circle in order to greet all surrounding him. "Grace to you and peace from God our father and the Lord Yeshua, the Mashiah." He paused briefly, and then continued, "Brothers and sisters, will you pray with me."

Heads bowed down.

"God of the heavens and the earth, who created the fish of the sea and the beasts of the land, the flowers in the field and the rains from the sky, and humankind in your own image, we give you thanks and praise for your creation; may you continue to sustain us and provide us with all that we need."

His lips moved, and sounds rolled off his tongue, but his mind was blank. His speech came from somewhere other than conscious thought, and Paulos seemed to float with the dust above the courtyard, listening to the words that poured from his mouth.

"God of Abraham, you chose your people and promised that we would become great and that through us all the persons on your good earth would be blessed; may you grant us wisdom and guidance that we may be a blessing to all nations."

A few scattered "amens" murmured in the crowd.

"God of Moses, you covenanted with us and gave us your Torah to guide us and protect us; may you now fulfill your promises in the new covenant, forgiving and forgetting our poor failures to obey your Torah."

A few more amens rose up from the Nazarenes, and Paulos' mind was returning to his body. His thoughts slowed and cleared as he found his rhythm.

"God of the Prophets, you have promised your redemption and your deliverance through your Mashiah; may you soon send Yeshua to reign in triumph over your kingdom, in fulfillment of your promises. Amen."

With the final amen, heads unbowed, and faceless eyes fixed on the foreign-born preacher, waiting. Except for the rush of hot winds overhead, the courtyard was dead silent, waiting. Paulos drank down a cup of water as the crowd watched, waiting. Self-awareness had returned to him, but it was more than that—he felt in command of the crowd and the situation, and the exhilaration of that surged through him.

"I am Paulos, a Jew from Tarsos in Cilicia. Circumcised on the eighth day, a member of the people of Israel, of the tribe of Benjamin, a Hebrew born of Hebrews; as to the law a Pharisee; as to zeal a persecutor of the Damascus *ekklesia*; as to righteousness under the Torah, blameless."

He offered his Hebrew credentials, but who was truly blameless? This was the time for hyperbole not true confession, and God would understand.

"On the road to Damascus, the risen Lord came to me and transformed me. On the road to Damascus, the risen Lord called me to be his apostle to the Gentiles. By the grace of God, I am what I am, and his grace toward me has not been in vain."

Although he focused on the faces in the crowd, Paulos kept a weather eye on Barnabas. Barnabas exchanged a nervous smile with Titos.

Paulos continued speaking. "In Antioch, that great city of the Romans, we have established a foothold for the Mashiah. Our numbers grow among the Jews of Antioch but especially among the Gentiles. Our mission has spread to Kypros and many cities of Anatolia. The kingdom of God is at hand!"

Barnabas searched the listeners for their reaction. His eyes asked, "Do they have ears to hear? Do they *really* listen?" His furrowed forehead said he could not read the crowd.

"We know that you have uplifted us in your prayers, and we ask for your continued support of our mission to the Gentiles. In you and through you, we are realizing God's will that Israel should be a blessing to the nations."

When Paulos finished, he introduced Titos, the tiny young man with the beardless face.

"Titos is from Tarsos, my own student in the synagogue in which I grew up at the knee of Eli the sage. Since he cannot speak Aramaic, please allow him to speak to you in Greek."

Titos replaced Paulos on the table. He was shaking, and his high-pitched voice cracked at his first attempt at speaking.

"Give him water to drink," a voice from the crowd shouted, and someone passed him a cup of water.

Paulos remembered the day many years earlier when he had first encountered the loyal, puppy-dog eyes of young Titos on the steps of the Tarsos synagogue. This was the moment for the protégé to deliver.

Titos began again. "I am not a Jew; I am an uncircumcised Greek, but I am your brother in Christos. Thank you for being a blessing to me as God promised Abraham."

He said a bit more, but no one heard his words. The uncircumcised Greek stood there in the midst of them calling them brothers and sisters. As Titos stepped down with a big smile directed at Paulos, there was a collective sigh in the crowd, a collective stepping back, a collective gathering of thoughts. The silent crowd began to murmur. As the whispers swelled, Ya'akov ascended to the tabletop and gestured for silence.

Ya'akov thanked the speakers from Antioch and praised their work. "Many of you remember the words of Yeshua: *love your neighbor as yourself*, which is basic Torah teaching. Yeshua was our great Torah teacher. Yeshua the Mashiah has established his kingdom, his holy Temple, and we who are his heirs must continue to build what Yeshua started until he comes again."

Ya'akov nodded to acknowledge the grunts of approval from the assembled Nazarenes.

"We all know that Torah tells us that the command to *love your neighbor* refers to the Gentile as well as the Jew. We also know that Torah tells us that God created all humankind, Gentile and Jew, in God's own image. And finally, as the speakers before me have correctly reminded us, the blessing of the Jews carries with it the obligation to be a blessing to all the nations."

The shrug of Barnabas' shoulders said he was surprised, and the look on his face said he was pleased with the words of Ya'akov, but

Paulos didn't trust the man, even if he was the brother of the Lord. Were there thorns on his olive branch?

"And so we welcome our Gentile brother here with us today," Ya'akov said, "and we welcome all our Gentile brethren all over the world into our *ekklesia* of God."

Paulos hadn't expected Ya'akov to be so generous, but Ya'akov wasn't finished, and a shift in tone confirmed Paulos' skepticism.

"Together with Moses and all God's people, we were forever changed on Mt. Sinai. God spoke to us, and we were overwhelmed. God revealed his hidden and unknown name to us, and *all the peoples of the earth shall see that you are called by the name of the Lord.*"

Ya'akov picked up his cadence, and the norm that hung from his neck swayed rhythmically.

"Torah is more than mere wisdom, it is our destiny. Torah is not empty words writ on papyrus scrolls but our essence. Torah defines us before the world. God is always present to us in Torah."

Paulos searched the crowd for their reaction, but their faces were blank. He worried what they were thinking.

"God commands us to be holy as he is Holy. We are called to holy deeds as a reflection of God's own holiness. In our Torah observance, we reflect a spark of the divine presence in the midst of a profane world. In our holy deeds of Torah, God is present to us and through us to the world."

The wind above picked up in ferocity, and a cloud of dust sifted down over the assembly.

"And so, as we welcome Titos and all the Gentiles into holy fellowship with us and with God, we merely ask that they too reflect the holiness of God, that they too encounter God in the simple holy deeds of Torah, that they too exhibit a spark of God's presence to the rest of the world through their holy deeds."

Why did that infernal builder's square always dangle around his neck? It seemed menacing, as a weapon at the ready, and Paulos remembered the story told by Gamaliel many years earlier, the story of the rigid sage named Shammai who chased away the Gentile with his builder's square.

"We merely ask that through the badge of circumcision, the holiness of God be exhibited to all the nations."

The sound of crashing timbers somewhere outside the villa accompanied the howling wind.

Ya'akov stepped down before the hushed crowd that only then realized the ramifications of the issue before them. Would they support a Gentile mission without requiring circumcision? The murmuring began again and gradually reached a crescendo.

A shrill female voice pierced the buzz. The crowd quieted, and a petite gray-haired woman ambled to the table as the crowd parted to let her pass. Men lifted her onto the dais.

The bantam woman smiled and looked around at the circle in front of her. Paulos knew her but couldn't place her. Ya'akov stared slit-eyed at the female who dared to speak. The crowd held its breath to hear the words of the woman, which was a good thing because she had a dainty voice.

"I am a woman. According to some, I should not be speaking in the company of men, but Yeshua accepted women into his circle. Yeshua broke bread with us. Yeshua drank wine with us. Yeshua our friend loved us, accepted us, and welcomed us into his company. In many ways, Yeshua broke down Torah boundaries between men and women."

Paulos cocked his head to listen to the woman, still unsure of her identity. Ya'akov's lips moved as if silently cursing the petite speaker.

"There were other friends of Yeshua who also shouldn't have been with him, according to Torah. Yeshua broke down boundaries and welcomed prostitutes, tax collectors, and others not ritually pure."

Ya'akov's face turned red, and his silent lips moved faster.

The woman continued her speech. "We are followers of Yeshua.

Let us live by his example. Yeshua did not allow Torah boundaries to stand between him and the people he loved, the people he invited to be in communion with him, and neither should we."

The trim woman in the silk robe extended her hand, palm up, toward Titos. "Brother Titos, you are welcome here, and you are welcome in God's kingdom."

As the men lifted her from the table, Paulos remembered the friendly woman from Magdala who had once promised to help his ministry. With a big smile, he whispered to Barnabas, "Maryam Magdalene."

The crowd was briefly silent, and then the whispers started again, quickly swelling into chattering. The owner of the villa who hosted the assembly climbed atop the table.

"My friends, the hour is late, and the sun is setting. It is time to adjourn for the day."

He pointed in turn at Ya'akov, Cephas, and Yochanan as he spoke, "We have three wise and able leaders. Let us place the matter in their hands; they have heard the words spoken today, and I am sure they will be happy to hear what any of you care to say to them in private on the morrow."

Paulos shook his head. No. No. Decide now!

"After they have heard what is on your heart, let Ya'akov, Cephas and Yochanan come together with the men of Antioch. We trust that God will guide them, and they will make an agreement that we will all accept and support."

The crowd nodded its approval. The pillars would decide. The numbness returned and Paulos mindlessly followed the others as they trudged to Cephas' home.

Chapter Forty-one

The winds howled through the night. Ya'akov's partially completed thatch roof rattled, hummed, and then ripped apart into splinters. The *ruah qadim*, the desert winds from a far-off land, scattered thatch through the streets of Jerusalem.

The morning after the assembly, Paulos bent over in the bushes, hands on his knees, his stomach churning with dry heaves. He had not eaten anything in more than a day. There was nothing to vomit. He was empty.

The Antioch delegation had retreated to their isolated hilltop while the three pillars received visitors in their homes in order to gauge the mood of the assembly. The storm winds had waned, but sagging dust choked the sun that crept along its arc in the salmon sky; nervous men bantered the day away, munching on figs and stale bread. Paulos ate nothing.

Finally, they returned to Cephas' house just before the orange-red sun dipped behind the hills. When Cephas saw them, he raised both arms in greeting, and his grin touched his ears. "The sense of the Nazarene assembly is clear," he said. "Your position is receiving strong support. I have spoken to Yochanan, and he agrees."

Did he hear right? Paulos canted his head sideways to allow Cephas to speak straight into his good ear.

"Many were persuaded by the words of Maryam," Cephas said.

The smiling, green eyes of Charis flashed into Paulos' thoughts, the Gentile woman who had been God's agent in his transformation. Now, another woman had been decisive for his ministry.

Cephas reached a bony hand and tousled Titos' bushy blond hair. "And the presence of this one was also critical for your cause," he said.

Paulos patted his protégé on the back before questioning Cephas further. "What does Ya'akov say?" Paulos asked.

Cephas sucked in a deep draught of air before blowing it out through pursed lips in a way not quite a whistle. He averted his eyes as he answered. "He senses the mood of the Nazarenes but remains unconvinced; he is a wounded lion," Cephas said.

Cephas lifted his face and smiled into Paulos' eyes as he finished. He couldn't help himself, and his smile erupted into his trademark twitter as he spoke. "Yochanan and I will each support your position; whether it will be unanimous or whether Ya'akov will ultimately dissent remains to be seen."

There were hugs all around, and someone opened a bottle of wine, the start of a long and boisterous evening. Even Paulos drank his share. Cephas' rooftop swelled with dancers and singers and jokesters and eaters and drinkers and Jews and a Gentile.

A few blocks away, Ya'akov's house was quiet, and the lamps went dark early.

A day later, the Jerusalem leaders and the Antiochene leaders met on Ya'akov's veranda, his home turf. Paulos, Barnabas, and Cephas walked up the stairs together in silence. Yochanan was already there awaiting their arrival with Ya'akov and his brother, Jude. The newcomers sat around a table with Ya'akov and Yochanan while Jude paced in the background.

Paulos looked directly at Ya'akov, but Ya'akov avoided eye contact. Paulos wanted to speak to the sturdy Nazarene: to say he was sorry, even though he was not; to commend him for his loyalty to the traditions, even though he disagreed; to assure him that he respected Jerusalem's authority, even though he did not; to express friendship, even though he didn't feel friendly. He wanted to speak, but he could not and would not because he had everything to say, but nothing. He would neither gloat nor argue; the undiplomatic diplomat would remain silent.

Cephas looked at Paulos then Barnabas then Yochanan and finally Ya'akov. Who would be the first to speak?

Cephas broke the awkward silence. "Well, are we in agreement?" He looked at Yochanan who nodded slightly and then at Ya'akov who sat with head bowed.

"Ya'akov?"

With great effort, Ya'akov pushed himself up from the table and plodded to the edge of the veranda, staring blankly down the street. He rocked back and forth from his toes to his heels, wriggling his shoulders awkwardly as if to loosen stiff muscles.

"Paulos, you feel yourself entrusted with a mission." He spoke slowly without facing his listeners. He carefully measured each word.

"To you has come a revelation that provides you with a sense of vocation ... are you confident of your special revelations?" He drew several deep breaths, exhaling them slowly.

"I find your self-assurance ..." he searched for the right word, "... staggering," he finally said. The contempt in his voice hung with the dust in the heavy air.

Paulos tugged at his nose as he considered his response. Of course, he was sure. "Yes, I know in the depths of my being that God has called me. You know my story on the road to Damascus when Yeshua spoke to me—

"Yeshua spoke to you!" Ya'akov whirled and glared at Paulos. Just like that day on Golgotha, he would dismiss the vision of the come-lately usurper from a foreign land.

"Yeshua spoke to you, a stranger?" Ya'akov stomped back to the table and hovered over Paulos, breathing heavily, hands at his side, fists clenching and unclenching.

"How can you be so sure Yeshua spoke to you and told you things he never told me, his own brother?"

Paulos' own anger flared. Once again, this brute questioned his Damascus experience; no, not merely questioned it, but disparaged it.

Once again, Ya'akov dismissed his message and his ministry—and his own standing before God—as if they were not true. There was truth in Damascus, and the proof was in his transformed heart and soul.

Paulos nearly rose to face the Nazarene who towered over him, but Cephas intervened and placed a hand gently on Ya'akov's shoulder. Ya'akov relaxed, and he stepped back, clasping his hands behind his back as if to restrain himself. Jude stepped from the shadows and stood behind his brother. Cephas remained standing between Ya'akov and Paulos.

Ya'akov's rising voice squeaked and cracked. "You, who would guide the blind, instruct the foolish, and teach babes. You, who would convert the world; are you confident *your* message is *God's* own truth?"

Paulos struggled to hold his tongue.

Then Ya'akov lowered his voice, and his tone changed from questioning to accusing. "Have you received God's revelation or merely self-delusion?" He paused to let the accusation sting. "Is it freedom from the law or lawlessness that you proclaim?"

Ya'akov looked into their eyes, each one in turn, before focusing on Paulos. He spread his hands wide and asked, "How can you be so damned sure of yourself? How can *anyone* be so cocksure?"

Again, Paulos nearly jumped up to defend himself, but Yochanan's voice intervened.

"I know that you're not convinced of Paulos' message, but don't question his call—

Before Yochanan could continue, Ya'akov held up his hand as if to say, "Let me finish."

"Your mission to the Gentiles is important, but the traditions of our elders are also important. Torah is our identity and our essence; I believe that strongly as I believe Yeshua did also."

Paulos filled his lungs and held his breath.

"We must remain strongly identified with our Jewish past. If we are lax in our Torah observance, we become isolated from the rest of Jerusalem, which only makes it easier for the Romans to scapegoat us."

Ya'akov hesitated then looked straight at Paulos. "Despite my concerns, I will not *insist* that your Gentile converts become circumcised. But, it is my hope that the Gentiles will choose circumcision *voluntarily*."

With that, Ya'akov extended his hand to Paulos. Paulos unfilled his lungs as a cool breeze swept through the veranda, dispelling the hot air that lingered from the dust storm and the tension along with it. Cephas slapped Paulos on his back and chuckled. Yochanan stepped forward and shook hands with Paulos then Barnabas. Jude stepped back into the shadows and glared.

Later in the day, Ya'akov spoke with his kin. "What else could I do? Could I overrule the assembly?" He said as much to himself as to his brothers. "But I extracted a promise from Paulos, an agreement that his *ekklesias* would gather a collection for our poor. A collection will pay homage to the ascendancy of the Nazarenes."

"If you accept gold and silver from the Gentile *ekklesias*, does that not acknowledge their legitimacy?" asked cousin Symeon.

Ya'akov collapsed hard onto his stool, bumping the table and sending a tin cup clattering across the floor. Even as he imposed conditions on Paulos, it would seem that the so-called Pharisee from Tarsos had bested him.

The triumphant Antiochenes returned home, self-satisfied in their victory, confident in the agreement. Titos remained uncircumcised. Paulos would not bar the front entrance only to have a thief sneak in through the back door. Did Ya'akov really think that he would allow Titos to submit voluntarily to circumcision?

Unknown to the Antiochenes, this was a drama in two acts; after an intermission that lasted more than a year, the scene would shift to Antioch and the second act would begin.

Chapter Forty-two

The incident in Antioch started innocently enough when Cephas and Raziah arrived unexpectedly. Was it the first summer after the apostolic assembly in Jerusalem or the second? Paulos wasn't sure, but when he heard a heart-warming cackle at the door to Julius' shop and looked up at a familiar toothy grin, it seemed that time had not passed at all. It was the sixteenth year since the crucifixion of Yeshua and the seventh year of the reign of Emperor Claudius, 49 C.E. Unknown to Paulos, it would also be the last summer of his happy sojourn in Antioch and the end of his friendship with Cephas and Barnabas.

Cephas and Raziah had departed Jerusalem months earlier, visiting the towns and villages of Galilee, successfully establishing a few Jewish *ekklesias* here and there. Now they had come to Antioch, and Raziah tapped her foot on the granite street as a juggler distracted her husband and Paulos as they walked from Julius' shop to the synagogue. In the decade since Paulos first arrived in Antioch, he had grown accustomed to the cosmopolitan city, but now he laughed at the street entertainers as if he first noticed them.

The din of the marketplace swallowed Cephas' high-pitched giggle. Bowed under the weight of packs on his back, he leaned against his head-high walking stick with both hands grasping the top and laughed at the antics of the juggler's monkey. When the primate placed his tiny hands over the eyes of his master, sending balls bouncing in every direction, Cephas' twittering giggle erupted again, but Raziah merely grunted. Heavy packs burdened her also, but her sturdy frame carried them well, straight and tall. She had refused Paulos' offer to carry her load.

Finally, Paulos stepped out and led his guests through the crowd and toward the synagogue. His gait would carry him ahead a few paces, and he would stop and wait bright-eyed before striking out again. It was good to have his friends here with him, an opportunity to repay the hospitality he had received twice over on his visits to Jerusalem. There was also pride in having this pillar, the greatest friend of Yeshua, here to honor the Antioch *ekklesia* and to stamp his imprimatur on the Gentile mission. For the moment, Ya'akov and the Nazarenes of Jerusalem seemed a world away.

"There it is. The building with the columns." Paulos, Cephas, and Raziah were enroute to the home of Barnabas, but with an intermediate stop at the synagogue.

Paulos gestured to those who were conversing in the synagogue portico. "Come inside. Come, come all of you. We have special guests." They followed Paulos inside, joining other *ekklesia* members already in the meeting room.

"We have honored guests from Jerusalem." Paulos half-shouted so all in the meeting room could hear. "This is Cephas, friend of Iesou, leader of the disciples, and a leader of the Nazarenes. And this is Raziah, his wife."

Wide-eyed Antiochenes fawned over the famous leader from Jerusalem. The frown on the face of Raziah said she knew better. Then they were off to find Barnabas, leaving the synagogue buzzing.

Raziah and Cephas became houseguests in Barnabas' posh villa. "I will do that myself, thank you," Raziah said to the servant who offered to wash their clothes. Raziah also insisted on helping prepare the meals, much to the bemusement of the household staff.

Then it was the celebration at the riverside arranged by Paulos: the organizer, planner, dreamer, and schemer. He hoped and expected to impress his guests with the size, vitality, and worship style of the Antiochene *ekklesia*.

Paulos, Barnabas, Cephas and Raziah were among the first to arrive for the Orontes riverbank gathering of all the *ekklesias* of

Antioch on the first day of the week, the day after Sabbath. Paulos led a donkey carrying blankets, an amphora of wine, and baskets of flat bread. Soon others began to arrive by twos and threes, each one bringing food, mats, clay plates, and cups.

"Hello. How do you do? I'm Cephas. Nice to meet you, I'm Cephas."

His self-introduction was unnecessary; everyone knew about Cephas, and they all wanted to shake the hand of this very important person from Jerusalem. Cephas did not shy away from the role even under the scolding eyes of his wife.

The crowd was even bigger than expected, and the excitement higher. A little behind schedule in the late afternoon, Barnabas ascended to a flat rock that would serve as the speaker's dais. He quieted the crowd, extended a greeting to all, introduced Cephas and Raziah, offered a prayer, and then announced the meal, inviting Cephas and Raziah to the head of the line.

The honored guests chose from a variety of fruits, breads, cheeses, meats, fishes, and—too many choices.

"Please, please have a little of this," one woman said.

"You must try this; it's my husband's favorite," said another.

"Strange and rich food for simple folks such as us," said Raziah.

Cephas and Raziah sat down with heaping plates next to Titos and several of his friends. Busy Paulos joined them, pleased that Titos had Cephas safely under his wing, pleased that Cephas appeared to be enjoying himself, pleased that the day was going so well.

"This is a splendid location," said Cephas as he looked at the rocky-river bed with fast flowing and clear water of the Orontes River. He also praised the feast that had been set before them. "And what is this tasty morsel?" he asked as he chewed on a salty piece of meat.

"Pork belly," answered Titos.

Raziah coughed, and she discreetly spit out the contents of her mouth into her hand as she caught her husband's eye, but he continued chewing. He popped the last bite of pork into his mouth and smiled at Raziah as he did so. He ate everything on his plate. Raziah did not finish.

The common meal ended, and the worship service began with a prayer followed by hymn singing. When the honored guest-preacher ascended the rock to speak, the crowd hushed expectantly.

Cephas was not a polished preacher, especially in Greek, and he spoke informally, stringing remembrances of Iesou together in no particular pattern. The night before, Raziah had reminded him of a few stories that would be especially meaningful to the Gentiles. Iesou's ministry had been almost exclusively to Jews with little contact with Gentiles, but there was that Samaritan woman and the soldier's servant in Capernaum, and there were others.

Cephas concluded his sermon to the mostly Gentile listeners, "And Iesou said, 'I tell you, many will come from east and west and will eat with Abraham and Isaac and Jacob in the kingdom of heaven.'"

The Antiochenes broke into sustained applause as Cephas stepped down from the flat rock. A few women seated around Raziah reached out to touch her arm or pat her on the back. Her proud smile was as big as her husband's grin.

Then followed the reenactment of the Lord's Supper with bread and wine. As Paulos repeated the ritualized story, Cephas' grin disappeared, replaced by a furrowed forehead, but when those around him stood to move forward to receive bread and wine, Cephas arose also. Paulos watched Cephas' reaction, but he was too far away to hear the brief exchange between Cephas and his wife.

"But the story isn't true," Raziah said.

"It's true enough," Cephas replied.

Cephas reached for her hand and lifted her to her feet. The Nazarene husband and wife from Jerusalem joined with the Antiochenes in the ritual of bread and wine. When Cephas extended his cupped hands to receive the chunk of bread that Paulos had broken from the loaf, the moment was timeless.

The Lord said to Abraham, "I will make of you a great nation, and I will bless those who bless you, and make your name great, so that you will be a blessing, and in you, all the families of the earth shall be blessed;" the Lord said to Moses, "You shall be my treasured possession out of all the peoples, you shall be for me a priestly kingdom and a holy nation;" the Lord said to David, "Blessed are those whose iniquities are forgiven, and whose sins are covered;" the Lord said to Isaiah, "On this mountain the Lord of hosts will make for all peoples, a feast of rich food, a feast of well-aged wines;" the Lord said to Jeremiah, "I will make a new covenant, for I will forgive their iniquity, and remember their sin no more;" the Lord said to Ezekiel, "Eat what is offered to you, eat this scroll, and go speak to the house of Israel;" a stormy wind came out of the north, a great cloud with brightness around it and fire flashing forth continually, seated above a throne was something that seemed like a human form, this was the appearance of the likeness of the glory of the Lord; Paulos and Cephas were standing at the foot of the throne, fresh as scrubbed newborns, together with all the saints, living and dead.

When Cephas took the bread and ate it, a solitary tear trickled down his cheek.

Days turned into weeks and spring into summer. Even Raziah warmed to her role as the wife of an esteemed elder statesman. The revered Nazarenes were popular houseguests, widely feted in the homes of the Antiochenes, but their happy tarry in Antioch would not last.

****

Ya'akov's knees ached. He took a break and sat on the plank scaffolding that bridged two sawhorses; Jude continued working with a wooden mallet on the opposite end of the scaffold. Ya'akov reached for a water skin and drained it, drinking deeply of its refreshment, finishing with an open-mouthed "aaaah."

Ya'akov was in a surprisingly good mood considering the news from Antioch. His elation stemmed not from the news but from his reaction. He had acted. Decisively. Authoritatively. By the book.

When he first heard that Cephas had become the fool, eating forbidden food with unclean Gentiles, he was mildly surprised. The man had no backbone; his pride and the fawning attention of the Gentiles led him astray. Spun around by the winds of praise, the spineless scarecrow forgot Torah.

But when he heard of the ritual of eating the body of Yeshua and drinking his blood, he was shocked beyond surprise. One didn't need to study with the Pharisees to know the command of God. *I will set my face against the person who eats blood.* Sacrifice? This was Greek mystery cult and not Hebrew religion. The Lord? The Son of God? The Gentiles interpreted these Hebrew titles differently than the Hebrews themselves understood them.

Paulos the misinterpreter. Paulos the dreamer who chased after visions. Paulos the latecomer who never walked with Yeshua. Paulos the so-called Jew who talked, acted, and thought like a Gentile.

Ya'akov's ambiguous attitude toward the Gentile mission was resolved; there could be no half measures. The Gentiles of the Antioch *ekklesia* must observe Torah, or the Hebrews of Antioch must avoid contact with them—no middle ground was possible.

No mixing and mingling—was that not the essence of Torah boundaries? The vine grower must not sow his vineyard with a second kind of seed; the farmer must not plow with an ox and a donkey yoked together; the warp of the weaver must not be wool if the woof was linen. God's people must distinguish between the holy and the common, the clean and the unclean. He saw it clearly now, and he had acted. He knew he was right, and his confidence swelled with his decisive action.

Ya'akov placed the edge of his norm atop the scaffold. The straight and true builder's square revealed the sagging of the plank.

He reached for a basket of prunes, popped a few into his mouth, chewed, spit out the pits, swallowed, burped, and smiled.

****

The sound of knocking was nearly lost in the rumbling thunder. Barnabas' servant swung the door open to find a short man silhouetted against the lightning flashes.

"I'm looking for Cephas. Is he here?" The pelting rain did not affect the slicked up orange hair, like a banty rooster's crown, atop the diminutive stranger.

"No, but I expect him later. Please come in out of the rain to wait for him."

"No. Tell him Phinehas will call on him on the morrow." Ya'akov's henchman turned and disappeared into the darkness.

"Allow me to speak boldly, my friend," Phinehas said, "and I speak to you with the greatest respect."

Cephas never liked the brash loudmouth who could respectfully say disrespectful things.

"My dear friend and respected leader, I must say that your conduct is shocking. Have you forgotten who you are? Do you so quickly turn your back on the traditions of the elders in order to curry favor with unclean Gentiles? Do you so easily break the commands of God's covenant to please your belly?"

Cephas' first instinct was to give this youngster his comeuppance, but the harsh criticism of Phinehas echoed the gentler rebuke of his own dear Raziah. In his own mind, he wondered: Had he sinned? Had he become unclean? Had he allowed the esteem heaped upon him by the Gentiles to affect his judgment? There was no grin on his face now.

Perhaps Ya'akov was right. Even if he was wrong, he was the brother of the Lord, the leader of the Nazarenes, the heir to the throne of his master. No, Cephas would not stand against Ya'akov, regardless of the merits of the disagreement.

Phinehas had tugged at a loose thread, and the fabric of the unified Yeshua movement had begun to unravel.

Chapter Forty-three

Paulos awakened from sleep early as usual and had already completed several pieces of work at the tentmaker's shop when he heard Julius making water in a chamber pot in his sleeping quarters. The round-bodied Roman staggered out in rumpled robes and went straight to the water vase. He scooped a cup, drank it down, and scooped another. He puckered his unshaven face and pressed his belly with his fist as if to force out a belch.

"Sore gut," he said. "Rich foods," he added. He sipped on the second cup of water.

It was then that Barnabas burst into the shop with the news that Cephas had withdrawn from table fellowship with the Gentiles. What was worse, he was advising the Jews of the Antiochene *ekklesia* to do the same.

"What! Cephas did what! What an insult to the Gentiles!" Paulos threw his tools on the floor and banged his fist on his workbench. "Call a meeting! Barnabas, we must call a meeting!"

Barnabas arranged a meeting at the synagogue for all members of the Antioch *ekklesia* to discuss their Torah-free behavior. Cephas would be there also.

The evening before the scheduled meeting, the *ekklesia* leaders came together at Barnabas' villa for a discussion that lasted late into the night.

"Is God the God of Jews only? Is he not the God of Gentiles also?" Paulos stood on a table speaking to his friends, Gentile and Jew, but he directed his message primarily to his Jewish kinfolk. "Apart from circumcision; apart from calendar observances; apart from food laws—the righteousness of God has been revealed—*apart from Torah*. There is no distinction between Jew and Gentile for we all are weak and incapable of claiming God's blessing by our own merit; it is God who claims us and blesses us despite our unworthiness."

Paulos' voice grew louder, and he spoke faster.

"Shall we Jews boast in our circumcision or in the foods that we eat? Shall we claim God's blessing ahead of the uncircumcised Gentiles who eat different foods?" The questions hung in the humid air of midsummer. Paulos stepped down from the table and drank down a cup of water and then another. He wiped the sweat from his brow and listened to the murmurings of his listeners.

After a few minutes, Barnabas cleared his throat and raised his hand. One by one, the others in the room fell silent. "Paulos, my dear, dear friend. You have spoken the good news most eloquently. Your strength of mind overwhelms me. Yet, I must confess that I have a question. May I be so bold as to raise my concern?"

A concern? Barnabas questioned him? Never before had Barnabas disputed with Paulos in public. What question could he raise?

"Speak, dear friend. Ask your question."

Barnabas shifted his weight from one foot to the other. "You have argued convincingly that Torah observances are not necessary, and none of us gathered here observe Torah dietary rules—even those of us who are Jews."

Paulos nodded.

"But what of the Nazarenes who choose to keep Torah?" Barnabas asked.

"What of those who are uncomfortable with breaking with the teachings of the elders?" Barnabas lifted his hands in a way that matched the questioning tone of his voice.

"May the Nazarenes continue to honor Torah if that is their choosing? May they continue to eat only what they believe to be clean? May they continue to circumcise their sons on the 8th day?"

He dropped his hands and his voice as he concluded. "Would you have the Nazarenes of Jerusalem turn their back on that which has been their identity?"

Paulos quickly responded, "Of course, they may continue to follow Torah. The point is that Torah observance is irrelevant," he said. "It neither accomplishes one's standing before God nor detracts from it. Dietary practices, Sabbath observance, festival observance, circumcision, these boundary markers no longer have meaning."

Glancing quickly at the Jews in the room, he added, "But, I would not suggest that the Jews should cease acting according to their custom and their culture—if that is what they choose to do," he said as he watched for signs of affirmation, but he saw only blank faces.

Barnabas then raised the conundrum.

"How then may Jews and Gentiles mix? Torah precludes mixing. Whether Torah is mandatory or voluntary, the result is the same— no mixing. What of the common meals at the *ekklesia*? What of the ritual meal of bread and wine?"

Paulos stroked his nose as he listened.

"Please help this simple-minded soul to understand. It seems either the Jews must abandon Torah purity rules, or the Gentiles must honor them in order that we come together as a united *ekklesia*. Please help me to see my way through this difficulty."

Paulos did not have an easy answer, and he stood mute.

Titos spoke, "We shall leave further discussions to the two of you. For us, it's time to return to our homes. The hour is late. Good night all."

Paulos and Barnabas remained alone.

"My dear friend, Paulos," he said. "I am neither as wise nor as learned as you, but is not Ya'akov the brother of our Lord? Is not Cephas the man who was the best friend and confident of our Lord? Are not the Nazarenes of Jerusalem the bedrock of our Iesou movement? Even though I may agree with you on principle, I cannot support open disagreement with Jerusalem."

As a tear rolled down his cheek, Barnabas announced his decision, "Paulos, I love you as a brother, but I must support Cephas' in this matter. If he chooses to follow the wishes of Jerusalem, I too will follow the wishes of Jerusalem."

Paulos stared blankly at Barnabas.

Barnabas spoke again, "My dear Paulos, I know that you have strong feelings. But, for the sake of unity, for the sake of our continuing mission, for the sake of the *ekklesia* of God, I beg you to put aside your personal feelings and support Jerusalem also."

Paulos responded with a torrent of arguments.

"This is a retreat from the basic newness of the Iesou event."

"What happened to the new covenant if the old covenant is still controlling?"

"Jerusalem seeks to rebuild the boundaries that separate us after Iesou tore them down!"

"There will be a split in our *ekklesias*—some will be Gentile and some will be Jew, but there will be no mixing and mingling."

"Blind submission to the authority of Jerusalem does not create true unity especially when Jerusalem is so wrong."

"Unity means equality and communion between Jews and Gentiles."

"Torah observance is not a shining attraction but a stumbling block."

The words poured out of his mouth as he looked imploringly at Barnabas. Barnabas stared at the floor without speaking or looking Paulos in the eye.

"Well?"

Barnabas remained silent, and Paulos didn't see his bald chin quivering.

Paulos stormed out, never to return to the home of Barnabas. He aimlessly wandered the suddenly unfamiliar streets of Antioch. He felt as he had in Petra, a lifetime ago—a stranger in a strange and hostile land.

What had happened? He replayed the dream-like events in his mind. Surely, he would awaken, and everything would be as before. He tripped and skinned his knees, but he quickly moved on, knees

numb, oblivious to the ache. He grieved Barnabas' soft lullaby voice
and his preening before his silver mirror. Barnabas, O my friend, let
us turn back time and go back to yesterday morn! O, that he could
erase the day, that Phinehas would never arrive, that Cephas would
never waver, and that Barnabas would not desert him! O that he
could return to the way it was!

Then he raged. His best friend had betrayed him. Cephas also.
Ya'akov was behind all this. Ya'akov and his insecurities and his
envy. Spineless, mindless, heartless backstabbers.

Clouds blotted out the stars and the moon, and he stumbled over a
sleeping dog that snarled and snapped at him, then barked as Paulos
retreated; the barking triggered a chorus of howling hounds that
echoed through the valleys of city streets and alleyways; each mutt
warning Paulos against intruding on its territory.

Perhaps Barnabas was right to follow Cephas, and Cephas was
right to follow Ya'akov, Paulos thought. Perhaps he had been hasty
and headstrong. Perhaps he should be contrite and concede to
Ya'akov along with Barnabas and Cephas. He would bargain with
them, and they would reach an accord. If he fulfilled his promise
to send a collection for the poor of Jerusalem, then the Nazarenes
would accept his Gentile mission.

But as the dark hours passed, he realized that the meeting
scheduled for the following day had a foregone conclusion. His
chances of persuading Cephas and Barnabas to return to table
fellowship with the Gentiles were nil; he assumed that the other
Jews of Antioch would follow Cephas and Barnabas. Unless he
relented and encouraged the Gentiles to become Torah observant, a
split was inevitable.

He imagined averting eyes, face after face, friend after friend,
turning away from him, embarrassed at his humiliation. He had
nowhere to go. Hostile Jerusalem was Ya'akov's own turf. Antioch
was suddenly alien. Kypros belonged to Barnabas. Would he retreat
to Tarsos—a sage with no standing, a diplomat without credentials,

and a shepherd with no flock?

Hah! Never! He was right, and they were wrong. True unity meant accepting the Gentiles—apart from circumcision and apart from food laws—not blind obeisance to Ya'akov and Jerusalem. Why did Jerusalem not see that Torah boundaries were walls between the Jews and the Gentiles? Paulos would not accept Jerusalem's attempt to rebuild the boundary walls.

So be it. He would speak his mind and accept the consequences. The new day was dawning.

Paulos wandered the streets until the sun arced high overhead. He revisited the familiar and the favorite for the last time; he sauntered along avenues, drank from the fountains, and cooled in shaded arbors. By the time he made his way to the synagogue, the crowd had already gathered. The Hebrew faces that clustered together on one side of the meeting hall appeared as strangers while the Gentiles squeezed against the opposite wall seemed frightened children.

Paulos marched right down the middle to where Cephas and Barnabas awaited him at the far end. Cephas' familiar grin had disappeared, replaced by a frown frozen on his face; there was an *almost* look to him like he *almost* said something, but he remained silent and rigid. Barnabas' unkempt hair, stubbly face, and bleary eyes revealed dried out and drained emptiness inside.

Paulos brooked no explanations, and he launched into an immediate tirade against his friend from Jerusalem whose sloped shoulders hunched as if under a great weight.

"Cephas, I must question your hypocrisy," Paulos said. "You have not kept Torah, yet you now require the Gentiles to do so or you withdraw from fellowship with them. If you, though a Jew, live like a Gentile and not like a Jew, how can you compel the Gentiles to live like Jews?" Paulos gestured with an open palm toward the Gentiles lining one wall of the chamber.

"We ourselves are Jews by birth and not Gentile sinners," he said as he made a similar sweeping motion with his other hand toward the stone-faced Jews lining the opposite wall. "Yet, we know that a person is justified not by the works of the Torah but through faith in Iesou Christos."

Paulos spoke the toneless words without rancor or expectation that they would change things. They just needed saying, or, at least, *he* needed to say them, for the record.

Cephas' lips moved but no sound appeared. He tried again. His squeaky voice cracked several times as he spoke. "My dear friend, forgive me if I have hurt you. I act not as I choose but as I must, and I pray that you do not turn your back on your Hebrew past and your Jewish brethren." When he saw that Paulos appeared unbowed, Cephas looked at Barnabas, and his eyes asked for help.

Barnabas cleared his throat and straightened his stooped back. He smoothed his hair and tossed his head back. "In my heart of hearts," he began, "I know that you are right and Ya'akov is wrong, but he is Ya'akov, the brother of the Lord and the leader of the Nazarenes who are my brothers, and yours. The Christos has torn down the wall that kept the Gentiles separated from God; don't build it up again only to keep the Jews out. Temper your speech and your passion. Set your face kindly toward Jerusalem."

When he finished, Barnabas offered his hand to Paulos.

Paulos would not temper his speech. *Apart from Torah.* This was no mere scholarly debate at the knee of Eli; this was the truth of his existence; this was the truth of his standing before God; this was the truth of his redemption and that of all humankind. He would not compromise the truth. If the Jews took offense at the truth that he spoke, whose fault was that?

Paulos rejected the hand of friendship offered by Barnabas and stalked out, believing that Cephas, Barnabas, and the others were the stiff-necked Jews in the room. He didn't see Titos shrug his shoulders, arms out, palms up. He didn't see Barnabas place his hands firmly on the shoulders of the tiny Greek, and he didn't hear

Barnabas half-whispered plea, "Take care of my friend."

Ya'akov and the Nazarenes had flexed their muscles. They had asserted their claim for control and primacy. Cephas and Barnabas had fallen into line for the sake of unity. Paulos would not, and he would not allow the Gentiles to become poor cousins. He would not set his face toward Jerusalem, but toward Rome.

Paulos sat on a large rock on the edge of the Orontes throwing stones into the river, his long legs dangling his feet in the cool water. It seemed like yesterday when Cephas had stood on the same rock while delivering his sermon to the full assembly of Antiochenes. Paulos pondered the next phase of his life. There was no going back.

"Hello friend." Titos and a few others had come to commiserate with him. His well-wishers included Lucius and Agathe, their eight-year-old son, Loukas, Julius, and other Gentiles but only a few Jews.

Paulos spoke to his Gentile friends. "I am embarrassed at the actions of my brethren. If they refuse to mix with you," he hesitated, and his voice cracked as he finished, "they are suggesting you are inferior."

"What do we do now?" Lucius asked the question as he sat next to Paulos on the rock.

"Stand fast for the Torah free message. Perhaps the Jews will return to table fellowship with you," Paulos replied.

Lucius looked at Paulos with alarm. "What do you mean 'with you'? Don't you mean 'with us'? What about you? Are you giving up the fight?"

Paulos mussed the curly hair of young Loukas as he answered the boy's father. "You don't know me well, my friend, if you think I'm retreating."

Part Six
On the Road
49-56 C.E.

Before I formed you in the womb I knew you,
and before you were born I consecrated you;
I appointed you a prophet to the nations.

Jeremiah 1:5

Chapter Forty-four

Paulos slapped the ass with a loud *whack*. The pack ass finally moved forward with Silvanos pulling and Paulos whacking. Fortunately, only one of their four donkeys was stubborn. All their worldly-goods, including clothing, tents, and a few cooking utensils, were loaded into packs and carried by the donkeys. They also carried Paulos' knives and awls. The ass balked at the steep climb into the Cilician Gates of the Taurus Mountains.

"We'll make camp here," Paulos said as he looked back, down the gully, and over the valley of the Kydnos. As a youngster surveying the world from his father's rooftop, he had dreamed of the Cilician Gates and the mysterious unknown beyond the mountains. He now savored the long-anticipated moment of ascending the rocky gorge that had tantalized him in his youth.

The missionaries could have gone farther up the narrow ravine since the sun was still high in the sky, but Paulos chose this vantage because it offered a wide view of the plain they left behind. He had already lived longer than most—over forty years—and he sensed he would not pass through the valley of his youth again, and he would say his goodbyes.

The two men and four donkeys had recently departed Antioch; instead of wallowing in defeat, Paulos embarked on a mission of conquest. If Ya'akov and the Jerusalem Nazarenes stifled his message of inclusion in Palestine and Antioch, he would go to the far corners of the Empire, beyond the reaches of the "Judaizers" who would impose the old boundaries of Jewish religion. Unfettered of the control of Jerusalem, he would be free to answer his grand calling.

"Please take me with you," Titos had asked.

Titos would have been an able companion, but Paulos turned

him down. "We need your leadership in the Gentile *ekklesias* in Antioch," Paulos had said.

Lucius and Agathe must stay with their children. Julius, good old Julius, would have gone if asked, but—he was Julius. Paulos settled on Silvanos, a Jew, to accompany him for companionship and for safety; Silvanos was short and stout with thick and curly black hair and a beard to match. He carried a club in his belt. Paulos' bodyguard was steady and solid; stodgy and stolid, some might say, one who cared little for the niceties of religious thought. He went not for the cause but for the adventure of it.

It was mid-summer but chilly in the high pass of the Cilician Gates. Silvanos built a fire of tall flame while Paulos parsed the rocky gorge to find the best vantage to soak in the dusk as shadows seeped over the plain. Paulos climbed atop a granite perch to survey the river valley and the city that shimmered in the summer haze. The day before, he had lied to his widowed mother and sister when he promised to return. In his heart, he knew he would not pass this way again; already, the city was indistinct in the distance, visible only in his memories. He had departed the city of his youth for the final time, a lonely man, dogged by the disapproval of Jerusalem and Antioch, and driven to prove his enemies wrong.

The Damascus road had defined him as a child of God, *apart from Torah*. More than a mere notion, a*part from Torah* was his essence, his standing before God, his theology and his identity. By denying *apart from Torah*, Antioch had rejected *him*, challenging his very being. He now belonged to nothing and nobody except an executed man and his cause, the cause of *apart from Torah:* God's own cause—the good news of the Christos—the gospel of inclusion to the Gentiles. Uprooted from Antioch and without community, the lonely pilgrim was free to be what God had intended him to be, the apostle to the Gentiles. With each new convert and each new *ekklesia*, the transforming experience of the Damascus road, *apart from Torah,* would occur again, validating his own existence.

He turned his face away from the east and the past, and he looked up the maw to the west and the future, away from Jerusalem and toward Rome. Was Arsenios still there? A dozen years had passed since Arsenios sailed out of his life, but he floated still through Paulos' thoughts. The memories were more frequent again since Antioch, but they were different, less guilt and more regret. Paulos was older, wiser, and more mature than when he had last seen Arsenios; perhaps his thorn in the flesh had withered, a mere indiscretion of youth. Perhaps he and Arsenios would reunite as friends and companions but no more than that. The man alone hoped it could be so. As Paulos embarked on his westward journey, Rome would always be on the horizon; would Arsenios be there?

Twilight turned into moonless darkness, and Silvanos sat alone in the aura of the campfire; when the cold, lanky man finally emerged from the blackness, he stared blankly into the flames.

"Figs?"

Paulos huddled close to the fire but said nothing.

"Salt fish?"

Paulos looked up at Silvanos and shook his head.

"Bread?"

"Thank you, but I'm not hungry."

Paulos was self-absorbed with the consequences of what lay behind and the unknown difficulties that lay ahead.

"Well," said Silvanos, "I'm going to turn in. I pulled extra blankets for you. Good night." He crawled into the tent.

Paulos allowed the fire to burn down, and darkness closed around the pale aura of yellow light. A thin feather of gray smoke disappeared into the darkness. After a while, the last flickers of flame gave way to glowing red embers. Finally, when the coals cooled and died to white ash, he shivered and stood on his feet. One leg was already numb with sleep, and he rocked from one foot to the other before attempting steps. His breaths hovered about his face and followed him as he trudged toward the dark shadow that was his tent. A meteor shower splashed across the moonless sky as he pulled the flap shut behind him.

The men and donkeys climbed until midday when they finally reached the summit of the gorge. After a quick glance back, Paulos took the first step down the slope, eyes fixed not on the coarse gravel that crunched beneath his sandals but on the far western horizon. He had set his face toward Rome even as he knew it would be a year, or several, before he would climb the seven hills of the Imperial capital city. For now, his mind formulated immediate plans for this day, the next, and the remainder of the summer.

For a day and a half, they would trek down the mountain before they reached the Anatolian plain, and Paulos decided that their immediate destination would be Lystra, the home of Eunice the Jewess who did not keep Torah and Timotheos, her uncircumcised half-breed son of a Roman soldier. Paulos would seek rejuvenation and affirmation from an *ekklesia* that was his, beyond the influence of Jerusalem, *apart from Torah*.

A handful of years had passed since he had spread his good news on the Anatolian plain and established an *ekklesia* in that Roman city; he knew that much could have changed. Had the *ekklesia* survived in his absence? Could he dare to hope that it had thrived? He was anxious to rekindle a friendship with Eunice and the *ekklesia* in her home, but with each passing day on the road, Timotheos came to dominate his thoughts. He had something to say to the trim son of a soldier.

During their descent down the backside of the mountain, Paulos was back to his talkative self. He wasn't aware that Silvanos didn't always listen to him closely—or understand him—but when Silvanos nodded or grunted in the right spots, Paulos kept talking. And so the unlikely pair passed the days on the well-traveled road as they approached Lystra. Paulos talked and Silvanos grunted, nodded, and tugged on the halter leads of their pack animals.

"My husband is dead. All I have now is Timotheos," said Eunice when the road-weary missionaries arrived at her home in Lystra. She was shorter and chunkier than Paulos remembered. After her husband died, she had cropped her brown hair, now streaked with gray. Paulos passed callused fingers over his thinning gray hair and supposed he had aged also.

Paulos and Silvanos stayed with the widow Eunice and Timotheos for several weeks. Paulos had many new followers to greet and instruct in the *ekklesia* that had grown under the leadership of Eunice and Timotheos.

Timotheos was now nearly thirty, tall and strong like his Roman father, intelligent and poised like his Jewish mother, literate in both Greek and Latin, unmarried, and an uncircumcised follower of Iesou. Paulos' critical eyes watched him interact with *ekklesia* members, vendors in the market, and patrolling legionaries. He engaged all with a lithe manner, confident yet unpretentious, quick with a joke and a disarming smile. His demeanor soon confirmed Paulos' hopes; he would be the one.

"May I speak with you from the heart?" asked Paulos, leaning into the hilly incline, as he returned from the agora with Timotheos and Eunice.

Timotheos carried several freshly filled wineskins slung over his shoulders while Eunice balanced a basket on her head, filled with fruit and vegetables, fresh and sweet.

"We must leave soon," Paulos said. "We're planning to head north to Galatia. It's already early autumn, and they say the winters are harsh in central Anatolia. We must put our feet to the ground before the weather changes."

"Timotheos and I shall miss you and will anxiously await your return," replied Eunice.

Paulos walked a few paces in silence before he spoke as matter-of-factly as he could, "We would like Timotheos to travel with us," he said.

The basket fell from Eunice's head and spilled its contents. A cabbage rolled down the hill as she sagged into a sitting position. Her pleading eyes that scanned Paulos before fixing on her son said she already grieved. The cabbage bumped and bounced as it rolled down the dusty road.

Timotheos' face was harder to read, and he said nothing as he helped his mother to her feet and refilled her basket. His eyes seemed wider and his dimples deeper. His lip lines portended neither grin nor frown. He squared his shoulders, raked his coal-black hair off his copper brow, and threw his head back as they continued up the hill in silence. Somehow, his well-favored appearance convinced Paulos that he had picked the right man.

When they reached their home, Timotheos said, "I will speak to my mother before I give you my answer."

The next morning, Eunice and Paulos were the first to arise, as usual. The heavy-set woman in a flour-specked apron pounded on bread dough as Paulos joined her in the kitchen.

"I spoke with my son well past the moon's rising," she said, "and I barely slept through the night. My son is not yet married. Will grandchildren never crawl in my lap? This is an unfair request to make of an old widow woman. I must confess great anger at you." Eunice averted her eyes from Paulos as she wrestled with her bread dough.

Paulos had heard her pacing. He had not slept either.

"Now I must ask you, do you truly believe God requires you to take my only son from me? Do you truly believe this is God's calling for my son or is it merely your own selfish request? Before answering, please search your heart."

Paulos silently considered his response. Timotheos was bright, eloquent and able to speak to the Romans in their own Latin tongue. The uncircumcised son of a Jewish mother and Roman father, he personified the mixed Jewish/Gentile message of the good news. Was he not God's own choice?

Before Paulos answered, Eunice spoke again, continuing to pummel the bread dough that was beyond readiness for her stone oven.

"Don't speak; the answer is already clear to me, and we decided last night. It's but a small sacrifice for me to offer my son to the service of the Lord, but I'll miss him greatly."

Her wide frame quaked with sobs, and Paulos drew her trembling body close to his own slender frame. He understood her heartbreak and sacrifice, but he stifled a smile. After all, Timotheos was perfect for the task; God had placed him in Paulos' path for a reason, for God's own purpose. Was this not a calling and God's own doing? Eunice dabbed at her face with her sleeve and pushed Paulos away without looking into his eyes. She turned to shape a loaf of dough, and she spoke without looking at him.

"You must promise to take care of my son and to return him to me often. That the Lord calls him shall be my consolation. That he returns to visit me in my old age shall be my hope," she said. "Now go. You must go quickly."

The three missionaries departed that same day with their faces set toward the northern high plains of Galatia.

Chapter Forty-five

Slowly, ever so slowly, they trudged forward on their tedious journey across the central plains of Anatolia through barren land, consisting of rolling hills and a few woodlands, toward the Celtic city of Pessinus of Galatia. The autumnal countryside was bleak—even the gleaners had finished with the picked fields of grain. Flocks of sheep with thick woolen coats crowded into pens, ready for the first blast of winter.

The hiker's spirits lifted when a range of mountains, overlooking the city of Pessinus, first appeared in the morning sky. As if to welcome them, a warm breeze sifted down the brown slopes and gullies. On an unseasonably warm day, the rumpled travelers set an early camp near a swift stream. They would bathe before entering the Galatian city.

In the frigid waters, Paulos saw the trim and muscular frame of Timotheos for the first time. The young Roman's skin glowed as he kick-splashed his way to the shore, legs pink from the stinging cold water. Paulos and Silvanos stood thigh deep in the river, not yet finished with their gooseflesh baths. On the grassy bank, Timotheos arched his back, tossing his head, running splayed fingers through his limp locks, squeezing out moisture. When he leaned forward again, a tangle of hair spiked upward.

Paulos suddenly squatted, neck deep in the eddying pool, with a worried glance at Silvanos, who hadn't noticed what had mortified Paulos. Silvanos waded ashore as Paulos remained submerged. Despite the bone-numbing water, Paulos did not join his naked fellows on the riverbank. He remained sunk to his chin until the men dressed and departed. He was different, a clam in a sea of fishes, and the wretched man felt alone.

Later, Silvanos and Timotheos engaged in high-spirited banter over their meager supper of dried figs and stale bread, but Paulos sat unspeaking, eyes glazed over, and he ate little. Long after snores seeped from the tent of Silvanos and Timotheos, Paulos lingered around the fire.

He had hoped that he had matured beyond youthful passions, but the thorn in his flesh had not withered and now stung again, an enduring reminder of his guilt before God. He resolved to bathe alone and avoid the presence of naked men. It was good that Timotheos shared a tent with Silvanos. It must always be so, yet Paulos' tent seemed so apart. His lonely eyes stared blankly into the embers with only a hooting owl as a companion.

He longed for the panorama from his parent's rooftop, the smell of fresh goat leather in his father's shop, the taste of his mother's fresh bread dipped in honey, the feel of goat's milk warming his throat, and the splashing melody of the river rapids. It was all so long ago and far away. Rome and the university teacher with the wayward curl seemed even more distant. Long after the coals cooled to white ash, the solitary man shivered his way to his tent.

During the night, the weather changed. Paulos smelled rain in the freshening breeze when he poked his morning face out of the tent. Silver-gray clouds chased the wayfarers as they set out toward the hard brown mountains. By midafternoon, the sky had eerily darkened, hours early.

"We should set up camp under those trees," Silvanos said.

Silvanos pointed to a small oak grove at the side of the road. The few remaining brown leaves on the oaks resisted the winter winds and clung tightly to their branches, but the unrelenting gusts whisked them away, each in its turn.

"The storm will soon catch us," Silvanos said.

Paulos looked at Silvanos, then the oaks, and finally the roiling clouds. He turned and looked ahead along the trail; the mountain range appeared to be close. For a moment, he thought he saw city smoke, soon lost in the swirling winds. He reluctantly agreed to stop, "I suppose you're right. Make camp," he said.

The three men had barely raised their tents when the first wind-blown raindrops began to sting their faces. There was no time for a fire and hot supper, and the men retreated to the relative sanctuary of their tents. Silvanos and Timotheos sat in their tent eating apples, raisins, the last of their smoked cheese, and hard bread. Slanting rain pelted against the linen tent walls. A clap of thunder crackled through the small grove; a few seconds later, Paulos yanked open their tent flap and crowded inside.

"My tent blew down," he said.

He wore two thin linen robes over a light tunic. His clothing was soaked through, and he shivered in the darkness without a blanket. The wardrobe of the men from the coast was not suited for the harsh climate of the high plains. As the night passed, the drumming of the raindrops on the tent wall ceased; later the wind fell silent.

Paulos awoke from his nodding position when Silvanos returned from his morning piss.

"Snow," Silvanos said. "There's snow on the ground!"

Silvanos and Timotheos crawled out, and Paulos could hear them laughing and rolling in the snow, but they sounded far away. Paulos seemed frozen to the ground, and he couldn't move his legs or arms. When he didn't emerge from the tent, Silvanos poked his head back inside.

"Hey man, it snowed," Silvanos said. "Come and look at the snow!"

Paulos looked at him as through a dream.

"What is it?" Silvanos crawled into the tent. "Your face matches the gray tent wall," Silvanos said, as he reached his fingers to touch Paulos' face. "You're burning up!"

"Start a fire! A big fire! Paulos is feverish!" Silvanos shouted to Timotheos. Silvanos removed Paulos' wet clothes and wrapped him in blankets.

Timotheos kindled a fire and tossed all the deadfall he could find in the patch of scrub oak onto the smoldering heap; soon, tall flames leaped in the chill air. He boiled water to make porridge.

"Here man, you must eat." Silvanos forced Paulos to take a few swallows of porridge that seemed too hot, but Paulos didn't object.

Bright sunshine belied the biting cold. "Should we stay here a day and let you rest?" Silvanos asked, but Paulos heard the question as a cry from afar, an unreal voice from a dream, and then all went dark.

Chapter Forty-six

Many persons visited Paulos, as he lay unconscious and delirious.

There were Ya'akov, Cephas, and Barnabas huddled together, then at his side, shaking their heads in disapproval before conspiring again, whispering and nodding. Eli floated by on billowing incense clouds. Paulos saw eyes: white eyes sunk deep into a hollow face, seeing but not seeing, leering and laughing. Naked Timotheos dived beneath the waves, arched high like a dolphin, and then splashed back into the sea while teary-eyed Arsenios watched from a ship's deck. The ship sailed into the sun with the frolicking dolphin-boy trailing behind.

A whirlwind tossed Paulos in the tree-lined tabernacle along the road to Damascus, thunder rolling and lightning crackling around him. In purplish clouds with yellow edges, he saw a face, then a hand reached toward him—a warm, soft, and gentle hand that caressed his brow, cradled his head, and coaxed him up.

Heavy eyelids opened to a feline, gray-haired woman in unfamiliar clothing sitting next to Paulos' bed, holding a damp cloth, purring.

"Well, so nice to see that you are feeling better," his nurse said. "My name is Tatiana. Welcome to my home. Mariana, come. Our guest is awake."

A thick, slope-shouldered woman waddled through the door with a steaming bowl of goat stew. Paulos greedily slurped the soup while Tatiana talked. "Your friends brought you here three days ago. We weren't sure you would live. The fever finally left you last night."

"Let me get you another helping," Mariana took the empty bowl and left the room.

"Where are my friends?" asked Paulos.

"Working. They are mucking stalls at a stable."

Mariana returned with another hot bowl of chunky stew; Paulos took time to savor the tangy aroma, and he spooned in the second bowl more slowly than the first.

Mariana and Tatiana each wore sleeveless, full-length dresses. Stripes lined Mariana's dress, and a checkered pattern marked Tatiana's. Paulos was accustomed to the pale robes of Palestine and the warmer climes around the Great Sea. Both women wore jewelry.

Tatiana had been a widow for many years. When she was still a young wife, her mercenary husband never returned from a far off campaign, fate unknown. She stood tall, straight, and thin with well-combed silver hair. Graceful and stately. Mariana was nearly as tall as Tatiana but considerably rounder, shaped like a droplet of her stew hanging from a spoon. Recently widowed with a houseful of grown children and grandchildren, Mariana had accepted Tatiana's invitation to share her spacious home.

The outside door creaked open and slammed shut. Mariana called, "Come, come and see. Paulos is awake."

Timotheos burst into the room and rushed to give Paulos a hug. Paulos' arms hung limply at his side, and his body knotted up.

"We didn't know if we were going to lose you, old man," Timotheos said.

Paulos never thought of himself as an old man; uncomfortable with the overt affection, he pushed Timotheos back and discovered strange clothing on his Roman friend. He wore a checkered shirt and brightly colored trousers! He had shaved the dark beard acquired on the trail, and his copper cheeks and dimples had reappeared.

A few hours later, Silvanos arrived. Drunk. The stable master had introduced him to fermented honey mead. At least he didn't wear trousers and still wore the familiar robe and tunic of Palestine and the coastal regions of the Great Sea.

Paulos endured a rough winter holed up in Tatiana's house in Pessinus. His beak-nose drained constantly, and his coughing fits shook the house. His companions continued to muck stalls, and their income paid for the room and board they received from Tatiana. Paulos' confinement allowed him to engage in long conversations with Tatiana, Mariana, and their friends, and an *ekklesia* centered in Tatiana's home grew rapidly as the cold months passed.

Silvanos worked hard in the stables and was a dutiful aide to Paulos even if he did little work as a missionary. Meanwhile, Timotheos proved himself an able surrogate for Paulos. His affable manner endeared him to many Galatians who sampled the *ekklesia* gatherings simply because of the warmth of his personality.

On the edges of Paulos' thoughts, where the dim line between conscious and unconscious dulled, Timotheos the Roman and Arsenios the Greek sometimes switched places. When it occurred to Paulos that he imagined that Arsenios was here as his associate, he rebuked himself and pushed such thoughts aside. Once, when his recurring nightmare of Arsenios sailing away featured Timotheos' face, he awoke feeling doubly guilty—not only at his persistent stinging thorn but also due to a vague sense of betrayal. For a few days after that, he had snapped at Timotheos without cause, and the wounded look on the protégé's face said he was confused and hurt by Paulos' random coolness that neither man fully understood.

During the winter, Paulos heard about the cult of Cybele and Attis that had its principle temple in the nearby foothills of the mountain range. Mariana recited an old poem.

> Come away, go to the mountain forests of Cybele together, together go, wandering herd of the lady of Dindymus. Let dull delay depart from your mind; go together, follow to the Phrygian house of Cybele, to the Phrygian forests of the goddess.

Paulos listened with a mixture of curiosity and revulsion. Years earlier, he had run to Eli the sage with a report of the eerie rituals of the Mithras cult. Now, the mysteries of Cybele intrigued him, and he seized the first opportunity to explore the temple grounds. He was guided by a former member of the cult who had recently converted to the *ekklesia;* Gallus was a eunuch who had previously castrated himself during a drunken orgy of the cult.

Dust swirled and clogged their nostrils as they crossed the barren landscape surrounding a semicircular amphitheater that served as the steps leading up to the cut-stone Temple. At the top, Gallus pushed, and a massive stone door to the temple creaked open. The men stepped inside and wandered through the empty chambers, their footfalls echoing off the rock walls. In the flicker of their oil lamps, bloodstains on the walls leapt about, triggering visions of the orgiastic cultic rituals that occurred here, but Paulos' imagination fell short of reality.

"Attis loved Cybele the mother of the gods, but he was betrothed to another," Gallus said as he recounted the cult legends. "Cybele appeared at his wedding, and Attis castrated himself in his frustration. He died from his wounds, but Cybele raised him from the dead." Gallus' matter-of-fact words belied the anguished moans of Attis that seemed to waft on whispers through the chambers.

Paulos lifted his lamp to look closely at the inscrutable face of the man who had sliced off his balls with a piece of flint. Absurd, of course ... yet, he now lived without sexual urges. Was he the better for it? His blank face said nothing.

"Is it true that you castrated yourself?" Paulos asked. "Is it true that others have done the same?"

"Yes, it's true," Gallus said. "We drink, and we dance, and we slap our swords against our shields. Priestesses arouse the men, if you know what I mean. Usually the ceremony involves cutting the balls of a bull, but personal castration occurs sometimes." Gallus laughed at himself and shook his head. "First, I drank a gutful of mead, I must say."

The man had crucified the flesh with its passions and desires. A rush of air swept through the chamber, stirring the flame in his lamp, and Paulos again heard the wail of Attis.

"But why?" Paulos asked. "Why would you do such a thing?"

Gallus shrugged his shoulders. "To achieve the immortality of Attis and participate in his rebirth—just like drinking the blood of Iesou and eating his body."

Just then, voices came from an outer chamber, and Gallus gestured to Paulos. "We must leave now," he said, and they did.

Paulos never asked him if a sharp-edged flint stone had made him a better man.

The missionaries spent nine months in the Celtic cities of Galatia, and when they headed west in midsummer, *ekklesias* had been established not only in Pessinus but also in Ancyra and Tavium. The missionaries joined a caravan along the ancient Persian Royal Road without stopping along the way in Anatolia. For weeks, they trekked west toward Europe and the cities of Macedonia. Paulos planned to spend the fall and winter in Macedonia; in the spring, they would finally head toward Rome.

Strangely, his relationship with Arsenios had changed even though they had not seen each other for many years. Paulos felt nagging remorse that he had somehow betrayed his old friend in the icy stream. The hope for a reunion continued to tug at him, but the need to apologize—for what?—added to the pull toward Rome.

Chapter Forty-seven

When God created the earth, He separated Anatolia from Macedonia by water, and the route of the missionaries required a sea crossing. When they finally arrived on the eastern shores of the Aegean Sea, they boarded a small merchant galley sailing from Troas, headed toward the Macedonian port of Neapolis.

With fair winds, the passage to Neapolis should have been a trip of one to two days, but favorable weather was not to be their fortune. The first day had been pleasant enough, but in light winds, the ship had made little headway under oar power alone. Gales stole upon them at night while the men were sleeping, whistling through the sails with an ominous hum, before the mainsail burst with a crack like a tree trunk snapping in a storm. The rending of the sailcloth, a simultaneous ripping of many frayed seams, was as dangerous as a broken mast. Without sail power, the captain and crew lost control of the galley that groaned as she lurched sideways at the mercy of wind and waves.

"Man overboard! Man overboard!"

With the sudden twist sideways, a massive wave had splashed over the ship and swept a helpless sailor overboard; he soon disappeared in the angry seas as the wind whisked the ship away. The same wave thumped Timotheos hard against the gunwale, and his body lay limp, in danger of washing away with another crashing wave. With one hand firmly grasping the rail, Silvanos crawled to Timotheos' unconscious body, and he clutched him close in his lap.

"Man the oars! Man the oars!" The captain shouted above the howling wind.

The crew scurried about with one hand for the ship and one hand for themselves. "Get out of the way! Move!"

Not sure what to do, Paulos crawled away from the sailors. He would have gone to Timotheos, but Silvanos seemed in control.

"Portside pull, pull! Starboard push! Push, damn it, push!"

Broadsides to the wind with waves smashing amidships, the small vessel was in danger of breaking up. If she didn't come apart at the seams, she would bob in the waves, pushed uncontrollably by the wind toward dangerous shoal waters. The oarsmen must point the ship downwind to regain a semblance of control.

"You there. Help the oarsmen." The captain shouted to Paulos and Silvanos. "Leave the body and man the oars!"

Silvanos' strength helped him crawl to his position, dragging the dead weight of Timotheos along with him. He protected his Roman friend under his legs as he grabbed the oar to assist a sailor. Paulos clumsily sat on the deck next to an oarsman, doubling up on an oar. He was on the starboard side directly across from Silvanos and limp Timotheos on the portside. Thank God for the strong and cool-headed Silvanos who was proving his worth as an able bodyguard.

One side pushed and the other side pulled as the oarsmen attempted to spin the boat against the pounding seas. Slowly the vessel turned away from the wind, her nose pointing downwind with the stern facing wind and waves.

"Pull! Pull! Both sides pull!" the captain shouted.

With the bow pointed downwind and both sides pulling, the vessel moved naturally with the wind, averting the danger of breaking up. All hands faced the ship's stern, pulling blindly on the oars; only the captain could see the way forward. Paulos' glassy eyes fixed on the limp body of Timotheos, waiting for a sign of life that did not come. Was the son of Eunice dead? He had promised to take care of her boy. Had he failed?

When the ship shuddered on a massive sea swell, Paulos jerked his eyes toward the sea; he was sure he had spied a beast in the wave trough. Did God send a great fish to swallow him like Jonah? Surely, God could see that Paulos embraced his mission, unlike Jonah who had evaded God's call. Why then, if he did God's bidding, did the sea rise up to challenge him?

Or, was he Job, confronted by the chaos of Leviathan, the uncontrollable monster of the deep? Job, a righteous man brought low by unkind fortune, deserved a blessing but received a curse. *My face is red with weeping, and deep darkness is on my eyelids, though there is no violence in my hands and my prayer is pure.*

Doubt clouded his addled mind. Squinting through the salt spray, Paulos searched the roiling waters, but his smarting eyes could not capture the elusive creature of the sea. How could Paulos answer God's call if he died a watery death? *Teach me, and I will be silent; make me understand how I have gone wrong.* He clenched his eyelids tight and grimaced at the sting. An image appeared, a caterpillar on a leaf, rafting the currents of the Kydnos River, before the winds and waves of the Great Sea buffeted him. The tempest raging above pulled his gaze upward and taunted him. *Have you an arm like God, and can you thunder with a voice like his?*

Pelting rain stung Paulos' upturned face. Unconsciously, he released the oar and stretched his arms outward, palms up. Resigned to his lot, he silently mouthed the words, "Do with me as you will."

"Land ahoy! I see land!" The cry of the captain jolted the men back from the dead, and a spark of hope returned.

Paulos was almost too tired to look. Blood dripped from his blistered hands that burned in the salt spray. His lungs heaved and his taut muscles felt ready to snap. With much effort, he turned his head and looked forward. At first, he saw nothing except sea swells as high as a house, but then as the crest of a wave lifted the ship up, he saw the dark outline of land before the ship settled again into the valley. Landfall was near; was that a good omen? Racing along at the mercy of the wind, the ship might flounder on shoreline shoals. Fear wrestled with hope.

"It is Samothrace!" The captain identified the island, as he leaned hard on the rudder, attempting to influence the drift direction of the ship. "Ready men. Be ready! I mean to navigate around the peninsula ahead, into the lee of the land. Portside be ready to push—starboard keep pulling. Ready men. On my command—now!"

The men had no strength left, but they redoubled their effort nevertheless. One side pushed on the oars and the other pulled to spin the boat. The captain slammed the rudder hard. The bow of the boat swung to starboard and toward land.

"Pull! Both sides pull! Damn it, I said pull!"

For a few moments, the ship was again broadsides to the wind, and sea swells crashed over the starboard gunwale, splashing over Paulos and streaming across the deck. Silvanos released his oar to grab onto the lifeless body of the young man from Lystra; rushing water swept the pair aft along the port rail until they slammed into the legs of the captain, knocking him off the rudder as all three sprawled in a jumbled heap on deck.

Screeching sea gulls awakened Paulos. He squinted into the sun, already high in the sky, as he lay flat on his back on a sandy beach. He rolled over and looked around at the others sleeping in the sand. The captain sat under a palm tree, pondering his ship aground in the shallow sandy bay.

Timotheos sat next to the captain. Timotheos! Alive! Praise God! Paulos ran to the boy and hugged him. The grace of God had saved them all!

The captain roused all hands from their sleep and led them on a short walk to a fishing village. As the winds quieted, the captain, crew, and passengers, assisted by a few local fishermen, worked to pull the ship from the sand shoal. At high tide, they easily floated the ship off the bottom.

The tattered mainsail was beyond repair, and there was no spare. The captain paid a dear price for several small sails purchased from the fishermen, and Paulos stitched them together into what must pass for a mainsail. It was much smaller than normal, but it would work in good weather.

After three days on Samothrace, the ship again set sail for Neapolis; favored by the winds, the ship reached Neapolis in less than a day, but the shipwreck was an ominous beginning to their European journey.

Nevertheless, Paulos was doubly convinced that God ordained his mission. Had God not saved him from fever in Pessinus? Had God not established *ekklesias* in Galatia? Had God not rescued the missionaries from shipwreck? More than ever, Paulos believed that he did God's bidding, that his was a divine calling, and that God chose him to spread the good news to the Gentiles. Adversity overcome was proof of God's favor. Battle scars were badges of honor. He soon forgot his helpless plight at sea, and he reclaimed control of his journey. Even though Paulos had said that a man could not accomplish his own worthiness before God, he would run the good race. He would press on toward the goal, seeking the prize.

Chapter Forty-eight

Colonia Augusta Julia Philippensis. Philippi.

After setting foot on European soil at the port of Neapolis, the missionaries walked a few miles inland to the wealthy city of Philippi of Macedonia. Nestled between gold and silver laden mountains to the north and swamp and sea to the south, Philippi guarded the main east-west highway, the *Via Egnatia.* A century earlier, Romans had spilled their blood on the plains near the city, the site of the decisive battle of the Roman civil war, and the victorious generals rewarded their troops with local land grants.

Ancient rock walls guarded the inner city, but the stones were less foreboding than the omnipresent legionaries. Paulos understood that this was the place for the Latin tongue of Timotheos, and the son of a Roman soldier did their talking.

"Is there a synagogue in the city?" Timotheos asked in the marketplace.

"There are no Jews here," grunted the vegetable vendor, "only Romans. Sometimes you can find Jews at the river, but there is no synagogue."

Paulos felt the glare of several soldiers as the missionaries exited the agora. Not much happened in Philippi without the helmets noticing.

The men camped on the river adjacent to the highway. Silvanos and Timotheos set up the tents while Paulos surveyed the river, lost in thought. As Paulos plotted strategy on the riverbank, he barely noticed two young men walk past him to fill an amphora with water. According to their garb, simple brown tunics without robes or sandals on their feet, the men were slaves. They waded into the stream near a fat man who sat on a rock washing his feet in the river. Paulos had earlier exchanged a greeting with the man who happened to be a Jewish seller of precious stones, traveling along the *Via Egnatia.*

"Away with you," the portly merchant said to the slaves. "Fill your vase elsewhere. You pollute the river here."

The slaves moved a short distance down river and filled their vase. Each one grabbed a handle at the side and carried the sloshing water toward the highway where their companion waited with a donkey.

Two helmets intercepted the slaves. "Stop right there. What's that you are carrying? Is that a pisser?" One of the soldiers urinated into the vase while the other laughed.

Paulos saw it all and exploded. He galloped up the grassy slope, his long legs barely touching the ground. "Goons! Apologize to these men."

"Piss off. Mind your own business."

At that moment, a larger contingent of soldiers came down the road with their commander on horseback, and Paulos gave a full report as he walked alongside the officer on the gelding.

The commander said nothing as they approached the offenders, but the sour look on his face said the men were well known to him as troublemakers. He dismounted and approached the foot soldiers, who eyed him nervously. He picked up the vase and held it high, pouring half over each offender, who stood rigidly at attention.

"Now rinse it and fill it again," the officer said as he remounted and led the troop toward the city.

Paulos' anger still flared, and he raced back down the hill to the fat man. "Are you a Jew? I'm a Jew, and you embarrass me. Does your circumcision make you better than these?" Paulos turned and gestured at the slaves who were now loading the vase onto a donkey. "You sit with your stinking feet in the river, and you complain that these poor souls pollute the water. Now it's your turn to apologize. Apologize, I say."

The fat Jew would not contend with the man whose blood was running hot, and he apologized to the slaves.

The next day, Paulos sat outside his tent as a well-dressed woman in a purple robe approached him. Gold earrings dangled from her ear lobes and bracelets jangled on both wrists. Her name was Lydia, a traveling merchant, and the owner of the slaves Paulos had defended. She thanked Paulos for his unexpected kindness and asked why he confronted the brutality of the Roman soldiers and the haughty attitude of the Jewish merchant. It was rare that anyone actually *asked* Paulos to speak, but he grabbed the opportunity to tell Lydia his story and the story of Iesou.

Lydia was his first convert on European soil. A few days later, Paulos baptized her in the river. "Lydia, you are baptized into the death of Christos Iesou and are buried with him," intoned Paulos as he slowly lowered her under the water in a complete immersion. Then, he quickly raised her up from the water, saying, "Lydia, you will be raised with Christos Iesou and will walk in the newness of life. If you have been united with him in a death like his, you will certainly be united with him in a resurrection like his."

Paulos continued to speak as she stepped from the river and Timotheos wrapped her in dry robes over her soaked garments, "Lydia," Paulos said. "You are baptized into Christos and have clothed yourself with Christos. There is no longer Jew or Greek, there is no longer slave or free, there is no longer male and female; for all of us are one in Christos Iesou."

Paulos repeated the rite as he baptized the slaves. A number of interested observers watched from the roadway at the strange ritual of the river baptisms, and Paulos seized the opportunity and spoke to the curious. Paulos didn't know him yet, but one of the listeners was a young man named Epaphroditus who returned the next day with his older sister in tow to witness the spectacle at the riverside. Euodia was a wealthy widow of a Roman officer. The brother and sister returned the next day also. At the end of the week, Paulos baptized them in the river along with others.

The three missionaries moved from their river encampment to

become houseguests at Euodia's villa that became the site of Paulos' first *ekklesia* on European soil.

"Why do you attract the widows?" Silvanos teased Paulos.

Paulos saw the truth of it—Eunice in Lystra, Tatiana in Galatia, and now Euodia in Philippi—even if he didn't understand the why of it; he had no answer other than that he felt comfortable with these women, and they with him.

Paulos rolled over on his featherbed; spider webs of sleep tangled his thoughts. A snow-covered mountain filled his open window, and the chilly vapors of a seacoast winter seeped in. He crawled deep under his wool blanket, allowing his protruding beak to savor the smells of morning-bread. The lazy, idyllic humors of Antioch warmed him, and he expected Barnabas' servant to step into the room to announce breakfast. Suddenly, his eyes popped open, the cobwebs cleared, and he remembered that he had left Antioch nearly two years earlier, and now he luxuriated in the hospitality of Euodia in Philippi.

He threw back his covers; there was work undone and a race to be run. The Philippian *ekklesia* grew stronger each day; the last days of winter would soon greet the fresh flowers of spring, and the missionaries must ready the *ekklesia* for their leaving. West to Thessalonica and then onward to Rome. Already there was an inviting fragrance in the warming breezes that sifted in from the west.

But instead of a measured farewell, the Edict of Claudius would prompt an unplanned departure. When Paulos had dressed and appeared in the villa courtyard, Roman soldiers arrested him. Timotheos was already there, hands bound behind his back. Silvanos was missing.

The iron bolt slammed shut on the prison door with an echoing *clank*. "What is the meaning of this outrage? I'm a Roman citizen!" Paulos shouted from the cell. "I must speak to the magistrates! I'm a Roman citizen!"

Later in the day, the prisoners appeared before a magistrate. "It is charged that you are Jews, proselytizing the Romans," the magistrate said. "What say you?"

"I'm a citizen of Rome," Paulos said. "Here is Timotheos, also a citizen of Rome and the son of an army veteran." Paulos didn't answer the question directly and didn't acknowledge his Jewishness. He knew the charges were true; they proselytized in direct violation of the Edict of Emperor Claudius, and he chose an indirect defense to the charges.

"We're citizens of Rome," he repeated.

The puckered face of the magistrate said that he was confused. After a moment of deliberation, he spoke to the jailor, "Release them into the custody of soldiers to be escorted to the edge of the city." Turning back to the prisoners, he warned, "Leave this city now, and you will be released, but if you remain in the city, you will be charged."

Their victory was short lived; Paulos recognized the two soldiers he had embarrassed earlier amongst the detail of legionaries. As soon as they reached the countryside beyond curious eyes, a soldier kicked Paulos in the groin.

"Ooof!" Paulos fell to the ground, and Timotheos soon joined him.

It would not be the last beating Paulos would receive at the hands of the Romans, each one adding stripes to his coat of arms. He only felt the blows to Timotheos and not to his own flesh.

But where was Silvanos? Had the bodyguard abandoned them to save his own skin? Or, had a harsher fate befallen him?

Chapter Forty-nine

Paulos and Timotheos huddled in the bushes. Traffic along the highway had slowed with the coming of the foggy night. As a group of travelers passed by, the outlaws held their breaths. The threat moved down the road until it vanished into a chorus of croaking frogs.

Timotheos felt his nose, as if to ask, "Did it bleed, still?" Paulos wanted to tell him that all would be ok, but would it? Had they reached the end of their journey? He had nearly succumbed to fever in Galatia, they had barely survived shipwreck, and now they suffered a beating at the hands of Roman soldiers. And what had become of Silvanos? Should they turn back and return Timotheos to his mother's bosom? An image of a cabbage rolling down a roadway intruded into Paulos' thoughts. He picked up the cabbage and returned it to the vegetable basket of Eunice.

How could they go anywhere, forward or back? They had no funds or supplies. Even his tentmaker's tools were gone. He was about to put their predicament to Timotheos, to gauge his mind, when muted voices threatened from the roadway.

"They come again!" Timotheos muttered.

A lamp glowed in the evening mist, swinging in rhythm with the steps of a man on foot.

"Down! Down!" Timotheos whispered. "Lie down in the weeds and let them pass!" He pressed his own nose against the musty soil.

"Paulos? Paulos?" A voice came from the road.

Like a squirrel in the grass, Timotheos' head popped up, and he stared in the direction of the light, a black lump of mud caked to his nose.

"Paulos? Paulos?" The voices drifted closer.

Timotheos jumped up, waving his arms. "Silvanos, we're here! Epaphroditus, we're here!"

They traveled forward. Paulos decided without consulting Silvanos or Timotheos. Neither of his associates exhibited disagreement; perhaps they knew resistance to Paulos' plans would be futile. They walked west on the *Via Egnatia* toward the Macedonian capital city of Thessalonica and Rome beyond.

For five days, the trio of missionaries merged into the traffic flow on the *Via Egnatia*—pedestrians, soldiers, and animal carts—never out of sight of a village, a vegetable market, or a well. The Roman superhighway connected the Bosphorus Strait on the east with the Adriatic Sea on the west, and Rome lay just across the sea. Their journey to Thessalonica would be around one hundred miles.

Epaphroditus had supplied them with clothing, food, and a purse full of Roman gold coins—each aureus was worth twenty-five denarii—to speed them on their way. Paulos provided their energy. His long strides set a pace that the others struggled to follow, even with a slight hitch in his gait, a reminder of the bruised hip sustained in the beating. He had long since worn out the willow cane he had inherited from Eli, but he always found a replacement, which he claimed he didn't need—an ornament not an implement—but which set the rhythm for his long strides and propelled him forward at a quick pace.

Along the way, Paulos pressed Silvanos for an explanation why the Romans had not arrested him. At first, Silvanos was evasive, but he eventually explained that the soldiers had not arrested him because he was … well, he had been with a woman that night. Paulos wanted to chastise him for succumbing to the pleasures of the flesh, but somehow it didn't seem appropriate at that time, and he held his tongue, satisfied that they were all safe and moving forward again.

The commercial center of the Roman province of Macedonia,

Thessalonica perched at the end of a long bay of the Aegean Sea. Many Jews resided in Thessalonica, unlike Galatia and Philippi, and a synagogue served as the point of entry for the missionaries. First, they secured accommodations and employment through the Jews of the synagogue, and later, they preached in the synagogues without fear of Roman interference. What the Jews did in their own synagogues was of little interest to the Romans. Paulos adopted the pattern established years earlier when he and Barnabas missionized in Kypros and Anatolia—proclaiming Iesou as fulfillment of the Sabbath readings and Hebrew festivals. By the time the spring blossoms turned to green apples, the missionaries had realized the first fruits of their Thessalonica mission.

As always, the Gentile listeners at the door of the synagogue, the *theosebeis*, were especially responsive to the inclusive, Torah-free message of the missionaries. One of these Gentile listeners was Jason, an early convert, who brought his family, including his elderly father, Justus, to the *ekklesia*.

"I'm an old man, soon to die," Justus said to Paulos as they shared a bottle of wine with Jason.

Jason and his father were short men with bandy legs. A full head of white hair and a wizened face witnessed to the elder's age. His high-pitched voice crackled as he spoke.

"Is any man ready for his death? I'm as ready as anyone is, but that doesn't lessen my fears. I'm afraid of the unknowing—yes, and the missing of it—life I mean—and the friends and the family."

"But that's the good news, my friend, we needn't fear death because the Christos will return and eliminate death for his beloved," Paulos said.

Pharisees taught that there would be a general resurrection of the dead on the last day; Paulos preached that God resurrected his son as the "first fruits", the sign that the kingdom was at hand, the end of death as promised. Eternal life in the presence of God would be

God's greatest gift to his beloved family.

"The prophet Isaiah promised, *He will swallow up death forever*," Paulos said to Justus. "Where, O death, is your victory? Where, O death, is your sting?"

Justus was not entirely convinced. "I fear I will die before the Christos returns," he said.

****

When Maryam, the mother of Yeshua, Ya'akov, and the others had died months earlier, her passing seemed natural to Ya'akov. She was a withered old woman who had lived a long life filled with children, grandchildren, and even Anina, a great grandchild, Ya'akov's own gentle granddaughter. Feeble as an elderly matriarch, Maryam's bright eyes remained alert to the end. It was her time, and even the great sadness of her life, the cruel death of her eldest son at the hands of the Romans, had dimmed with time and the bounty of a family that sprouted around her. Ya'akov briefly mourned her passing, and accepted it without regret; he only wished he had done more to advance his brother's kingdom during her lifetime.

But now Shera, the wife of Ya'akov and mother to his daughter, was dead, and hers was a different death. One day she had been healthy, robust, and filled with life, and the next morning, Ya'akov awakened next to her cold, stiff body; by evening, she lay in a tomb outside the city, washed and anointed with oil and spices and wrapped in bands of linen by her daughter and granddaughter. Much later, her family would store her bones in a stone box, an ossuary, to await the general resurrection expected by the Pharisees. A month passed, and emptiness replaced Ya'akov's initial numbness.

Ya'akov's household now consisted solely of Joses, his youngest brother. Seema, the treasured daughter, the only child God had given to Ya'akov and Shera, had married and lived with her husband and their daughter, Anina. Since Shera's death, Seema and Anina visited Ya'akov regularly to cook, clean, and to buoy his spirits. In this, they were mostly successful, especially young Anina, aged ten years, who was the answer to her grandfather's prayers. She prayed with him, too, kneeling alongside him on his prayer mat; often he remained silent, listening to her angelic voice intone the prayers of the elders, smoothing her brownish, matted hair with his callused hand, peeking at her high cheeks that always seemed to be pinched pink, and inhaling the scent of cinnamon that always swirled about her. Prayer had always been an important part of his daily ritual, but praying with his granddaughter added luster to grey days and pride in his progeny that respected the teachings of the elders.

Evening had come to Jerusalem, and Ya'akov sat on his lamp lit veranda with his councilors: Jude his primary lieutenant, Joses the youngest brother, and cousin Symeon. Simon was absent as usual with his own demanding family. It had been nearly twenty years since the Romans crucified Yeshua, their oldest brother, and he had not returned as they expected.

Now Shera had died, and Ya'akov felt old. Many years of bearing his heavy frame resulted in a stooped posture and chronically sore knees, stiff in the morning and painful when he knelt to pray. He was careful to slide a stool next to his kneeling pad to use as a crutch.

Joses dared speak the thoughts that flitted through his brother's minds from time to time like a dark shadow spoiling the sun. "Perhaps Yeshua will not return in our lifetime."

Ya'akov did not rebuke his brother's skepticism. He wished he understood the inscrutable ways of God. Ya'akov half-heartedly warned his brothers that the people failed to observe Torah, the Jews were not yet worthy, and that was the reason their brother had not returned.

"Hah, when will the Jews be worthy?" Joses scoffed.

Later, after his brothers departed, Ya'akov knelt for evening prayer. His aching knees barked at him as he leaned against his stool, lowering his heavy body to the floor. The skepticism of his youngest brother yapped at him also—not because Joses was wrong but because he might be right.

Ya'akov felt ill. His damned stomach agitated him again, and the mutton he ate for supper rumbled in his gut. His belly churned, and he spewed hot, stinking bile into his chamber pot. As he wiped his lips with a rag, unbelief heaved inside his heart. He could control neither his queasiness nor his qualms.

Was Yeshua truly the Mashiah? Shera had died; time was taking its toll; where was Yeshua?

Chapter Fifty

The branches in the Thessalonica orchards sagged under the weight of plump red apples. Paulos plucked a low-hanging specimen and bit into its crisp sweetness as he wandered in the countryside just outside the city gates. His forenoon strolls, before the hot summer sun reached its peak, had become his favorite time to think and plan for his Thessalonica flock. The harvest had been plentiful, and the *ekklesia* flourished.

Absorbed in his thoughts, he didn't notice the hornets that swarmed over a fallen apple, and when his sandal mashed the overripe fruit, an angry wasp stung him. Paulos leaned against a boulder and daubed mud over the pink, slightly swollen, prickly patch of skin on his forearm. It was then that he first noticed the youngster trotting in a beeline straight toward him. Somehow, he sensed bad news.

The breathless boy stammered, "Jason sent me. Please meet him in the market after sundown. Go alone."

Jason had been an early convert, a Gentile, the son of old Justus. Paulos had often been a guest in his home. Why meet in the market? Alone? After dark?

Jason appeared edgy as he walked with Paulos on a back street of Thessalonica. His eyes darted to every movement and every sound. In fits and whispers, he reported his encounter with a pair of Roman soldiers.

"'Have you been proselytized by a Jew?' They startled me with the question as I exited the synagogue," Jason said. "One grabbed my arm while the other interrogated me." Jason stopped talking and lowered his face as they met a passing stranger. After a quick glance to make sure the stranger was beyond earshot, Jason continued.

"'Why'd you go into the synagogue?' my inquisitor asked. 'To listen to the ancient stories of the Jews,' I said. 'I go of my own free will to hear the old legends.'"

There was no law prohibiting the Romans from attending the synagogue; the Edict of Claudius prevented the Jews from actively encouraging Roman proselytes—directed not at the Roman listeners but the Jewish tellers. Paulos was shocked that the soldiers accused one of their own.

"The soldier who spoke narrowed his eyes and spit at my feet, staring at me as if his icy glare would elicit my confession. 'Release him,' he finally said to the soldier who pinched my arm. 'But I warn you and your Jewish friends. I've heard reports of Jews proselytizing Romans, and we'll keep our eyes on you and the synagogue. Stay away from the Jews if you know what's good for you.'"

When he finished, Jason stopped and looked straight into Paulos' eyes. "You must leave the city," he said, and his imploring look said the same. "It won't be long before the Romans arrest you. It's dangerous for both of us that we even speak." He jumped at the noise of a crashing pan in a nearby house before smiling weakly.

Paulos had listened patiently, but he seethed inside. As he started to speak, Jason touched a finger to his lips.

"Say nothing, but depart the city at once with Timotheos and Silvanos. Camp along the creek—you know the place—and I'll meet you there. Then you can speak your heart."

Paulos stomped around the campsite, smashing dead branches against tree trunks, kicking clumps of dirt, and hurling rocks into the lazy brook that sidled past their campfire. Roman meddling had increased as the missionaries neared Rome. Never a problem in Antioch, Anatolia, or the remote cities of Galatia, the strict enforcement of the emperor's edict in Macedonia was an unexpected challenge.

"Damn the stiff-necked Romans!" Paulos ranted. "We bring them good news and they respond by beating us and throwing us in jail. They despise the richness of God's kindness, forbearance, and patience, and by their hard hearts, they invite God's wrath. They choose their own fate," he said. "And they'll incur God's fury, they'll see." He nodded and smirked, as if pleased that God would punish his enemies. The one who tore down walls—who preached a ministry of reconciliation, forgiveness, and inclusion—invoked holy wrath.

For a moment, he stared blankly into the creek. The muddy swirls he had stirred slowly cleared in the flow of freshwater. His anger against the stiff-necked persecutors receded, replaced by concern for the hard reality facing his persecuted flock. How could the fledgling Thessalonian *ekklesia* survive in the face of Roman oppression?

"What will happen to you if we leave?" he asked Jason.

"We'll lie low for awhile," Jason said. "I'm sure we'll be alright, and this will pass soon enough."

Paulos was not convinced, but no easy solution came to him. Perhaps this was God's way of encouraging him onward to Rome. Perhaps it was time for an *ekklesia* in the hub of the empire to spider the message outward. Perhaps Arsenios awaited him there—it was irrational, he knew. He pictured Arsenios splashing in the Kydnos, the sun glistening in his blond hair, a stray curl dangling over his forehead. With a resolute nod of his head, he told the others to prepare for a journey to Rome.

"Are you crazy?" Timotheos nearly choked on an olive pit. "The Romans beat us bloody in Philippi, they seek to arrest us in Thessalonica, and you would have us continue down the *Via Egnatia?* Through Macedonia? To Rome itself?" Timotheos looked at Silvanos who shook his head and shrugged his shoulders; Jason raised his eyebrows.

"We cannot go to Rome," Timotheos said for himself and the others. "We would travel many miles through Macedonia before we reach the sea and Rome beyond. We have worn out our welcome in Macedonia, and we must head in a different direction. It's not the time for Rome."

"God calls me to spread the good news, and where better than Rome itself?" Paulos said.

"You can't preach from prison."

"I have a friend in Rome that I would like to visit."

"Will he visit a jailbird?"

Paulos squatted down and flipped sand pebbles into the stream. He *wanted* to stay in Thessalonica to protect his *ekklesia* in the face of persecution, but he recognized the danger in that. He *wanted* to travel to Rome, but he knew his fellows were correct. He wished God would clear the paths he *wanted* to follow.

"If not Thessalonica, then where?" he asked. "If not Rome, then where? Where would you have us go?"

Silence. It seemed as if the brook ceased gurgling, the songbirds ceased singing, and the leaves in the bushes ceased rustling.

"Corinth."

Everyone turned to stare at Jason, the speaker.

"Corinth," he said again, louder. "Corinth is a crossroads, not as great as Rome, but important enough, and the welter of religions of that city will lessen the danger of Roman persecution. The incense of many religions mingles in Corinth, and the Romans pay little heed. Your missionizing will not draw attention, and you will be safe in Corinth."

Timotheos looked at Silvanos, and they nodded at each other. Paulos continued to splash sand pebbles in the water. He *wanted* to stay in Thessalonica; he *wanted* to travel to Rome.

The trio of missionaries journeyed south to escape Macedonia and entered the province of Achaea; their destination was the cosmopolitan city of Corinth at the south end of Achaea, but they made slow progress. Instead of his usual determined gait, Paulos set a choppy pace, and he often lagged behind the others.

"Come on, you're dragging. You walk as if your feet are in sand,"

Timotheos said to his mentor.

Paulos stood on the trail looking back.

"Come on, man!"

Paulos jammed his walking stick down hard and stomped toward the others. Before he caught up with them, they turned up the trail again, and Paulos shouted.

"Stop, damn you!"

This time they waited until he reached them.

"We must go back," Paulos said. "It's my fault; the Romans want me, and the Thessalonians shouldn't suffer on my behalf. We must go back."

Paulos turned as if to go back, but Timotheos stood his ground.

"We can't go back," Timotheos said, "and we have discussed the reasons overmuch already. It's too dangerous for you in Thessalonica where the Romans seek you as a Jew proselytizing Romans. You're a wanted outlaw in the whole of Macedonia."

As he finished, Timotheos turned and started up the trail, followed by Silvanos. After a brief hesitation, Paulos also followed. At first, he glared at the backs of his associates, but as the miles passed beneath his well-worn sandals, he gained a grudging appreciation for the independence of the young Roman—and his courage in standing up to him. It was good to have a clear thinking assistant to temper his passion. Even as he gradually agreed they had chosen the right path, Paulos was unaware of the dangerous scheme fermenting in the mind of Timotheos.

As their journey turned into a week, and then another, Paulos' long strides returned. He again took his place at the head of the pack as they curled around Mount Olympus along the seacoast, trudged up the rugged Tempe Valley of the Pinios River to the town of Larissa, raced southerly across the Thessaly plains, meandered through a coastal pass between mountains and sea known as the *hot gates*, and accelerated across the region known as Boeotia. After three hundred miles in four weeks, they arrived in the classical city of Athens. They didn't missionize along the way; they soldiered forward until mountains, plains, and forests barricaded them from Macedonian authorities.

When they reached Athens, Timotheos revealed his intentions. "I'll return by ship to give comfort to the Thessalonians," he said. "I'm not circumcised, which is always the conclusive test for the Romans. I can speak to the Romans in their own tongue. As far as the Romans are concerned, I'm not a Jew, and I can always mention my legionary father."

Paulos canted his face sideways to allow his better ear to hear the bold plan. His breathing quickened.

"I'll book passage on a ship and sail to Thessalonica," Timotheos said. "After I encourage the Thessalonians, I'll return with a report."

Paulos stroked his pointy nose as Timotheos' eyes offered assurance of his earnestness. It was a solid plan, and Paulos' appreciation for the maturation of his able assistant grew the more. But, it was a dangerous plan too, and Paulos' pinched insides spoke of his worry for his affable friend. Although he had his reasons for keeping personal feelings at a safe distance, Paulos wished away the reserved coolness he sometimes exhibited.

Much as he would miss the companionship of Timotheos, Paulos would give him free rein like a young stallion, to run where he would. A day later, Paulos stood alone on a dock in the harbor in Athens and watched him sail away.

Chapter Fifty-one

Paulos did not anticipate the malaise that would afflict him after the departure of his protégé. A month passed without any word from Timotheos, not even a letter, and Paulos regularly paced the docks of the Athens harbor, as if his watching would encourage Timotheos' return.

Paulos evangelized listlessly, and he seldom visited a synagogue; the monuments, artwork, and historic sites of Athens—the great city of Classical Greece and home to Plato's Academy and Aristotle's Lyceum—all failed to interest him. He worried, and he was lonely. Stodgy, silent Silvanos was no substitute for the boyish exuberance of Timotheos.

"It's time to move on." Silvanos placed his hand on Paulos' shoulder as he spoke. Paulos stood on a dock, staring blankly at the harbor. "We must go. He's in God's hands; let's move on to Corinth," said Silvanos.

Paulos said nothing to Silvanos, but he muttered a prayer. "Dear Lord, return him safely to me." Paulos turned to Silvanos and started to speak, but his words caught in his throat. He sucked in a heavy breath and started again. "I'm ready," he said with one last glance at the harbor.

"Not everyone is able to go to Corinth." That was the saying around the Aegean Sea. The bustling commercial city, known officially as *Colonia Iaus Iulia Corinthiensis,* overlooked the shipping lanes between east and west. The Romans had destroyed the Greek city two centuries earlier, but Julius Caesar rebuilt it and repopulated it with a mixture of Romans, Greeks, Jews and émigrés from around the Empire. A polyglot harbor proletariat of dockyard workers and ship's crews added to the overall heady mix of the city.

With the foreigners came their deities. Isis was there from Egypt with Osiris, her consort. Demeter and Persephone had not traveled far from their homeland near Athens, Cybele and Attis had come down from Galatia, and Mithras from Tarsos. Dionysus brought along his wine flasks for his bacchanals. Aphrodite was gone, but her temple prostitutes lingered—now less religious and more commercial.

"Not everyone is able to go to Corinth." Too opulent. Too decadent. Too extravagant.

Paulos and Silvanos accepted employment in the seaport village of Cenchreae, a few miles outside the main city of Corinth. Paulos repaired sails, toiling in a small stall on the docks that faced the harbor to the west.

His employers were twin sisters, Chloe and Phoebe, who managed the shipping business they had inherited from their father. The women lived in a wood frame building at harbor's edge, the same home they had known since the days they were harbor urchins, about three decades ago, but Paulos was not a good judge of age, nor could he tell the hulking twins apart—big-boned, hippy, and broad-shouldered. Deeply etched frowns garnished their sun-ripened faces. They seldom covered their tangled reddish-brown hair, and they sported trousers—unheard of for Roman men much less for a woman—influenced by who knows what odd foreigner that weltered through their harbor. They swore like sailors and accepted no guff from any man. Only in Corinth.

Silvanos also toiled for the unmarried sisters as a dockworker. Often, Silvanos did not return to his sleeping mat in the stall on the docks—Paulos was uncertain which of the twins favored Silvanos—maybe both.

"Shun fornication!" Paulos warned Silvanos one day as their work on the docks ended and Silvanos headed toward the home of the women.

"Is the pious virgin envious?"

The taunt cut more deeply than Silvanos could have known. His mocking tone stilled the tongue of Paulos, and he never again confronted Silvanos over the twins.

A month passed and then another. Late one day, as the afternoon rays pierced his stall, a shadow settled in front of Paulos, a dark shape outlined by the aura of the sun. Paulos tilted his head back, squinted, and shielded his hand against the brightness. "Silvanos, is that you?"

"You blind old man?" A familiar voice jeered, "I'm not Silvanos; I'm Timotheos."

An hour later, Paulos tumbled into the harbor with a resounding splash. His head bobbed with a grin spread from ear to ear. The man was neither a good dancer nor a good drinker, and he had stumbled from the pier into the water. Silvanos doubled over, howling with delight.

The sounds of merriment drew Chloe to her window. Paulos the inebriated swimmer waved at her as she pulled back a tattered curtain. When she shook her head, he knew that she wondered at the foolishness of her recently hired mender of sails, but he didn't care.

"Would you like more wine?" Timotheos leaned over the water, squeezing a wineskin just enough to allow a few drops to spill over Paulos' head.

Paulos turned his face upward and opened his mouth wide; another burst of belly laughs erupted from Silvanos. Paulos opened his mouth wider. Timotheos had returned. The Thessalonians were safe. God was good.

With Timotheos back at his side, Corinth would become Paulos' base of operations for the next eighteen months. In the two years since leaving Antioch, he had walked over a thousand miles— maybe two thousand miles—along the highways of Anatolia and Greece. His mission activities were successful, even if he had not met his own high expectations. Paulos and his two companions had established solid *ekklesias* in a handful of cities in Galatia and Macedonia, and now their sojourn in Corinth would be a time to regroup—and to found the largest *ekklesia* yet.

The day after Timotheos' arrival, Paulos and Timotheos walked together through the streets of Corinth; Paulos' long strides and quick pace had returned, along with his enthusiasm for mission, and they explored the city to identify synagogues.

"You're sure Jason and the Thessalonians are well?" Paulos needed reassurance.

"Yes, despite continuing persecutions from the Romans, the *ekklesia* is standing strong, and they have added a few new members."

Paulos smiled, nodded, and gently stroked his nose as they walked.

"But there are concerns as well," said Timotheos.

As they turned a street corner, a chill draft swept down from the brooding black mountain that towered over the city. Paulos had heard rumors of the ancient rites of the temple atop the rocky cliffs.

"What concerns?" Paulos asked as he kept a suspicious eye on the sinister mountain.

"Jason's father, Justus, is dead."

Paulos whirled to face Timotheos. "The Romans?"

"No, no, it is nothing like that. He died naturally."

Paulos drew a deep breath and began walking again.

"But what does this mean?" Timotheos spoke for Jason but also for himself. "We proclaim eternal life as part of the new covenant, and we baptized the Thessalonians into the resurrected Christos, but Justus has died. What does this mean?"

Paulos hesitated briefly and looked at Timotheos. He tugged hard on his beak-nose and said nothing. He resumed walking. What did this mean? How would he reassure Timotheos and Justin? Why had Iesou not yet returned?

From the shaded portico of a synagogue, Paulos composed a letter to the Thessalonians. He dipped his reed pen into water and wiped the tip across the dry ink. He placed the tip onto the papyrus and methodically formed the Greek letters, a single stroke at a time. Papyrus was expensive, and the work was time consuming; it was important to get it right the first time.

παῦλος καὶ σιλουανὸς καὶ τιμόθεος τῇ ἐκκλησίᾳ θεσσαλονικέων ἐν θεῷ πατρὶ καὶ κυρίῳ ἰησοῦ χριστῷ χάρις ὑμῖν καὶ εἰρήνη

Paulos, Silvanos, and Timotheos, to the *ekklesia* of the Thessalonians in God the Father and the Lord Iesou Christos, Grace to you and peace.

Paulos answered the concerns of the Thessalonians, arising from the death of Justus, about the destiny of those who died before the expected return of the Lord.

But we do not want you to be uninformed, brothers and sisters, about those who have died, so that you may not grieve as others do who have no hope. For since we believe that Iesou died and rose again, even so, through Iesou, God will bring with him those who have died. For this we declare to you by the word of the Lord, that we who are alive, who are left until the coming of the Lord, will by no means precede those who have died. For the Lord himself, with a cry of command, with the archangel's call and with the sound of God's trumpet, will descend from heaven, and the dead in Christos will rise first. Then we who are alive, who are left, will be caught up in the clouds together with them to meet the Lord in the air; and so we will be with the Lord forever.

Paulos' theology had become singularly spiritual. The return of the Christos would animate the dead, who would unite with Iesou eternally in the heavens, joined also by the living. In Paulos' apocalyptic duality, Iesou was spirit not flesh, the kingdom was not of this earth, and the new age of the new covenant was eternal life in the presence of the Lord. Yeshua—the Hebrew from Galilee, the Torah teacher, the prophetic voice of justice, the political Mashiah of the Nazarenes, and the one who would be king to liberate Israel—had died on the cross. Iesou—the Christos, the Lord, and the Son of God—had risen from the dead.

The short letter to the Thessalonians was personal, meant for a few, and for the limited purpose of encouraging his friends; if he had written for a broader readership, he might have chosen his words more carefully. He might have remembered the plea of Cephas: *I pray that you do not turn your back on your Hebrew past and your Jewish brethren.* He might have recalled the admonition of Barnabas: *Temper your speech and your passion and set your face kindly toward Jerusalem.* He thought he was merely encouraging his small circle of Gentile friends in Thessalonica, and he wrote words that would sting unintended readers: "The Jews, who killed both the Lord Jesus and the prophets, and drove us out; they displease God."

Chapter Fifty-two

Paulos often trod the well-worn cart path from the village of Cenchreae to Corinth to preach in the synagogues. One day, while leaving the city to return to the village, he sensed a stalker, and as his mind flashed back to the thugs of Petra many years earlier, his heart raced. He furtively glanced back at the strangers scurrying about the busy street. Did someone follow him? Which one? Why?

He started again, slowly, listening closely to catch any telltale sounds behind him. He stole nervous glances to his left and his right. Should he run? Should he turn and confront his pursuer?

He continued forward. The footfalls on the cobblestone street behind him came nearer, accompanied by heavy breathing. Paulos wheeled to face a little round man with a sweaty, drooping face.

"Are you a follower of Iesou the Christos?" squeaked Aquila the tentmaker, gasping for breath. "So am I."

In the evening twilight, Paulos brought Silvanos and Timotheos back to the city, bearing gifts of food and wine, joined by their recent converts, the coarse sisters from Cenchreae. Reaching the agora, Paulos stopped to get his bearings.

"He said his shop was just here, on the west end of the agora."

"I've seen the tentmaker's shop also." Silvanos wrinkled his nose as he surveyed the street. "There, there it is."

The tentmaker and his wife greeted their guests at the door. Aquila the tentmaker appeared older than Prisca, his wife, but both were younger than Paulos—early thirties. The husband and wife could have been siblings for their similar shapes: slope-shouldered, flabby, plump, and stumpy. Aquila was silent; Prisca was not. She spoke for both of them, except for the occasional joke Aquila offered to tease

her, which she ignored, but which left the Cenchreae twins slapping
their trousered knees and giggling.

"We've been here a year," Prisca said. "No, is it two years
already?"

Aquila shrugged.

"We first heard about the Christos in Rome—

Paulos interrupted, "In Rome?" Who preceded him to Rome?
Who preached the good news before him?

Prisca proceeded to tell their story.

"'The King is dead! His slaves are free!' That shout on the lips
of a slave who came to our synagogue was the start of it," she said.
"When King Herod Agrippa of Judea died suddenly—is it five years
already? Six? Seven? Never mind, when the king died many years
ago, his slaves became freedmen."

Paulos knew that was the law, and he knew that Agrippa's family
villa in Rome may well have had Hebrew slaves from Palestine
serving there. They would have become freedmen upon Agrippa's
death. The story of Prisca rang true.

"Well, one of the slaves named Abdel had become a follower of
Iesou in Judea and when he became a freedman, he came to our
synagogue in Rome and jubilantly proclaimed that Iesou freed him."
Prisca looked at Aquila. "Do you remember when scrawny little
Abdel hopped on a table and danced on his bandy legs?"

Aquila nodded.

"That was the day an *ekklesia* started in our synagogue," Prisca
was breathless as she finished.

Abdel the slave? Paulos remembered an undernourished slave
named Abdel from the caravan to Damascus decades earlier. That
one was slave to Azariah the Sadducee, not King Agrippa. Must be
a different Abdel.

Although disappointed that he would not be the one to establish
an *ekklesia* in Rome, Paulos was also encouraged; if he merely
visited an established *ekklesia*, it would be unlikely that the Romans

would arrest him. Rome, as his ultimate destination, again caught his imagination, but with an existing *ekklesia*, it also seemed less urgent.

"But how did the two of you end up in Corinth?" Timotheos asked.

Aquila perked up and laughed the laugh of one who knows a private joke. He pointed at his wife. "That one is a troublemaker," he said. "She got us kicked out of Rome." He chuckled again.

All eyes turned to the squat woman who seemed harmless enough. There was more to this story, and all eagerly listened. Silvanos stepped forward and refilled the storyteller's cup to the brim with dark, red wine.

"I'm afraid I got into a squabble with the leader of the synagogue," she said. "He was angry that the followers of Iesou invited Gentiles to the synagogue." The smile on her face said she enjoyed telling the tale.

"It was more than just a little squabble," Aquila chimed in, and all the faces in the room turned toward him. "It was enough that it came to the attention of Emperor Claudius who sent his centurion to intervene."

All eyes swung back to her. Her widening smile said it was true and she wasn't sorry. "Well, the centurion came and said to me and to the synagogue leader, 'Each of you has three days to arrange your affairs and leave the city.' That was that, and here we are. Corinth is now our home, but our friends in the Roman *ekklesia* keep it strong even if they have now moved from the synagogue into a private home."

Paulos liked her spunk.

The contingent of missionaries grew to include Prisca and Aquila, Jewish followers of the Christos, troublemakers deported from Rome. Paulos moved into Corinth and briefly slept in the double-roomed tentmaker's stall, before moving into the spacious villa of Titius Justus, an early Corinthian convert. Titius was a Roman, the son of a wealthy Corinthian merchant. As a young man, he had dabbled in the various cults, but the stories of the ancient God of Israel drew him to the door of the synagogue next to his house. He was one of many *theosebeis* who joined the swelling ranks of the Corinthian *ekklesia*. Timotheos also moved in as guest of Titius, but Silvanos remained with the sisters in Cenchreae.

Months later when Silvanos decided to return to Antioch, Paulos was not entirely surprised; Silvanos had been a steady companion, but a missionary he was not. Silvanos gave no reason for his departure, but his tangled relationship with the sisters from Cenchreae had ended shortly before he informed Paulos of his pending return to Antioch.

Paulos imagined the response of Ya'akov, Cephas, and Barnabas to the report of Silvanos. *What? Paulos established ekklesias across Anatolia? And Macedonia? And Corinth?*

Paulos smiled inwardly. As he looked back upon the journey since departing Antioch, the sum of his successes loomed larger than they had seemed at the time. Even his tribulations fit into God's plan, he could see with hindsight. The more Paulos thought of it, the better he liked the idea of Silvanos returning to Palestine with a report; if he had not decided on his own, Paulos would have sent him.

Paulos had been in Corinth for a year when another missionary joined their band; his name was Apollos, a Diaspora Jew from Alexandria in Egypt. The massive cargo ships from Alexandria, the grain suppliers for the western empire, often made port in Corinth when hauling their grain tonnage to Rome, and many Alexandrian merchants, sailors, and others settled in Corinth. Apollos helped to establish an *ekklesia* in Corinth consisting largely of Egyptians.

Paulos experienced a brief encounter with the Roman authorities following a complaint from certain Jews of a synagogue, angered at his preaching—especially because the synagogue leader, Crispus, converted to the Christos sect, taking many Jews with him. The Roman Governor quickly dismissed the charges.

"Why should I care what superstitions the Hebrews choose to follow?" he said to the complaining Jews who had lost their synagogue to Crispus and his cohorts who followed the Christos. "I won't side with one faction or the other. This is the business of the synagogue," he said, "not the governor."

After eighteen months in Corinth, Paulos spent less time as a preacher than as an administrator. Apollos led his own Egyptian *ekklesia,* Chloe and Phoebe—the twin sisters of Cenchreae—directed an *ekklesia* centered in their seaport village that attracted a rainbow of personalities from the port-city proletariat, while Crispus—a Jew and leader of a synagogue—led a synagogue-based *ekklesia* with numerous Jewish participants, and Titius Justus guided a mostly Gentile *ekklesia* from his own home. Paulos and his missionary band had established a diverse handful of *ekklesias* consisting of rich and poor, male and female, Jews and Greeks—not to mention the Romans, Egyptians, and others from around the Empire. Many of the converts brought prior experiences of the mystery cults.

Only later, after Paulos left Corinth, would this welter of Corinthians disintegrate into squabbling.

Chapter Fifty-three

Spring arrived early in the eleventh year of the reign of Claudius, 53 C.E., and so did the shipping season. Swarms of sailors from afar clogged the streets, and the markets hummed with strange dialects. The influx of ship's crews triggered Paulos' wanderlust; after eighteen months, it was time to move on, but to where?

Paulos decided to ascend to the summit of the mountain that overlooked Corinth. The black cliffs that had seemed so sinister when he arrived had now shriveled into a benign curiosity. Perhaps the panoramic view would inspire plans for the next leg of his journey, as if he could see the whole world from the mountaintop; besides, he was curious about the temple ruins there.

Paulos chomped down a breakfast of fresh bread, figs, and goat cheese with Titius Justus, his host and guide for ascending the acrocorinth. As they ate, they surveyed the dark rock visible from the villa portico. Today they would scale the heights. Would they find God in the heathen Temple there? Would they pierce the heavens hidden in the clouds? Paulos laughed inwardly at the foolishness of men who sought God through their own works: those who erected mountaintop Temples; those who built brick towers in Babel; and those who circumcised their foreskins.

An hour later, they were halfway up the steep, twisting path to the tabletop plateau atop the cliffs. "It seems higher up close," Paulos said.

Titius was younger than Paulos, but he could not match the pace of his long-legged elder. "Slow down, man," Titius said.

Titius leaned against a rock and sucked thin air while Paulos impatiently tapped his walking stick on the hardscrabble path. They finally arrived at the top by mid-morning, under a high, bright, and clear sky. On such a day, you could see God's earth and all that was in it. Puffy clouds floated in the heavens above the pilgrim climbers.

The temple to Aphrodite was a ruin of hewn stones, cluttered in the weeds as silent witnesses to the orgies of a former time. For more than an hour, Titius sat alone on a stone that had once been part of the temple while Paulos surveyed the world from all edges of the windswept tabletop.

For a long while, Paulos gazed to the northwest; Rome was in the far off clouds. Was his future that way? Once, he thought *he* would be the one to establish Rome as the center of the *ekklesias* of the Christos, but an emancipated slave had won the race years earlier. Still, Rome could be his hub, his stepping off point to the whole of the empire. Was it time for Rome?

What of Arsenios? Could he be in Rome? Probably not, since a decade had passed since they had exchanged letters. Better to let go of that hope ... or was it merely a temptation? Better to avoid temptation, better to avoid the prickly thorn, better to look in another direction.

Paulos leaned in and lapped cool water on his face from a spring-fed pool. Cupping his hands, he drank deeply of the sweet water. Delicate white flowers sprouted from the rocks around the pool. He picked one, sniffed its fragrance, and then slowly plucked the petals, one by one. They floated around his lonely reflection. He was surprised to see a thick vein of gray beard along his cheekbone with smaller smears of gray mottling his thinning, auburn hair. Friends, faithful and true, surrounded him in Corinth. Yet, when his mind drifted toward Rome, he felt hollow and alone. He crumpled the last white petal over his sorry old face and walked across the flat top to the opposite side of the summit.

From the eastern edge of the mount, he saw many faces of his past. Did his mother still live? What happened in Antioch with the return of Silvanos? What of his friends in Antioch: Lucius, Agathe and their toddlers? Good old Julius? Titos, his protégé from Tarsos? Barnabas? Paulos' anger toward his friend had cooled in the nearly four years since Barnabas sided with Jerusalem, and Paulos' heart warmed at the thought of the tall man preening in front of his mirror.

What of Ya'akov in Jerusalem? Paulos' great successes had proven Paulos right and Ya'akov wrong. He hoped the stubborn Nazarene had received a report of his far-flung network of *ekklesias*. That would stir him up. A slight smile crossed his face at the thought of the Nazarene jerking so hard on his norm that he ripped it off his neck.

To the northeast, he pictured a regional void in his network of *ekklesias*. Earlier, in his haste to travel from Galatia to Macedonia, he had bypassed the westernmost portion of Anatolia. This was the Roman province of Asia, encompassing the eastern shores of the Aegean Sea. The principal city, Ephesus, was the fourth largest metropolis of the empire after Rome, Alexandria, and Antioch. The region was ripe for evangelization, and Ephesus would be a perfect hub from which to manage Paulos' own empire.

Hah! What would Ya'akov think of that?

A hot breeze whistled up the cliffs and over the pilgrim, swirling his robes around him. The Apostle to the Gentiles heard the call of Ephesus.

Despite the departure of Silvanos, Paulos' entourage had grown; Prisca and Aquila joined his cause and sailed with him to Ephesus. Of course, loyal Timotheos remained Paulos' trusted aide and associate. Apollos the Egyptian had joined Paulos' ministry in Corinth and would soon follow him to Ephesus.

The merchant ship that had carried them over two hundred miles, across the Aegean Sea from Corinth, swung at anchor in the Ephesus harbor; dockworkers busily unloaded the ship's cargo onto barges. For three days and nights, the missionaries had camped in their tents on the deck of the galley, enjoying favorable winds and weather for their open sea crossing.

Paulos, Timotheos, Prisca and Aquila stepped off the barge onto the docks of Ephesus, mingling with the crowd that ignored the new arrivals. Hawking calls of vendors shrilled above the clatter. The smells of the city—spicy pudding pots, donkey dung, wood smoke, fresh bread, and fishmonger booths—merged with the salt air of the harbor. In the morning mist, the liquid sun flowed over the eastern mountains, seeped through the hills that ringed the city, and spilled into the city streets. Did the others feel the same thrill of anticipation Paulos did?

Paulos had grand plans for Ephesus, which would become his home base. The missionaries would evangelize in this great city and establish *ekklesias,* but they would also fan out to the entire region. The location of Ephesus would be perfect for centralized administration. The Phrygian *ekklesias* to the east, the Galatian *ekklesias* to the northeast, the Macedonian *ekklesias* to the northwest, and the Corinthian *ekklesias* straight west formed an arc, with an equidistant radius of several hundred miles to Ephesus in the center. From this centralized location, Paulos would preside over his domain.

Ephesus was a major seaport on the mouth of the Cayster River that spilled into the Aegean Sea, following its short journey from the slopes of Mount Tmolus to the east. The ancient and enduring Persian Royal road terminated in Ephesus, at the western end of a caravan trail that stretched far to the east, connecting the cities of Anatolia, the eastern Roman Empire, and Persia beyond. The Hellenistic city boasted an outdoor theater that seated nearly 25,000 persons. Perhaps one day Paulos would preach to an overflowing crowd! Doubtful, of course, but he could dream.

The day after their arrival, the four missionaries toured the city together, and they soon found themselves staring at the monstrous Temple and sprawling Temple grounds of the goddess Artemis, the daughter of Zeus and twin sister of Apollo, according to Greek mythology. Timotheos read aloud from an inscription posted outside the Temple:

I have set eyes on the wall of lofty Babylon on which is a road for chariots, and the statue of Zeus by the Alpheus, and the hanging gardens, and the colossus of the Sun, and the huge labour of the high pyramids, and the vast tomb of Mausolus; but when I saw the house of Artemis that mounted to the clouds, those other marvels lost their brilliancy, and I said, 'Lo, apart from Olympus, the Sun never looked on aught so grand'.

Paulos was less impressed than the others who gawked at the brilliant structures. He also scoffed at the steady stream of visitors that ebbed and flowed through the temple gates. Every one of them an idolater. Inside the temple, priests functioned as silversmiths, imprinting coins with the likeness of Artemis, and as bankers, processing currency exchanges. Paulos was offended that the coin of the realm bore the image of a false god, but one day, he would confront these idolatrous priests with their idol-coins.

The four missionaries rented a two-room apartment near the agora and a public latrine. They preached and missionized through synagogues, and established *ekklesias* by summer's end.

On one of the first cool days of early autumn, Paulos finished his cold supper alone. The others had eaten earlier, but he had returned to the apartment late in the day.

Paulos looked up from the table to the knock at their door. Half-asleep Timotheos leaned on an elbow and raised his head from his mat; Prisca poked her head from the room she shared with Aquila. Who would call at this hour? Paulos drained his wine cup, wiped his lips with a cloth, and walked slowly to the door, holding a flickering candle in his hand. When the door creaked open, candlelight spilled onto a yellow-haired man of slight build, standing on the stoop.

"Hello teacher," said Titos.

Paulos grabbed his friend from Antioch and wrapped his long arms around him, hugging him into the room. "Come in. Come in, my son."

Prisca took a step closer, and Aquila appeared at her elbow. Timotheos sat up, fully awake.

"My friends, this is my dear friend Titos—first from Tarsos and then from Antioch," said Paulos.

Prisca and Aquila stepped into the main room to greet their guest. Timotheos remained seated on his mat.

"When Silvanos returned to Antioch with tales of your travels, I decided to join you," Titos said. "First, I sailed to Corinth, and your friends there told me you had moved to Ephesus. Here I am."

When Paulos introduced Titos to the others, he finished by saying, "brightest student I ever had."

Prisca set cups on the short-legged table in the middle of the room, and Aquila opened a bottle of wine. They all reclined around the table, except Timotheos who remained on his mat in the corner. Paulos didn't notice.

Titos updated Paulos on nearly four years of news from Antioch. "Barnabas left Antioch shortly after you did. He returned to Kypros and nurtures growing *ekklesias* on his island home. When you departed Antioch, you left a grieving hole in his heart."

A flood of bittersweet memories of the tall Kypriot washed over Paulos. "Barnabas, ah Barnabas, one day we will meet again," he half-whispered to no one in particular.

"Lucius and Agathe are parents again."

"How is young Loukas," Paulos asked.

When Titos said that Loukas, the firstborn son of Lucius and Agathe, was now a young man, Paulos felt old.

"How are the *ekklesias*—especially the Gentile *ekklesias*?"

"They do well even though the *ekklesias* are now either strictly Jewish or Gentile without much interaction. Silvanos' reports of the success of your missionary campaign raised quite a stir and boosted the morale of the Gentile *ekklesias*."

"Hah, I knew it," Paulos said and he slapped his knee. He gulped a big draught of wine, and wiped his lips with his sleeve. All the news

was good; could there be more? "What of Jerusalem," he asked as
he leaned toward Titos. "How did they react?"

"I haven't heard any reports."

Ah well, sooner or later grumpy Ya'akov would have his supper
spoiled when word filtered down from Antioch. Paulos should have
instructed Silvanos to go to Jerusalem straightaway to render a
report.

Titos moved away from the table to the pack he had deposited
in the corner. The others watched with curiosity as he rummaged
through his belongings. When he didn't immediately find what he
was looking for, a worried frown formed on his pale cheeks.

"Ah, there it is," he said, and he held up a faded and tattered goat-
leather purse. He returned to the table, and dropped the purse in
front of Paulos. "Look inside," he said. "Do you remember?"

Paulos slipped his long fingers into the purse and extracted an
old shekel, a Hebrew coin with the Greek letter "χ" on one side and
a date palm on the other. No one could see his lower lip and chin
quiver under his mottled beard, but the tears that streamed over his
wrinkled face told them that this was a special token of his past.

"My belonging coin," he said, and he hugged Titos long and hard
as his body quaked with sobs.

No one noticed Timotheos slip out until they heard the door slam
behind him.

"He must be visiting the latrine," said Prisca.

After several bottles of wine, Prisca and Aquila finally retired to
their room. When Titos spread his sleeping mat on the floor, Paulos
realized that Timotheos had not returned, but he guessed that a hot
belly kept him close to the latrine, and he quickly fell asleep. When
Paulos awoke in the morning, Timotheos snored from his mat, and
Paulos assumed all was well.

Chapter Fifty-four

The first winter spent in Ephesus was unusually cold and uncomfortable. Always wet in the winter, the cold rains persisted day after day with occasional snow fleecing the mountain villages surrounding the city. Paulos paid little heed to the sour moods of Timotheos that matched the weather.

Winter kept the missionaries close to home, but Paulos planned an expansive campaign to coincide with the warm breezes of springtime. First, he would send missionaries up the valleys into the many small cities and villages within a day or two of Ephesus. For the first time, Paulos would direct missionary activities to an entire region and not just a single city. Second, he would send a contingent to revisit the *ekklesias* of Phrygia while another group would travel to the Galatian *ekklesias*.

"We must water the seeds we have planted. The tender shoots need nourishment," Paulos explained to the others.

He had another motive also, "At the Jerusalem assembly, I promised to collect funds for the Jerusalem poor," he said. "Now is the time to fulfill that promise. I look forward to the surprised look on the face of old Ya'akov when we plop sacks full of gold coins on his table. Then he'll see the legitimacy of my mission to the Gentiles."

When Paulos and Ya'akov had agreed to the collection, neither man saw charity in the gesture; for both, it was a symbolic statement of power and prestige. For Ya'akov, it spoke to the ascendancy of the Jerusalem Nazarenes, but for Paulos, it said the Gentile *ekklesias* were legitimate. Since then, Ya'akov had rejected Paulos' Torah-free mission to the Gentiles, but sacks bulging with gold would swing the advantage back to Paulos.

Prisca suggested that Timotheos should lead the group to Phrygia. After all, that was his homeland, and he could revisit his mother, Eunice. According to her plan, Paulos and Titos would travel to Galatia. Paulos didn't notice the scowl on Timotheos face, and he was surprised when Timotheos later offered his objections in private.

"Why not me?" Timotheos asked. "I've been your faithful assistant, and now you take this newcomer as your travel companion?"

"My trusted friend, don't you see that because of your experience, I need you lead your own travel party?" Paulos busied himself with packing his tentmaker's tools into a goatskin bag. "Prisca's plan is a good one, and we will follow it," he said. He didn't understand the explosion that followed.

"Damn Prisca's plan," Timotheos barked. "Let the woman be silent with full submission. You should permit no woman to have authority over a man; she should remain silent."

Paulos set down his tools and searched the face of the Roman, but he discerned no clues to explain this outburst.

"What sour words foul your mouth," Paulos said. "In Christos, there is neither male nor female, and where would our cause be without the leadership of women? Surely, you speak not from your heart."

Paulos reminded Timotheos of Charis, the prostitute's daughter in Damascus; Mary Magdalene at the Jerusalem assembly; Eunice, Timotheos' own mother; Tatiana the Galatian of Pessinus; Euodia of Philippi; and now Prisca, their faithful coworker from Corinth. Timotheos face was pinched and blanched, and his lips pressed together tightly; too late, the words had already slipped out.

"Please don't tell Prisca what I said. You know I didn't mean it."

The embarrassment in his eyes said that his apology rang true, but what Paulos didn't see was that the root of the anger was not Prisca, or any woman, but the recent arrival of the tiny man from Antioch.

Traveling through springtime greenery with an eastbound caravan, Paulos and Titos followed the Persian Royal road northeast from

Ephesus to Sardis; Paulos' previous journeys had been in the company of Silvanos, the stout bodyguard with a cudgel at his belt, and Timotheos, the athletic son of a soldier. The current pair of travelers—an old man whose cane had stretched into a shoulder height walking stick, now a necessity and not merely an adornment, and a bird-boned tiny man whose strength was his intellect—required the security afforded by a caravan. Each man led a donkey carrying packs of supplies.

During the three-day walk to Sardis, Mount Tmolus dominated the eastern horizon. Each morning, the gray crags seemed so close; yet by evening, they seemed barely closer. Only the gradual appearance of black forested slopes beneath the stony summit marked their progress.

"There Pan sang his songs, flaunting among the gentle Nymphae, and played light airs upon his pipes." Titos repeated a line of a popular poem about the gods of Mount Tmolus, followed by his whistling imitation of the pipes of Pan.

Titos played his own light airs upon their conversation, providing a call and response to Paulos' musings. In this, he was different from Timotheos; Titos' intellect was inquisitive while Timotheos' mind was administrative. Titos asked questions; Timotheos haggled with vendors, arranged employment and lodging, and managed the finances of Paulos' ministry.

Then too, Titos had been with Paulos in Tarsos and the apostolic assembly in Jerusalem, and he had witnessed the Antioch incident; these common experiences allowed Paulos a look back. Paulos was glad of the company of his former student from Tarsos—not that his conversation was better than with Timotheos, but it was different. In his four-year dash across the continents, Paulos had relied on Timotheos' steady hand to build his empire; now it was time to set his mind upon Antioch and Jerusalem and to finally respond to the slight of Ya'akov and the Nazarenes.

Had it been merely a slight? With the passage of four years and from his perspective as the leader of his own network of *ekklesias*, the sting of Antioch had lessened; Paulos had forgiven Cephas and Barnabas, and he expected his mission successes would soften tough-skinned Ya'akov; and hefty purses filled with gold wouldn't hurt either!

Upon arriving in Sardis, Paulos dispatched Titos to the market while he explored the city looking for synagogues. Hours later, they reunited. Titos carried a basketful of foodstuffs including fresh bread, smoked cheese, figs and dates, and several jars of foul smelling garum—fermented fish sauce that would not spoil during their journey.

"We must send missionaries to Sardis," Paulos said. "I found the largest synagogue I've ever seen, and *theosebeis* hung on the doorstep like ripe fruit on the vine ready for plucking."

The tall man and his short companion walked inexorably toward the eastern horizon; Mount Tmolus gradually receded behind them, as the high plains of central Anatolia loomed before them. Their conversations became shorter, and Titos whistled to pass the time, but with Tmolus no longer dominating their vista, he varied his tunes. By the time they arrived in Pessinus after two weeks of tedious walking, Titos had stopped whistling altogether. Titos stood behind his leader, leaning against his own walking stick as Paulos knocked on the door of Tatiana and Mariana, his Galatian nurses during his wintertime illness several years earlier.

Mariana, the round-shouldered and thickset woman with unkempt hair, shrieked when she opened the door. "Oh Paulos, is it really you?" she said with a gap-toothed grin. Raising her throaty voice, she called to Tatiana. "Come quickly and see who's here!"

Tatiana came from the kitchen, wiping her hands on a towel. Even while doing household chores, she wore a fine peplum dress of multicolored patches. When she saw Paulos, she dropped the towel, and her hand covered her gaping mouth. After a moment, she rushed to him and hugged him before she stepped back to regain her prim posture.

Both women appeared fit. Mariana's tangled hair was thinner with bald spots showing through while Tatiana's neatly combed hair had turned beyond gray to white; she was more elegant than Paulos remembered. The robust-bodied Mariana had grown heavier, and her mouth had fewer teeth.

Word spread rapidly that Paulos was back in the city, resulting in a boisterous party that evening—even Paulos drank his share of honey mead as he enjoyed the evening spent with friends, old and new. The *ekklesia* had grown since he had first visited several years earlier, and Paulos basked in the adulation of the newcomers who only knew him by reputation; the role of returning, conquering hero fit him well. Titos sat alone in a corner, smiling at the adulation poured on his mentor.

For a week, the visiting dignitaries socialized. In the absence of major issues, Paulos merely dispensed with minor details of business in the prospering *ekklesia* of Pessinus. Finally, he raised the issue of the collection for Jerusalem.

"Iesou lived in Palestine, the land of his Jewish kinfolk. His family still lives in Jerusalem, and I would like to make a gesture of good will by offering a collection of funds to the poor of Jerusalem," Paulos explained to Tatiana. "Such a gift will unify the wide-spread *ekklesias* of Christos," he said, without mentioning the rift in his relationship with Ya'akov and Jerusalem.

Tatiana inhaled a deep breath and leaned back in her chair for a moment before she rose and filled her cup with water from a large vase in the kitchen. "I like the idea," she said as she returned to her seat. "Will you make the same request of the *ekklesias* of Ancyra and Tavium?"

"Yes. Titos and I will leave soon to visit those cities."

Tatiana rocked forward and back, her whole body nodding as she made soft clucking sounds with her tongue. "Yes, yes. We will do it," she said softly.

With a single clap of his hands, Paulos bounded to his feet, grabbed

Tatiana's fingers, and pulled her up for an awkward dance. When he noticed Titos' bemusement, he guided her back to her chair. He wiped his smile away with long fingers over his mouth and down his beard. With a long exhale, it was time to plan for their next step.

Paulos was absent from Pessinus for nearly a month while he and Titos visited the *ekklesias* of the other Galatian cities, where his request for a collection received an equally favorable response; the Galatians were proud to gather a collection for the poor in honor of the family and friends of Iesou in the city of Jerusalem.

Paulos and Titos retraced their path to Pessinus to spend a few last days among friends before leaving Galatia for the return journey to Ephesus. On the day they returned to Pessinus, Paulos and Titos reclined with the two widows, finishing supper when someone pounded on the door.

"Paulos, will you see who that might be," asked Tatiana as she began to clear the dishes.

Paulos opened the door but quickly stepped back; a menacing Celtic warrior filled the doorframe, wearing body armor and a metal helmet with silver wings extending from the sides. Straw-like hair protruded from under his helmet like a threshing basket turned upside down, and black eyes glared under brows thick as moustaches. Breadcrumbs clung to his tangled red beard. The man-giant hoisted a large shield with a colorful checkered pattern, slapping a long sword against the shield. A flowing purple cloak hung over his back. Paulos saw murder in the eyes of the monster whose gruff voice boomed as he raised his sword.

"Are you Paulos the Jew?"

Paulos shrunk further into the room, and the man let loose with a belly laugh and stepped forward with a bear hug for the startled Paulos who stood with arms dangling at his side. Mariana slapped her knee and howled with open-mouthed laughter that soon became a rib-splitting paroxysm of coughing. She gulped down a cup of water and laughed again. Even prim Tatiana giggled at poor Paulos in the clutches of their warrior friend.

"This is our friend, Caesar," Tatiana said. "Yes, that is really his name. Don't you think our collection of gold coins will be safe with Caesar leading our delegation to Jerusalem?" teased Tatiana. "We will collect funds through the winter and send Caesar and a delegation to Jerusalem in the spring."

Paulos could not help a wry grin as he pictured Caesar knocking on the door of Ya'akov's home.

On a bright summer day, hot in the highlands of central Anatolia, Paulos and Titos departed for their return to Ephesus. Each day, they chased the sun as it arced across the heavens. When Mount Tmolus appeared on the horizon, Titos again whistled his pipes-of-Pan tune. By the time they reached Sardis and the foot of the mountain, Paulos had joined in. They were nearly home.

"Look at the mosaics inlaid in the tile floor," said Timotheos, as he proudly escorted Paulos through the luxurious terrace home he had secured for the missionary band. He had returned from Phrygia a month earlier. "From the terrace, you can see the whole city and the sea," he said, pointing in the direction of the docks. Paulos nodded his approval, and Timotheos beamed.

Hilly ground on the south side of the city marked the foothills of a mountain range, and a series of terrace homes housed the wealthy citizens of the city. The missionary's terrace rested atop the roof of the house below them on the steep slope. In turn, their rooftop served as the terrace for the next house, in a continuous pattern up the hill.

In the fullness of late summer, Paulos was flush with the triumph of his collection journey to Galatia. Timotheos reported similar success in Phrygia. It was good to be home in the gracious company of friends, surrounded by the comforts of a splendid terrace villa. Moreover, Apollos, the Alexandrian Jew who had been with them in Corinth, had arrived to join the missionaries. Paulos, Timotheos,

Titos, Prisca, Aquila, and now Apollos made six.

Apollos updated Paulos on news of the still-growing *ekklesias* of Corinth. He warned Paulos of growth pangs and quarreling between the *ekklesias*.

"Tis late in the season," Paulos said, "and the weather will soon turn. I'll visit the Corinthians in the spring, or perhaps I'll send Timotheos." Paulos was not in the mood to hear bad news, and he paid little heed to Apollos' warnings of strife in Corinth. "For now, let us enjoy a quiet winter as we thankfully consider our great victories this year and pray for continued success in the year to come."

Chapter Fifty-five

Despite his aching knees, Ya'akov relished the fresh air of springtime, as he limped along a country path outside Jerusalem, in the company of Anina, his granddaughter. According to her mother, Anina was now a young woman who had started to bleed, but Ya'akov refused to notice the budding breasts under her swelling tunic.

Returning from a visit to the tomb where the bones of Shera, his dead wife, now rested in a stone ossuary, they paused under a silvery-green leafed olive tree. Anina plucked a small white blossom, and cradled it gently in her palm. He would avoid these country visits to Shera's tomb except for the urging of dear, sweet Anina. She would also insist that they dally here in the shade of the olive branches where he would remember great-uncle Yeshua for the inquisitive child.

"Was uncle Yeshua a Pharisee?" she asked.

The wrinkles in her grandfather's face softened, and he grunted approvingly at the child's curiosity. *Wisdom is in the question, not the answer.* So said the sage who taught him many years earlier.

"He had no formal training, like I received," Ya'akov said. "Yet, he had the heart of a Pharisee. He was our great Torah teacher, demanding holy deeds of justice and mercy. *Blessed are the poor*, he often preached. That is why we share bread and honey with those in the humble streets of the city." He chided himself for his own recent laxity and resolved to do better—and to bring young Anina with him as a lesson.

"Some say he was a breaker of Torah: that he supped with unclean sinners," Anina said.

The wrinkled face of the old man hardened. Why had his brother been so foolish? Certainly, his lapses were not intentional, merely irresponsible, but it made his own task of strictly defending Torah more difficult.

"Yeshua did not come to abolish the law, as some might have you believe," Ya'akov said. The so-called Pharisee from Tarsos had seized upon his brother's indiscretions to rebel against the wisdom of the elders. "Yeshua came to fulfill the law," Ya'akov continued. "Until heaven and earth pass away, not one letter, not one stroke of a letter, will pass from the law. Whoever breaks one of the least of these commandments, and teaches others to do the same, will be called least in the kingdom." There was an edge to his voice as the face of his beak-nosed adversary roiled his thoughts.

His anger reminded him that there was pressing business, and they soon departed the idyllic grove. He trundled back to the city as fast as his feeble legs could carry him for an important meeting with his brothers.

Ya'akov fumbled with his norm as he listened to his brothers argue. Reports had filtered from Antioch, detailing Paulos' trek across Anatolia and around the Aegean, establishing cells in the major cities.

"He fills old wineskins with fresh wine, and they will surely burst," said Jude. "*New creation*, he preaches. He is right about that, but it isn't God's new creation but that of his own making. Paulos does not preach the religion of our forebears or the teaching of Yeshua, our brother."

Jude was right, Ya'akov thought. The spiritualized "Christos" of Paulos bore little resemblance to Yeshua, their flesh and blood brother.

Joses, the youngest, opposed Jude. "Twenty years. Two decades. A generation. That's how long it's been since Yeshua died on the cross," Joses said. "Look around and you see nothing but Roman tyrants. There's fighting in the streets. Jew fights Jew. Assassins lurk with their daggers. Is this the kingdom Yeshua promised?" argued

Joses. "Paulos preaches that flesh and blood will not inherit the kingdom of God. We need to consider seriously the message of this man and not reject it simply because he goes to the Gentiles."

Joses was so young, thought Ya'akov. He was a tiny tyke when Yeshua died. Did he remember his brother? He didn't appreciate the message of Yeshua; yet, he also spoke the truth—the kingdom had not arrived as the brothers expected. Could it be that the kingdom would not be of this earth as Paulos claimed?

Shera's bones lay in a cold stone box in a lonely tomb. Would Ya'akov ever see her again? The words of the Teacher of old haunted him: "All is vanity. All go to one place; all are from the dust, and all turn to dust again." But Isaiah the Prophet gave him hope: "Your dead shall live, their corpses shall rise. O dwellers in the dust, awake and sing for joy! For your dew is a radiant dew, and the earth will give birth to those long dead."

The angry voice of Jude snapped Ya'akov from his thoughts. "The kingdom hasn't arrived because the people don't honor God by respecting Torah. Paulos, the apostate, leads his followers astray. Perhaps it's his blasphemy that delays the kingdom," Jude said.

Ya'akov squeezed his norm so tightly that he broke the skin on his palm, but he did not notice.

Cousin Symeon seldom spoke, but when he did, he often offered a middle ground. "Send an emissary. Instead of relying on hearsay reports about the *ekklesias* of Paulos, send a reliable truth-seeker."

"Send Phinehas," said Jude.

"He isn't a diplomat; he's a troublemaker," said Joses.

Joses was right, thought Ya'akov. Phinehas was a hothead, but who else would stand up to Paulos? Phinehas had backbone.

"Send Phinehas but instruct him to keep a low profile and not stir up trouble," Ya'akov said.

Jude instructed Phinehas, Paulos' nemesis from Antioch, to sail to Greece to find Paulos.

Chapter Fifty-six

It had been an unusually warm spring across the regions of the Great Sea in the thirteenth year of the reign of Emperor Claudius, 54 C.E., and searing summer winds would blow like a bellows stoking a forge. Three sets of travelers departed on separate journeys one spring day; later, in scalding summer heat, their paths would cross. A separate entourage, the fourth, set out soon after.

Phinehas stood on the docks of Caesarea of Palestine, the Roman capital city of Judea, two day's journey from Jerusalem. He impatiently waited for the captain's signal to board the merchant galley that would sail north along the coast before heading west toward Corinth, the last known location of Paulos. Phinehas and the Nazarenes were unaware that Paulos had moved to Ephesus. Phinehas' pale skin burned in the blistering midday sun, and he was anxious to board and set up his linen awning for shade. At least the sea breeze across the docks kept the heat tolerable.

Ya'akov had dispatched him to probe the *ekklesias* of Paulos, and to encourage Paulos to respect the Torah traditions. Ya'akov would allow his courier discretion in the details, and Phinehas' mind already schemed. He would hold the false-Pharisee's feet to the fire.

As Phinehas waited, he surveyed the resplendent palace built generations ago by King Herod the Great, now the residence of the Judean Governor, lackey of the Romans. The castle would belong to the Nazarenes in the new kingdom, Phinehas thought to himself.

Frigate birds with long wingspans soared over the castle, whose gold-leafed rooftops glistened in the sun, and sea gulls squawked their squabbles over dead fish floating in the water. Finally, the captain blew his whistle and waved for Phinehas and the other passengers to climb aboard the ship.

That same day, Timotheos departed from Ephesus also bound for Corinth. He would travel the land route around the Aegean, planning to visit the *ekklesias* of Philippi and Thessalonica along the way. There were reports of bickering amongst the Corinthians, but Paulos saw no urgency; he was sure that Timotheos would calm the waters in Corinth after his extended journey around the Aegean.

Paulos was more concerned about the petty squabbling that existed between his two young protégés, which he didn't understand. The two had shared a room, but their constant bickering resulted in moving Apollos in and Timotheos out. Paulos had planned to visit Corinth himself, but he worried about the infighting that might occur in his absence. Better to separate the two by sending Timotheos. Again, Timotheos had questioned why Paulos sent him rather than Titos, but since he knew the *ekklesias* and they knew him, he was the obvious choice. Even he could see that, he admitted, but he departed in a foul mood.

Unknown to Paulos, a contingent *from* Corinth departed the seaport of Cenchreae for the short passage across the Aegean, seeking a face-to-face meeting with him in Ephesus. Of the three travel parties that departed that day, the Corinthian delegation arrived at their destination first.

Stephanas was spokesperson for the Corinthians. He had brawled his way to his position as foremost ship's captain in all of Corinth. He could out-drink, out-swear, and out-fight any sailor, and his scars bore silent witness to encounters too numerous to remember. The last he knew of his nose, it was in the mouth of a sailor who bit it off during a disagreement at sea; the last he knew of that sailor, he was flying overboard, thrown into the sea by the remorseless captain, like a spoiled sack of grain.

Stephanas now commanded the fleet of half a dozen merchant galleys owned by sisters Chloe and Phoebe of Cenchreae; through Chloe's influence, he had joined the *ekklesia* in their home which had softened his gruffness a wee bit—he didn't throw disobedient sailors overboard anymore—but his strength of character remained. Despite his coarse behavior and speech, Chloe chose Stephanas to confront Paulos, whose single-mindedness would disarm a lesser man than her ships' captain. Paulos had not responded to Chloe's messages that dissension gripped the Corinthian *ekklesias*. With the first stable weather of spring, Chloe had dispatched Stephanas to Ephesus to solicit Paulos' immediate intervention.

Stephanas stood in front of Paulos in the shaded portion of the Ephesian terrace home; his muscles bulged beneath a sleeveless goat-leather jacket that smelled of sweat and saltwater. Paulos would not have trusted the swarthy sailor except for the letter he carried from Chloe. After reading the letter a second time, Paulos looked up at the sea captain with the hideous, nose-less face.

"Would you like wine and bread?" asked Paulos.

"I prefer beer if ya gots it. I likes the barley beer brewed in good ol' Ephesus."

Paulos filled the biggest cup he could find and set it before Stephanas.

"Chloe's note says there's trouble in the *ekklesias*. What trouble?"

Stephanas drained the beer in one large gulp and clanked the empty tin cup on the table. "Got any more?"

Paulos filled the cup again as he listened.

"Chloe says they heared ya too hard."

Paulos canted his head sideways as if to listen with his better ear; he was uncertain what Stephanas meant by "heared ya too hard."

"New, ya said. Everything is new. Ya said in the new age, of the new covenant, we're a new creation, filled with new life and freedom. They listened to ya alright, but they heared ya too hard." He drained the cup again.

Was Stephanas criticizing his preaching? His message?

"They says, if I got a new life in the spirit, then what I do with my body is of no matter. If I screws my neighbor's wife, it don't matter.

If I drinks too much wine when we gather, it don't matter. Looks at me, they says, I'm in the spirit, and I can dance or sing or babble in gibberish. I'm united with God through baptism, and what I does on this here earth don't matter."

Paulos poured the last of the beer into the sea captain's cup, and Stephanas nursed the dregs to make them last.

"Enthusiastics, that's what they is. Ya lit a fire under 'em, and now they're enthusiastics, better'n everyone else as they live in their glory. They heared ya too hard."

Paulos was stunned. He hadn't anticipated that his flock would backslide, or were they moving too fast? This wasn't his fault; well, maybe he left Corinth too early, but must he always be the nursemaid? The decadent, self-indulgent Corinthians had twisted his message of newness to justify their pleasures of the flesh. He was convinced that there were evil forces at work to thwart his ministry, and he must formulate a plan of battle.

The next morning, Paulos hustled to the market with an empty amphora; a vendor filled it with fresh brewed beer. For the next few days, Paulos listened as Stephanas talked; the more cups of beer Stephanas drank, the more lucid the answers became, and Paulos saw the picture; he began to compose a letter that Stephanas would carry back to the Corinthians.

The new age had dawned and would be fully realized when the Christos returned—soon, but not yet. Paulos needed to rein in the reign of God for these heavenly and perfect—in their mind—"enthusiastics" for whom expectation had become actualization.

"Already you have all you want," he wrote.

"Already you have become rich. Apart from us you have become kings." The words flowed freely from his pen onto the papyrus.

"Knowledge puffs up, but love builds up. If I speak in the tongues of mortals and of angels, but do not have love, I am a noisy gong or a clanging cymbal."

In their own glory, the Corinthians stormed the gates of heaven; Paulos reminded them that they still lived on this side of death and the cross. He criticized their pride and boasting.

"What have you got that you did not first receive? If you have received all this, why glory in it."

Stephanas carried Paulos' letter back to the Corinthians. He arrived the same day as a redheaded troublemaker from Jerusalem. Timotheos was still miles away, traveling slowly by foot, oblivious to the developing crisis in Corinth.

Chapter Fifty-seven

Ya'akov sat in the shade and watched the others pound and saw and chisel; because of his knees, he mostly superintended the construction projects of his builder brothers. As the afternoon shadows lengthened, Ya'akov whistled, signaling the end of the workday. Jude and Simon departed for their own homes; Ya'akov's once burgeoning household had shrunk to just him and his youngest brother, Joses, and they trudged in silence along the dusty streets of Jerusalem to return to their home and their supper. Ya'akov grimaced with each painful step as he mounted the stairway to the second story veranda while Joses prepared a simple meal of bread and garum.

As they ate in silence, a noisy ruckus in the street stirred Joses from his stool; he walked to the veranda's edge to look down at the hubbub. When he surveyed the scene below, he let out a throaty laugh and gestured to Ya'akov, "Come, come. You must see this spectacle."

"Tell me what it is," said Ya'akov, reluctant to move from his comfortable chair.

"Come and see for yourself," Joses said with a laugh.

Placing his hands on the table, Ya'akov hoisted himself slowly and shuffled to the edge of the veranda to see what so intrigued his brother. He looked down upon a contingent of strangely garbed foreigners, parading down the street. Instead of the lightly colored tunics and robes of the locals, the strangers wore multi-colored checkered shirts and rarely seen trousers. Instead of robes, they wore cloaks fastened around the neck by a metal brooch. A sad looking donkey pulled a wooden wheeled cart that groaned as it clattered along the bumpy street.

The fourth set of travelers had arrived at their destination.

Towering above the others, wearing a bronze helmet with silver wings jutting from either side, a giant in full battle dress dominated the scene. The warrior wore chain armor over a brightly colored striped shirt and trousers, rhythmically beating his sword against his shield in menacing fashion, but the broad smile on his face assured the Jews that he was all pomp and show. His fellows laughed as they engaged the locals in friendly conversation.

Suddenly, the Jews pointed up at Ya'akov and Joses, and the warrior stepped forward and growled at them in a gravelly voice that filled the street.

Ya'akov was dumbfounded at the comic scene. Or, was it dangerous? Nothing made sense. He meekly raised his hand without speaking.

The warrior in battle garb stepped to the stoop, "We bring you gifts. May we enter?"

Ya'akov looked at Joses then back at the man-at-arms and stammered a welcome. Joses ran to the front door and ushered the foreigners up to the veranda where Ya'akov waited. Looking up at Caesar was even more shocking than looking down at him. Caesar stepped forward and engulfed Ya'akov with a massive bear hug. The stench of the man!

Caesar turned and gestured to others from his party who carried heavy bags from the cart. "Set the bags on the table," he said to his cronies. To Ya'akov, he said, "Look, look. Look inside these bags. These are gifts from the Galatians. Look what we have brought for our poor brothers and sisters of Jerusalem, according to the instructions we received from Paulos the apostle."

Joses opened a bag, and snatched a handful of gold coins; sifting them through his fingers, they clinked as they dropped back into the bag, and his mouth dropped, too. Caesar looked expectantly at Ya'akov, but Ya'akov stood mute and hospitality was not forthcoming. Ya'akov couldn't move; he couldn't speak; he could neither offer hospitality nor refuse it. A dreamlike haze gripped him. Finally, after a few awkward moments, the Galatians bade farewell and slowly clattered back down the street. Ya'akov again waved feebly as they departed.

Joses ran to fetch his brothers. When they returned, they found Ya'akov stalking around the veranda, slapping his walking stick against the waist-high wall and across the table. His fog had lifted.

"Damn Paulos. He sends unclean, Gentile barbarians into our city and into my home. These impure foreigners insult us with their filthy coins, as if we need the charity of Gentiles. Hmmph! What of our reputation in Jerusalem? What must the Jews think of us? What must the Pharisees think! I'm sure the tongues of the rumor-mongers wag tonight!" He whacked his walking stick across the table; it cracked into flying splinters. The brothers retreated to the edge of the veranda as Ya'akov stomped about.

Three days of stifling heat passed, but Ya'akov's anger did not dissipate; instead, he grew angrier by the minute, by the hour, by the day. "Did you see the way that stinking Gentile grabbed me?" he said repeatedly to no one in particular, as he shook his head while shuffling from one spot on his veranda to another.

He was angry with the Gentile warrior, and he was angry with himself. Why did he invite these obscene barbarians into his house? Why did he accept their gift? The bags remained on his table, taunting him. What should he do with the contaminated gold? Mostly his rage coalesced on Paulos who had humiliated Ya'akov in front of all Jerusalem.

"I tell you, this mission to the Gentiles will be the ruin of us." Ya'akov said to his brothers. "Yeshua said to a Gentile woman, 'I was sent only to the lost sheep of Israel. Only Israel ...'" Ya'akov's voice trailed off.

Joses defended the Gentile mission. "But, the story also tells us that Yeshua relented and said 'Woman, great is your faith! Let it be done for you as you wish.'" The brothers raised a familiar point and counterpoint in the Nazarene discussions about Gentiles, and both men were familiar with the well-worn arguments.

Cousin Symeon spoke, "If Paulos is converting the heathens to the cause of Yeshua's kingdom, is that such a bad thing?"

Ya'akov did not relent. "When the day comes and Yeshua returns to usher in his kingdom, do you really think these barbarians who are in league with the Romans will side with the Jews? I hear the Galatian warriors hire themselves to the highest bidder as mercenaries. Can we count on such as these to stand up for mother Jerusalem? How can we count on those unwilling to experience circumcision and to adhere to the Torah? Is their heart truly with us?"

Ya'akov continued to voice familiar arguments. "A true convert, a true proselyte, must wear the badge of Torah as a sign of fidelity to the God of Israel. A true convert must undergo circumcision. A true convert must eat as Torah prescribes. A true convert must honor the Sabbath and keep the festivals in due season. Then and only then can a conversion be trusted as sincere. Then and only then can a convert truly earn the right to be part of the family of God."

He should never have consented to a Torah-free Gentile mission during the Jerusalem assembly. He should have insisted that Titos and all other Gentiles submit to the knife. He was weak then, but he would be strong now. Ya'akov stood at the edge of his veranda staring blankly down the street, tugging hard on his norm.

"Where is Phinehas?" asked Ya'akov. Jude reminded him that Phinehas had shipped west, headed toward Corinth. "Too bad. Phinehas would have the backbone for the mission I have in mind," said Ya'akov.

Jude chose four other young men of the firebrand group of Phinehas to travel from Jerusalem to Galatia on behalf of Ya'akov and the Nazarenes. They would set the matter straight. They would make it clear that circumcision and strict Torah observance would be required of all who claimed to follow Yeshua of Nazareth.

"We shall learn who is sincere and who truly is with us," Ya'akov said to the four as they departed Jerusalem. "And be sure those Galatians understand that Paulos is not a true apostle since he never knew Yeshua. Be sure and tell those Galatians that Paulos was a persecutor." It was time that he confronted Paulos, who never walked with Yeshua, yet claimed to be an apostle.

Ya'akov watched the four depart, trailing pack donkeys laden with gold—the Galatian gift refused. The frayed leather cord around his neck snapped, and his builder's square clanged on the street below the veranda.

Chapter Fifty-eight

Paulos barely tolerated the torrid summer in Ephesus as he awaited Timotheos' news from Corinth. How would the Corinthians respond to the letter Stephanas had carried to them? While waiting, Paulos seldom ventured from the terrace house. In the mornings before the white sun scorched the city, he paced on the outside terrace, squinting at the ships entering the harbor, as if he could identify the one that carried tidings from Corinth. By midday, he retreated to the breathless humidity of the shaded house; open windows invited transient breezes to no avail. When the late day sun sunk toward the horizon, shadows slanted over the terrace, and he returned to his harbor vigil.

"I'm sure the Corinthians will heed my letter," Paulos would tell anyone who came near, but then he would look toward the sea and mumble words lost in the offshore breezes.

On the hottest day of the infernal summer, storm clouds roiled over the Aegean. Sheets of falling rain swept across the chop. Above that, charcoal clouds bulged with silent lightening. Higher still, where the sky met the heavens, powerful white crowns watched over all. When Paulos saw billowed sails emerge from the squall, pulling a vessel in a race against the wind, he expected a cargo of unfavorable news. The mist that swallowed the harbor blurred his sight, and Paulos could not discern the indistinct beings who disembarked, but he sensed that Timotheos was among them.

Paulos turned his attention away from the harbor to the cobblestone road in front of the terrace home. He fixed his gaze on the street corner where he expected his messenger's first appearance. Long minutes passed. Fog choked the twilight. Finally, Timotheos materialized out of the mist. Paulos strained his eyes to search the beardless face of the young Roman for a sign. What news? Timotheos bowed low as he leaned into the steep hillside; he revealed nothing.

Paulos moved to the top of the stairway, watching the hatless head rise toward him. He heard Timotheos heavy breaths before he tasted his sour words.

"Foreign missionaries are in Corinth," Timotheos said, "and they refute your teachings."

Prisca appeared with a cup of water that Timotheos gulped down. "Another, please," he said as he handed the empty cup back to her. He drank the second cup more slowly as if delaying what he had to say. He stole a glance at his mentor then averted his eyes; finally, he spoke. "What's more, they question you," he said. "They say you can't know Iesou because you weren't there."

When the first raindrops splashed across the terrace, the others retreated to the sanctuary of the terrace home, but Paulos stood alone in the wind gusts and pelting rain. Prisca gingerly pranced across the wet tiles and led her friend with the blanched and drained face under the rooftop. The others scurried about, closing windows, stuffing rags in leaks, and placing pots to catch the drips through the porous roof, but Paulos dripped alone as the late summer deluge poured down upon Ephesus.

Paulos was already busy at the table when Prisca stumbled out of her bedroom the next morning, shielding her eyes against the sharp yellow sun. The storm had passed, followed by a clear, cool morning and high blue skies. The torrid weather pattern had broken. Paulos barely noticed as she poured a cup of water from the pitcher on his table nor did he observe her curious eyes survey the silver shekel that rested atop a tattered purse, glinting in the morning sun.

The meddlers in Corinth could only be from Jerusalem. Sent by Ya'akov. That Ya'akov would interfere with his *ekklesias*, his Gentile, Torah-free *ekklesias*, shocked him. So much for the agreement at the apostolic assembly in Jerusalem. So much for the hand of fellowship extended by Ya'akov.

It took Paulos less than a week to compose another letter to the Corinthians, and Paulos decided to send his other protégé, Titos, by ship to deliver the letter. Timotheos and the others listened as Paulos handed the scroll to Titos and issued his instructions.

"You were in Jerusalem during the assembly. Tell the Corinthians about the agreement that I would be sent to the Gentiles; tell them that I was offered the hand of fellowship by the pillars of Jerusalem; tell them also about the mischief in Antioch caused by the Nazarenes."

Just as he had protested earlier when Paulos sent *him* as emissary, Timotheos now pouted over the selection of Titos. "It's not my fault," he said when he was alone with Paulos. "The foreigner had already swayed the Corinthians before I arrived. I did the best I could to dissuade them. Titos will see. You'll see. It wasn't my fault."

"I didn't say it was your fault," Paulos said. "Titos was in Jerusalem, and he can testify to the events of the apostolic assembly. He also knows many from Jerusalem; perhaps he can identify this meddler." Maybe it *was* Timotheos' fault, Paulos thought, and he hoped Titos would be a better advocate.

Paulos' short letter was conciliatory toward the Corinthians, sarcastic regarding the outside agitators, and forceful in presenting his credentials as the Corinthians' founding missionary. "We are not peddlers of God's word like so many, but as persons sent from God and standing in his presence." Correctly assuming that the Jerusalem agitators promoted Torah observance, he reminded the Corinthians that they were God's beloved, not by observing the letter of the law but by the spirit given in the new covenant, "the letter kills, but the Spirit gives life." He spoke of his own transformation and theirs, "And all of us, with unveiled faces, seeing the glory of the Lord as though reflected in a mirror, are being transformed into the same image."

Less than a month later, Titos returned by ship. "The Corinthians are unbowed," he said. "The situation is even worse than you feared. Your accuser is the same Phinehas who tormented you in Antioch."

Paulos had sent letters and each of his protégés as emissaries, to no avail. Would he lose Corinth as he had lost Antioch? The bastard, backstabbing Phinehas had turned Barnabas and Cephas against him. Would he contaminate his Corinthian friends also? At stake was the truth of Paulos' gospel, revealed to him on the road to Damascus, *apart from Torah*. By questioning his message, they questioned the truth of his own being, his standing before God, the gift of grace he had received on the road to Damascus, *apart from Torah*. To him, this was no mere dispute about ideas; it was an existential battle over his own soul. If Damascus had not happened, he was doomed. If Damascus had not happened, humankind was doomed.

He must counterattack. In person. This time, he would send no surrogate. Paulos booked passage on the first ship headed for Corinth.

Southwesterly breezes steady on the nose resulted in a foul crossing from Ephesus to Cenchreae. The cargo ship followed a zigzag pattern of tacks upwind—back and forth, back and forth, endlessly back and forth. Heavy seas pounded uncomfortably against the groaning vessel. In his haste, Paulos had not carried sufficient food for the voyage so he parceled out meager rations for the last days of the extended journey. He arrived tired, wet, and hungry; in the harbor mist, he knocked at the door of Chloe and Phoebe, the Cenchreae twins.

"So, you have finally come yourself," Chloe said half-joking, half-accusing. Paulos shivered into a chair. Despite his empty belly, he had no appetite for the hard bread and cold fish she offered, and he merely picked at his meal. He would have preferred sleep, but Phoebe lumbered off to spread the news of his arrival to his supporters, and soon a small crowd gathered, which raised his spirits even if his body lagged.

"Phin-e-hasss." Paulos said the name slowly, accentuating each syllable, and holding the end, producing a hissing effect. "I know this deceiver." Paulos explained the role of Phinehas in the Antioch incident. "At last, I'll confront the snake who poisoned Antioch for me."

Paulos should have slept in. He should have recuperated from the chill he caught crossing the sea. He should have eaten heartily to restore his strength. He should have better prepared for the confrontation, but events swirled out of control. At high noon the following day, Paulos met Phinehas in the spacious courtyard of a private home before the assembled Corinthians.

Phinehas the aggressor seized the moment, and he hopped atop a table to speak. "I know Ya'akov considers you to be his friend. In deference to Ya'akov, I will respect you," the short man with slicked up hair said, as he proceeded to assault Paulos with great disrespect. Phinehas leered at Paulos—even as he addressed the Corinthians—perhaps to gloat, to ogle his victim, to savor Paulos' suffering at his stings, to salt the wounds left by his bite, or to add intimidation to his strike. There was something menacing in the way he kept his face twisted toward Paulos, glaring at him while he spoke to the Corinthians.

"Has Paulos told you he never met Yeshua? Oh, he claims to have seen a vision? Well, who can trust a vision? Whom did he see in his vision? He tells you he saw 'the glory of God', but has he seen Yeshua? Has he seen the man of flesh and blood, the man who ate and drank, walked and talked, and who had brothers and sisters? Has he seen the Yeshua who was friend of Cephas, brother of Ya'akov, and son of Maryam?"

Phinehas turned away from Paulos to face the Corinthians, adding tension before he would answer his own questions. "I tell you he has not," he hissed. Phinehas smiled broadly at the Corinthians before he returned his gaze to Paulos to continue his biting attack.

"He was not among the followers when Yeshua walked the roads of Galilee or when Yeshua followed his journey of destiny to Jerusalem, and he certainly is not one of the disciples of Yeshua who now take up the mission of the Mashiah and the mantle of his leadership. If he now claims to be an apostle, let me tell you more."

Phinehas paused and glanced at the Corinthians. He drank from a cup of water as if to allow his venomous words to pulse through Paulos' veins toward his heart. With an exaggerated motion, the undersized showman set the cup down and glared again at Paulos, with a disarming smile.

"Has Paulos told you that he persecuted the followers of the Mashiah? In Damascus, Paulos opposed the *ekklesia*."

Paulos had never denied it, but it seemed so sinister when reported by Phinehas.

"Now Paulos tells you that Torah no longer matters, that for him, 'all things are lawful.' He turns his back on his own heritage. Not only does he cut himself off from God, but he is an apostate who leads others astray with his false teachings." As he finished, Phinehas smiled with great self-satisfaction and slithered into the crowd.

Perhaps it was his weakened condition. Perhaps it was the unexpected vitriol against him personally, rather than a reasoned debate. Perhaps it was because the charges were true; after all, he had not walked with Iesou, he relied on his vision, he had been a persecutor, and he disputed Torah, but the naked way Phinehas expressed Paulos' own life stripped it of meaning.

Whatever the reason, Paulos had no antidote to fend off the stings of Phinehas. As poison coursed through his veins, he staggered to the dais. Sweat streaked his blanched face under the hot gaze of the faceless crowd. His starved belly rumbled, and the empty man had no answer. He muttered toneless words of self-defense with a crackling voice. He did not recognize the suddenly anonymous faces of the Corinthians, who said nothing, their silence a telling judgment. He was defeated, and he knew it.

A humiliated Paulos retreated to Ephesus. With favorable winds, the return journey passed quickly. At first, Paulos hardly noticed, absorbed with a mixture of self-pity and self-doubt, but as the winds distanced him from his defeat, his anguish turned to anger then to resolve. He did not wait for the sailors to warp the ship into a berth at the docks of Ephesus; he dived overboard, swam to shore, and galloped up the hill to the terrace house to write another letter "out of much affliction and anguish of heart and with many tears." This time he would be the aggressor.

Paulos rewrote the letter several times to get it just right, but his hand was unsteady so Timotheos acted as his amanuensis, his secretary, who penned the script onto the papyrus. He meant to attack Phinehas, a "false apostle," without appearing mean spirited, he meant to criticize the Corinthians without antagonizing them, and he meant to bolster his own credentials without boasting.

He apologized for the poor appearance he made in his recent visit, acknowledging that his bodily presence was weak and his speech contemptible, but then he built his credentials out of his own failings "for whenever I am weak, then I am strong." He warned the Corinthians against "false apostles, deceitful workers, disguising themselves as apostles of Christos," who preached a false gospel and a false interpretation of Iesou—"someone comes and proclaims another Iesou than the one we proclaimed." Not having walked with Iesou of Nazareth mattered not since "visions and revelations of the Lord" had revealed all to him.

Paulos hurried to finish the letter before the *mare clausum*, the seasonal cessation of shipping due to winter weather, and he dispatched Titos with the letter on one of the last ships to leave Ephesus that season. It would be months before Titos would return by land following a slow slog around the Aegean, and Paulos settled in for a long winter's wait.

Chapter Fifty-nine

Titos had been gone for less than a month. In the mountain pastures around Ephesus, morning dew became frost, and highland ponds glazed over with a thin veneer of ice. On the seacoast, sodden clouds hung low and gray over Ephesus. Autumn was ending, and winter was nigh. Paulos idled impatiently, but then came the unexpected knock on the terrace house door.

Epaphras, a visitor from the new *ekklesia* in Colossae up the valley of the Meander River, answered the door and Roman soldiers immediately arrested him. Paulos heard the commotion and emerged from a back room.

"That's him. That's the Jew bastard," accused the soldier's witness, a priest of the Artemis temple. "That's the Jew who spreads his superstitions. Arrest the bastard!" The silversmith priests of the Artemis temple didn't appreciate Paulos' meddling in their commerce, claiming their gods were false but his Hebrew God was true, and they alerted the authorities.

Paulos' worries about Corinth across the sea abruptly paled next to the danger to his own life and limb. Poor Epaphras from Colossae had the misfortune of visiting the wrong person at the wrong time, and the soldiers escorted him away in shackles, too.

Eight prisoners, including Paulos and Epaphras, crowded into the holding cell, measuring five paces by seven paces. Each day, the Roman guards paraded the prisoners into the sunlight to allow cleaning of the ramshackle wooden building. The last-to-arrive inmates swept the cell and tossed fresh wheat straw onto the wooden-planked floor. The guards assigned a special task to Paulos; he held his breath as he carried out the bronze pot filled with human waste and dumped it in the swamp behind the building. The daily ritual concluded with a meal of hard bread, water, and rancid meat of unrecognizable origin.

The roll of prisoners changed regularly; the cell was merely a temporary holding station for petty thieves and misdemeanants who awaited their hearing before the magistrate. Once they were tried and their punishment exacted (usually beatings with a rod and sometimes banishment to exile), they did not return.

Weeks passed as Paulos and Epaphras waited for their court date. After a month of sitting in the holding cell, the day of their appearance before the magistrate finally arrived.

"Stand before the magistrate," said the centurion as he poked his lance in the prisoner's backs.

"What say you to the charges of proselytization?" asked the magistrate. "Are you Jews who spread your religion in violation of the decree of the Emperor?

"We are Roman citizens, sir," said Paulos.

Upon a signal from the centurion, soldiers stepped forward and ripped the garments from the two prisoners, stripping them naked before the judge. Paulos' hunched shoulders slumped all the more, and his chest hollowed. The blotched skin of an old man sagged in folds around his slight paunch. His long arms seemed detached as he awkwardly covered then uncovered himself, uncertain what to do with his hands.

The judge looked at the uncircumcised member of Epaphras then addressed the centurion. "This one is uncut. Are there witnesses against him?"

"No, sir," said the centurion. "But he was with the one named Paulos when we arrested him."

"Release that one," said the magistrate with a dismissive wave of his hand.

Paulos was relieved as Epaphras picked up his garments and scrambled toward the door. Paulos' nodded at him when he briefly hesitated before disappearing into the sunlight. The magistrate then stared at Paulos circumcision.

"You claim to be a Roman citizen," he said, "but you bear the mutilation of the Jews."

Paulos stammered unintelligibly.

"Are there witnesses against this one?"

"Yes, sir. Many. He is well known as the leader of a Jewish sect that promotes its superstitions among the citizens of this city."

The magistrate clenched his jaw and glared at naked Paulos who stood mute, feeling puny and helpless; his guilt was visible for all to see.

"Do you deny it?" The magistrate's tone was accusing not questioning.

Paulos had gone under the rod before, and he would do it again. He was neither brave nor defiant, merely resigned. He knew that he was guilty according to the law of the Romans, and he would accept his punishment. The magistrate waited a moment for an answer, but Paulos stood mute. Hearing no defense, the magistrate pronounced judgment.

"Guilty. I find the prisoner guilty, and I sentence him to a beating with a rod in the manner prescribed by law."

"But, sir, he is a repeat offender with a long history of ignoring the decree of the Emperor," said the centurion. "Death. A death sentence is appropriate for this one."

Paulos stiffened and gulped the air; he stood naked and helpless before the magistrate who suddenly controlled his fate.

Sweat beads formed on the brow of the magistrate. He chewed on his lips as if he did his thinking with his mouth. The magistrate alternately glared at the centurion and Paulos; finally, he dropped his eyes and muttered, "I must confer with the Governor. I cannot impose the death sentence without orders from the Governor."

The soldiers paraded Paulos, now a convicted criminal, back to the holding cell. He clutched his tattered robes in his hands to cover his nakedness in front of the hooting crowds.

Paulos knew little of the governor, and he didn't know what to expect when the governor and the magistrate would meet to resolve his fate.

"Cut off his head! Cut off his balls! Cut off the rest of his mutilated prick! What do I care?"

The rotund Governor reclined on pillows on the tiled floor of his airy veranda; the magistrate stood rigidly in front of him. Even on a cool day of early winter, both men perspired heavily—the magistrate sweated nervously while the fat man with pallid, sagging skin did so naturally. The Governor poured the last of a bottle of wine into his cup; he threw the empty bottle over the balustrade at the edge of the veranda, shattering it in the courtyard, already the third smashed bottle of the morning.

The Governor had greater worries than the fate of a damned Jew; he feared for his own neck. Emperor Claudius, his benefactor, the distant cousin who had appointed him to this plum position, was dead, poisoned by his own wife. Agrippina had assassinated the emperor, her third husband, in a palace coup that elevated her sixteen-year-old son to the throne. Nero the man-child was the new Emperor, the new Caesar. Out with the old and in with the new.

Of course, Nero would send his own crony to replace him as Governor; the fat man knew that. Would Nero demand his life? His drooping jowls puckered as he looked with alarm at his wine cup. Did he detect the sickly, sweet taste of hemlock? He dashed the cup across the floor, splattering its contents on flowered mosaics. He pulled a stiletto from its sheath and pricked his palm, deliberately drawing blood. For a moment, he stared at a maroon droplet before he smeared it across his green sash. Perhaps he should hug the dagger now and be done with it! The magistrate jumped even while attempting to appear dispassionate as the Governor flung the blade in his direction, missing by a wide margin.

Tangled in his robes, the Governor awkwardly pushed himself up from his pillow, staggered to the edge of the veranda, and pissed through the marble balusters onto the courtyard below, indiscreetly fouling the air with audible flatulence.

"Piss on the Jew," he mumbled. "Cut off his head and send him to Hades! I don't care what you do with the damned Jew."

The magistrate turned and bounded down the steps, apparently eager to leave the presence of the Governor, but just as he reached the gate to the street, the Governor called to him.

"Wait! Don't do anything with the Jew." Caution suddenly seized the soon-to-be-former Governor. "Let him sit. I'll wait to see which way the wind blows from Rome."

A week later, Paulos stood in the sunlight with the other prisoners while the putrid holding cell received its daily cleaning. Two guards approached him.

"Come with us, Jew."

When Paulos realized they followed a different street than the one to the magistrate, he feared his life was about to end, but the guards merely transferred him to a long-term cell. As they arrived at the garrison, one of his guards opened the door to a wooden shed attached to the outside of the barracks.

"This is your new jail."

The shed boasted a window, a sleeping mat, and stools. Compared to the holding cell, Paulos' new home was a luxurious apartment. Paulos paused on the threshold and turned to thank the guards. As he did so, he spied Aquila; his short friend stood across the street with an impish grin, holding his coin purse high and shaking it.

Paulos spent the winter months in relative comfort and with unexpected privileges from his jailors, thanks to Aquila's bribes. Paulos regularly received guests who provided him with fresh bread, garum, figs and dates, and often a pot of warm stew. One of his visitors came all the way from Philippi. Epaphroditus, the brother to Euodia, Paulos' wealthy benefactor, arrived during a stretch of wet, cold weather, suffering from a fever and wheezing. Aquila promptly brought him to Paulos' cell. The slight man appeared as gray and delicate as the papyrus letter he carried from the Philippians. He also offered a bulging purse of gold coins, placed in the care of Aquila who had a special purpose in mind.

"Put him to bed and summon a physician," Paulos instructed Aquila. While Epaphroditus recuperated, Paulos penned a reply letter to his Philippian friends.

To all the saints in Christos Iesou who are in Philippi, with the bishops and deacons: I thank my God every time I remember you… I am fully satisfied, now that I have received from Epaphroditus the gifts you sent, *a fragrant offering, a sacrifice acceptable and pleasing to God.*

His mission was God's mission. A gift to him was a gift to God.

Letter writing and the affairs of the Ephesian *ekklesia* kept Paulos busy through the winter, but he worried often about the situation in Corinth. As spring approached, he expected Titos to return with news at any time.

Once again, events would intervene.

It was late in the day and late in the winter. Paulos' cell door squeaked open and the round figure of Aquila loomed in the doorframe.

"Come quickly. We must leave," Aquila said in a voice barely above a whisper.

Paulos was confused, and he stared blankly at his stubby friend, silhouetted against the afternoon sun.

"Listen to me. I've paid dearly for this opportunity, and you must come now!" Aquila said, louder and more demanding than before.

Paulos was not accustomed to the assertive tone of his friend, but he arose from his squatting position on the floor and followed Aquila out the open door of the cell-shed.

"The guards will soon return. Hurry!"

The escapee and his accomplice scurried down a back street as quickly as they dared, without drawing attention to themselves.

Turning a corner, they found Timotheos waiting with Prisca and two donkeys packed with supplies. Gaunt Paulos was breathless from the exertion of his escape, and he could barely stand up under Prisca's tearful hugs.

"Paulos. Paulos," she said repeatedly.

Timotheos smiled through moist eyes.

Three years after their arrival, the four missionaries fled from Ephesus, leaving a regional network of *ekklesias* behind. Under the bright stars of a moonless night, they trudged slowly— atrophied and out-of-shape Paulos held them back—north along the Persian Royal Road. When miles separated them from Ephesus, they settled into a routine of walking during daylight and camping at night. It would be a long march through the western regions of Anatolia before they would reach Troas, the coastal city far to the northwest, the jumping off port for Macedonia.

A week later, they arrived in Troas, beat and broke. Aquila's hefty bribe had nearly emptied his coin purse even before they departed Ephesus. They lingered in Troas while they raised funds to book sea passage to Macedonia and the friendly *ekklesia* in Philippi. Timotheos and Aquila toiled on the docks; Paulos' atrophied body regained vitality with daily walks to the harbor to greet ships arriving from the west; Paulos expected Titos to arrive with news of Corinth. Two weeks after their arrival in Troas, Aquila's coin purse again jangled, but Paulos was reluctant to leave.

"What if we pass Titos at sea?" With each passing day, he grew more apprehensive. "What if something happened to the boy?"

After waiting another week, the others persuaded Paulos to press on to Philippi. Amidst squawking gulls and harbor hubbub, the missionaries waited impatiently on the docks as dockworkers loaded cargo onto the galley that would carry them to Macedonia. Paulos was uncommunicative and grumpy as he squatted apart from the others, lost in thought. Jarring images of young Titos agitated

Paulos' consciousness.

The leering red snake opened his jaws wide, squirting stinging venom over Titos; a wolf with the head of Phinehas snarled at the boy; boars, bears, and other beasts of the forest encircled the lad who retreated to the edge of his mountain campfire; crackling lightning ripped open the black clouds and a deluge extinguished the campfire; all was dark.

In his stupor, Paulos heard the voice of Titos call to him.

"Paulos, is that you?"

Paulos shot up from his squatting position, willing his ears to hear the sweet cry again. Did he dream? Did he imagine the voice?

"Paulos, is that you? It's me, Titos!"

Paulos swung on his heels and stared up at the figure aboard a ship that dockworkers warped to the dock. Paulos shielded his eyes against the morning sun as Titos waved at him. The dockworkers pulled on thick, hemp ropes, slowly swinging the galley toward the dock; Titos leaped over the lessing gap and rushed to the embrace of Paulos. Paulos cupped Titos' head in his hands and repeatedly kissed Titos' face as tears spilled down his own cheeks.

Aquila paid for an additional passenger for the voyage west while Timotheos and Titos hustled to the agora, returning with arms filled with plump wineskins for an onboard celebration. It seemed that even Timotheos was excited at the safe return of Titos; Paulos was glad that his protégés forgot their rivalry, at least for the moment.

"Do tell, how are things in Corinth?" Paulos asked. "Is Phinehas still deceiving them with his venomous lies? What of Chloe, Phoebe, and Stephanas; are they still with me?" Paulos' words could not keep up with the worries of his mind, and he peppered Titos with questions as the ship's crew rowed the boat from the harbor to the sea.

Titos smiled and held up his hand, signaling Paulos to be quiet. "All is well. The Corinthians expelled Phinehas from the community, and he sailed back to Jerusalem. Your friends are in control and the leader of the enthusiasts is contrite."

Paulos screeched a gleeful shout, and he passed the wineskin again.

"Even before I arrived with your letter, Phinehas' welcome had worn thin. His personal attacks offended many of the Corinthians, and his insistence upon Torah observances alarmed the Gentiles."

Paulos stood and paced along the gunwale with one hand grasping the rail as he listened to Titos' report, oblivious to the rolling ship and occasional salt spray.

"When I arrived with your letter, I read it to the assembled *ekklesia*, leading to much debate. Your friends spoke in your favor, and they asked me to speak also; I reminded them that Cephas, Ya'akov, and Yochanan had each extended the hand of friendship to you and your mission to the Gentiles. As I sensed the mood was swinging in your favor, I kept applying the pressure."

Paulos stopped pacing and stared out to sea as a subtle smile twitched the corners of his mouth.

"Phinehas also sensed that he had lost momentum, and he began to attack your friends. Finally, he challenged Crispus and the other Jews to stop worshiping with the uncircumcised Gentiles. Until then, Crispus had been silent, but when he stood up to speak, the battle was over."

"Crispus, yes. Crispus. I knew I could count on Crispus," Paulos said with a firm nod as he pounded his fist on the gunwale. Crispus, the Jewish leader of a Corinthian synagogue, had been an early convert, and now he had proven to be a loyal friend.

Titos finished the story. "Crispus said he would continue to worship with his brothers and sisters of the *ekklesia* whether they were Jew or Gentile. Then he looked straight at Phinehas and said, 'But I do not care to worship with you. I think it best if you leave Corinth. Now!'"

The warmth of the springtime sun caressed Paulos' cheeks as refreshing sea breezes lifted the ship forward. Years earlier, this same sea passage had resulted in shipwreck, and he had feared Timotheos would be lost at sea. Paulos looked at the son of a Roman soldier sitting comfortably next to Titos, and his eyes welled. Aquila and Prisca, the plump married couple, leaned against the gunwale, their stubby fingers intertwined. Just a few days ago, Paulos had been a condemned convict. Jerusalem had contended with him over the soul of his Corinthian *ekklesia;* he had fought the good fight and emerged victorious. Soon, friends in Philippi would greet them.

Paulos stood at the bow of the ship; he lifted his face to sea and sky, wind and waves, closed his eyes, and smiled, "Aaaah, life was good. God was good."

Chapter Sixty

The Macedonian springtime greeted the arrivals in Philippi: cool nights for sleeping; early sunrises; cheery mornings that awakened the blushing blossoms in the apple orchards; afternoons hot enough to make a workman sweat, even shirtless in the shade; and twilight evenings filled with children's laughter that lingered into the night. Philippi perched on a hilltop against a mountain backdrop, and Euodia's villa boasted views of snowy peaks girdled by black forested slopes. Paulos presided over a summit of his Philippian followers on the villa terrace; pine-scented breezes filtered down the valleys and floated over the terrace as if the mountaintop eminences signaled their approval of the planning session.

"I promised to collect funds for the poor of Jerusalem. Now is the time to press that effort," Paulos said. Philippi had always been generous with financial support for his mission; Paulos rightly expected more of the same for the Jerusalem collection.

Two months later, Paulos and his entourage departed for Thessalonica, the next stop on his collection journey; donkey packs bulged with gold and silver coins, given by the Philippians. The entourage had grown: Secundus, a merchant accustomed to managing money, became the bursar; Aristarchus, a former Roman soldier, brandishing a sword and shield, served as security for the entourage and their valuable cargo. Aristarchus reminded Paulos of Caesar, the Celtic warrior. Paulos wondered if the Galatians had delivered a collection to Jerusalem; if so, how had Ya'akov responded? He would learn soon enough. For now, Paulos remained optimistic that a collection would heal the rift with Jerusalem. Only later would he learn the opposite.

The entourage would change further once they reached Thessalonica. Titos would return to Corinth carrying Paulos' final letter to the Corinthians, a letter of reconciliation and of instruction regarding the collection, promising the Corinthians that Paulos would return soon to finish the collection efforts. Prisca and Aquila would also leave the group when it reached Thessalonica.

They broke the news to Paulos one night as they camped along the *Via Egnatia*, the road to Thessalonica.

"Paulos, we, we—

Prisca broke into tears and couldn't continue. She usually spoke for Aquila, her husband, but now he spoke for her.

"My dear friend, forgive us, but we've decided to return to Rome. It's our home, and it's time to return now that Emperor Claudius who expelled us is dead," Aquila said.

Paulos rubbed his back against the trunk of a fig tree without looking at either of them, the stubby husband and wife who resembled each other, his loyal companions for the past five years, the conspirators who saved his neck in Ephesus. Only the lonely chorus of chirping crickets broke the silence. Prisca wiped her eyes as she awaited a response from the leader she dearly loved.

Finally, Paulos forced a smile and looked into the eyes of his dear friends. "Of course. Of course," he said.

For a fleeting moment, Paulos nearly said he would join them; like a rogue wave, the old allure for the city of seven hills almost knocked him off course, an unexpected swell of emotion long subdued but never forgotten. With the passage of many years, Paulos rarely thought of Arsenios. Now, sweet melancholy pinched his heart once more, and he wondered about the blond Greek with the wayward curl hanging over his forehead. The image of his crestfallen friend at the rail of the departing ship stung him again.

Paulos began to speak, coughed, cleared his throat then started over. "One day soon I'll join you there. After we finish this collection, and after I deliver it to Jerusalem, I'll journey to Rome. I have business there, too ..." His voice trailed off.

Chapter Sixty-one

Paulos and Timotheos settled into the home of their old friend, Jason, in Thessalonica. Prisca and Aquila departed for Rome and Titos for Corinth, carrying Paulos' letter of reconciliation. The Philippians who had joined Paulos' collection team, Aristarchus and Secundus, stayed in the home of another *ekklesia* member.

Meanwhile, Paulos was unaware that a courier was tracking him. From Ephesus, around the Aegean to Troas, across the sea to Philippi, and along the *Via Egnatia*, the messenger finally caught up to Paulos in Thessalonica. The courier carried a letter from Tatiana, Paulos' Galatian friend, with ominous news from Galatia.

On the heels of his victory over Jerusalem in Corinth, Paulos learned of a new battlefield in Galatia. As soon as he finished reading the letter, Paulos raked his arm across the table, strewing plates, cups, and utensils clattering onto the plank decking of Jason's kitchen.

"Damn you, Ya'akov!" he shrieked as he kicked over an amphora, spilling water that gurgled down the cracks between the floorboards.

Jason, Timotheos, and the courier stared at Paulos with their mouths hanging open. Paulos put both hands alongside his head and tugged on his gray hairs as if he could pull the bad news from his brain. "Damn it, damn it, damn it," he said, softer each time, as he stumbled out the door into the streets of Thessalonica.

By the following morning, Paulos' rage had cooled to a controlled simmer. He read and reread the letter:

To Paulos and our friends in Christos in Ephesus or wherever this letter may find you. Blessings to you from your friend Tatiana in Pessinus of Galatia. Your friend Mariana and others here also send their greetings.

It is with great dismay that I must tell you that we have received unexpected visitors who arrived soon after the return of our own delegation that carried gifts to Jerusalem. The visitors from Jerusalem are critical of you personally and critical of your teachings. They dismiss your apostleship because you were not a follower of Iesou during his lifetime. They say you are inferior to the Jerusalem leaders. Did you really persecute those in Christos in Damascus as they claim?

Sometimes the truth can be the most damnable lie. Of course, he had never known Iesou during his lifetime; he never claimed otherwise. But he had Damascus. When the skies opened and God spoke to him, he received all he needed directly from the Lord.

We must also tell you that the Jerusalem emissaries are imposing the law of the Jews upon us. Some of our members have quit the *ekklesia*. Others accepted these requirements. For the men, the requirement of circumcision is painful and dangerous. Does the Jewish Torah bind us?

It was not surprising that circumcision frightened the Galatians. Evil crept out from the Temple of Cybele in the Galatians' midst, and circumcision must seem as bewitching as the cultic castration of Attis. The Judaizers did not advance the kingdom, they cut the Galatians off from the Christos.

We know you and love you, and we are sure you have answers to these charges. Please help us as we defend your name to the others here in Galatia.

If you are able to visit us personally, I am sure you will set things right. If you cannot make a personal visit at this time, please send a letter that we can circulate to all *ekklesias*. We anxiously await your assistance.

Your sister in Christos, Tatiana.

"I must return to Galatia to battle these Judaizers," Paulos said.

"And then where?" Timotheos asked. "Will you merely follow the arsonists who torch your *ekklesias?* First Corinth then Galatia, where will they next appear?" Timotheos asked hard questions.

They walked along in silence. As Paulos' strides lengthened, Timotheos tugged on Paulos' sleeve, and the gangly man slowed.

"Then I will go straightaway to Jerusalem and confront Ya'akov face-to-face," Paulos said.

"Yes, Jerusalem. You must go to Jerusalem," Timotheos said. "But are you ready now? Should you not first send a careful reply to Tatiana and the Galatians? Should you not finish gathering the collection and assemble an entourage so that you go to Jerusalem with strength? Jerusalem, yes, but only when you're ready."

They talked themselves to the edge of the city, crossing the *Via Egnatia* highway as it passed from east to west. They climbed atop a nearby hillside that afforded a countryside view. Timotheos rested on a boulder adjacent to a grove of fig trees while Paulos paced, considering his options.

After gazing west along the *Via Egnatia* toward Rome, then south in the direction of Corinth, then east toward the land of the sunrise and Galatia, his eyes fixed on the sea that extended far beyond his vista. Jerusalem lay across the Great Sea. Twice in his life, he had been to Jerusalem—a generation ago when he spent a fortnight as the guest of Cephas after fleeing Damascus, and a dozen years later when he led the Antioch delegation to the apostolic assembly. More than half a dozen years had passed since the assembly, and he was anxious to return, but Timotheos was right—he would return in strength, laden with bags of gold and a supportive entourage.

Raindrops jarred Paulos from his thoughts as storm clouds rolled in from the sea. Timotheos did not complain about pace as they jogged back to Jason's home just ahead of a late summer thunderstorm.

"Paulos an apostle ... sent neither by human commission nor from human authorities, but through Iesou Christos and God the Father ... to the *ekklesias* of Galatia ... For I want you to know, brothers and sisters, that the gospel that was proclaimed by me is not of human origin; for I did not receive it from a human source, nor was I taught it, but I received it through a revelation of Iesou Christos."

Timotheos read the words penned by Paulos' hand, the opening stanza of his letter to the Galatians. Timotheos would recopy the letter since Paulos' penmanship had become unsteady.

"That should make it clear that I am not inferior to Ya'akov or dependent upon him or Cephas for my mission," Paulos said when Timotheos finished reading.

For the next month, Paulos carefully drafted his letter to the Galatians with Timotheos as secretary while Jason directed the collection efforts with the assistance of Aristarchus the soldier and Secundus the money-manager. Paulos established a pattern; early in the morning before the sun overheated the city, he walked with Timotheos while they discussed the letter—actually, Paulos did most of the talking and Timotheos mostly listened, often urging Paulos to slow his pace. During the afternoon, Paulos would dictate and Timotheos would put pen and ink to papyrus; after supper, Jason would join them for a discussion of the day's entry.

Paulos dictated the letter as a speech or legal argument, relying upon his rhetoric training. First, he set forth a correct account of the facts to rebut the lies of the Judaizing Nazarenes. He told the Galatians about the Jerusalem agreement. He alone had authority to go to the Gentiles and the Nazarenes did not; Ya'akov and Cephas had given their word sealed with their handshake! He reported on the Nazarene meddling that caused the Antioch incident, and he criticized Cephas' waffling behavior. After a few days of writing, the factual foundation was complete, and Paulos turned to his argumentation.

"Torah is a curse, you know," Paulos said, as he and Timotheos reached the cluster of fig trees outside the city that had become their venue for daily ruminations. Paulos reached up and plucked a fig from a low hanging branch. He popped it into his mouth, chewed, and swallowed. Paulos meant to provoke a response from Timotheos, but the Roman leaned against his favorite boulder and said nothing.

"Torah is a curse because it deceives us into thinking that we are in control," Paulos continued. "We make idols of our own efforts and ourselves. We forget that God is God and we are not." Paulos grabbed a few more figs to chew on while they walked back to town.

That evening, Paulos read aloud what he had dictated and Timotheos had penned that afternoon:

> We know that a person is justified, not by the works of Torah, but through faith in Iesou Christos. And we have come to believe in Christos Iesou, so that we might be justified by faith in Christos and not by doing the works of Torah, because no one will be justified by the works of Torah.

"I don't understand this idea of justification," said Jason.

Much as he appreciated Jason, Paulos often became exasperated with him during these evening discussions because he didn't understand what seemed so clear to Paulos. "Don't you see? It's not human works; it's God's gracious act of forgiveness, of acceptance, of justifying the unworthy."

A scowl replaced the blank expression on Jason's face. "Is there no human responsibility?" Jason asked. "If it isn't human action, effort, deeds, merit, or accomplishment that God requires, what's the human responsibility? If there's a requirement that humans must satisfy, what is it?"

Paulos answered quickly. "It's faith. Those who have faith are the family of God."

"And what is faith?" asked Timotheos, tilting his stool on two legs as he leaned against the doorpost. The room was stuffy, but Timotheos breathed the cool vapors of the night from his doorway perch.

"Belief. Believers. Those who believe the gospel that I preach are the family of God."

Timotheos' stool clunked on the wooden floor planks when he rocked forward from his leaning position. He stepped outside to escape the stifling air inside. He continued to listen from the street as he pondered the stars. For a moment, all was silent before Timotheos spoke. "What of the Nazarenes? What of the Jews?" he asked, standing in the fresh, evening air but looking back into the sultry room. "Are they no longer of the family of God because they believe differently than you teach?"

Paulos grasped his walking stick that was leaning in the corner of the room, and he too stepped outside, sucking a deep draught of night air. He joined Timotheos, and they both gazed at the wash of stars across the moonless sky. *I will make your offspring as numerous as the stars of heaven and as the sand that is on the seashore.* No, he could not nullify God's promise to Abraham. How could he uphold the promise to the children of Abraham *and* include the Gentiles in the promise? He would think on that.

The next morning outside the fig orchard, Paulos droned on about his insistence on *belief in his gospel* as the boundary marker for the *ekklesia* of God. He didn't notice that Timotheos was barely listening, distracted by a child playing outside a mud-brick hut.

A fully-grown fig tree shaded the humble building that apparently housed a family. The young boy could not reach ripe figs hanging from drooping branches, and he climbed the tree with great determination to reach the sweet figs. With legs straddling a horizontal branch, the youngster pulled himself forward until he was able to stretch and pluck a few figs. After eating the sweet fruit, he realized his predicament; he was afraid to back down the branch, and he was stuck.

"Momma! Momma! Help me!"

The child began to wail; just as Timotheos was about to walk over to help the child, the mother came from the house. She stood directly under her boy who clung to the branch just beyond her outstretched arms.

"Momma! Momma!" he cried.

"Just let go, I will catch you," she said with her arms extended toward the boy.

He didn't loosen his grip.

"Don't cry my little one. Momma will catch you. Just let go."

The whimpering stopped as the child appeared to be summoning courage.

"Trust momma, I will catch you."

The child let go, falling safely into his mother's arms.

"Are you listening to me? Did you hear what I said?" Paulos' voice called Timotheos back.

When Timotheos turned his face toward him, Paulos saw an expression that betrayed doubt or disagreement. There was an *almost* quality to the look, as if the protégé was about to argue, to challenge his mentor for the first time. Paulos glared as he waited for Timotheos' words that never came.

Paulos didn't hear what Timotheos wanted to say but could not: that Paulos was overreacting to his dispute with Ya'akov; that he diluted his own pure gospel of the unconditional grace of God, *apart from Torah;* that belief was no less human effort than works. Was a gracious God willing to forgive transgressions of Torah but unwilling to forgive an uncertain heart?

Finally, Timotheos turned toward the fig tree and pointed. "Did you see that boy fall into his mother's arms?"

Chapter Sixty-two

"See what large letters I make when I am writing in my own hand!"

Paulos concluded his letter to the Galatians with a personal greeting added to the end of Timotheos' transcription and dispatched a courier to carry it straightaway to Tatiana. Aristarchus the Philippian soldier and Secundus the bursar had completed their collection efforts in Thessalonica earlier, and they were anxious to move on. Already the autumnal nights were cooler; it was time to head south to Corinth before snow clogged the mountain passes. With the epistle safely enroute to Galatia with a copy for Philippi and one for Ephesus—in case the Judaizers would appear at either place—Paulos was also ready to move on, and his focus shifted again to Corinth.

Paulos marched at the head of a donkey caravan while spear-wielding Aristarchus covered the rear. A few Thessalonians had joined Paulos' entourage, and their caravan snaked along the sea around Mt. Olympus. They raced through the mountains and plains of Achaea. Paulos pushed himself to his limits, and the others barely kept up. He knew how the others saw him: thinning brown hair that grayed at the edges; stooped shoulders; and a hitch in his gait—he had grown old. He had walked many leagues, but there were many more yet to go, and he would lead on.

Each day it seemed that they departed earlier in the morning and trudged later in the evening as Paulos pushed forward, oblivious to aught but the goal of Corinth. He didn't hear the grumbling of his Roman compatriots, he didn't see the thick coats of the goats and sheep, he didn't feel the chill of the autumnal air, he didn't smell the decaying leaves and grasses, he didn't taste the cold suppers of late evening; he only sensed the ever-nearer Corinth. Titos had assured him that the Corinthian controversies were resolved, but Paulos needed to see for himself.

On the last day of their journey, the road weary travelers trudged well past sunset to reach the village of Cenchreae and the home of Chloe and Phoebe. Paulos approached the stoop and pounded on the door of the familiar, old rickety building at harbor's edge. Light flickered through the cracks in a back window; he followed the glow as it flowed through the house, window by window, crack by crack, until it clutched at his feet across the doorsill. The door creaked open slightly, and candlelight fell warmly on his face. Chloe flung the door wide when she recognized Paulos, rushed to hug him, and smudged his cloak with the candle that still dangled in her hand.

Paulos' reunion with the trousered sisters of Cenchreae was a happy portent of the warm welcome accorded him by the Corinthians. Titos was right, the contentious *ekklesias* had calmed, and the former conspirators embraced Paulos as returning champion, a role that fit him well.

A winter of contented calm followed the nervous frenzy of the autumnal trek across Greece as Paulos settled comfortably into Corinth. Paulos, Titos, and Timotheos established headquarters in the spacious villa of Gaius, overseeing the collection for Jerusalem that was already well underway; the wealthy Corinthians proved to be generous.

Not even bad news from Philippi dented Paulos' high spirits. The Judaizers had reached Philippi as he expected, claiming that the followers of Christ must be circumcised and eat proper foods. Paulos was confident that the Philippians would repel these evil workers: the Philippians were strong in their faith; they had seen his earlier letter to the Galatians; and he had forewarned them of the danger of those who spread a false gospel.

"Beware." That was the thrust of the short letter he wrote to remind the Philippians. Beware the evil workers who "mutilate the flesh" and whose "god is the belly."

Paulos received good news as well. A cheery letter arrived from Prisca in Rome; she and Aquila had safely returned to their Roman environs to discover that many new members had flocked to the *ekklesia* in their absence.

"Your reputation has reached the city of seven hills," she wrote. "When our old and new friends learned that we had been with you, we were treated with great respect. Please come soon. Your Roman friends in Christos will welcome you heartily."

Paulos imagined a triumphal reception, hordes of followers, and a populace eager to hear his message. He would springboard from a successful Roman visit to the far western frontier of the Empire— soon the whole world would hear his good news, and the Christos would return in triumph.

Paulos wondered about his old friend Arsenios; he had not seen him in nearly two decades—could he still be in Rome? The images that had jarred Paulos over the years had become less frequent and less troubling, but the ashen cheeks of the young Arsenios on the Rome-bound ship came back to Paulos now and once again stirred a cloudy mix of guilt and affection—and hollow loneliness.

Before realizing his long held goal of Rome, Paulos must first finish the business of the collection for Jerusalem to stop the meddling of Ya'akov and the Nazarenes in *his ekklesias*. He would personally carry the collection to Jerusalem when the sea opened in the spring; surely, these gifts and a face-to-face meeting with Ya'akov would settle the matter.

In the meantime, he would compose a letter to the Romans that would prepare them for his impending arrival; it would also systematically address his issues with Jerusalem as a brief in anticipation of his hearing before Ya'akov. He would send a copy to Ya'akov via the *cursus publicus*, the Roman postal and courier service.

Gaius, his host, allowed Paulos to use his personal secretary to write down what Paulos dictated. The letter to the Romans was unique in that it was to an *ekklesia* that Paulos had neither founded nor visited. It was also unique in that it did not deal with particular problems or local issues.

Paulos had moved beyond administration. Titos and Timotheos, his lieutenants, tended to the affairs of the Corinthian collection and his far-flung network. The rivalry between the pair had lessened over time, as their status within Paulos' team evolved into complementary roles. Timotheos was clearly the first lieutenant and Titos was second but with his own important sphere. Timotheos, the son of a Roman soldier, naturally assumed leadership during Paulos' absences. Titos, the more scholarly of the two, relished his role as the intellectual foil for Paulos' theologizing and letter writing. Each had served Paulos well as his surrogate and emissary to his *ekklesias*. What is more, they had become friends to Paulos' great satisfaction.

Paulos was free to be the elder statesman, the sagacious philosopher and theologian, and his letter to the Romans served up the rich fruit of his ripened thought. The tang of his words remained sharp but was less bitter.

The central and overriding theme was the universal action of God in accepting broken humanity, both Jew and Gentile, into his beloved family:

But now, *apart from the Torah*, the righteousness of God has been disclosed ... the righteousness of God through faith in Iesou Christos for all who believe. For there is no distinction for all have sinned and fall short of the glory of God; they are now justified by his grace as a gift ... For we hold that a person is justified by faith *apart from the works prescribed by Torah* ... Or is God the God of Jews only? Is he not the God of the Gentiles also? ... While we were still sinners Christos died for us ... 'Those who were not my people I will call my people, and her who was not beloved I will call beloved'.

"Master Paulos, if Torah is not required, does not 'law free' mean 'lawless'?" Tertius, the secretary asked. "Does this mean that morality has become irrelevant? Does this cheapen God's grace?"

The impertinence of the secretary, a slave, surprised Paulos. His education and intellect belied his lowly status, but that wasn't unusual; many slaves of the Romans were well bred and well read. Paulos stroked his beak as he mulled the slave's challenge. It occurred to him that the question was one that he had wrestled with before but never resolved. May we steal? May we murder?

Paulos suspended his dictation to Tertius the slave for a couple of days while he thought the matter through. Of course, morality remained important, but right behavior did not determine one's status before God. When he returned to the discussion, Paulos dictated and Tertius scribed, "What then are we to say? Should we continue in sin in order that grace may abound? Should we sin because we are not under Torah but under grace? Do not let sin exercise dominion in your mortal bodies."

And then the slave asked another unresolved question, the same question that Timotheos had raised when he scribed Paulos' letter to the Galatians. "What of the Jews? Is God's promise to Abraham a nullity because the Jews don't believe as you teach?"

It was true enough that many Jews had hard hearts toward Iesou the Christos, but it was also true that they remained the people of the promise. God was faithful to his promise even if his chosen people were not. "They are beloved, for the sake of their ancestors; for the gifts and the calling of God are irrevocable." A gracious God would forgive the hard hearts of the Jews, and not just the Gentiles. All had been disobedient, but God would be merciful to all.

Perhaps time had softened the memories of Ya'akov's rebuke on Golgotha, of betrayal at Antioch, of the bitter speech of Phinehas at Corinth, and of the backstabbing attacks of the Judaizers in Galatia; perhaps it was the serenity of a winter spent in repose and reflection in Gaius' comfortable villa; perhaps it was his victory in Corinth and the expectation of a triumph in Rome; perhaps it was the anticipation of greeting Ya'akov face to face, with reconciliation, recognition, and respect for his Gentile mission to follow. Perhaps it was all these things and more, but Paulos' letter offered an olive branch.

Gone was the curse upon those who insisted on following Torah. Yes, his Gentile followers would remain Torah free, but he did not criticize the Nazarenes who chose to eat kosher: "Those who eat must not despise those who abstain, and those who abstain must not pass judgment on those who eat." And, the Nazarenes would be free to observe Sabbath and the festival days as they chose: "Some judge one day to be better than another, while others judge all days to be alike." Let the Nazarenes do it their way, and Paulos' *ekklesias* would do it theirs. "Let us therefore no longer pass judgment on one another, but resolve never to put a stumbling block or hindrance in the way of another." Surely, Ya'akov would respond with a gesture in kind.

Except for the final greeting, the letter was complete. Tertius called the letter Paulos' great work, his *magnum opus,* using the Latin words. The inquisitive slave had been an unexpected foil for Paulos' thoughts. Once, Titos had rebuked the slave. "Don't talk back to Paulos," he had said, perhaps envious of the deference Paulos was paying to the insights of the secretary. "Slaves must be submissive and give satisfaction in every respect and show complete and perfect fidelity to their masters," Titos had said.

After that confrontation, Paulos took Titos and Gaius, the slave's master, aside. "Let me tell you about Philemon and his slave," he said. Paulos told them about the runaway slave he had encountered in the Ephesus prison and about Paulos' letter to Philemon that encouraged emancipation.

When he finished, he put one hand on the shoulder of each man as he asked, "What words do we speak when we baptize?" Neither man replied to the question that was not a question but a reminder. Titos dropped his gaze that said he knew the answer that remained unspoken: *In Christ, there is neither Jew nor Greek, male nor female, slave nor free.*

Paulos spoke directly to Gaius. "Your slave has been of great service to me. Now that I have finished my letter, you may take him back but no longer as a slave but more than a slave, a beloved brother. Refresh my heart in Christ. Confident of your obedience, I know that you will do even more than I say." Gaius speechless mouth hung open as Paulos and Titos departed. Paulos' cane *scritch, scritched* on the tiled villa floor as he shuffled along.

Lengthening days and warming breezes signaled that the Corinthian winter had nearly run its course. It was time to make ready for Paulos' journey to Jerusalem. Phoebe of Cenchreae would hand-carry the letter to the Romans aboard her own ship. Tertius, the recently emancipated slave, posted a copy of the letter with the *cursus publicus* for delivery to Ya'akov.

Tertius had come up with a private nickname for Paulos, their leader. "Swallowtail" he called him because of the double point in his beard that appeared following Paulos' habit of resting his chin on his cane as he dictated. Titos and Timotheos secretly called him Swallowtail also; Paulos knew, and he didn't mind.

The letter to the Romans concluded on an ominous note, "Join me in earnest prayer to God on my behalf, that I may be rescued from the unbelievers in Judea, and that my ministry to Jerusalem may be acceptable to the saints, so that I may come to you with joy and be refreshed in your company."

PART SEVEN
JERUSALEM REVISITED
56-59 C.E.

Jerusalem remembers, in the days of her affliction and wandering, all the precious things that were hers in the days of old. When her people fell into the hand of the foe, and there was no one to help her, the foe looked on mocking over her downfall.

Enemies have stretched out their hands over all her precious things; she has even seen the nations invade her sanctuary, those whom you forbade to enter your congregation.

Lamentations 1:7 & 10

Chapter Sixty-three

Old Ya'akov was a proud grandfather. Anina, his dear granddaughter, would soon wed. The Nazarene elder had gladly said "yea" to the young Pharisee who had asked for his blessing. Anina's own father was long dead, so the honor fell to Grandfather Ya'akov. Not only was the suitor a proper Pharisee, he was the nephew of old Gamaliel, Ya'akov's friend and Sanhedrin leader who had recently died. Ya'akov could not be more pleased with the match, even in such troubled times.

According to the Hebrew calendar, it had been 3816 years since God had created the heavens and the earth, 56 C.E. Emperor Nero had reigned for two years and had turned eighteen years of age. In that year, the discord in Jerusalem reached a new pinnacle—a Jew assassinated the High Priest. The assassin was a Zealot, a *sicarii,* a dagger man, who plunged his stiletto to its hilt between the shoulders of the High Priest as his entourage wound its way through the agora. The murderer melted into the crowd and disappeared.

Not a good time for the young couple to start a marriage, Ya'akov worried. He had counseled a long betrothal, followed by marriage when the time was right, after this affair of the assassination of the High Priest died down. Undoubtedly, the bastard deserved it, but ...

Insurrectionists, rebels, and brigands were always Galilean. Everyone knew that. Nothing good could come from Galilee. All the Galileans living in Jerusalem came under suspicion, especially those known to be hostile to the Temple priesthood.

Ya'akov was not surprised at the knock on the door that came late in the day.

"Enough!"

At the command of the centurion, the Roman soldier ceased whipping the bloodied back of the helpless Hebrew prisoner. Ya'akov writhed on the dirt floor of a cell within the Fortress Antonia, the Roman military garrison next door to the Jerusalem Temple. The centurion chugged a cup of water as the old Jew twisted himself into a heap in the dust.

"This is your last chance; give me the name of the dagger man," the centurion said.

With great effort, Ya'akov shook his head and mumbled through swollen lips, "I can't; I don't know who the assassin was; I wasn't involved; he was no Nazarene." He didn't expect the centurion to believe him, but he did.

The centurion flung his tin cup against the rock wall. It was still clanging as he stomped through the cell door. He gave an honest report to the family of the slain High Priest and the circle of Sadducees. The old Nazarene spoke the truth, he said. According to the centurion's investigation, Ya'akov was not involved in the assassination, and the centurion ordered the prisoner released.

As Ya'akov limped away from the Roman garrison, he passed under the high walls of the Temple. In the lowlight of evening, the white marble had lost its luster and appeared gray. The aristocrats of the Temple hierarchy would remain convinced of his guilt, and they would await their day of righteous revenge; he knew that.

The bloody Romans and their sympathizers would one day be the death of him, he feared, and then he remembered the letter he had received from Paulos, trumpeting the return of the Jew who acted like a Gentile.

Chapter Sixty-four

Secundus the bursar became a goldsmith; Aristarchus the bodyguard became a tailor. Secundus converted heaping stacks of copper coins into smaller stacks of more valuable silver coins; in turn, he converted the silver stacks into still more valuable gold coins; finally, he melted the gold coins into flat bars. Aristarchus sewed the gold bars into the folds of the robes and cloaks of the delegation to Jerusalem that would carry a secret treasure to Ya'akov.

The mariner with the bit-off nose, Stephanas, captained the merchant galley that would carry them in a circular route around the Aegean Sea. Along the way, Paulos would revisit his *ekklesias* for a final time, bolstering his treasures of Jerusalem delegates and gold. He would have preferred to sail straightaway to Jerusalem, but Timotheos had counseled return visits to the Aegean *ekklesias* along the way, and Paulos had grown to trust the advice of his first lieutenant.

On a balmy day of early spring, their ship departed Cenchreae. After a day of comfortable sailing, the ship pivoted around the tip of mainland Greece and struck a northerly heading along the coast, dead into the wind. For three days, the ship's sails remained furled, and the ship's crew pulled hard on oars, slowly propelling the galley into the headwinds that funneled down the valley of the sea between the mainland to port and the mountainous island of Euboia to starboard.

By sunset each day, the weary crew and passengers enjoyed copious quantities of barley beer, safely anchored in protected coves along the coast of the island. As was his custom, Stephanas abstained from strong drink while aboard ship, keeping his weather eye clear. Aristarchus, in charge of security, also avoided the merriment at dusk.

By mid-afternoon of the fourth day of rowing, the galley reached the island village of Khalkis. "We overnights here but departs early in the morn to shoot the straits," said Stephanas; his crew understood, but the passengers did not.

The crew awakened the passengers before sunrise; a sullen gray blanket of clouds cloaked the eastern ridge; the cloud edges turned pink as morning ascended the backside of the mountains. The crew quietly rowed the ship in the calm waters of a breezeless dawn only to stop and wait when they reached the straits. Paulos stood in the bow next to Stephanas, whose clever eyes measured the rippling current streaming toward the ship. For nearly an hour, the ship's crew maintained their position, poised for a signal from their captain to spring ahead.

"Thar 'tis! Rip, ya bastards!"

The ship lunged forward so quickly that Paulos nearly lost his balance. Stephanas sprinted aft to grab the stern rudder, leaping past the grunting sailors who pulled the oars that rammed the vessel forward into the narrow pinch point between mainland and island. As the ship accelerated to a speed faster than a man could run, the captain spread his feet wide to brace against the rudder. The slightest steering error would send the careening craft smashing into the cliffs, less than the length of a tall pine from either side of the slender galley. Paulos clutched the rail, and the apparent wind welled tears in his eyes as the ship sluiced through the gap.

"Yowwee!" The captain screeched in delight. "Pull, ya son's of whores! Pull!"

As quickly as the race through the straits began, it was over, and the crew relaxed, leaned on their oars, wiped their sweaty brows, and laughed at their confused, frightened passengers.

"Tis the tidal current, doncha see!" The captain teased the uninitiated who had not passed this way before. "The whole, damned bay rushes through the neck then turns around and hurries back to where she come from. If ya times her right, ya can ride her like a whore whats enjoys her work, but if ya times her wrong, she'll kick ya in the balls and send ya back through the door ya come through!"

Paulos wished the entire journey would speed on the currents, but he expected foul winds and seas ahead—as the past, so the future.

A week later, the galley crew rested comfortably in the harbor of Thessalonica after a slow slog northward against the wind. The worst of the trip around the Aegean was over. Paulos and the others spent three days visiting Jason and other friends of the Thessalonian *ekklesia* before sailing west to the port of Neapolis near Philippi. The sailor's work was much easier heading east as the northerly winds blew over the port beam, allowing the galley to move under sail power.

Tears flowed freely as Paulos boarded ship after three days in Philippi. His Philippian friends, especially the siblings Euodia and Epaphroditus, had been among his first converts and had remained his most faithful supporters. Despite his eagerness to move on, Paulos would not pass this way again, and he had delayed their departure an extra day. His cheery goodbye was dishonest and masked the sadness of a final farewell. He would not see these dear friends again except, perhaps, in the hereafter.

Stephanas' ship departed Macedonia and Europe and sailed east to Troas on the northeastern corner of the Aegean, the gateway to Anatolia and Asia. Paulos impatiently remained behind in Troas a few days while the others traveled to Ephesus to reconnoiter. It had been a mere year since Paulos had escaped from the Ephesus prison, and Timotheos would gauge the safety of his return.

When his ship pulled into the Ephesus harbor a few days after the others had arrived, Paulos scanned the hills, searching for the terrace villa that had been his home, before he turned to watch for a friendly face on the docks. Soon he spotted the waving arm of Titos. When Paulos stepped onto the dock, Titos grabbed his elbow and turned him back toward the harbor.

"It's not safe for you here. You're still a wanted man by the Ephesian authorities who seethe over your escape. We must sail south where Timotheos and the others are waiting for us."

Anxious to move on, Paulos didn't disagree. As the ship's crew rowed the galley out of the harbor, Paulos kept a nostalgic eye on the terrace house high on the hill, his home and headquarters for nearly three years. The pair sailed to Miletus less than fifty miles down the coast where they joined the others as well as many friends from Ephesus and inland cities. More gold and more delegates! An entourage of more than a dozen—Paulos, Timotheos, Titos, Aristarchus, Secundus, and a handful more from the scattered *ekklesias*—boarded Stephanas' galley for the remaining voyage out of the Aegean to the port city of Patara on the Anatolian coast of the Great Sea. Jerusalem on the far shores seemed ever nearer and ever more distant.

Paulos booked passage on a ship to Palestine while Stephanas arranged a westbound cargo for his galley's return voyage to Corinth. Paulos' delegation of more than a dozen transferred to a *strongyla ploia,* a larger sea-going vessel that relied primarily on sail power instead of oar power. The round *ploia* was beamier than the sleek oar-powered galleys of coastal waters. Paulos stepped off the ship's dimensions—nearly ten paces wide and over thirty paces long, easily the largest ship he had ever boarded.

Paulos' entourage rented rooms in an inn for nearly a week before the *ploia* departed for Palestine. First, they waited while the ship's cargo was loaded, and then a storm kept them in port a couple of extra days. It seemed the fates plotted against his return to Jerusalem, and Paulos stalked the docks, willing the ship's departure. Finally, a tugboat rowed the round vessel from the harbor, and the ship's company unfurled her sails for the downwind run across the Great Sea.

They were four days at sea with favorable winds. The prevailing northwesterly breezes blew strong and steady across the port side of the stern quarter. The boom that held the foot of the mainsail was eased to starboard; with fair winds and following seas, the vessel sailed smoothly in a constant broad reach—the most comfortable and speedy point of sail. They raced along at nearly one hundred miles a day, sailing by sun during the day and the moon and stars at night.

Paulos, now an experienced sailor, had ensured that the entourage enjoyed the luxury of small tents for sleeping on deck. Their packs contained more than enough food, and water was readily available from the amphorae stacked in the ship's hold.

Along the way, they sailed near the southern shores of Kypros, and the western city of Paphos was in clear sight as they passed. Alongside the ship, sleek gray dolphins darted beneath the waves, then jumping, then diving, and finally departing for other amusement. Dim images of the Aphrodite temple and festival smudged his memories, but the heady mood of the open sea soon prevailed as Paulos regaled his travel companions with stories from the Kypros missionary journey more than a decade earlier, lifetimes ago. He spoke fondly of Barnabas, long since forgiven for abandoning him in the conflict with Cephas in Antioch. Paulos had heard that Barnabas was home in Kypros.

Paulos leaned on the port rail on the high side of the ship and gazed at Paphos passing by in the distance. The sea breeze carried his whispered prayer for Barnabas.

Barnabas was indeed in Kypros where he was the leader of a network of *ekklesias* stretching from Salamis to Paphos. He happened to be in Paphos at that moment spending time with his brother Chariton in the family villa.

"Whatever happened to Paulos your friend who was here with you many years ago?" asked Chariton as he and Barnabas sat on the veranda with a cup of wine.

"The last I heard he was in Ephesus or somewhere in Macedonia. I understand he has done well as a missionary," replied Barnabas.

His lips moved silently and his heart offered up a prayer for his friend Paulos, as his eyes followed a passing *ploia* silhouetted against the half-sunk, orange-red sun.

Paulos ignored his awe-struck companions who gawked at the gold-roofed palace built by King Herod the Great, half a century earlier. They had arrived in Caesarea of Palestine, a Roman enclave in the land of the Jews, a Hellenistic city with a large Gentile population, and the home of the Roman governor of Judea who resided in the palace. A two, maybe three, day hike inland would bring them to Jerusalem.

Titos, who had attended the apostolic assembly as an uncircumcised Gentile, was the only member of the delegation who had previously visited the homeland of the Jews. Timotheos, half-Jewish and half-Roman, and the rest who were Gentiles, arrived in Palestine for the first time. For all, this was a pilgrimage to Jerusalem—not as the mother-city of the Jews and home to the Temple—but to walk where Iesou had walked, to breathe the air that he had breathed, and to visit the hallowed ground where he had died for them.

But Paulos was no wide-eyed pilgrim, on this, his third visit to Judea. Nearly a quarter century had passed since Damascus, the day of his rebirth. Yet, there was one who would deny him his birthright, and Paulos had come not as a humble penitent but as an heir to demand his inheritance. In the moment he stepped from ship to shore and his foot touched the dock, his journey—from Antioch to Galatia, to Macedonia, to Corinth, to Ephesus, and then to each again—had come full circle to Palestine and Ya'akov. After countless miles underfoot and too many sunrises to remember, he was here, and the hilltop city of Jerusalem beckoned beyond the horizon. He would have struck out straightaway to Ya'akov's domain, but the setting sun said otherwise.

The entourage set up lodging in several Caesarea inns, and all would remain there except Paulos, Timotheos, and Titos who would journey alone to Jerusalem. They would send for the others in due course. By cockcrow the following morn, the wayfarers were well on their way toward the first glimmers of dawn over the eastern mountains, their faces set toward Jerusalem.

Chapter Sixty-five

Drenched in sweat, Paulos gasped for breath and stared into the blackness. He groped his way to a vase of water, and he gulped down a cup. The hot, dead air of the windowless room prevented slumber. Although Ya'akov had agreed to a meeting with the foreign missionaries, he had not extended the hospitality of lodging, and they slept in the tiny abode of a Hellenistic Jew in Jerusalem.

Paulos scooped a second cup of water and sipped it slowly. He dragged his mat onto the dusty street and lugged it behind him as he mounted the wooden rungs of a rickety ladder to the rooftop and the fresh air of the Jerusalem night. Wispy clouds veiled a pale moon. In his fitful sleep, Paulos dreamt.

God the father sat on his heavenly throne with clouds swirling about and dimming his face. Ya'akov approached the father to receive the blessing that was his due, but the father sent him to hunt among the Jews.

"Bring me my people that I may savor my portion."

When Ya'akov had departed, Paulos stole into the presence of God, bringing with him many Gentiles, which he offered to the father. "Lord, here is your portion," he said, and the father blessed Paulos instead of Ya'akov.

Paulos escaped into the wilderness, but a pursuer knocked him off his feet, and he wrestled with his assailant—first Ya'akov, and then Iesou, and then the father, and then Arsenios, and then his own double.

When he awoke, the clouds had dissipated, and the moon had sunk below the horizon, leaving a multitude of twinkling stars. He descended the ladder gingerly due to an aching hip, and he aimlessly limped through the streets of Jerusalem, awaiting the dawn.

It had been over two decades since Paulos first visited Jerusalem and Ya'akov had rejected him as a coworker. A dozen years after that first visit, the two had opposed each other at the apostolic assembly. Shortly after the assembly, men sent by Ya'akov to Antioch incited discord between the Gentiles and the Jews. Conflict heightened further when Nazarenes from Jerusalem appeared in Pauline *ekklesias* in Corinth, Galatia and Philippi, refuting Paulos and his teachings.

The stars dimmed then disappeared as fog blanketed the city. Paulos continued to wander. He regretted his own hot-tongued, name-calling in his letters. In his Corinthian correspondence, he had labeled the Jerusalem missionaries "peddlers of God's word," "false apostles," and "deceitful workers," implying they were ministers of Satan. In his letter to the Galatians, he had cursed "false brothers" who were confounding the Galatians by offering a message contrary to his own. In his second Philippian letter, he had called the Judaizers "dogs" and "evil workers." For the first time, it occurred to him that his letters may have fallen into the hands of the Nazarenes and reached Jerusalem. Had his hot words burned the ears of Ya'akov?

Dawn was slow to break as brooding, gray clouds hung low over the city. When Paulos saw a faint glow gilding the Temple domes and turrets, he returned home to wash and prepare. Later in the day, he would meet Ya'akov, the Nazarene leader and the brother of the Lord, for the third time.

Together with his brothers, Jude and Joses, and cousin Symeon, Ya'akov sat silently at his table under his veranda roof, awaiting the arrival of the Jew who acted like a Gentile. He did not notice the welts that still smarted, following his beating by the Romans weeks earlier, nor did he notice the chronic ache in his worn out knees. He had not ventured from his veranda since his release from Roman custody, and the loose folds of skin that sagged on his big-boned frame witnessed to his poor appetite.

He stared vacantly toward the temple as he awaited the knock on the door. When it came, he merely blinked as Joses skipped down the stairway to escort their expected visitors to the veranda. Upon returning, Joses stood with Paulos, Titos, and Timotheos at the head of the stairway, awaiting a word from the Nazarene leader who sat with his back toward them.

"You claim him, and you deny him to me," the old Galilean said, without facing the men who couldn't see the tear that coursed through the wrinkles on his face.

Joses nudged the emissaries toward stools at the table, and they all sat down.

"You claim my own brother, and you deny him to me," Ya'akov said again, louder than before, as he lifted his eyes to the usurper that had stolen his brother and his blessing.

"Yeshua and I suckled at the same breasts; as bare-assed young whelps, we pissed on the same tree; our fingers gripped the same hammer handle worn smooth by our father's callused hand; we ogled the same young virgins in our village; and we wept together when we buried our father. But now, he comes to you in your dreams, and he is yours." Beneath a gray beard, his knit chin quivered. He had been angry before, and he would be angry again, but now he was merely sad.

After moments of pregnant silence, Paulos spoke. "We bring you much gold and silver for your poor."

Ya'akov glared with wide, dark eyes; he snorted hot breaths; and his heart pounded. Rage replaced sadness in an instant. His fist came crashing down on the table, splashing wine and scattering tin cups, clinking across the mud-brick floor.

"You would buy my brother from me with a bribe!" He erupted.

He grasped the underside of the table with both hands and tipped it atop Paulos who fell from his stool to the floor. Timotheos grabbed Paulos by the arm and tugged him to his feet; Paulos retreated down the stairway with Titos and Timotheos trailing behind. That was the end of the parley for that day.

Titos and Timotheos jogged to keep pace with long striding Paulos who muttered and gestured with his hands as he ranted, oblivious to the pleading of his companions to slow down and think the matter through. He stalked past their lodging, toward a city gate, toward Caesarea, and toward the western empire—not even the Great Sea would slow him down, it appeared. He would kick the dust off his sandals and depart Jerusalem and Judea. Finally, just before passing through the city gate, his protégés each grabbed one of his arms and stopped him.

"T'is late in the day, and we should spend the night before departing," Timotheos said.

After some discussion, Paulos relented, and they returned to their host's small house. He did not eat the food set before him, and he spent the evening shuffling around the rooftop, mumbling to himself.

Cockcrow found him slumped against the wall in a corner of the rooftop. Awakened in dawn's twilight, he pissed into a chamber pot, stumbled to his mat, and slept again. When he awoke, he peered up at four shadows that blocked the sun. He shielded his eyes from the searing rays. It was Timotheos and Titos together with Joses and Symeon.

"We come with an apology from Ya'akov for yesterday," Symeon said.

Paulos rubbed his eyes, grabbed his walking stick, and hoisted himself to his feet.

"Please return for further discussions," added Joses.

Paulos smoothed the wrinkles in his robe with the palms of his hands. Had Ya'akov truly sent them or had they come on their own? He glanced at Timotheos and Titos, and they each offered a subtle nod.

"Very well. Allow me to wash up and eat something. I'm famished! We'll return after midday."

After Joses and Symeon departed, Paulos was in a buoyant mood. "Ya'akov is envious of our missionary successes, and the offer of a gift pricked his wounded pride. When we return, I will not brag, and we will allow Ya'akov his due." Paulos devoured all the bread and fruit provided by their host.

When Paulos and his two associates returned that afternoon, they expected a contrite and conciliatory Ya'akov. They were mistaken. The Nazarene leader had prepared an interrogation.

Jude gestured at the empty stool next to Ya'akov, and Paulos sat down. Two scrolls, partially unrolled, lay on the table in front of the old men. Ya'akov didn't acknowledge Paulos and appeared to be concentrating on one of the open scrolls. When Paulos slid his stool forward, the scraping sound on the mud brick floor grated in the stillness. The sonorous breaths of Ya'akov filled the silence as if no one else dared breathe. Even though he expected Ya'akov to speak, Paulos was startled when Ya'akov's voice suddenly exploded.

"I am God, and there is no other," Ya'akov said, reading from the scroll in front of him. "To me every knee shall bow, every tongue shall swear." For the first time, he acknowledged Paulos by turning to face him with a burning gaze. "Tell me, do you know these words from the scroll of Isaiah?" he asked.

"Certainly," Paulos replied.

"Who is the speaker?"

"God, of course."

"The one God?"

"Yes."

"The true God?"

"Yes, of course."

"And there is no other?"

Paulos nodded without speaking. He knew what was coming next. He would not shy away from a serious debate—he welcomed it.

Ya'akov reached for the second scroll, a tattered epistle, and pushed it under the nose of its author. "Is this your letter?"

"Yes." Paulos knew his own words even in the hand of an unknown copyist.

"With a lump of charcoal, I have smudged a mark next to several lines in your letter. Please read those lines to us."

Paulos narrated the words aloud as requested by Ya'akov. He would play along.

Christos Iesou, who, though he was in the form of God, did not regard equality with God as something to be exploited, but emptied himself, taking the form of a slave, being born in human likeness.

As Paulos read the familiar words, a musical tune lilted through his memory.

And being found in human form, he humbled himself and became obedient to the point of death— even death on a cross.

He shut his eyes, but continued to speak the words he knew so well. He pictured a choir singing at one of his *ekklesias*—was it Corinth? Or Ephesus? Or ... it could have been any of them.

Therefore God also highly exalted him and gave him the name that is above every name, so that at the name of Iesou every knee should bend, in heaven and on earth and under the earth, and every tongue should confess that Iesou Christos is Lord, to the glory of God the Father.

When Paulos finished, he explained, "This is based upon a praise song to your own brother, the Christos. The Gentile *ekklesias* sing it with great adoration."

"Ha!" Ya'akov said as he slapped his palm on the table. "Your Gentiles sing a silly ditty, but you have bastardized a core passage of Hebrew belief in the God-Who-Is-One and applied it to Yeshua," he said.

Paulos couldn't deny it. He didn't look into the face of his adversary and didn't see Ya'akov's sagging skin twitch beneath bulging eyes.

"Your song grates on my Hebrew ears," Ya'akov said. "You have composed a discordant canticle about my flesh and blood brother, twisting the Hebrew Scriptures into a Hellenized misunderstanding of messianism."

Paulos lips moved without speaking. He pushed hard against the anger that welled within. *Does this fool not have ears to hear or eyes to see?* He rejected the impulse to argue. "This is what God has revealed to me." Paulos said as matter-of-factly as he could without intending to provoke.

The wrinkles in Ya'akov's face softened, and the fire in his eyes cooled as the men sat silent. After a few moments, Ya'akov awkwardly pushed himself to his feet and shuffled to the edge of the veranda, leaning forward with both hands on the waist-high wall, gazing at the domes and turrets of the temple.

"You claim my own brother, and you deny him to me," Ya'akov whispered his words from the day before. He straightened up and rolled his shoulders as if he loosened stiff muscles. Far off, a fool rooster crowed, thinking it was morn, unknowing the setting sun from the rising.

"I tell you, I *want* to believe the lofty claims you make for my brother." Ya'akov spoke the words softly without turning to face the others. "But how can we *choose* what to believe? How can I will my mind to believe what my eyes did not see and my ears did not hear?"

When he finished, he glanced at Paulos, and their eyes locked briefly before each turned away. There was vulnerability in the soft, brown eyes of Ya'akov, but it was Paulos who was instantly disarmed. For over two decades, he had contended with Ya'akov in a series of thrusts and parries, attacks and counterattacks, and harsh words met with harsher replies, but the humility in Ya'akov's glance melted Paulos' hard heart. In a battle of ideas, self-assurance was necessary armor, but when Ya'akov dropped his shield, he penetrated Paulos' defenses.

For the first time, Paulos saw a human like himself rather than an iconic adversary: a man of doubts and worries and wonderings. With his halting, timid confession, Ya'akov exposed Paulos' own uncertainties, long ago crusted over to protect from both external attack and internal angst. Neither man said anything, but they knew they had reached an accommodation but never an agreement; each in his own way revered Yeshua, despite contrary understandings, and it would remain so.

Paulos mumbled, and headed for the stairway. He hesitated at the top step, and his gaze again met Ya'akov's; their eyes spoke more than either man had intended or expected that day.

Titos and Timotheos traipsed along behind their mentor who led them through the city gates and up a steep incline to a barren hill.

"This is Golgotha where they crucified him," Paulos said.

Paulos leaned against a boulder and sucked in a deep breath of holy air. It tasted sweet and moist and said rain was coming. *I am God and there is no other.* Paulos scooped a handful of dust and sifted it through his fingers, scattered by the freshening breeze. *To me every knee shall bow.* To whom shall we bow? *Every tongue shall swear.* What shall we swear? *Iesou Christos is Lord.* Who died on this hallowed ground? A man, said Ya'akov, his own flesh and blood. Paulos' eyes swept over the gray hilltop, searching for that which couldn't be seen.

"Who do you say?" Paulos said after a moment. His two protégés stood near, silent, and the sheepish look on their faces said they were confused at his odd question, but he wasn't asking them anyway.

"I have often joked about the teasing promise of my teacher, Eli the sage, who said that I would paint my own picture." Paulos stared north toward Tarsos, another place and another time. "Are my colors too bright? My edges too sharp? My outlines too broad and bold?" He expected no answer.

"Ya'akov, the brother of the Lord, doubts my teachings but today he said he *wishes* that he could believe." Paulos dropped his voice to a whisper. "He *wishes* that he could believe."

Paulos looked suddenly at the two men as if he was surprised they were there. He turned his face toward the roiling clouds. Questions rushed over his mind and spilled out his mouth. His staccato queries swirled in eddying breezes, whisked away unanswered. "Do we wrest control from God? Do we let go only to take it back? Do we deny God's grace?"

Paulos rubbed hard on his nose as raindrops began to pelt the men on the hilltop. Timotheos began jogging down the path to the city.

"Come on," Timotheos shouted as thunder shook the ground.

Paulos' nod said to Titos, you go too. Titos looked deep into the eyes of the old man who was behaving strangely. "Go," Paulos said. "It's alright."

Titos followed Timotheos back to the city, but Paulos remained alone in the cloudburst, limping around the hilltop, barely noticing his soaked robe and tunic. When the rains came the hardest, he lifted his face and spread his arms, and a cry came from deep in his gut, low and wordless, but swelling into a shout as the wind howled and his arms lifted higher.

When the storm had passed, a pale, cool sun appeared in the western sky, yellowing the edges of gray clouds. With a wisp of a smile, Paulos headed down the path to the city. *Do you forgive Ya'akov for the error of his thought? Do you forgive me?*

Chapter Sixty-six

Paulos never saw Ya'akov again, and he never offered the collection that now seemed unimportant; Ya'akov would probably have refused it anyway. Although Paulos had not achieved the full-fledged recognition he had sought from Ya'akov, and he realized he never would, the leaders had reached an unspoken understanding, an implicit agreement to disagree, with a grudging measure of acceptance if not respect. Timotheos, Titos and the others would return the funds to the *ekklesias*, and Paulos would finally journey to Rome.

Before departing, Paulos felt compelled to visit the Temple a final time. He didn't gaze upon the white marble walls, and he didn't wash himself as he entered the Court of the Gentiles; he marched straightaway to a bird vendor. He pressed two copper coins into the palm of the merchant and wrapped his long fingers around the blue-gray dove he purchased. There was a fearful look in the eyes of the helpless creature. Paulos paused briefly at the first inner wall, shaking his head as he read the signs prohibiting Gentile entry. He stalked straight through the Court of Women into the Court of Israel. A priest approached him and reached for the offering, expecting to take the dove into the Court of the Priests for sacrifice according to the custom, but instead of handing the bird to the priest, Paulos thrust his hands upward and released it. The disoriented creature flapped its wings and hovered briefly and then lifted into the sunshine and disappeared.

"Hah," Paulos said to the priest who watched slack-mouthed. Paulos spun on his heels, stomped out of the inner courts, and returned to the outer Court of the Gentiles.

That's when it happened.

Paulos saw the red fury named Phinehas at the same time that Phinehas spied him. For a moment, they glared at each other, but Paulos had plenty to say to his nemesis at Antioch and Corinth. When Paulos took a step toward the short man with the slicked up hair, Phinehas began to shout.

"Unclean! Unclean! That man is an unclean Greek who has polluted the Temple!"

A crowd encircled Paulos and picked up the chant, "Unclean! Unclean!"

Paulos lost sight of Phinehas, who melted into the crowd. The threatening mob pushed forward and jostled Paulos who fell to the ground, but a trio of patrolling soldiers intervened before Paulos was injured.

"Back off! Back off, I say!" ordered one of the soldiers, pulling his sword from its sheath for emphasis.

The rabble stepped back with the arrival of the soldiers. Two soldiers lifted Paulos by his armpits and dragged him away while the third legionary brandished his sword at the taunting crowd. The soldiers escorted Paulos to the Fortress Antonia for his own protection while the centurion sorted out the charges.

Word spread rapidly of Paulos' arrest. He worried alone in the squalid cell of the Fortress, filled with the stink of former prisoners, dark without windows. He was unaware of the swirling rumors that would decide his fate. He was Greek; he was Roman; he was Corinthian; he was Ephesian; he was a Jew; he was a Gentile.

"He was seen entering the house of Ya'akov the Nazarene," reported the advisor to the recently appointed High Priest.

The doting old man merely smiled. They called him Ishmael the aged. Already nearing eighty years, Ishmael had served as High Priest decades earlier; following the recent assassination in the market, the Roman governor had reappointed Ishmael in order to restore respect for the priesthood. That Ishmael was nearly deaf and could not hear his advisors was of no consequence; he was also senile. The Sadducees that comprised his Privy Council wielded his authority.

Half-truths and rumors were good enough for the Privy Council who willingly claimed the worst—Paulos and Ya'akov had conspired to assassinate the former High Priest. The Sadducees would strike at the followers of Yeshua, the false Mashiah. That this one was also a Pharisee made him the perfect scapegoat. His crimes against the temple and against the priesthood would expose the seditious Nazarenes and their Pharisee friends. On behalf of the High Priest, his opportunistic councilors demanded that the centurion surrender the prisoner to the temple police.

Paulos squatted in a corner with his hands tied behind his back, listening as the soldiers spoke of him as if he didn't exist.

"Damn the infighting, infernal Jews! Why didn't the legionaries just allow the mob to do its dirty work? Why must he be my problem?" the centurion muttered as he looked from the garrison window over the temple grounds next door.

"The Jews attacked him because he was a Gentile in the Temple," a soldier reported to the centurion, "but the end of his prick is cut off. He's a filthy Jew like the rest."

Paulos squirmed.

Another soldier offered another report. "We have a request from the High Priest that we surrender him to the Temple police. The Sadducees say he was a conspirator complicit in the death of the High Priest."

"The prisoner says he is a Roman citizen," said a third soldier.

The centurion looked at Paulos, a frightened heap in the corner. "Is that true?"

Paulos nodded.

"Good," said the centurion who had his solution. "Transport him to Caesarea. Let the governor deal with him."

****

Ya'akov brooded alone in the dark after hearing the news. He had absolutely no influence with the Romans, and his own neck was in danger. There was nothing he could do, even if he would.

The sun had set hours ago, but Ya'akov had not stirred from his solitary veranda vigil. With a roof overhead, he was unaware whether the night sky was clear or clouded, and his ears did not hear the nocturnal sounds of the city—barking dogs, a muffled argument between a husband and wife, or the beery chorus of young revelers determined to drain an amphora of fresh barley malt.

Five and twenty years. The Romans executed Yeshua five and twenty years ago, give or take a year, and he had not returned. The seedling doubts that Ya'akov could never weed out now ripened into full bloom. Had his labors been for naught? Had he been inadequate for the task? Had he misunderstood?

There would be no resolution of the worsening Roman oppression anytime soon and certainly not in his lifetime, what little was left of it. He wrinkled his nose; there was blood in the air.

Ya'akov pushed himself to his feet, and he shuffled to his bedroom to piss in his pot. He was thirsty, but he only allowed himself a few sips of water from the vase in the corner, or he would be up all night. He returned to the veranda table and dropped heavily into his chair.

Could Paulos be right?

No.

For the dreamer of dreams to elevate Yeshua to "equality with God" was absurd, Hellenistic blasphemy. Lord! Son of God! How this false-Pharisee had twisted these traditional Hebrew notions. The grudging accord he had reached with the Jew who acted like a Gentile didn't mean he had to accept his false teachings.

Torah observance was unnecessary; all that was required was faith—so said Paulos the apostate, but who could believe his Greek notions! Faith without works was dead, and Pauline rejection of Torah was dangerous. The Nazarenes must hold fast to the traditions of the elders, Ya'akov reminded himself as he clucked with his tongue between his teeth. Straight and true. In these dangerous times, the people must have a norm to guide them. Torah. He rubbed the straight edge of his iron norm that still dangled around his neck even though he had not toiled as a builder for longer than he could remember.

With a grunt, Ya'akov lifted himself from his chair and trudged to his bedroom. He pissed once more before he eased himself onto his aching knees for evening prayer.

Paulos claimed that Yeshua's kingdom was not of this earth. A spiritual kingdom. A kingdom of heaven. A kingdom of eternal life in the presence of God. Could Paulos be right in that much, at least? Who could know? As the tired Nazarene slipped into sleep, his last thoughts and his dreams were of Shera, his departed wife.

****

Governor Felix did nothing with the Jew who claimed to be a Roman. He could not surrender a Roman citizen to a Hebrew court, but the Sadducees would be outraged if he released the prisoner, so Paulos sat in the Roman prison in Caesarea. After a fortnight, Titos and Timotheos visited him.

"You must lead the others back to their Aegean *ekklesias*," said Paulos. "You must return the gold also. I'll travel alone as soon as these false charges are cleared up."

Paulos faced his friends, placing a hand on the shoulder of each one.

Titos' bare chin quivered. "Paulos, my dear Paulos, allow me to stay in Caesarea," Titos said. "I'll visit you daily, and I'll lobby the governor on your behalf," Titos struggled to say the words.

"I'll soon join you," Paulos said. "You'll see."

Timotheos squeezed his master's hand. "We have a treasure," Timotheos said. "Perhaps a well placed bribe will do the trick. It worked in Ephesus."

Paulos pursed his lips, clucked with his tongue between his teeth, and tugged on his nose as he briefly pondered this suggestion. This was no mere prison guard to deal with; this was the governor under pressure from the Sadducees. No bribe would be possible. After a moment, he gave a quick shake of his head before he patted Timotheos' shoulder.

"No need. The Romans will soon free me. Anyway, this collection should be returned to the *ekklesias* to be used in the service of the Lord."

Timotheos' eyes moistened and he bit his lip, hard. A brief sob escaped from Titos as Paulos gently turned his dearest friends toward the cell door and pushed them forward.

"Guard, open the door please," Paulos said, and his own voice cracked.

Then they were gone.

For over two years, or was it three—he lost track of the days, Paulos languished in the Roman prison in Caesarea. He hoped, despite the unrelenting passage of untold time, and he prayed daily for his release so that he could head for Rome, his destiny. Joses and Symeon visited occasionally with fresh fruit and clean robes, always assuring Paulos that Ya'akov would have come himself but for the lengthy journey and his poor health, but Paulos remained skeptical.

And then the shifting political currents whisked him away to Rome, not as a conquering hero but as a prisoner in irons aboard a massive ship. Emperor Nero's newly appointed Governor of Judea quickly accomplished a solution to the problem of the Jewish prisoner who claimed to be a Roman. Once more and for the last time, Paulos became a pilgrim wayfarer, carried on the winds for the last leg of his journey to the city of seven hills.

PART EIGHT
ROME
59-62 C.E.

On her forehead was written a name, a mystery: "Babylon the great, mother of whores and of earth's abominations." And I saw that the woman was drunk with the blood of the saints and the blood of the witnesses to Jesus. I will tell you the mystery of the woman, and of the beast with seven heads and ten horns that carries her. The beast that you saw was, and is not, and is about to ascend from the bottomless pit and go to destruction.

The seven heads are seven mountains on which the woman is seated.

Revelation 17:5-9 , selections

Chapter Sixty-seven

It was in Portus—the man made harbor at the mouth of the Tiber River, near the village of Ostia, fifteen miles downriver from Rome—that Paulos finally set foot in the homeland of the Romans. As he disembarked from the massive grain ship from Alexandria that had carried him to Rome, Paulos expected that he would soon have his day in court, followed by freedom.

Despite his prisoner status, and his withered, atrophied legs, Paulos felt exhilarated as the seven hills of the city came into view. During his forced march from the seaport, he barely noticed the gibes of his Roman guards who jerked on the tether to his bound wrists as if he were a balky donkey. He limped along as gamely as he could, his once forceful gait long since diminished.

The prisoner and his guards passed by the Colosseum and the Pantheon. Fresh water fountains abounded, supplied by aqueducts; theatres garnished the streets, or a gymnasium, or bath complexes, or libraries. Elegant palatial villas on Palatine Hill contrasted with swollen, impoverished ghettos. Horse and chariot traffic clattered on the cobblestone streets, frightening the detainee as they rumbled past.

Finally, they arrived at *Carcer* in the heart of the city. The centuries old dungeon known as *Carcer* reeked with the stench of death. The Romans shoved those marked for execution into a pit to starve before plunging their stinking carcasses into the sewers beneath the dungeon for the short swim to the Tiber River.

Initially, Paulos found himself in a common holding cell with others, awaiting a hearing before a magistrate. At least the holding cell in Ephesus had received a daily sweep out, followed by a sprinkling of fresh wheat straw, but in *Carcer,* the inmates pissed and shit straight through a hole in the floor into the sewers below. When they bothered.

Paulos' status in the Roman prison was the same as it had been in Caesarea. He was no thief. He was no murderer. If he had been a common criminal, the authorities would have understood how to deal with him, but he was a political prisoner, and his jailors didn't know what to do. So, he sat. And waited.

The original charges from Jerusalem, that he had breached Jewish religious law, were meaningless to the Romans, and that is why he expected an immediate release. But, his reputation as a Jewish agitator, a proselytizer, kept him holed up in *Carcer*: too important to be released, but too unimportant to be brought to trial—especially in the absence of local witnesses to testify against him. To the Jews of Palestine, he had been too Gentile, but to the Romans, he was too Jewish.

After a couple of weeks in limbo, Paulos finally heard his name called, but it was not for trial. Soldiers transferred their undernourished, dehydrated, and depressed Hebrew prisoner to a private cell for reasons unknown to him. He received sweet fruit, washed vegetables, and fresh baked bread. Clean clothing appeared, together with tent maker's tools. Daily, his guards replenished the fresh water in the vase in his corner. His spirits soared—surely, this was portent of an imminent release, but it did not happen.

The cut-stone cubicle without windows, above the *Carcer* dungeon, became his home. When his old friend Aquila appeared for a visit, Paulos understood the source of his special treatment from his jailors. The squat tentmaker from Corinth and Ephesus understood how to place a bribe. The look-alike couple, Prisca and Aquila, residents of Rome, became his protectors.

Paulos kept himself busy by repairing leather goods brought to him by the Roman guards, developing a pleasant relationship with his jailors who paid him with crisp apples and fresh baked flatbread and the courtesy of receiving guests. The jailors placed a pair of stools and an oil lamp in the dank cell that seemed rather cheery compared to the putrid holding cell. A steady flow of visitors from the Roman *ekklesia* passed through his cell-home.

Paulos had been in *Carcer* for a few months. His guard announced that he had a visitor, and the cell door creaked open. Paulos glanced up from his stool, tools in hand, at the stranger standing in the backlit doorway. He appeared to be about the same age as Paulos although in much better physical shape: tall, lean, and muscular. His flowing toga identified him as an affluent Roman and not a Jew, with a full head of oiled and coiled silver hair; one lock dangled over his forehead.

"Who is there?" asked Paulos as he rose unsteadily to his feet.

The distinguished visitor stepped forward without saying anything and looked straight into Paulos' eyes. Paulos knew those eyes, deep as a well.

It was Arsenios.

Paulos lurched back and stumbled. Arsenios caught him before he fell and helped him onto his stool. The dear, dear friend from Tarsos sat down on the second stool.

Neither man spoke for a long while as the past filled the moment. They were young again: plum juice dribbled down their chins in the Tarsos market, the chill waters of the River Kydnos stung bare skin, fish and clams boiled over an open fire, flames leaped like gazelles in their eyes, swaying grain fields laughed at the tickling breeze, a barge floated on lazy river currents, a ship sailed west toward Rome with a pair of young passengers; but then, the images went dark and Paulos longed for what might have been but was not, and he grieved the loss of years and love.

His eyes moistened and then a solitary tear trickled into his sparse gray beard, matched by the single tear that coursed down Arsenios' shaved cheek into his dimple. Chins quivered. More tears followed. The men stood as one, and hugged, and sobbed, and shook, and then kissed full on the mouth. Then they laughed before they cried some more.

The years were lost, but thank God for the moment.

****

The barefoot, spindle-legged, blotchy-skinned monarch wore only a dirty sleeping robe that unflatteringly accentuated his plump belly. He burped as he listened to his advisors in his bedchamber. His gut was unsteady from too much grape the night before.

Nero was twenty-four years of age and in the eighth year of his reign as Roman Emperor. He had become emperor upon the death of his grand uncle, Emperor Claudius. Nero's mother, Agrippina, had poisoned Claudius, her third husband, to assure that her son would ascend to the throne. Nero laughingly lauded mushrooms, the vehicle for the poison, as "the food of the gods." He learned his mother's lesson well, assassinating her, in turn, when she attempted to exert influence over him.

Despite personal excesses, Nero's reign was effective during the early years of his reign, due to the beneficial influence of his two advisors. Then one died and the other retired, and their replacements were cruel fools.

Rufus was Prefect of the Praetorian Guard. The Praetorians were the Emperor's bodyguards but also his henchmen. Rufus was the head bully, a career soldier with a battle scar on his face from a knife wound. Tigellinus was a doughy, effeminate man with a pimply face; a wealthy horse breeder; and a friend of Nero, whose long list of personal indulgences included horseracing.

"We have just received a dispatch from Caesarea in Judea. Our Governor has died," Rufus reported to Nero. "A replacement needs to be appointed immediately. Who knows what the rebellious Jews will stir up in the void created by this death?" Tigellinus nodded vigorously, but the emperor paid no heed. Rufus continued, "The Jews are killing each other in the streets. We need to send a strong man to keep a lid on that boiling cauldron."

Always those accursed Jews, Nero thought to himself. The distant regions of the Empire seemed so far away and difficult to control. Trouble in Palestine would ripple throughout the Empire. The damned Jews lived everywhere, always keen to the situation in Palestine. He didn't need trouble in Palestine that might leak into other provinces.

The slovenly sovereign nodded slightly as he burped again.

Despite his soft appearance, Tigellinus was a tyrant with a stock solution for all problems. Find scapegoats and kill them. "Arrest local leaders of the Jews in Rome and publicly execute them," Tigellinus said. "Let news of the executions filter back to the Jews of Palestine."

Nero blinked his weak, blue eyes at Tigellinus and then looked away, thinking of breakfast.

The horse breeder continued, "For years, a Jewish leader has rotted in *Carcer*. Paulos is a Jew who agitated for the sect of the Christians with influence in many cities of the Empire. Start with him, and make a public spectacle of it."

Nero clapped his hands and a slave appeared. "Bring me bananas and berries in fresh cream," the emperor said.

When he saw the impatient faces of his councilors, he shrugged his shoulders. "Do as you wish. Bring the Jew into court and instruct the magistrate to order his crucifixion," he said and burped again.

"Hurry with the bowl of fruit," he shouted after the slave.

Chapter Sixty-eight

As was his custom, Ya'akov awoke well before the sun's early rays pierced his east-facing window on the first floor of his two-story house. To avoid the stairway, he had moved down to the first floor a few years earlier. In the dim light of dawn, the house was quiet except for the creaking floorboards as he shuffled to the kitchen for a cup of water.

He slumped into his chair at his table, peering out a window to watch the city come alive while he munched on his breakfast of bread and figs. A rooster crowed nearby, alerting the neighborhood to the arrival of dawn's first glimmers of gray light. Dogs began to roam the dusty streets, and an occasional clanging pot or slamming door signaled that Jerusalem awakened.

He wondered at the news of Anina, his granddaughter. She was pregnant again, and she had carried the baby a full nine months; earlier children had miscarried. This time she would give birth to a healthy son, he was sure.

The morning sun arced over nearby rooftops, suffusing the room in yellow light, and Ya'akov could no longer look out the window into the glaring brightness. The arrival of the sun in his kitchen coincided with the completion of breakfast, and Ya'akov popped the last fig into his mouth and drained his cup of water.

He filled a washbasin with water from the vase in the corner. He splashed water on his face and washed himself, and then he began the painful process of lowering himself to his knees for his morning prayers. His first prayer was for Anina and her unborn child.

Rhythmic *clump, clumping* of marching troops drowned out the random sounds of the awakening city and interrupted his prayer.

"Halt."

Ya'akov looked up from his kneeling position as a young Roman officer kicked his door open.

"Are you Ya'akov of Galilee, the Nazarene?"

Ya'akov could only nod.

The officer turned to his troops. "Arrest him."

Two legionaries stepped forward and each grabbed an arm. They dragged him away in his bedclothes, to the villa of the High Priest. With the death of the Governor, there was no Roman in Judea powerful enough to prevent the illegalities of the High Priest, who usurped executive authority in the absence of a Governor. Seeing a window of opportunity to strike at Ya'akov the Pharisee and leader of the Nazarenes, the High Priest persuaded the Roman centurion to arrest Ya'akov and deliver him to the custody of the Sadducees in the High Priest's circle.

After a quick trial in the garden of the High Priest, before the good Pharisees of Jerusalem got wind of the outrage, a handpicked mob of thugs shackled the prisoner and led him away. When they departed the garden, a swelling crowd followed them.

"Ya'akov!"

The voice of Joses cried out from the crowd as Ya'akov shuffled along with feet fettered and hands bound behind his back. Cousin Symeon was with him. Ya'akov glared at his lieutenants as if to say, "Begone! You're in danger here, and you must take my place as leader of the Nazarenes and as head of the family."

Joses jutted his jaw, pursed his lips, and bobbed his head slightly. That was the way with the brothers; they communicated with a smile, a nod, a grunt, or a glance. With a slight wave of his hand, Joses spun and retreated down a dusty alley followed by Symeon; Ya'akov's eyes followed them until they were gone. Farewell my brothers. God be with you.

Like Yeshua a generation earlier, Ya'akov stood condemned to death for the cause of the kingdom of God, both of them victims of an irregular trial before the bastard high priest. Only the manner of their executions would differ—Yeshua died by crucifixion at the hands of the Romans, and Ya'akov would die by stoning by a mob of Jews, henchmen of the high priest.

The scum escorted him from the villa of the high priest, through the streets of Jerusalem, toward a ravine lying outside the city walls, the would-be site of his execution. Ya'akov was a well-known man in Jerusalem, and murmurs swelled as they passed Jews on the street. Only a few joined the mob; most of the onlookers jeered his captors.

The rabble that surrounded him walked mute; the only sounds were the clumping of feet and muffled whispers. Ya'akov scanned the faces of strangers, whose eyes bulged with morbid anticipation, awaiting the spectacle of his death. Who would be the first to cast a stone, he wondered? Poor, foolish Jews. Couldn't they see that he had attempted to rescue them from the Roman tyrants, that he attempted to improve their lot, and that the kingdom he proclaimed was for them?

Snarling dogs with beady red eyes circled with the crowd, tongues dripping and hanging from long snouts. The hounds knew they would soon lap his spilled blood.

In the heavy air, the stench of unwashed humans hovered over the slow moving mass. Sweat trickled down Ya'akov's forehead and dripped from his nose. He cast his eyes on the sun now high over God's Temple, towering over the east edge of the city. Did God watch from the Temple?

The fools hobbled the feet of an old man with crippled knees. Did they think he would attempt escape? "Slay me here and be done with it!" The whispered words slipped out his dry mouth. "I am ready," he said to no one in particular; then he said it again, louder, "I am ready!" He looked again at the temple and nodded as the edges of his mouth crept upward in an expanding smile. He knew that God approved of his sacrifice. Unlawfully convicted. By the High Priest. In a secret trial. For the cause of God's kingdom. Yes, his death would mirror that of his honored brother, the Mashiah.

Ya'akov's smile continued to grow.

Would he soon see Yeshua? And Shera his dear wife? Perhaps in that much, at least, Paulos was correct—God's kingdom was not of this world, a spiritual kingdom, a heavenly kingdom, an everlasting kingdom in the presence of God. Yeshua would be there. And Shera.

Then he saw her: dear, sweet Anina. Granddaughter Anina. She followed the crush with a bundle in her arms. When she caught the eye of the great grandfather, she removed the wrap and raised her newborn above her head. Her newborn! A scrawny, pink, squirming, man-child! His legs kicked and arms flailed as if he climbed a ladder toward heaven! She had birthed a son! A gift of God!

"Mattithyahu," the old man shouted, "gift of God. His name shall be Mattithyahu." The crowd stepped back from the old man and away from the young mother. Proud tears streamed down his face, and he muttered softly, "Teach him. Teach your son well. Teach him the stories of Uncle Yeshua. Teach him the wisdom of the elders."

Anina nodded resolutely through her tears.

Then they were at the place, and Ya'akov wondered how he had arrived so quickly at his death's door. After a last glance at Anina, who continued to hold the child above her head, he craned his neck and looked straight up at the white sun overhead, haloed by sundogs. He exhaled a great sigh and extended his arms upward as the stones rained down upon him.

Chapter Sixty-nine

"Guilty. I find the prisoner guilty and impose a sentence of death to be carried out on the morrow."

Escorted by his jailor, the condemned prisoner shuffled back to his *Carcer* cell on withered legs that had once tramped across continents. He slouched with head bowed against the brightness of the day; in his windowless cell, his eyes knew only darkness and the dim glimmer of an oil lamp. Now, he squinted in the piercing sunlight, shadows and flashes darting past his watery eyes.

In *Carcer's* hallway, the prisoner raised his bound hands, and the jailor clumsily untied the knots that rubbed his wrists raw. "I'm sorry, Paulos," the jailor muttered without looking into the face of his inmate.

As the jailor swung the cell door open, the condemned man's own stench seeped out and over him, an unfriendly greeting from his confining quarters these past few years. With gnarly fingers, Paulos rubbed his eyes, sore from the sun, and stepped into the blackness. The door slammed behind him; the clank of the iron lock echoed against the rock walls of his cell. The jailor forgot to light the lamp in the cell, and Paulos huddled darkly on his mat in the corner.

He rubbed his numbed hands together to restore life. Slowly, he began to feel the calluses where his knives and awls had nestled over long years becoming living things, extensions of his sinews, knuckles and flesh. His wrists burned where the rope had chafed him.

Guilty. The magistrate pronounced him guilty and sentenced him to death. Tomorrow, he would die.

He knew that the Roman magistrate merely followed orders. More powerful men than the petty magistrate had uttered his death sentence. Damn Romans! Was he guilty? By whose law? Not by God's!

His eyes searched the darkness, and he struggled to breathe in the oppressively hot air. Sweat streaked down his face and dripped from the tip of his beak-nose; he licked his parched lips, not bothering to pour a cup of water from the jar in the opposite corner.

He wished he had a window to catch the sun that would climb over the hills of Rome in the morn. Cockcrow: the last time. Oh, to behold the sunrise once more!

Damn the Romans, but damn the Jews too! *Unclean, unclean,* cried his Jewish accusers, his own kinfolk.

He wheezed the raspy breaths of an old man as he leaned against the hewn stones of his prison wall. Slowly, he breathed away his resentments toward the Romans and the Jews, and he blamed himself—and God.

"I will not restrain my mouth; I will speak in the anguish of my spirit; I will complain in the bitterness of my soul." Job's holy lament inspired him to boldness.

He never expected to face death. He awaited the return of the Christos to annul death. "Iesou, where are you? For nigh unto thirty years, I have awaited your return—your absence taunts me."

God called him to his mission. Yet, obstacles challenged him at every turn. He had endured beatings, stonings, and imprisonment; now, he faced a death sentence.

"Why?"

His whisper echoed off the dank walls, returning to him unanswered. Perhaps he had failed God. Did he not follow God's call? Or was he the fool? Had he not served God well? Would his death serve God? Nothing seemed clear to him in the darkness of his deathwatch.

Just a handful. Just a handful of followers here and there. That was all. Not much. Not many. Assaulted by the Romans and harassed by the Nazarenes. The Nazarenes led by Ya'akov. Ya'akov, the brother of Iesou. Why Ya'akov—the one who should have known Iesou the best but who understood so little? Why had Ya'akov opposed him?

His tin cup rattled on the stone floor as he bumped it from his stool. He stabbed for it in the darkness, crawled the few paces to the water jar, and gulped a cup of water, then another. He returned to his mat with a sigh.

He closed his eyes to remember friendly faces. Good and faithful friends blessed his journeys. "You know them, Lord, protect and preserve them. Inspire and lead them!" The words spilled out of his mouth and echoed down the prison hall.

"What's the matter?" The jailor checked at the cell door.

"Nothing. I'm fine."

The jailor grunted and left him alone again.

A man should die surrounded by sons and daughters, grandchildren, his lover. Of these, he had none. He would die alone. Was that God's choice? Or his own?

He did not fear death. No! Death terrified him, and God knew his fearful heart.

"Lord, give me the strength to trust!"

Was he guilty? "Yes" he admitted. By the laws of the Romans, he was guilty. By the laws of the Jews, too. By God's law? He sucked a deep breath and exhaled slowly as he rubbed both hands over his brow, lacing his fingers behind his head. Was he guilty before God?

With the thumb and forefinger of his right hand, he tugged on his long nose. He leaned back against the unforgiving stones, pondering the path that led him to his date with the Roman executioner.

He had been the teacher of many. He had offered his strength to the weak. He had lifted those who stumbled. But now it had come to him, and he was afraid. Had he not answered God's call? Had he not been a dutiful servant? Had he not earned his place in God's kingdom? Was not his work his hope and his confidence?

Deep sleep finally came to him and then a dream.

Was someone there? "Who is it?" He reached out and grasped at the air, now cold. His body shivered.

A whisper. Did he hear a whisper? His ears strained to hear the icy words: "Can mortals be righteous before God? Can human beings be pure before their Maker?"

He awakened, suddenly serene. Even in the darkness, he could see clearly now. What he had taught, preached, and written now returned to him—for him. He had *not* earned his place; his work was *not* his hope and his confidence; he was *not* righteous before God or pure before his Maker.

Nevertheless.

In the hour of his death, Paulos felt vitally alive. He did not know, he could only trust. He knew less than he thought he did, but rather than haunting him, his uncertainty strangely calmed him. He understood his lack of understanding; God was in his unknowing; and faith must be blind to be faith.

In the darkness, he smelled a sweet lily and spotted scarlet petals, glowing from a crack in the rock wall. He struggled to his feet and ripped off his ragged robes. The naked beggar, unclean in his own filth, raised his hands above his head and shouted to the unseen heavens, "I am guilty! Dear Lord, your pardon is my only hope! I fall before you! Catch me, Lord, there is none other!"

The prison door creaked open, and a warm glow spilled into his cell. Shadows crossed the face of the jailor who stood in the flickering flame of the oil lamp in his hand.

"Is it time?" Paulos asked.

"No, it is still early. Put on these robes, and I'll be back in a moment." He left the oil lamp.

The condemned man dressed in the fresh garments. He rummaged through the ragged clothes he had tossed in the corner until he found his coin purse, and he tied it to his waist with a sash. The old, worn leather felt good in his crippled fingers. He pulled out his belonging coin that glistened even in the low light of the oil lamp. His fingers seemed young and nimble again as they rolled and rubbed the shekel. After he slipped the coin back into the purse where it belonged, he squeezed it through the supple leather as the guard reappeared.

Paulos trudged slowly behind the jailor who opened the prison door to the still night of the city streets. For a moment, Paulos paused on the stoop and filled his chest with a deep draught of fresh air.

"Sit there." The jailor pointed to a stool, propped against the eastern wall. A smile struggled against the jailor's tight jaw muscles; Paulos' eyes thanked him for this last courtesy.

The sinking moon paled in the mists of the far horizon; the sea was there glistening in moon-glow, Paulos knew, but it was beyond sight. At first, his pricked ears heard only silence but then came the familiar trill of the Calandra lark. On many morns, the dull, distant, warble had seeped into his cell to herald the breaking day; now the full-throated aria of the fair bird swelled in the night. Deep in the breast of God's creature was a stirring, a knowing, a trusting that morning was nigh even under the cloak of darkness. Paulos' lips moved silently, miming the melody, and his heart sang along. When dawn's first glimmers finally appeared, Paulos heard a rush of wings as the Calandra took flight.

Silhouettes shuffled in the gray shadows of the street. Paulos rubbed his eyes, squinted and craned his neck toward their muffled voices. There were Prisca, Aquila and many others from the *ekklesia.* Friend by friend, Paulos' eyes greeted theirs. Paulos leaned back against the wall, and the eastern glow bathed his face in pale yellow.

Then Paulos saw Arsenios. The Greek forced a smile, but his lips trembled and tears spilled down his cheeks and soon Paulos' face too. Paulos loved the man, and the man loved him.

The golden orb rose too fast over the city. Paulos silently watched in awe and wonder as the shadows disappeared and the day chased the night. O glorious day!

He was ready to die. Death held no sting for him. After awhile, he became numb to the pain, and he let go. *Catch me Lord.*

In the late afternoon heat, the riverside meadow was a shimmering blur of scarlet poppies. A swallowtail butterfly bobbed over the field of red. For a moment, the wisp alit atop a sweet-smelling bulb, black-and-tan wings gently flexing up and down. When a faint breeze stirred the redheaded stalks, the butterfly took wing toward the setting sun. Above the fixed melody of countless honeybees, the lark trilled its descant.

Notes

What happened to the Nazarenes after Ya'akov's death?

In 66 CE, a few years after the deaths of James (Ya'akov) and Paul (Paulos), the political firestorm in Jerusalem burst into the conflagration of civil war: sect against sect, class against class, brother against brother. Josephus, a Hebrew aristocrat, provided an eyewitness account.

> Now after these were slain, the zealots and the multitude of the Idumeans fell upon the people as upon a flock of unclean animals, and cut their throats; and for the ordinary sort, they were destroyed in what place soever they caught them. But for the noblemen and the youth, they first caught them and bound them, and shut them up in prison, and put off their slaughter, in hopes that some of them would turn over to their party; but not one of them would comply with their desires, but all of them preferred death before being enrolled among such evil wretches as acted against their own country... the terror was upon the people so great, that no one had courage enough either to weep openly for the dead man that was related to him, or to bury him.[1]

After a few years of Jew spilling Jewish blood, the Roman legions stepped in and destroyed what was left, including the Temple, and Hebrew society changed forever. The Sadducees and priesthood disappeared along with the Temple, the zealots made their last stand on Masada, and the Essenes vanished, hiding their sacred writings

---

[1] Flavius Josephus, <u>The Great Roman-Jewish War</u>, The William Whisten Translation As Revised by D.S. Margoliouth (Mineola, NY: Dover Publications, 2004) 250-251.

in clay jars in mountain caves, only to be discovered as the Dead Sea Scrolls nearly two millennia later. The fog of war obscured loyalties and factions, and it was uncertain who killed whom, but tradition says the Jewish followers of Yeshua did not fight but fled Jerusalem, as did many others. Tradition has them escaping to Pella, a small city in nearby Syria.

But their fate was sealed. With the destruction of Jerusalem, they had lost their power base and their close alliance with the Pharisees; the hatreds and slit-eyed suspicions of bloody factionalism lingered. A decade and a half later, when a remnant of the Pharisees regrouped outside of Jerusalem as rabbinical Judaism, the rabbis scorned the Yeshua movement that was now mostly Gentile, that contended with them for the synagogues, and that had not shed blood for mother Jerusalem against the Romans. With the loss of their connections to Judaism and Jerusalem, the marginalization of the Jewish Christians was perhaps inevitable. Their adherence to Torah left them ill equipped to contend with Torah-free, Gentile, Pauline Christianity outside of Palestine.

The Jewish branch of Christianity had become enfeebled and dominated by the Gentile branch, but the Jewish Christians survived in pockets here and there. However, by the end of the following century (c 180 CE), an influential bishop named Irenaeus reflected the developing orthodoxy when he declared in a treatise entitled, Against Heresies:

> Those who are called Ebionites [Torah observant, Jewish Christians] agree that the world was made by God; but their opinions ... represented Jesus as having not been born of a virgin, but as being the son of Joseph and Mary according to the ordinary course of human generation, while he nevertheless was more righteous, prudent, and wise than other men ... They use the Gospel according to Matthew only, and repudiate the Apostle Paul, maintaining that he was an apostate from the

law... they practise circumcision, persevere in the observance of those customs which are enjoined by the law, and are so Judaic in their style of life, that they even adore Jerusalem as if it were the house of God.

Pauline, Gentile Christianity had become normative, and Nazarene, Jewish Christianity had become heretical.

I didn't know Jesus had siblings. What is the source of that information?

James appears numerous times in the New Testament. The clearest gospel statement, but not the only one, is from Mark 6:3 on the occasion of Jesus' return to his home synagogue in Nazareth: "Is not this the carpenter, the son of Mary, and brother of James and Joses and Judas and Simon, and are not his sisters here with us?" Paul mentions James several times in his letters and refers to him as "the Lord's brother". Gal 1:19.

At three major junctures, the book of Acts refers to James in Jerusalem: praying with the disciples following Jesus' death ("with Mary, the mother of Jesus, as well as his brothers." 1:13-14); during the apostolic assembly when James appeared to be the leader with the last word ("I have reached the decision ..." 14:13-21); and upon Paul's return to Jerusalem with the collection many years later ("Paul went with us to visit James; and all the elders were present." 21:18). Lastly, the Book of James in the New Testament is attributed to him (probably incorrectly), but the attribution reflects his reputation as a proponent of Torah.

James is also mentioned by Josephus, the aristocratic Hebrew eyewitness to history, who wrote that the illegal execution of James by the High Priest caused a great stir in Jerusalem. James also figures prominently in non-canonical gospels such as the Gospel of the Hebrews and the Gospel of Thomas, which treats James as Jesus' handpicked successor.

But as Jewish Christianity receded and the church became Gentile and Torah free, memories of James faded. The process became complete when James and the other siblings were marginalized as mere cousins of Jesus by an ascetic, celibate monk and papal advisor, later revered as St Jerome, whose doctrine of the Perpetual Virginity of Mary gained ascendancy around 400 CE.

According to Jerome, a leading proponent of celibacy, James the Just was a fine man and devoted disciple, but he was neither Mary's son nor brother to Jesus. The Virgin remained a virgin, according to Jerome's influential writings, and Joseph and Mary, husband and wife, were untainted by carnal stains, and the sinful seed of Adam had not despoiled her holy womb. The birth of Jesus was miracle not human, and Mary experienced no bloody pangs of childbirth. There was no human branch on the divine family tree of Mary and the Son of God.

Due to Jerome's powerful influence, this understanding came to be Roman Catholic dogma. Since James was no longer the brother of Jesus, any lingering interest in the erstwhile bishop of the church quickly waned. Thus it was that James the Just, the eldest brother of Jesus, and the leading figure in earliest Christianity, became a forgotten man.[2]

The novel seemed to have too many letters to the Corinthians and didn't even mention other New Testament letters attributed to Paul. Why is that?

The novel referenced four letters to the Corinthians, not two as indicated by the canon of the New Testament. Scholars agree that the Corinthian correspondence within the canon is the product of ancient cutting and pasting of multiple documents. Indeed, there

---

[2] Jeffrey J. Butz, The Brother of Jesus, (Rochester, Vermont: Inner Traditions, 2005), 171.

may have been more than four letters from Paul to the Corinthians.
Seven of the thirteen New Testament letters attributed to Paul are clearly authentic—albeit some are chopped up and pieced back together and there may be small accretions added here and there. Of the remaining six, a couple are questionable, and the others are clearly inauthentic and referred to as *pseudopigrapha* or even "pious fraud." In fact, not only were the Pastoral Epistles (1st and 2nd Timothy and Titus) not written by Paul, some scholars suggest they were falsely attributed to Paul in order to soften or correct his radical views, especially pertaining to women and slaves.[3] Paul's bad rap as a misogynist is mostly unwarranted for this reason. The novel follows this view.

Was Paul really gay? What is the evidence for that?

What was his mysterious "thorn in the flesh" that he alluded to without explanation? Why did he never marry as his Hebrew heritage would have expected? It is impossible to answer these questions with certainty. If this was a court of law with rigid standards of evidence and burden of proof, the claim would fail. The evidence is insufficient.

Yet, there are hints implicit in Paul's own words, and this novel is not the first to suggest that the man who wrote harsh words about homosexual behavior was himself a conflicted gay man. Paul's writings are replete with negative assertions about human sexuality. Here is a sampling:

"[D]o not gratify the desires of the flesh." Gal 5:16b

"[T]hose who belong to Christ Jesus have crucified the flesh with its passions and desires." Gal 5:24

"I punish [pummel] my body and enslave it" 1 Cor 9:27a. Does this refer to self-flagellation?

---

[3] Marcus J Borg and John Dominic Crossan, The First Paul, (New York: HarperCollins, 2009)

"God gave them up in the lusts of their hearts to impurity, to the degrading of their bodies ... God gave them up to degrading passions. Their women exchanged natural intercourse for unnatural, and in the same way also the men ... were consumed with passion for one another. Men committed shameless acts with men". Romans 1:24-26

"Therefore, do not let sin exercise dominion in your mortal bodies, to make you obey their passions." Romans 6:12

"I am of the flesh [carnal], sold into slavery under sin ... I see in my members another law at war with the law of my mind, making me captive to the law of sin that dwells in my members. Wretched man that I am! With my flesh, I am a slave to the law of sin." Romans 7:14, 23-24a

Why such a negative attitude toward human sexuality? There would have been nothing in either his Hebrew culture or Greek environment that would engender an abhorrence to *heterosexual* passion, and Paul actually spoke favorably about the mutuality of conjugal relationships between marital partners.

To the contrary, the Hebrew attitude toward *homosexual* behavior was strikingly negative; it was an abomination for a man to lie with a man as with a woman, said the holiness code of Leviticus— punishable by death. According to the Torah teaching imbued in Paul since his youth, such behavior was inconsistent with his kind as a man, as a Jew, as a child of God. Paul probably knew the harsh injunctions of the *Book of Jubilees*: "God's people should cover their shame, and should not uncover themselves as the Gentiles uncover themselves," said the book in a probable euphemistic reference to homosexual behavior.

Could homosexual urges be the reason his writings drip with sexual angst? Is the inference that he was a self-loathing gay man a reasonable conclusion?

To me it is a beautiful idea that a homosexual male, scorned then as well as now, living with both the self-judgment and the social judgments that a fearful society has so often unknowingly pronounced upon the very being of some of its citizens, could nonetheless, not in spite of this but because of this, be the one who would define grace for Christian people... grace was the love of God, an unconditional love, that loved Paul just as he was.

A rigidly controlled gay male, I believe, taught the Christian church what the love of God means.[4]

[4] John Shelby Spong, Rescuing the Bible from Fundamentalism, (New York: HarperCollins, 1991) 125.